Praise for *Vanquish of the Dragon* ...

"Reminiscent of Hitchcock Thrillers,..."
PACIFIC BOOK REVIEW

"...sharply written, fast moving thriller."
RECOMMENDED BY US REVIEW OF BOOKS-
FEATURED BOOK OF THE MONTH, APRIL 2016

"...an undeniable page turner...well-written and highly entertaining read."
BLUE INK REVIEW

"This is a highly entertaining story that works well in part because of several interesting and layered characters."
FOUR STAR RATING, CLARION REVIEW

Praise for *Dark Vanity*

"For thriller aficionados who enjoy a nail-biting "who done it,", Dark Vanity: Not Your Typical Hollywood Murder is your next best read."
HOLLYWOOD BOOK REVIEW, EXCELLENT MERIT

"Four out of Four Stars. I recommend this book to anyone interested in mystery thrillers and adventure fiction. Also, I recommend it to anyone that enjoys fast-paced thrillers and suspense novels."
ONLINEBOOKCLUB.ORG.

"Dark Vanity is an intensely absorbing mystery beginning with a bang and not letting up an iota."
STARRED REVIEW, PACIFIC BOOK REVIEW

"Granted that the characters are well developed and the plot equally rich, but what stands the book out as a classic is its fast-paced nature and lots of red herrings that will keep the reader on the edge as the story unfolds."
OFFICIAL REVIEW
ILoveUniqueBooks.com (4 our out 5 stars)

Gregg's second novel, *Dark Vanity, Not Your Typical Hollywood Murder*, is available now.

VANQUISH

of the DRAGON SHROUD

Third Edition

Murder, Intrigue, & the Hidden Wealth of the Red Nobility

Gregory E. Seller

ISBN 978-1-7371682-2-5 (paperback)
ISBN 978-1-7371682-3-2 (kindle)

Library of Congress Control Number: 2024903317

Paperback
Ebook

Published by Gregory Seller Consulting, LLC
Laguna Niguel, California

Author: Gregory E. Seller

Cover/interior design and layout:
Mark E. Anderson, www.aquazebra.com

AquaZebra™
Web, Book & Print Design

Printed in the United States of America

Dedication

For Dolores and Genevieve

Table of Contents

1

A Celebration, Interrupted

She burst to the surface gasping for air. The Pacific Ocean swells around her, forcing salt water and foam into her nose and eyes. It's a moonless night, the water dark and frigid. She struggles to stay afloat, fighting angry waves whipped by the wind.

The winds known to Southern Californians as the Santa Ana can be warm and balmy, but they aren't warm this dark October night. Salt spray from the wind is so strong that it feels like thousands of little pins against her face, burning her lips and stinging her eyes. Four-foot swells make the lights on the distant coastline appear and disappear with each passing wave. Maxine is disoriented and near panic.

Earlier this evening, she was enjoying a celebratory cruise on a beautiful yacht with her husband, his business partner and his wife, and their most important client. They had a toast to a record year and would be arriving on Catalina Island within the hour. The wind picked up, and it was getting chilly on deck, so Maxine went below to get a warm fleece from her cabin. Wrapping the fleece around her shoulders, she took the stairs back to the upper deck, hearing several voices, all speaking loudly. At first, it sounded like laughter, very loud and raucous. But as she climbed the stairs, she could hear that it was not laughter, but yelling.

The stairs took her to the salon, where she heard her companions arguing even more loudly. She had just opened the salon door to join the others on deck when suddenly there was an explosion. It knocked her to the floor, and the boat listed sharply to the port side.

Her husband, Logan, burst into the salon. His face was bleeding from a deep gash in his cheek. He pulled Maxine up off the floor.

"Oh my God, Logan! Your cheek! What happened?"

Picking her up in his arms, blood dripping from his face onto her dress, Logan simply said, "You'll forgive me."

He rushed her outside to the deck, but the others were gone. Before she knew what was happening, her husband lifted her up and threw her over the railing into the dark ocean.

She hit the water headfirst and went under. When she came to the surface, she screamed and looked back at the boat.

"My God, Logan, what are you doing?"

Logan was leaning over the railing and looking at her, but he did not jump in to save her. He had a pained look on his face and stared right at her. Blood was running down his face to his neck and over his white tuxedo shirt.

Max, struggling to stay afloat, yelled again for Logan. "For God's sake, Logan, please, help me!"

The boat was on fire, and the horn was sounding a distress call. The current was strong, and she could feel herself rapidly drifting away from the boat.

Logan stood at the railing for a moment. He then said something to her that she couldn't hear. He turned and ran back inside the burning boat.

Maxine screamed, "Logan! Logan!" but no one was on deck.

She tried to swim back to the boat, but the current was too strong. She had never been a good swimmer, though she was often described as having a "swimmer's body." She screamed for Logan, or for anyone on the boat who would hear her. No one came to the deck, which was now engulfed in dark smoke. She could hear voices in the distance and see the fire overtaking most of the boat. She fought to stay afloat while watching the sinking boat, still in sight but drifting away.

A few moments later, there was a bright flash and a large explosion near the bow of the sinking yacht. The explosion caused a large wave to sweep over her, and Maxine was underwater, not knowing which way was up.

When she came to the surface, the ship was gone. The air smelled of fuel, and the smoke was heavy. She was treading water among the debris from the ship, some of which was still on fire. Bits of burning debris and embers were falling all around her. She heard a voice in the distance, but it was too dark to see who it was. There was a fire on the water, probably an oil slick. She could feel the heat against her face as it came closer to her.

A wave crashed over her head, and she was underwater again. She surfaced, fought for air, and tried to yell for help, but nothing would come out. Her chest was tight, and she felt pressure like a steel chain wrapping around her. Was it a heart attack or panic? Her breathing was getting short and shallow, and she was shivering.

Will this be it? This is how I die?

In a flood of emotion, she screamed for Logan, both angry at what he had done and hopeful for help. But there was no one to hear her screams. Her mind was racing. *Why would he want me to die here, in this way? Murder by drowning at only thirty-five years old?*

Her chest was getting even tighter, and she began losing the feeling in her feet. At first, they had tingled, but now they were numb from the cold. She could feel herself slipping farther under the water with each passing wave. *How much longer will I have? I can't die this way.*

Debris from the exploded ship was now all around her. She saw a large piece of a plastic chair floating nearby, and she swam toward it. It was moving in the current faster than she was, but she knew she had to reach it. There were other pieces of debris but nothing as large as the piece of the plastic chair.

She finally reached the chair and placed it underneath her right arm. It helped to keep her head above the water. Still, she knew she would drown soon if she didn't get help. The waves were simply too big for her to fight them much longer.

On the verge of drowning, she thought only of Logan. She loved him so; how could he have thrown her into the water? And why? To kill her or to save her? Her heart told her it was the latter, but her mind told her otherwise. There were life rafts on the boat— and life jackets and life preservers. Throwing her into the water with a life jacket would have been different. But tossing her overboard into the cold, dark water with no life jacket could only mean he had wanted her gone. *But why?*

She reaches for her neck to feel the beautiful necklace Logan had given her on the way down to the boat that night. She clutches it with her left hand while her right arm clings to the floating piece of plastic chair.

Just before they arrived at the pier earlier that night, Logan pulled a small box from under the backseat of the limousine. "A little bon voyage gift," he whispered to her.

"What? For a trip to Catalina, I get a gift?" She'd opened the box, and her mouth dropped. It was an extraordinary platinum pendant with white and yellow diamonds. Red rubies spelled out "Maxy," which was what Logan called her since they had first met at college. It was large and somewhat heavy for a pendant. Logan had had it engraved with "Il Mio Cuore el il tuo per Sempre," which in Italian means, "My heart is yours forever." It was etched in beautiful script on the back of the pendant.

Max remembered smiling and shaking her head. "I don't believe it. I just don't believe it."

Logan then whispered to her, "Had it made for you. Wanted to give it to you on our anniversary, but it wasn't done yet. Your friend Julian is fast with the money but slow with the goods, if you know what I mean."

Julian was a jeweler in Beverly Hills whom Max's family has used for decades. He was in his eighties now, and while still very talented, he wasn't much good at custom jewelry anymore, unless you could wait forever to have it created.

Max was stunned. "You designed it, and Julian made it? I'm overwhelmed, sweetheart."

For the design of the pendant, Logan used an art deco pattern that Maxine loved. She called it "travel streamline," and it wasn't a feminine pattern by any means. In fact, it was rather masculine. But Max loved the art deco look and used it in many of her interior design projects. Why had he given her this special gift *tonight*, if he had planned to kill her the same evening? She couldn't make sense of any of it.

Feeling hopeless and exhausted, Max lets herself drift in the direction of the waves. The current carries her closer to some lights in the distance. More debris? Or perhaps another boat? Her eyelids are so swollen she can no longer focus.

The lights draw closer, but she is losing consciousness. She knows hypothermia is starting to set in. Her hands are numb, and her lips are painfully raw and burning from the salt water. The distant lights grow closer. It looks like a boat. She yells out, but as she opens her mouth, seawater rushes in. It makes her vomit, and she struggles to breathe.

A moment later, her eyes swell shut, and she slips out of consciousness.

2

Night Turns to Day

In the early hours of the next morning, while it was still dark, divers retrieve one badly burned body about five hundred yards from where the yacht went down. Four of the other passengers, plucked from the sea by the Coast Guard the night before, are now at Coast Hospital in Laguna Beach. One passenger is missing.

The yacht's owner, Ethan Chandler, and his wife, Jaclyn, are exhausted and confused but sharing coffee with their Coast Guard rescuers and the Coast Hospital Emergency Room staff. In an adjoining room, Viktor Lucienne and his assistant, Brigitte Archambault, are on the phone with Viktor's business associates in Paris. They're speaking passionately in French, assuring them Viktor is well. Aside from a bad cut on his right hand, Viktor is fine. Brigitte was not on the yacht last night, but rushed to Coast Hospital after Viktor asked his Coast Guard rescuers to call her early this morning.

The ship's captain is still unconscious and in intensive care. The first mate has a broken leg, face lacerations, and is in surgery.

The two other passengers, Maxine, and Logan Aronheart are missing. The survivors are certain that the charred body is either Maxine's or Logan's, and that the other likely drowned or, by some remote possibility, might still be floating in the waters off Dana Point Harbor.

Ethan becomes agitated. Running his fingers through his hair and wiping his brow, he looks at the name tags of his Coast

Guard rescuers. "Who is in charge of rescuing the missing passenger?"

"It's no longer a rescue operation, sir. It's a recovery," one of the Coast Guard officers' replies. They had just arrived at the hospital to interview the passengers their fellow crew members rescued earlier this morning.

Ethan's confused. "What do you mean a *recovery* and not a *rescue?*"

"We're looking for one more body, sir."

Ethan clears his throat, "What's your name and rank?"

"I'm Captain Westmore. It's my ship and crew that responded to your distress call last night."

"But that missing person could be alive, right?"

"Not likely, sir. We have two cutters and a helicopter still looking, but with the water temperatures and surf conditions, it's not likely the missing passenger will be found alive. Unless of course they're an Olympic swimmer."

Ethan isn't amused by Captain Westmore's comment, "How long will you keep looking?"

"There's not a definite time period, sir."

"But you will keep looking until you find the other passenger, right?"

"That's the objective, sir."

Ethan gets up from his chair and gazes at his wife for a moment. Standing over six feet two inches tall and with thick blond hair, Ethan still has that surfer look, although he grew up in Connecticut and not Southern California. Looking older than his thirty-six years, Ethan is still strikingly handsome. He is the only child of a wealthy Greenwich, Connecticut surgeon, has an arrogant, self-confident personality but can be very charming. Ethan and Logan met at college. Fast friends since freshman year at the University of Colorado at Boulder, he and Logan are like brothers. After graduation, they went to separate coasts to work, but remained close friends. Ten years ago, Ethan asked Logan to join him as a partner in a new hedge fund he was starting. Logan agreed, and for the past ten years, they both made more money than they ever imagined.

Ethan turns to Captain Westmore and asks him when the identity of the burned body will be known.

"That's up to the county coroner," he replies.

"Well, couldn't you tell if it's a man or a woman?" Ethan asks. "Surely you know that much?"

The captain hesitates for a moment and then says, "I'd be speculating, sir. I didn't see the body myself."

"Then speculate, damn it!" Ethan is becoming even more agitated and walks across the room to approach the captain. His wife follows him to try to calm him down.

Jaclyn pleads, "Ethan, stop! I'm upset about Max and Logan too but get control of yourself!" Jaclyn holds him by the shoulders and gives him a steady gaze, as if she is transmitting a thought to him. Ethan relaxes. Jaclyn, a former model, and child beauty queen is the epitome of think-before-you-speak training. Normally calm and collected, Jaclyn is hard to rattle and very aware of her appearance and demeanor. Ethan is the opposite, impulsive and animated. Their starkly different personalities make them a good pair—most of the time.

"I'd rather you speak with the coroner, sir," says the captain. He then motions to one of his officers to come forward. He takes a clipboard from the officer and approaches Ethan. "Sir, we have some questions for you and your ship's captain."

Ethan frowns. "Questions? What do you want to know? I wasn't the one sailing the ship."

"I understand that sir, but we're trying to determine the cause of the fire and explosion. As the ship's owner, we'd like to know if you are aware of any mechanical problems before the fire."

"I'm not a mechanic," Ethan snaps back. "I just own the damn yacht. You'll have to ask Clint about any of that mechanical stuff."

"Is that your captain's name—Clint?"

"Yes."

"Can you give me his full name?"

"Clinton Grays," Ethan mumbles.

"And your relationship with him?"

"Relationship? He's just my captain. Sails my yacht. Takes care of it, or at least he used to."

"How long has he worked for you?"

"Since I got the boat ... over three years."

"Do you have the maintenance records, sir?"

"No. You'll have to get all that from Clint."

"He's not in very good shape now, sir, so if there is anything at all you can tell us that would be helpful in determining the cause of the fire, that would..."

Ethan cuts him off, bolts out of his chair and points his finger at Captain Westmore. "Someone is dead! My best friend or his wife or both could be dead! You're concerned about the cause of the damn fire when someone is dead and someone else is missing? I want to know the identity of that burned body. That's the most important thing to me now. And you aren't doing *anything* about it! Is it Maxine or Logan's body that's in the morgue?"

The captain puts his hands up in the air and says, "Sir, please calm down. You'll have to speak with the county coroner. She has the body, and it's up to her to identify the deceased. My job is to try to determine the cause of the fire and locate any survivors. Everything else is up to the county coroner and the DA."

Ethan shouts back, "The DA? What the hell does the District Attorney have to do with it?"

"One of your passengers is dead, sir. Another is missing. You own the boat and employ the captain."

"Oh, now I get it! Well, that's enough! You can talk with Clint when he wakes up, and if you have any other questions for me, you can speak with my attorney."

Jaclyn gets up from her chair, puts both of her hands on Ethan's chest, and speaks directly into his face. "What's wrong with you, Ethan? These people rescued us. They saved our lives. Get a grip on your emotions. You're embarrassing me. And yourself."

"Sit down, Jackie. I know they saved our lives. But Logan and Max are missing or dead, and this guy is asking stupid questions instead of looking for them."

Captain Westmore waves his two officers away and tips his hat at Ethan. "Mr. Chandler, go home, get some rest, and we'll contact you later."

Ethan puts his hand on his forehead. He then shakes his head and waves the captain away, as if shooing off a fly. Jaclyn, with one hand on her hip, pushes Ethan in the shoulder with the other hand and leaves the room.

Standing alone by the window, Ethan stares out at the ocean. The hospital is across the highway from the beach, and it is a crystal-clear fall Sunday morning in Southern California. The storm has cleared out, and the wind has blown away the coastal haze. Catalina Island, about twenty miles offshore, is so clear that Ethan can see the white cliffs near the town of Avalon, at the southern tip of the island. Catalina was their destination last night. Ethan had arranged a surprise dinner in the Casino building, complete with a small orchestra. It was to be an evening of celebration, business success stories, and dancing. Instead, it became a night of terror and death.

Ethan stares at the ocean, wondering if Max or Logan could still be out there. What would life be like without either one of them? Ethan needs Logan; he keeps him grounded. Ethan made Logan a partner in his firm ten years ago because he knew he would need him. Banished from New York, Ethan came to California to start a hedge fund, and he knew he would need Logan to tend to the business details and keep him focused. Ethan, the boastful promoter, and charmer who could attract clients on his good looks and personality, needed Logan to run the business. It has always been that way with Ethan. He needs a business partner because he is just too lethal on his own.

After graduation from the University of Colorado, Ethan's father got him a plum Wall Street job with a brokerage firm. Never one to not capitalize on his gifts, Ethan attracted a following of Park Avenue matrons and young (mostly second or third) wives of business titans that formed the bulk of his clientele. His associates often chided him as the "gigolo of Wall Street." Long on good looks and sexual ability, Ethan spent more time in bedrooms, bars, and restaurants than he did at the brokerage desk. He brought in so much new money to manage that he humiliated some of the long-time brokers at the firm. Ethan didn't care that his coworkers despised him; so long as he was making money and having a good time, all was well in his world. That's the way it had always been with Ethan. His good looks, charm, and family money made most things in life easy for him.

Ethan was born into privilege, so he never wanted for much he didn't already have. But, as he would often say, "More is more, and even more is better!" Making more money is his way of showing he is accomplished. His "rich pretty boy" tag in college often made him feel diminished, like he had to prove he is smart, and not just good looking and rich. It served him well in New York, where being rich and good-looking opens just about every door, whether it be to the boardroom or the bedroom. Ethan felt he was living the perfect life.

And perfect it was, until he was plucked from his own bed one night by two men who beat him up and threw him from his apartment window. Fortunately for Ethan, the two attackers were a bit sloppy. They failed to realize that there was a balcony four floors below Ethan's bedroom window. What was supposed to be a fall of thirty-two floors was only four. One of Ethan's clients was the wife of a man who owned a big trash-hauling business in New Jersey. Being curious, he read his wife's brokerage account statement one night and concluded that if Ethan was hired for performance, it wasn't in the stock market. There are so many stock trades that the trading fees outstripped the earnings. In the brokerage business, that is known as churning the client's portfolio simply to generate more fees. The angry husband found a whole stack of unopened account statements; his wife had not bothered to even look at them. After having his wife followed for a few weeks, the trash-hauling titan decided a change of brokers was in order. Unfortunately, the balcony four floors below the bedroom window made the expected termination less than complete.

When Ethan was in the hospital recovering, he had a visitor who told him to leave New York forever or the next fall from a tall building would be permanent. Ethan left for California the day he got out of the hospital. His brokerage company quietly settled matters with his former New York clients to avoid tarnishing the firm's reputation. Since his former company swept all the wrongdoing under the rug, Ethan didn't lose his securities license, so he decided to make a fresh start in California. That was ten years ago.

Jaclyn walks back into the room to see Ethan staring out the window. "Ethan? Ethan?" He seems lost in his own thoughts, so she goes to him and touches him on the shoulder.

"Damn! You startled me!" He turns so quickly toward her, she steps back.

"I'm sorry. I'm just worried about you. You've been in here alone for almost half an hour, so I came to check on you. Let's go down to the Coast Guard office at the harbor and wait for news about their rescue efforts. No point waiting here."

"Are you out of your mind? I can't go sit in some Coast Guard office waiting for them to find who's still out there. I need to know whose body is in the morgue, so that's where we're going. Get your things, and let's get out of here." He turns to her, takes her by both hands, and stares into her eyes. In a soft voice, he says, "Jackie, I need Logan. *We* need Logan. If he's dead, we're screwed."

Jackie is taken aback. "What? What do you mean we're screwed?"

Ethan squeezes her hands tightly. "We're not just screwed; we're dead. I've got to know where he is. For your sake and mine, let's hope it's Max in that body bag in the morgue and that Logan is out there, alive, somewhere."

Jaclyn is stunned by his words. Max and Logan are two of their closest friends; how could Ethan choose which should be dead? She turns pale and pushes Ethan's hands away from hers.

Without saying anything more, Ethan grabs her by the arm, and they head for the stairway.

3

Beached by Strangers

Wet, cold, and lying face down on rotting wood, Max wakes up in a small boat. The waves are rough, and it is still dark. She hears a motor and smells diesel fumes.

When she turns over to look up, a voice says, "Hey, Sleeping Beauty. You, okay?"

Max wipes her forehead with her hand and pushes her wet hair out of her face. Her eyes are trying to focus on who is speaking to her. The boat is moving side to side and then front and back, making her nauseous. She shivers and her teeth are chattering.

"What happened? Who are you?" she asks.

"Fished you out of the water, ma'am. Saw the explosion and headed over, and there you were—slumped on that piece of chair and about to drown."

"Oh my God, yes, yes, I … my husband, is he here?"

"Who's your husband, ma'am?"

She can see that there are two men in the boat with her. One is at the helm with the motor, and the other man, the one with the Southern accent, is at the front of the boat speaking to her. It's a small boat, barely big enough for the three of them. "Logan. Logan Aronheart. He was with me on the boat. Please tell me he's okay."

"Don't know, ma'am. We only spotted you. Lots of debris, but we only found you."

"The others? There were others!"

"We only gots you, ma'am. Here, put these on. They're not your size, but they're warm and dry." He hands Max a heavy sweat suit—pants and shirt—like you'd wear for a workout or jogging.

"No, no, I don't care. We need to go out to find my husband. Please. And who are you?"

"Sorry, ma'am. No time. If you won't put these on, we'll just leave you with 'em on the beach."

"What? The beach? No, no, who are you? We must go look for my husband!" She looks back at the man at the helm, and he's silent. It's dark, and she can't see their faces. She feels sick to her stomach. "No, please. Don't leave me. Take me back out so we can look for Logan. Please. I'm begging you." She begins to sob as the boat is carried onto the beach with the waves. The man in front jumps out and holds the bow. The waves are strong and crashing around them. He guides the boat to a spot where it stops in the sand. The man at the back of the boat pulls her up by her armpits, and the man in the water grabs her legs. Confused and struggling, Max begs them not to leave her alone on the beach. Begging was not her style, but she is so bewildered and weak, she's behaving like someone else. "Please, can you call someone? Do you have a phone?"

The man in the water gives her a flashlight and the sweat suit, which is now in a plastic bag. He pulls her away from the water and onto the dry sand. "Go up to the hotel beyond the parking lot, ma'am. You'll be picked up there shortly."

And with that, the other man grabs the bow of the boat and the two of them turn it around and push it back into the sea. They both jump in, start the engine and plow through the waves. Max quickly loses sight of them in the darkness, and the sound of the engine fades away.

It's dark, and Max has no idea where she is. She's shivering, so she takes off her wet dress and puts the sweat suit on. Placing her wet dress in the plastic bag, she turns on the flashlight, and heads up the sand to find the parking lot the stranger mentioned. Barefoot, with her feet still cold and tingling, she starts walking into the darkness.

After only a few steps in the sand, she stops and falls to her knees. With the excitement of the past hours behind her (she has no idea how long she has been out there), she can finally think without being in a panic. *What happened? How do I make sense of this?* She stares down at the beautiful blue Chanel dress that is now rolled up in the plastic bag. As if the events of the past hours never happened, her thoughts now take her back to the start of the evening.

"Bottoms up, sweetheart. We're almost there," Logan whispered to Maxine.

They were in the back of the limousine, and she was resting her head on Logan's shoulder. She had one hand on his lap and the other holding her champagne flute. "I wish it was just the two of us taking that cruise tonight."

"Let's pretend it is just the two of us," Logan replied. He smiled and kissed her on the cheek. Logan is a striking man—dark hair that's turning gray on the sides, blue eyes, and just under six feet tall. His beard is tightly shaved and very well trimmed. He has a slight build and speaks in a soft but firm voice.

Max smiles, "Well, that won't be easy to do with your biggest client breathing down my neck all night—or should I say breathing down my cleavage all night?"

Logan cleared his throat and grinned. "He's supposed to be on his best behavior tonight."

"Really? Like he was on his best behavior the last time I saw him?"

"That, my dear sweet wife, is something we should try not to remember. You were such a trooper, and I won't ever forget it."

"My left tit won't ever forget it either!" Maxine smiled and grabbed Logan in the ribs. "Really, it was sore for a week. And black and blue too. That little man is so annoying."

"Well, he's French, so I guess it goes with the territory." Logan smiled broadly and winked at her.

"That's such a lame excuse. Just because you're French, you don't grab your dance partner's breast right in the middle of 'Some Enchanted Evening.'"

"I know. I know. No dancing with him tonight." Logan put his champagne flute between his legs so he could hug Maxine with both arms and give her a long kiss.

Maxine reached between his legs, grabbed the champagne flute, and put it to his lips after their kiss ended. She touched her glass with his, and they toasted each other in silence.

The limousine pulled into Dana Point Harbor, and they went to the dock where Ethan, Logan's business partner, keeps his yacht. It was a beautiful seventy-eight-foot Alfamarine that cost him over three million dollars. Ethan bought it about three years ago. While Logan thought it an excessive expense, their clients and employees loved to be taken out on it—especially clients like Viktor Lucienne, a Frenchman who was an investment middleman and their single largest client. He loved to be entertained, and in a big and extravagant manner. Though a little man by stature, Viktor had a large personality. With short dark hair and a stereotypical thin French mustache, Viktor looked like a French film star from the 1930s. Hair slicked back, cigarette holder, and flamboyant clothes, Viktor was a caricature of himself. He was meticulously groomed and very self-aware. With a strong family pedigree and an education at the Sorbonne-Paris, Viktor excelled at making business connections, at home and abroad. He speaks French, English, Russian, and Mandarin with ease. The fact he has a Chinese wife helps with learning Mandarin and making Chinese business connections. Viktor met Ethan during what he called Ethan's "former life" in New York, but the exact nature of the introduction remains a mystery to everyone else. Nonetheless, Viktor delivered billions in assets for Ethan and Logan's firm to manage, and he relished being their single largest client (at least in assets if not in stature).

Copious, as the yacht was aptly named, sat at the end of the pier, bathed in soft blue lights from bow to stern. It was a sight to behold. Even though Logan and Maxine encouraged him not to buy it, Ethan was the senior partner in the firm, and he bought this little treasure with his own money. All the operating expenses were, of course, charged to the business, including the costs for the captain who lived on the boat with his first mate.

"Permission granted to come aboard!" Ethan yelled out from the upper deck of *Copious* as Maxine and Logan stepped out of the car. He was dressed in a glitzy captain's uniform he loved to wear even on business cruises (though he was in fact *not* the captain). Viktor Lucienne was standing next to him in a beautiful blue Christian Dior suit with a white shirt. He was grinning from ear to ear. He hoisted his champagne glass and said something in French as Maxine and Logan climbed the stairs up to the boat deck from the pier. The first mate, Rick, got their bags from the limousine driver. As they reached the deck, Logan extended his hand to Viktor, saying, "Good Evening, Viktor. It's great to see you, as always."

"*Bonsoir, cher,*" Viktor said with a big smile as he hoisted his champagne glass to make a toast in the air. He then smiled at Ethan, and they clinked their glasses together.

Max rolled her eyes. Viktor made everything a flourish. Whether angry or happy, every sentence seemed to end with a grand gesture and a grin or a frown, just to be sure there was a little drama in every statement. Viktor was always on stage, the center of attention. Max often said that "Viktor played being French more than the part required."

Viktor then shouted out, "*Mon ange, Maxine!*"

Max cringed but then smiled. *Mon ange Maxine*, she knew, was French for "my angel Maxine," which Viktor always called her.

"Oh, my little *cochon*, how I have missed you," Maxine replied to Viktor with a big smile.

Viktor laughed loudly and hoisted his glass. *Cochon* meant "pig" in French, and Maxine loved to hear Viktor chortle when she would call him her "little pig." She often thought to herself that he wouldn't laugh if he knew how serious she was about that phrase. As the good corporate wife, Maxine knew she needed to charm the clients. She particularly enjoyed charming them while being just on the edge of an insult. Max considered that her specialty. It would sometimes unnerve Logan, but she never got caught at it. Logan often winked at her when she uttered an insult veiled as an endearment, and someone like Viktor would laugh wildly, as if it were a compliment. Maxine always told Logan that straight men were easy targets. They were looking at her boobs instead of her mouth, so a little veiled insult passed as charm. The only men who caught her innuendoes and veiled insults were her gay friends. They knew better. Max always said that if you were a gay man, dialogue was something you paid attention to. Boobs were just an accessory. For straight men, it's the reverse. Fortunately for Logan, most of the clients of his firm were straight men—and not only straight, but European, Russian, or Chinese, which made it even easier for Max to deliver her charmingly veiled insults because their English was usually imperfect.

That happy greeting on the yacht was hours ago. Now, there was no champagne and no Viktor Lucienne and no Logan. Cold and shivering, Maxine picks herself up off the sand and turns on the flashlight.

It looks like a berm or a hill ahead of her. If there is a parking lot, it must be above the beach at the top of the hill. She uses the flashlight to scan the hillside, looking for a trail or stairs to the parking lot. As she gets closer, she sees it isn't a berm or a hill, but a cliff that is very high and rocky. She can't see the top, but she scans the base of the cliff with her flashlight, looking for any way up. Then she sees it. Her flashlight comes upon a wooden sign in the sand that says, "Parking Lot Access." It has an arrow pointing to a walkway, and at the bottom of the sign, she reads, "Salt Creek Beach." She now knows exactly where she is, and it sends a shiver up her spine.

4

Such a Drag

"Hey, Lydia, you're up next!" yells the stage manager, Patrick. "Polly got her zipper stuck in her bra strap so she can't go out yet. Finish stuffin' all that in wherever it's supposed to go and get out there! Crowd's gettin' nasty!"

"You kidding me? My makeup's not finished. If Polly got her tits messed up, that's her fault. Shove her out there anyway," Lydia snaps back.

It's Saturday night at the Queen of Hearts club. The midnight show on Saturday is always packed, and this night is even more so since it features a famous guest headliner. The Queen of Hearts is the largest drag club in Los Angeles, and the midnight cocktail show follows the earlier 8:00 p.m. dinner show. The older crowd hits the dinner show, and the younger crowd prefers the midnight show, usually after partying earlier at other clubs. They show up full of liquor and other *party favors* and are always a noisy but fun crowd.

Tonight, the club features a guest performer from New York, an older, pioneering transsexual who makes the talk show circuit and is regular fodder for the tabloids. She was born a man but became a woman through a series of surgeries over thirty years ago. Vilified by some and admired by others, she is a celebrity of sorts. She has a great singing voice, and tells stories, including how she transitioned from a college football jock to a glamorous woman. She's not a drag performer. She is a woman, and therein lies the reason she is not always welcome at drag clubs. She is not a drag performer, so other perfomers often resent her performing at a drag club. That is the feeling at the Queen of Hearts club tonight. The drag queens don't like sharing the stage with her, and are unhappy with the owners of Queen of Hearts for bringing her in. Nonetheless, she is an attraction and a famous-for-being-famous celebrity who will pack the house tonight.

Lydia LaFon is a regular drag performer at the club. At six feet two inches tall and 180 pounds, he's taller and slimmer than most of the other drag performers. And that was how Lydia always refers to himself—not as a drag queen but a *drag performer*. Lydia has quite a following in LA because he can sing his own songs and doesn't have to lip-synch. Lip-synching songs is standard fare for most drag queens. It is unusual for drag performers to sing their own songs, so Lydia has a big and loyal following. The character of Lydia LaFon was carefully crafted as something uniquely her own and not an impersonation of a celebrity. A long black dress with silver sequins and a high white collar is the latest attire for Lydia, along with white satin gloves that reach from her fingers to her elbows, finished off with five-inch heels covered in silver sequins. Tall, slender, and sultry is an apt description of Lydia LaFon.

Lydia's character is a mixture of Judy Garland and Cher, with a little Bette Midler humor, and the crowd loves her. Between songs, she tells jokes and picks on members of the audience. She cut her first CD the previous year and has a good following in the LA and Palm Springs gay clubs. And, he has a successful day job, not as Lydia, but as a designer under his real name, Seth Boncola.

Patrick opens the door to the closet Lydia is using as a dressing room and says, "Hey, hon, I *really, really* need you to go out there. Polly's a mess, and the special guest from New York is in a snit, and the other girls are just suiting up so I'm begging you to go out there. Please!"

"Your own fault for bringing in that side show from New York. This is a drag club, not a science class. Make your high-priced New York tranny go out on stage!"

"Lydia, you know better. *Tranny* is a derogatory word. She is a transsexual. Transgendered. Nothing wrong with that."

"Yep, of course, you know it's more than okay with me. I'm all for someone being happy in their own skin. But she's made it an oddity by slapping her over made puss on every tabloid in the country. She behaves like a freak on that reality show. She does a disservice to the transgender community. She's her own circus. Every day, lots of people make the difficult decision to become what they believe they were born as. It's an honorable and serious decision. Something you do proudly and quietly. She's made it a freak show. Makes people think that's how you end up if you have a sex change; just tabloids and talk shows. Sends the wrong message. And this is a drag club, and she's not a drag performer."

"Okay, I get it. Everyone's mad about who she is, but she's here so let's just move on with the evening. Please. I'll give you *four* songs tonight. How's that? Four! All the other girls get only two. Even the special guest from New York only gets two! Now go out there, and I'll tell Mike he can spin four songs for you. Crowd's all excited. Get out there!"

"Well, well, desperation's a wonderful thing," Lydia says with a big grin. "Tell Mike I want my usual opener and then pull my CD background disc for the other three songs. I'll announce the numbers from the stage."

"Okay, but for cripes' sake, Lydia, get your butt out there. He'll spin whatever you want. Just get the crowd in the mood."

The crowd roars when Lydia makes her appearance on stage about a quarter past midnight. She can see that the room is jammed. People are standing everywhere, and photographers are there too. Tabloids, most likely. No doubt they're covering the New York special guest, but Lydia is pumped to start the show, and she brings the house down with her four opening numbers. She plugs her CD, which is for sale in the lobby, and that makes her even happier. Despite her earlier-than-expected performance, she's thrilled after she finishes her set, and runs backstage to hugs and high-fives from the other performers. Finishing her act early also means she can begin indulging in the free drinks the patrons will be sending over to her forthwith.

Patrick waves to Lydia, catching her attention, "Hey, Seth, you've got to get dressed and drive to Dana Point. Now."

"Dana freakin' Point? You crazy? Why? You didn't like my set?"

Patrick looks pale, and his forehead is sweating. He gets worked up during show nights, but this look is different. He looks frightened.

"Patrick, are you okay? What's wrong? You're killing my show buzz!"

"Seth, I'm sorry. We got a call at the desk at about 12:30. They asked for you. Told them you were performing, and they should call you back on your cell. They said it was a matter of life and death and that you were to go to the Ritz-Carlton in Dana Point and pick up your friend Max. They said to go right away, and don't tell anyone you're picking her up. It could endanger her life. And yours. Then they hung up. The voice was strange and made me shiver."

"Max? Max needs me to pick her up? She's on Ethan's boat tonight with the hedge fund bozos."

"Look, I've got to get back to the show. Do what you want, but it was a strange call. You did your gig tonight, so you're done until Sunday brunch this afternoon."

Seth grabs his cell phone and calls Max right away. No answer. He then calls Logan's cell phone. It goes right to voice mail. Should he call Ethan? What was up? Why did the caller say not to tell anyone that he was to get Max? It was now almost 1:00 in the morning. What would Max be doing in Dana Point at the Ritz-Carlton? She's on Ethan's yacht. And why wouldn't she call Seth herself?

Seth works for Max. He's been her assistant since he got out of design school. They are best friends, and next to Logan, Seth is the most important man in Max's life. They often call their friendship a sexless marriage, since they're as close as a gay man and a straight woman can be.

As a design assistant by day and occasional drag performer at night, Seth has a "charmed double life," as he often calls it. Seth adores Logan and Max and is loyal to them both, without reservation. When Seth had his crystal meth addiction, it was Max and Logan who took him in to rehab and cleaned him up. His own family rejected him when they learned he was gay and were nowhere to be found when he got hooked on crystal meth. After he was clean and started performing drag, he chose the name Christal Meth as his character, as a way of showing he was free from crystal meth and could laugh at it. It was all great for a while until another guy, who weighed about three hundred pounds and who also used the same drag name showed up one night and beat him up after his show. Hence, he created Lydia LaFon, for which he thought there would be no competition, at least name-wise.

"Shit. Come on, Max! Answer your damn phone. Where are you?" He then tries Logan again. Then Max. He hesitates for a moment and calls Ethan's cell phone. No answer.

Seth starts to take off his Lydia costume and makeup when Patrick comes in.

"They're on the phone again. Want to know if you have left yet. Please go speak with them, Seth. This just doesn't sound right."

Half dressed, Seth runs down the hall to the house phone at the hostess station. He picks up the phone, only to hear a dial tone.

"Damn it. They hung up. What did they say?"

Velma, the drag queen working the hostess desk, looks up at Seth and shakes her head. "Strange voice, asked why you were still here and said that this would be the last call for you to save your friend Max. It was creepy. What's up, Seth? What's going on?"

"Shit. It's already after 1:15a.m. I need to get to Dana Point."

5

The Unregistered Guest

Seth keeps calling and calling—Max, then Logan, then Max—but no one answers. He calls the office. He calls Max and Logan's home in Beverly Hills. Nothing.

His heart is racing as he speeds down the San Diego freeway toward Dana Point. He decides to call the Ritz-Carlton. Maybe Max checked in there and someone was phoning for her.

The hotel switchboard answers and transfers him to the front desk, where he is told they are not permitted to give out the names of guests in the hotel.

Seth is frustrated. "Okay, I get it, but is there a woman there named Maxine Aronheart waiting in the lobby? The bar? Anyone expecting Seth Boncola to pick her up?"

The voice on the line says, "There's no one in the lobby, sir. It's almost 1:45 in the morning."

"Okay, but can you please, please tell me if she is registered?"

"I'm so sorry, sir. You know I can't do that."

"How about a hint? I'm driving all the way down from LA to pick her up."

"Well, sir, I can only say that *if* you are driving down here at this hour expecting to see someone here by that name, well, it's perhaps a wasted drive, if you know what I mean."

"Shit."

"Sorry, sir?"

"So, she is not registered, damn it. Can you page her?"

"Sir, we don't have a paging system."

"Can someone go to the bar and tell me if there is a woman there named Max Aronheart?"

The night front desk clerk hears the desperation in Seth's voice. "Okay, I'm not supposed to leave the desk, but if you will hold, I'll run back to the lobby bar and see if she is there."

"Thank you! Thank you so much!"

"Will do, sir."

Seth waits on the phone for several minutes.

The voice then returns and says, "I'm so sorry, sir; there's actually no one in the bar, and the bartender has already closed up."

"Damn. Did he remember anyone that might be her?"

"I thought you might ask that, sir, and the bartender said it was a busy night—Saturday, lots of people, a wedding party, and some wealthy Mexicans from Guadalajara here to party. No one was hanging around waiting to be picked up, at least as best he could tell."

"Okay, thanks. I'm on my way. I'll check back later."

Traffic is miserable. It's practically 2:00 a.m. on a Sunday morning. Seth wonders aloud, "Where are all these people going?" He keeps calling Max's and Logan's cell phones for about the next hour and then gives up when he gets off the freeway and heads down the road to the hotel.

He calls the Ritz-Carlton again and asks the operator to transfer him to the front desk. It is now after 3:00 a.m., and it had taken almost two hours for the trip from West Hollywood to Dana Point.

"Front desk, this is Chad. May I help you?"

"Hey, Chad, it's me again, Seth, looking for Ms. Aronheart, Maxine Aronheart?"

There is silence for a minute, and then Chad says, "May I place you on hold for a moment?"

"Oh no, please don't do that. You know why I am calling. I'm almost there."

There is reply, but Seth cab tell he's on hold because the music was playing.

After less than a minute, another voice comes on the line. "Good evening, er, good morning, sir. May I ask who is calling?"

"Of course. I told you; my name is Seth Boncola. Who are you, and is my friend there? I'm pulling into your parking lot now."

"This is the hotel manager, sir. We have your friend, but she wanted to know who is asking for her. Please wait a moment."

"Damn it. Now what?"

"Hey, baby, it's me! You really on your way? What's going on? Where are you?"

It's Max. She sounds out of breath and frantic.

"Hey, hey, calm down! Yes, it's me. I'm just pulling into the parking lot. Where are you in the hotel?"

"In the manager's office, but I'll come out to the lobby." She hangs up.

Seth doesn't even bother parking. He goes right to the valet, stops the car, and runs into the hotel lobby.

He sees Max standing there. She's crying. As soon as she sees Seth, she runs to him, and they embraced like long-lost lovers. Now they are both crying, and Seth asks her, "Who called me? How did they know where I was? Why didn't you call me yourself? And what's with that terrible sweat suit you're wearing?"

"Who called you?" Max says, rather startled.

"That's just what I asked *you*," he replies.

"I don't know. I don't have my phone, and no one knows I'm here. Seth, the ship blew up! Logan is missing. They're all missing. I don't know why I'm here, and I'm so confused."

"Whoa, whoa, wait a minute. What do you mean the ship blew up? *Copious* blew up? When? How? Where is everyone else?"

Seth is stunned. He held Max in his arms and then pushed back to see her face. Speaking softly, he said, "What the hell happened, Max?"

Sobbing and shaking, she says, "I don't know. It blew up and, and …"

"And what? And what?"

"Logan threw me overboard after the first explosion. Then there was another and another, and I-I can't tell it now, Seth. I was brought here by two men in a boat. They dumped me on the beach. I walked up the hill to the parking lot and knew immediately where I was. In the parking lot of the Ritz-Carlton. I stumbled into the lobby, and after I shocked the staff with my appearance, a security officer took me to the manager's office. Said I was rambling, and they couldn't understand who I was or what happened."

"Oh my God. How could that be? Did you call the police?"

Before Max can answer, a voice behind Seth replies, "Yes, we did call the police, and they're here." Seth turns to see a nice-looking man in a suit and tie standing beside two Orange County deputy sheriffs.

The man extends his hand and introduces himself to Seth. "My name is Fritz Engel. I'm the manager, the night manager on duty, that is. I suggest we go to my office and let everyone discuss the situation with the deputies. I'm afraid something terrible seems to have happened."

"What do you mean?" Seth asks.

"Let's just go into my office so we don't disturb the staff or guests."

Seth holds Max close to him as they all walk into a small conference room adjoining the general manager's office. Mr. Engel had placed water, coffee, and tea on the table.

Before they were seated, Max says, "Please, please can we talk about looking for my husband and the others?"

The deputies look at one another, as if deciding who should speak first. The one deputy is tall and older, probably in his fifties, and the other is a younger Hispanic man who appears to be right out of the academy. He speaks first.

"Let me begin, ma'am, by introducing myself. I'm Deputy Reyes, and this is my associate, Lieutenant Rupert. Can you tell us what happened on that boat, and how you got here?"

"No, please, please, we can get to that later. What I need to know is if we can look for the others. Do you know anything?"

There is silence for a moment as the officers look at each other again, hesitating to speak.

"What the hell's going on here?" asks Seth. "There're people missing in a boat accident, and we're sitting here questioning her?"

"And you are who, sir?"

"I'm Seth Boncola, and this is my best friend, Max. Her husband and his business partner and guests are out there somewhere in the ocean. Is anyone looking for them?"

"You know the others on the boat too?"

"I know her husband and a couple of the others, yes. Enough about us. What do you know? Has someone reported all of this, or what's up?"

Deputy Reyes leans forward and puts his hands together on the table. "We got a radio alert about an hour ago that the coast guard was bringing survivors from a boating accident to the Dana Point Harbor. We had a 'stand by for assist if needed' notice. Then Ms. Aronheart here came in about thirty minutes ago, upset and crying at the front desk, so we were dispatched here on a disorderly conduct complaint from the hotel. When we got here, Mr. Engel told us a woman claiming to be a boat accident survivor was in his office."

"Where are the other survivors? Are they all, okay?" Seth asks.

"We don't know. We called HQ to get a status update, and they said they would get back to us after they contacted the Coast Guard."

"Oh my God, can we go to the harbor?" Max stands up from her chair as if to leave, when Seth grabs her and holds her arm.

Reyes looks at Max and says softly, "Ma'am, we aren't sure if they are at the harbor or were taken to a hospital. They're getting back to us."

"What we are curious about is how *you* ended up here and the others ended up with the coast guard at Dana Point Harbor?"

"I don't know," Max says. "I was picked up by two men in a boat. I was unconscious, and when I woke up, they were dropping me off at Salt Creek Beach. I walked here."

"And the name of the boat you were on?" asks the deputy.

"*Copious.*"

The deputy then looks to Seth. "And how is it, sir, that you're here?"

"Someone called me. Well, they didn't call me; they called the club where I was working."

"And what club is that sir?"

"Queen of Hearts. In West Hollywood."

"Who called you?"

"I don't know. I never spoke with them. Patrick, the club manager, took the call while I was performing."

"Performing?"

"Yes, that's what I said. Performing."

"What is it that you perform?"

"I am a drag performer, Officer."

"Drag?"

"Yes, drag. You know, boys dressing up as girls? Surely, you've heard of it, even here in Orange County."

"Oh, oh, I see."

There is silence in the room for a moment, and then Seth speaks up, "Look, what's this got to do with the boat sinking?" Seth is getting agitated and so is Max.

Deputy Reyes replies, "What time did you get this call?"

"I told you that I didn't get the call. The club manger did, and it was between midnight or a little after, and 12:30 a.m. because that's when I was on stage, approximately."

Max looks at Seth with a very confused expression. "Say that again, Seth. What time were you onstage?"

"A little after midnight, maybe for twenty minutes or so. Four songs. I was fabulous!"

"No, no, Seth, that can't be right. We were going to dock at Catalina about midnight, and we were running late, still offshore from Avalon when the first explosion happened, about 11:30 or so. You couldn't have gotten a call that early because I was still bobbing around in the ocean around that time. At least I think that's right."

"What? You mean you weren't here at the hotel when Patrick

got that call at the club? You were still on the boat or floating in the water?"

Max puts her head in her hands, closes her eyes, and begins to sob again. "I don't know. It all runs together. We never got to Catalina. It had to be close to midnight. We just had our big toast, and then there was the explosion."

"Ma'am, it's over twenty-two miles from Catalina to Dana Point. Takes the Express boat over an hour and a half to get there."

"I'm telling you that's what happened. That's all I know."

Deputy Reyes looks at Mr. Engel and says, "What time did she show up here in the lobby?"

"I guess about 2:45 a.m. I got the call in my office from security about 3:00, or thereabouts."

Now Seth is very confused and looking intently at Max. "Sweetie, how could someone call me at the club to come get you at this hotel when you not only weren't here but floating around in the water? How could they know you were coming here?"

The room goes silent.

Deputy Reyes leans forward and stares at Max.

"Ma'am, did you call your friend here from the yacht and leave a message, knowing that you were leaving the others and taking yourself here, in a boat on your own?"

"No, no of course not. How could I have called him?"

"And where did you get the clothes you're wearing?"

"From the men in the boat."

Reyes eyes the plastic bag with her dress and asks, "What's in the bag?"

"My ... my dress. The one I was wearing when the men in the boat picked me up."

"May I see it?"

Max hands him the bag. Without opening it, Reyes examines it closely. Though it is wet, he can see some residue on the dress and that the fluid in the bag is dark brown. "Is that a pattern on the dress that's making the fluid brown?"

Max reaches slowly for the bag, looks carefully at the bottom of the bag, and wipes her eyes. "Blood. It's my husband's blood. It's all over my dress."

Reyes looks at Rupert and sits back in his chair. "So, you have blood on your dress and somehow complete strangers showed up to rescue you, and they happen to have a change of clothes, which, by the way, doesn't fit you too badly. How many fishermen carry a new set of women's sweats when they're out at night looking for perch?"

Seth looks at Max and frowns. He wants to ask her something, but thinks it may make matters worse, so he stays silent.

At that moment, the deputy's phone rings.

"Oh. Oh, I see. Are you sure? No ID? You're sure? Okay, thanks. I'll be back with you."

Deputy Reyes is silent for a moment and then says softly, "The coast guard retrieved six people from the water after the boat explosion. They took them to Coast Hospital about an hour ago."

Max jumps from her chair. "Oh my God, who? Who are the six? There should be seven. There were eight of us. Eight. I'm here so there should be seven there."

Reyes is silent for a moment, then speaks softly, "One is dead, ma'am. One body and six survivors."

"Who? Who didn't make it? Please tell me!" Max is frantic.

"Don't know, ma'am. Badly burned body on the way to the county coroner."

Max bursts into tears and reaches for Seth. They hold each other, and Seth whispers, "I'll take you to the hospital, and we'll find out. Let's go."

Reyes interrupts, "Just a moment, sir. I'm afraid she's not going anywhere. Either are you, sir. Not just yet. She's in our custody as a person of interest in this matter. How could you have received a call to pick your friend up here, when it would be nearly two hours before she walks in the door? And she's supposedly floating around in the sea between here and Catalina? And someone is dead? You're both coming with us. Oh, and I'll take the bag with the dress. That's going to the county coroner."

6

Conflicted Angst

The sun is just coming up Sunday morning as Ethan and Jaclyn go down the back stairs of the hospital and out to the lobby. Sitting in the waiting area is an attractive Latino woman, thirty-one years old, dressed in heels and a tight green dress. She has been there a couple of hours, waiting for Ethan and Jaclyn. Her name is Maria, and she is Ethan's executive assistant.

"Maria!" Ethan shouts.

She looks up, sees them both, and runs over to greet them.

"Oh, Ethan, I'm so sorry. Where is everyone else?"

"All here, except Max and Logan."

"What? Where are they?"

"One is missing, and one is at the county morgue."

"Oh my God, no! Which one? Who is at the morgue?"

"That's what we'll find out. You have the car?"

"Yes, you can have mine. Here are the keys. It's parked right outside in the first space. Didn't have time to find a rental this early on a Sunday morning."

"And Viktor? You're going to take him and Brigitte back to the hotel when they're released?"

"Yes, of course. How are they?"

"Fine. We didn't tell them we're leaving. Tell Viktor I'll catch up with him at the hotel tonight, and we'll meet in the office as planned tomorrow morning. I'll let him know about Max and Logan as soon as I hear anything."

"Yes, don't worry. I have Terry coming to get us in about an hour."

Terry is the personal driver Ethan uses for business travel and for trips down to the boat, like the one last night.

"The phone? You got me a phone?"

"Yes, but the best I could do is give you my mother's phone for the rest of the day. I need mine to look after Mr. Lucienne and your other issues, so my mother said you could use hers. I'll get it back from you at the office tomorrow and get you a replacement first thing in the morning."

"Okay, thanks."

Maria puts her finger to her chin. "Um, you might get a lot of calls from people speaking Spanish so just ignore them, or don't answer the phone unless you see it's me calling."

Maria is very dedicated and efficient. She began her time with the firm eight years earlier as a trading clerk and then became Ethan's assistant five years ago. She's single, still lives with her mother, and makes herself available to Ethan around the clock. She was the first person Ethan had the staff in the emergency room call when the coast guard brought them to the hospital a few hours earlier.

Maria reaches inside her purse, "Here's some cash. I'll get you more tomorrow and a new ATM card when the bank opens."

"Okay, we're off. Let me know when you have Viktor and Brigitte back at the hotel."

"I will. Don't worry about them. What about Captain Grays?"

"He's still here. Just look after Viktor."

Ethan doesn't bother to tell Maria that Captain Grays is still unconscious. All that is on his mind at this point is getting to the coroner's office.

The Orange County Coroner's office is in Santa Ana, about forty minutes from Coast Hospital in Laguna Beach. Ethan and Jaclyn take Maria's car and drive directly there. When they arrive, the door to the coroner's office is locked, since it is Sunday. The county coroner is part of the sheriff's department, so they go to the main counter in the sheriff's department and inquire about seeing someone in the coroner's office.

"I'm sorry, sir. The coroner's office is closed until tomorrow morning," says the deputy on duty at the desk.

"I need to speak with someone," Ethan replies. "There was a body taken from a yachting accident last night, and I need to know who it is."

"Are you a relative of the deceased person?"

"No, I am not. My business partner and his wife were with us last night, on our boat. One is missing, and one was brought here."

"Sorry, sir, you'll have to come back tomorrow. And if you aren't a relative, I'm not sure we can give you any information until the medical examiner is through with the investigation."

"But isn't the body here? Can't you tell me if it's a man or a woman?"

"Really, sir, that's not why I'm here."

Ethan snaps back, "I want to see someone in authority!"

"Sir, you can see whomever you want, but you won't get any more information until the coroner's office is open tomorrow morning."

"Damn it! It's my boat, my business partner, and his wife! Why can't anyone tell me anything?"

"Your boat? Then you are a responsible party? Have you spoken with the sheriff's department about the accident?"

"No, but we've spoken with the coast guard."

"That's fine, and they will investigate the maritime issues about your boat sinking, but you've got someone who's dead. That an issue for the medical examiner and the sheriff's office. Wait here."

Ethan glances over at Jackie. "Shit. How'd we walk into this? Let's bolt."

Jaclyn looks shocked. "Bolt? Ethan, someone is dead. It's our boat. It's Max and Logan. What's wrong with you?"

As she finished speaking, a man in civilian clothes comes out from behind a door and introduces himself.

"I'm Detective Carter. I understand you have some connection to the boat sinking last night?"

"Yes, that was my boat, and I'm trying to find out who died last night."

"You apparently left the Coast Hospital without speaking to one of my associates who went there this morning. He's there now speaking with a couple of other passengers."

"Oh shit, who? Who's he speaking to?"

"I don't know, but I can tell you that we *do* need to speak with you. Can you both please come with me to my office?"

Ethan resists, "I want to call my lawyer, before I speak with anyone."

That statement irritates Detective Carter. "Really? Is there a problem? We just want to find out what happened last night."

"Problem? Of course, there's a problem! Someone is apparently dead, you won't tell me who it is, someone else is missing, and I'm the one getting the questions. I want some answers first."

"I understand, sir. But you'll need to file a report on what happened. The sooner we do that, the sooner we *all* get our questions answered."

Ethan looks at Jaclyn, and she can see that he's fuming. He's used to being in control, and when he's not, he doesn't behave rationally.

Jaclyn holds Ethan's hand and looks at Detective Carter.

"If we help you fill out the report, can we see the coroner about the body?"

Detective Carter nods, "I'll tell you what. If you give me the basic facts of what happened last night, I'll call you when the coroner or medical examiner gets here. I don't know if she's coming today or tomorrow morning, but it'll be up to her to answer your questions. All I can do is call you when I find out when she's coming in to examine the body."

Jaclyn looks at Ethan and says, "Let's fill out the report now, then go meet Viktor at the hotel. We can come back as soon as the coroner comes in."

Ethan looks at her and says, "Damn frustrating, but okay. I

do want my attorney on the line, so I'll call him and then we can answer the questions."

With that phone call, Ethan ruins his attorney's Sunday morning golf game. He has him on the phone as they answer questions for the detective for about an hour. Ethan knows so little about the boat, he deflects most questions to be answered later by the unconscious, and unavailable, Captain Grays. The final minutes on the boat were in fact quite eventful, but Ethan simply says there was an explosion and the next thing he knew he was in the water and the coast guard was picking him up. Jaclyn follows his lead and says she remembers even less, and that Ethan's account of the events is better than hers. Neither one of them wants to recount the *actual* events during the last fifteen minutes on the boat before it went down.

Obviously frustrated, Detective Carter ends the line of questioning. "Well, I'll keep my end of the bargain, although I can hardly say you've kept yours. After I get statements from your captain and his first mate, I'll need to get back with both of you."

"Fine," Ethan snaps. "We'll go now and expect your call as soon as the medical examiner shows up."

The detective turns to walk away and mumbles, "Yep."

Ethan and Jaclyn decide to drive back to Los Angeles directly from the sheriff's office.

As they enter the car, the borrowed phone from Maria's mother begins to ring. The caller ID says "Maria," so Ethan answers the phone. "Ola. What's up?"

"Ethan, Viktor is on the phone with ... Max."

"What? On the phone with Max? Oh my God, then she's alive?"

"Apparently so. But that means—"

"Logan's dead. He's the one in the body bag. Oh God."

Hearing Ethan's words, Jaclyn begins to cry. Ethan becomes nauseated with the news. He stares at Jaclyn and drops the phone on the car seat.

7

Someone or Something's Amiss

"You've said enough, Viktor. She's a mess." Seth was trying to console Max after Viktor just told her that "your being alive means Logan is *decede, mon ange*" (dead, my angel).

Just moments earlier, as they were leaving the Ritz-Carlton with the deputies, Max begged them to let her call the hospital. "Please, please, you can arrest me or do what you want, but if the others are at the hospital, please let me speak to them to see who is alive and who is … isn't. That's all I'm asking. Please call the hospital and let me speak to someone who can tell me who is there."

Seth chimed in. "It's the least you can do. She's missing her husband, and if the rest of the group is at Coast Hospital, please let her speak to them so she knows if her husband is there."

The lieutenant agreed. But instead of calling the hospital, he radioed HQ to ask the deputies at the hospital to call him. He knew they had been dispatched earlier that morning to interview the survivors.

All four of them loaded into the deputy's car for a trip to Santa Ana HQ when the lieutenant's phone rang. "Thanks for the quick call, Deputy. We have Mrs. Aronheart here in our custody. Is her husband there with the others you are speaking to?" The voice on the other end of the line gave a short answer, and the lieutenant looked at Max. "Two have left, two are in surgery, and there are just two there now being picked up by someone."

"Who? Who is there?" Max asked.

The lieutenant asked who was still there, and the voice on the other end said, "Mr. Lucienne and his associate."

"Mr. Lucienne is still there, Ms. Aronheart."

"Please, please, may I speak with him?"

"Deputy, please put Mr. Lucienne on the phone. I'm handing my phone to Ms. Aronheart."

Even before the lieutenant passed the phone to Max, Seth knew it would not be good news. If Logan was there, he would have tried to reach him on his cell phone hours earlier. Seth had his cell phone, and Logan knew the number by heart.

As Max took the phone, she said, "Viktor, it's Max. Is Logan there with you?"

Viktor, startled to hear that Max was alive, then uttered those three words in French that let Max know Logan must be the one dead if she was the one alive. Max put her head on Seth's shoulder and cried.

Seth grabbed the phone. "Damn it, Viktor! Couldn't you have thought of a better way to say that?" Seth was furious. He threw the phone back to the front seat where the deputies were sitting, and he wrapped his arms around Max.

At nearly that same moment, Maria hung up with Ethan, whom she called as soon as Viktor began speaking with Max. She tried calling Ethan back after he hung up, but he wasn't answering. Realizing that she needed to get Mr. Lucienne and Brigitte back to LA, she told them both to gather their things and that the driver would take the three of them to the hotel.

"What about Ethan?" Viktor asked.

"He will meet us at the hotel," Maria said, hoping she was right.

Ethan, still in the parking lot at the coroner's office, sat in the car staring out the front window, Jaclyn at his side. Maria kept calling Ethan on her mother's cell phone, but he wasn't answering. Jaclyn was wiping her eyes as Ethan sat there, stoically.

A tap on the car window startles them both. It's Detective Carter. Ethan just stares at him. The detective taps on the window again and motions for Ethan to put the window down.

"Sorry, Detective. You startled me."

"I can see that. Surprised to see you are still here. I looked out the window, expecting you to have left, and then saw the two of you sitting here. Anything wrong?"

Ethan hesitates, looks at Jaclyn and then back at Detective Carter. "I guess we don't need to see the coroner now."

"Why? I came out to tell you she just arrived."

"We know who's in the body bag. It's my business partner."

"And how exactly do you know that?"

"Because I just spoke to his wife. If she's the one alive, then Logan's the one who's dead. Logan, that's his name. Logan Aronheart." Ethan starts to cry but holds it back.

Jaclyn looks at him and can't tell if it was more anger than grief.

The detective doesn't say anything for a moment. He then puts his hand on Ethan's shoulder and says, "Well then, I'm sorry. I guess the coroner and medical examiner will be discovering the same thing shortly."

Wiping his eyes, Ethan says, "Do you mind if we leave? I mean, is there any reason for us to stay now? We'd like to get back to LA and see Max."

The detective looks confused.

"Oh, Max is Logan's wife," Ethan says quietly.

"I understand. Again, I'm sorry. We'd still like to speak further with you and your captain, but it can wait, for now."

"Thanks." Ethan puts his hand on Jaclyn's shoulder and starts the car. Detective Carter turns to go back inside headquarters. A news truck pulls up as Ethan is driving away.

Eyeing the news truck, Jaclyn says, "It's going to be on the news, Ethan. Should you talk with Viktor before we get to LA?"

Ethan says nothing and keeps driving, staring straight ahead.

Just as they are about to pull onto the Santa Ana freeway toward Los Angeles, Maria's cell phone rings. It shows an area code "714" number, which is Orange County. Ethan ignores it, and it rings over to voice mail. The phone rings again. It's the same "714" number.

"Ethan, you should answer it," Jaclyn says, as she picks up the phone and hands it to Ethan.

Ethan pushes the phone away.

On the third ring, Jaclyn answers the phone. "Hello? Who is this?"

Ethan scowls at Jaclyn but keeps driving. He can hear a voice on the other end.

Jaclyn looks startled. "They want us to come back."

"What? Back where?"

"To the coroner's office. It's Detective Carter. He said to turn around and come back. Right away."

"Let me talk to him." Ethan grabs the phone from Jaclyn. "Can't this wait? You said we could talk later."

"Mr. Chandler, we really need for you to come back. It's important. And it's urgent. If you don't come back right away, I'll send a highway patrol cruiser after you. I'll expect to see you here in twenty minutes, tops." The detective hands up.

"Shit. Now what?" Ethan takes the next off ramp and turns around to get back on the freeway going back toward Santa Ana.

"What do they want?" Jaclyn asks.

"You think I know?"

"Should you call Viktor?"

"And tell him what? Forget Viktor for now. We'll call Maria when we're back on our way to LA."

They are both silent until they arrive back at the Orange County Sheriff's office. There are now three news trucks and some reporters around the door to the coroner's office.

Near the entrance to the parking garage, they spot Detective Carter with two deputies. They motion them to a spot inside the parking garage that says, "OC Sheriff Vehicles Only." Detective Carter stands by the door of the car as Ethan steps out.

"We're going in a side entrance. Follow me."

"Why are we here? And what's all the commotion with the news trucks?"

Detective Carter doesn't respond.

Jaclyn is becoming upset and says, "What's going on, Detective?"

Detective Carter looks at them both and says, "We'll talk inside."

Once inside, they go downstairs through another door to a long hallway. At the end of the hallway stands a short, rotund lady with very short gray hair in a white lab coat. There is another lady standing by her side, much younger and slimmer. She appears to be Asian.

Before Ethan and Jaclyn could even introduce themselves, the larger woman says, "What, exactly, is going on here?"

Ethan looks at Detective Carter and says, "What? What is she asking? Who is she anyway?"

Before Carter can respond, the lady speaks again, "I'm the county coroner, and this my medical examiner, Catherine Honda. So, what's going on here?"

"I don't understand. What do you mean?" Ethan is clearly confused, as is Jaclyn. "Do you need for me to identify my partner? I can't do that, I'm sorry, not right now."

"There's nothing to identify. That's the problem, sir." The coroner stares at Ethan and then back at Detective Carter. "There's no body in the bag. Just some burnt clothing, body tissue, and blood. And maybe a body part or two. Your idea of a joke? Where's the body the coast guard told me they put in that bag early this morning?"

Ethan is stunned, and his face goes flush. He looks at Jaclyn, who is holding her mouth like she's preparing to vomit. "Oh, dear God, what do you mean?"

Jaclyn vomits, falls on Ethan, and they both land on the floor.

8

Convergence

The deputies stop the patrol car, pull to the side of the road, and look to the backseat where Seth and Maxine are embracing, sobbing.

"I'm so sorry, ma'am. Ms. Aronheart. Terribly sorry." Deputy Reyes is visibly upset, his own eyes tearing up.

Lieutenant Rupert gets out of the car and opens the back door of the patrol car where Max is sitting. He kneels beside Max, and gently places his hand on her shoulder. "I'm sorry you learned about this in such a despicable way. Who was that heartless man on the other end of the phone?"

Max, wiping her nose and her eyes, turns to Rupert and says, "He didn't mean it; I'm sure. It's just his way. He's … he's just … matter of fact and more dramatic than he needs to be. Can we go see Logan? Can you take me to where he's at? Please?"

Rupert glances at Deputy Reyes. Reyes shakes his head, as if to say that's a bad idea.

Rupert pats Max on the shoulder and says softly, "That's probably not a good idea right now, Ms. Aronheart. The coroner's office is a bad place to see your husband. His appearance could be, well…Why don't you wait until he's taken to a mortuary?"

"No, no, I know what you're saying, but if that's where they've taken him, then we need to go there. If you won't take me, then Seth will do it. What do you need me for anyway? Aren't you finished with me, at least for now?"

Seth chimes in and says, "Please, if you won't take us there, then take me back to my car. I'll take care of it from there."

Rupert stands up, closes the back door, and returns to the front seat. He looks to Reyes and says, "Tell HQ we're bringing Ms. Aronheart to the coroner's office."

Max puts her head in Seth's lap and whispers, "Thank you."

At the coroner's office, the scene is complete mayhem. Reporters and camera crews outside want more information on who's dead and who the passengers were on the boat the night before.

Ethan is sitting outside the women's restroom waiting for Jaclyn, who was cleaning up inside. Detective Carter is on the phone with the Coast Guard, attempting to speak with the crew who retrieved the body earlier that morning.

Jaclyn comes out of the women's restroom holding on to a female deputy who had helped her into the restroom after she vomited and fainted. Looking pale and disoriented, Jaclyn hugs Ethan and says, "What's going on? What kind of nightmare is this?"

Ethan hugs her and pats her on the back but doesn't say anything.

Meanwhile, Deputy Reyes pulls into the parking garage at the Orange County Sheriff's headquarters and finds a parking space close to the entrance. He and Lt. Rupert escort Max and Seth downstairs and into the hallway leading to the coroner's office.

Hearing footsteps coming down the hall, Ethan and Jaclyn look up to see four people coming toward them. Ethan blinks and then says, "Oh my God, it's Max!"

Jaclyn pushes the hair out of her eyes and yells out, "Max, Max, is that you?" Before Max can even answer, Jaclyn runs to her. They embrace, both sobbing.

Max holds Jackie tight, then places her hands on Jackie's cheeks and smiles.

"Oh, Jackie, I'm so glad you and Ethan are okay."

"It's a nightmare, Max, a nightmare. Where have you been? How did you get here? What happened to you last night?"

Max nods her head, "All of that later, sweetheart, but first I want to see Logan."

Jackie is stunned at what Max just said. "What? Haven't they told you?"

Wiping tears from her eyes, Max answers, "Yes, I know he's dead. I want to see him anyway.

"Uh, Ethan …" Jackie doesn't know what to say.

Ethan looks at the deputies and says, "Haven't you told her?"

Reyes looks confused and says softly, "Of course, we have. She knows her husband is dead. Who are you, sir?"

"No, no, that's not it!" Ethan says angrily. "There's no body in the bag. It's empty. Whatever or whoever was picked up by the Coast Guard early this morning is not in the bag."

"What? What are you saying?" Max is startled at those words and grabs the arm of Deputy Reyes. "Did you know this? Then where's my husband?"

Reyes and Rupert are both startled at what they just learned.

Rupert says, "Let me call Carter. He must know."

Ethan snaps, "He knows!" He then points down the hall and says, "There he is—on the phone with the Coast Guard trying to find who handled the body last night."

Rupert waves down the hall at Detective Carter and walks over to speak with him.

Max looks to Ethan, "Then he could be alive?" She begins to smile and says, "This is wonderful news. Then it wasn't Logan in the bag. It's someone else."

Ethan looks at both Max and Seth, who are now embracing and smiling. "It was someone. Someone was in the bag, and the Coast Guard said it was Logan. But the body is not there."

Max shakes her head in confusion, "Who can we speak with to find out what's going on? I need to know." Max walks down the hall to where Lt. Rupert and Detective Carter are talking. "Please tell me what's happening."

Lt. Rupert introduces Detective Carter to Max. Seth joins her, followed by Ethan and Jaclyn.

Detective Carter escorts all of them down the hallway and into a room with a table and chairs. It looks like a briefing room used by the sheriff or the county coroner. He closes the door. "I don't have a solid answer for you, but I can tell you what we know. The Coast Guard retrieved a badly burned body from the water early this morning, only a few hundred yards from where *Copious* sank. The Coast Guard crew put the burned body in one of their own body bags. They were ordered to return to sea to look for the other missing passenger, which would have been you, Ms. Aronheart. The other passengers were taken to the hospital, and they knew there was still one missing. The Coast Guard crew left the body bag on the dock with the port agent, who then gave it to the coroner's staff when they arrived. When the coroner and medical examiner arrived this morning to examine the body, it was gone."

Max is agitated. "Gone? How could that be? Was there nothing inside?"

"Bloody clothes, with some burned flesh and personal items. The coroner and medical examiner are analyzing all the contents to try and identify whose body was in there. Ms. Aronheart, this means the coroner will need to contact your husband's doctor to obtain his medical records, blood type, that sort of thing."

"Fine, of course, I can give him his phone number now. Where is the coroner? May I speak with him?"

"Yes, but the coroner is a woman, and she will be joining us here in a few minutes." Detective Carter looks at Lt. Rupert and says, "Do we have all the details on how Ms. Aronheart found her way from the burning boat to the hotel?"

"We have her statement. Her version of what happened. And statements from the hotel manager. But we haven't verified all of it, particularly the part about the fishermen who picked her up." Rupert seems uncomfortable describing the events that way, and he then turns to Max.

Frowning, Max looks at Rupert and Carter and says, "I've told you the truth. I'm confused too. I'd like answers to the same questions. Who picked me up? Who called Seth to come get me? But all I care about now is finding my husband."

The door opens, and the coroner walks into the room. She's holding a large plastic bag and a notepad. "Good morning. I'm Elizabeth Bearitz, the County Coroner. Call me Betty. May I ask that you each introduce yourselves? Of course, I already know the sheriff's deputies and Detective Carter." She then points to Ethan and Jackie. "Oh, and you, the vomiting lady, and blondie here, we never actually met when you were here earlier."

Ethan clears his throat, trying to contain his irritation at being called blondie. "I'm Ethan Chandler, and this is my wife, the vomiting lady, better known as Jaclyn."

The coroner writes down the names, and without looking up asks, "And your relation to the missing body?"

"Business partner. And friend. Logan Aronheart is his name, and he is my business partner and best friend."

Coroner Bearitz then points to Max and Seth, without saying anything.

Seth speaks up first. "This is Maxine Aronheart, the wife of Logan Aronheart. I'm Seth Boncola, business partner of Ms. Aronheart, and she and Logan are like my adopted parents."

The coroner looks up from her notepad and raises her glasses above her nose. "*Like* adopted parents. What's that mean?"

Seth raises his voice slightly and leans forward. "It means I view them as my parents, and they view me as their son. Is that clear enough?"

The coroner says nothing but makes a few more notes on her pad.

Tossing her notepad on the table, Ms. Bearitz pulls out a chair and sits down next to Max. She opens the plastic bag and shows Max a ring, which is badly burned. "Can you identify this Mrs. Aronheart?"

Max gasps and puts her hands over her mouth. She doesn't say anything. Seth puts his arm around her shoulders.

Max reaches out to touch the ring, but the coroner pulls it back. "I asked you to identify it, not to touch it."

"It's Logan's ring," she says softly. She begins to cry.

"Wedding ring?"

"No. A ring I gave him for our fifteenth wedding anniversary. He wore it on his right ring finger. Where did you get it?"

"In the bag."

"Were there other items? What else?"

"No other jewelry."

"What else then? Please tell me."

"Bloody clothes, this ring, and some other items I'm still examining. But no body if that's what you're asking."

The room is silent when Seth speaks up. "Okay, so what happens now? Logan is missing. Who's looking for him? When do we find out if Logan was in the bag and how he got out, if it was him? What is happening here?"

Detective Carter stands up and looks at Max. "There's a full-scale investigation, of course, already underway. Possible homicide. Possible kidnapping. Possible drowning. You name it. And as uncomfortable as it is for you, Ms. Aronheart, I'm going to have to ask you to come with me and Deputy Reyes and Lt. Rupert. We've got to get your story pinned down to every detail. And, Mr. Chandler, you and your captain are going to have to get very specific with us about the last fifteen minutes on that boat."

Ethan stands up and looks intently at Detective Carter. "Are you arresting us?"

"No. We just want to clarify your statements so we can investigate this mess and try to locate Mr. Aronheart. And determine exactly what happened to him, alive or dead."

Max looks startled.

Carter clears his throat and addresses Max. "I'm sorry for putting it that way, Ms. Aronheart."

Max shakes her head. "I understand. But let me ask you this—is the Coast Guard still looking for my husband?"

Carter and Rupert look at each other waiting for the other to speak first. The short silence is awkward. Carter finally speaks, "We have advised the Coast Guard that the body they retrieved is missing. And since we can't confirm who was in the bag at this point, we have asked them to keep looking for a body at sea. Captain Westmore, the Coast Guard captain in charge last night, is furious, as you would expect. He has a patrol cutter searching the vicinity of the sinking boat this afternoon. With the currents and sea conditions last night and early this morning, he's not optimistic about finding anything. I should also tell you that his crew is very definite that they retrieved a badly burned body in close proximity to the debris from the ship."

Ethan shouts, "Who the hell would steal a burned body? Really? And who brought the body here?"

Detective Carter looks at the coroner, who is staring down at her clipboard. "That would be a member of my staff."

Ethan moves closer to her. "Who, exactly, on your staff? May we speak with them?"

"My intern, that's who. And no, you may not … speak with him."

The room is silent for a moment.

Ethan doesn't let up. "Who is this intern? Is he an idiot?"

The coroner pushes back her chair and leans over the table at Ethan. "Not quite an idiot, Mr. Chandler. He is a forensic pathology assistant intern. Pathology residency in training from the University of California, Irvine. He's very sharp. And he also has better manners than you, sir."

Ethan sits up in his chair, speechless for a moment, but then says, "But a body just doesn't disappear on the way to the morgue, does it?"

Detective Carter puts up his hand to end the discourse between Ethan and the coroner.

"That's exactly what we want to know, Mr. Chandler." Detective Carter then motions to Max, Seth, Ethan, and Jaclyn to come with him to obtain more detailed statements from each of them.

Coroner Bearitz raises her hand and says, "Don't leave without giving me the contact information for Mr. Aronheart's doctor."

Max speaks up immediately. "Dr. Dorsett. Gale Dorsett. He's

a man. My cell phone went down with the boat, so I don't have his number. But he's at the Sunset Doheny Medical Plaza. I guess I should call him first and explain what's happening."

The coroner nods her head, "Yes, do that, and quickly. I'll need his blood type and medical records as soon as possible. I can send a messenger right away to retrieve them."

Seth uses the web browser on his phone to look up the website for Dr. Dorsett. "Max, I have his number here. He shows the number to the coroner, who writes it down.

The coroner tilts her reading glasses off her nose and looks at Max. "Do you know the doctor well enough that you can reach him on a Sunday?"

Max looks at Seth. "Please dial the number and ask his answering service to locate him. Tell him it's for me and it's an emergency."

Seth dials the number, the answering service comes on, and he asks that Dr. Dorsett be paged for an emergency.

As they are leaving the room for Detective Carter's office, Deputy Reyes looks down at his cell phone and then up at Max. "Ms. Aronheart, I guess you should know that Channel Four just ran a story saying your husband is apparently dead and in the county morgue. Says the other passengers are all accounted for."

"How would they have that information?" Max asks Detective Carter.

"Well, it's not 100 percent correct, is it? They apparently don't know the body is missing, but I assume they'll figure that out soon enough. The reporters are demanding a press conference with the coroner and the sheriff."

"And I will have to give them a formal statement this evening," says Coroner Bearitz as she leaves the room.

As they are going down the hall to Detective Carter's office, Max eyes the door to the women's restroom. "May I make a quick stop here at the ladies' room? Just be a minute."

Carter waves her in and says, "Sure. Take your time."

As soon as Max enters the restroom, Seth quickly follows and says, "Oh you forgot something, Max!"

Carter looks at the others and asks, "Did he just follow her in there?"

Inside the restroom, Max turns to Seth and says, "I know. I saw it too. That bag had some of Logan's other things."

Seth wipes his upper lip and whispers, "Yeah, like the business card holder I gave him for his birthday two years ago."

"Burned. Partly melted." Max replies, looking down at the floor.

"I know. But why didn't she ask you about those items?"

Max replies, "I don't know. She knows that I saw them, so why not ask? Is she afraid I'll be more upset than I already am? It makes no sense. Who steals a body and leaves the jewelry?"

"We've got to get into her office and see what else she has from the body bag."

"Exactly what I was thinking."

9

Fifteen Minutes

Detective Carter has an assistant with a digital recording device set up in an interrogation room near his office. Max, Ethan, Jackie, and Seth come in, along with Deputy Reyes and Lt. Rupert. They all take a seat around the table.

Seth is the last to sit down. He surveys the room and walks once around the table before taking a seat next to Max. "Cozy little interrogation room. Just like on TV. But isn't this where you interrogate the suspects? The perpetrators? The perps?"

Carter smiles and says, "Yep. You got that right. But you aren't suspects. Not officially. My office is just not big enough to get collective statements from all of you as a group. You've each given us statements separately, and now we have some questions to shed light on some discrepancies."

Ethan puts his hands together and pounds them lightly on the table. "But we've already given you statements. My wife and I were in your office hours ago and gave you everything we know. Max was interviewed at the hotel. What more do you want?"

Carter opens a file on the table. "It's the last fifteen minutes. On the boat. Your statements don't match. That's why we're here. Let's focus on the last fifteen minutes."

Ethan stands up from his chair. "For cripes' sake, Carter! What does that have to do with Logan missing? Isn't that all that matters at this point? Where is my partner? Max's husband? This other bullshit is irrelevant."

"Mr. Chandler, you can yell and swear all you want, but that only means we're here longer than we need to be."

Ethan sits down and pushes his chair away from the table. He frowns at Detective Carter and holds his hands out in an "all yours" gesture.

Carter leans forward across the table, looking directly at Ethan. "Mr. Chandler, you said there was a discussion between you, Mr. Lucienne, and Mr. Aronheart at the back of the boat and that an explosion interrupted your conversation. What was your conversation about?"

"Nothing in particular." Ethan pauses, rubbing his neck. "A little business from the office and some plans for the evening. That's all."

"You said that Mr. Aronheart left the deck after the first explosion?"

"Yes, that's right. He ran to get his wife."

"And you never saw him again?"

"No, no, I didn't."

"And you went on to say that you and your wife and Mr. Lucienne went to find the captain. Is that correct?"

"Yes."

"And you didn't find him before the second explosion, correct?"

"Right. When the second explosion went off, we went for the life raft at the stern. I looked for Logan and Max, but I couldn't find them. The boat was going down quickly so we got in the raft as fast as we could."

"What was the condition of Mr. Aronheart when you last saw him?"

"Condition? Are you crazy? He was frantically looking for his wife."

"Nothing else? Nothing physical before the explosion when he went to retrieve Ms. Aronheart?"

Max and Seth are listening to Ethan intently. They're waiting for the part where Logan got his injury. But Ethan says nothing.

Carter gets up from the table and stands over Ethan. "Ms. Aronheart's statement said that when Mr. Aronheart entered the salon to retrieve her, his face was bleeding badly."

Ethan looks briefly at Jaclyn and then turns to Carter. "I don't know about that. He was fine when he ran to the salon. Maybe he fell or something from the explosion."

Max speaks up. "Ethan, he had a huge gash—"

Carter quickly interrupts, "Please! Ms. Aronheart don't say anything. I'm asking the questions here."

Ethan stands up, looks at Carter and then at Max. "I don't know any more than I've told you. When he went to look for you, Max, he wasn't bleeding."

Max objects, "But it's not that far from the back deck to the salon door, Ethan! He was bleeding profusely! It was only seconds after the first explosion because I was still lying on the floor when he came in!"

"Okay, okay. Let's take a breath," Carter says. "What about Mr. Lucienne's bloody hand? Did you see how that happened?"

"No. No, I didn't." Ethan looks at Jaclyn, who is still silent. She looks back at him, wondering if she should say something to support him. She remains silent, and then stares at the floor.

Carter picks up a piece of paper from the file. "A bottle. Mr. Lucienne said he cut his hand on a bottle. That's what he told the nurse who bandaged him up at the hospital."

Ethan put his hands up and rises from his chair. "Look, I'm not quarreling with any of this. So be it. If Viktor cut his hand on a bottle, fine. What happened to Logan, I don't know, but if Max here says he was bleeding, I believe her. You're talking about a matter of minutes for all these events, and we were in a state of panic. It's not like this played out for hours."

"There was no argument on the deck?" Carter looks at both Max and Ethan.

Ethan glances at Max but doesn't say anything.

Max speaks softly, "Ethan, I heard yelling. That's why I was coming outside."

Ethan disagrees. "Max, you can speak with Jaclyn here or Viktor. We were laughing and talking but not arguing. Right, honey?"

Jaclyn looks at Max and then addresses Detective Carter, "It's all so confusing. The whole thing. But no, we weren't arguing with Logan."

Cater is frustrated. "Were you and Mr. Chandler arguing? Mr. Chandler and Mr. Lucienne? *Anyone* arguing about anything?"

"No." Jaclyn purses her lips and looks at the floor.

Carter stands up, pointing at Reyes and Rupert, and asks, "You two have anything relevant to add from when you picked up Ms. Aronheart and Mr. Boncola?"

They both shake their heads no.

"Okay. One last thing. Mr. Boncola, do you have any idea who called for you at the nightclub telling you to retrieve Ms. Aronheart?"

"That's the third time I have been asked that question, and for the third time, the answer is no. I never spoke to anyone. Both times it was a message from someone at the club who answered the phone."

"We will be in touch with them as well."

Seth shakes his head and put his arm around Max's shoulder.

Carter closes the file, opens the door, and says, "You are all free to go, but don't leave the city. No travel. Not until you hear from us."

As they leave the room, Ethan takes Max by the hand, and they stop in the hallway. "As if we all needed that. What happened in there is just … disgusting. Can we take you both home?"

Max looks at Seth and says, "No, thanks. We're going to get Seth's car at the hotel. He'll take me home. Or I may not even leave here until we find Logan. Might check in to a hotel and have some things sent down."

"I can do that for you, Max!" Jaclyn practically leaps out of her shoes as she spoke.

"No, no, it's fine, Jackie. Not sure what I'm doing yet."

Ethan let's go of Max's hand. "We'll need to talk, Max ... when you're up to it."

"Fine. I'll get a new cell phone and call you when I have it so you can reach me."

"Okay, right then. Please call me as soon as you hear something about Logan. I don't trust these goons here to do that."

Ethan and Jaclyn walk away. Seth stands behind Max as she watches them go down the corridor and out the door, not even looking back. Seth puts his hands on her shoulders and whispers into her ear, "They don't exactly seem bereaved, do they?"

After remaining silent for a few moments, Max turns to Seth and softly replies, "Enough of them. Let's get to the coroner's office."

Max and Seth go down the flight of stairs to the coroner's office, hoping they can go in without her being there. They think she would be at the press conference by now. Reaching the door, they quietly go in. No one is at the front desk. Seth knocks on the door to the morgue. No one answers. He tries the door, but it's locked. A few seconds later, the door behind them flies open and Coroner Bearitz rushes in like a bull out of a chute. She's as startled to see them as they are to see her.

"What are you two doing here? Do you have some more information for me?"

"Well, actually, we were hoping you had more information for us." Max points to the door to the morgue and says, "You have more of my husband's belongings in there. I want to see them."

"I'm the coroner. This is *my* office. You don't call the shots here, ma'am."

"I don't care who calls the shots, but I want to see my husband's other possessions you have in that plastic bag."

"Can't do that."

"Why not?"

"Still an active investigation. I'll let you know when you can inspect the other items."

Max looks at Seth and then walks a few steps to where Ms. Bearitz is standing near the door. She is about two inches from Ms. Bearitz, who is now backing up against the door from which she just entered. Now nearly face-to-face, Max clenches her jaw and then speaks softly to Ms. Bearitz, "You're going to open that door, and show me the items you have from my husband, right now. And if you don't, I'm going out there to the television cameras and tell them you're keeping me from seeing my husband's belongings. I'll also tell them that you're withholding information from me while my husband is missing or possibly dead. I'll play the bereaved widow, being trampled on by the county coroner. I play well to the camera, Ms. Bearitz. Open the door. Now."

The coroner is startled. She looks at them both but says nothing.

Seth comes closer to the coroner and says, "She means it. So do I. Open that door for her, or by the time she gets back from speaking with the reporters, you'll be ready for a body bag of your own."

"My God, are you two crazies?"

Max speaks up softly, "Just let me see what you have from my husband, and we'll leave. Quietly."

The coroner walks around Max and toward the locked door to the morgue. She opens it and waves them both past with her hand. Turning on the lights, she walks toward the wall where refrigerated vaults hold the bodies being investigated or autopsied. "Not the part of my operation I like people to see, especially people who may have lost their spouse. For the record, you're forcing me to do this against my better judgment."

Max nods her head and grabs Seth by the hand. "Of course. Call it want you like. I just want to see Logan's things in that bag."

The room smells of chemicals. Max feels faint as they walk toward the vaults. Seth pretends it doesn't bother him, but he feels queasy too. They hold each other's hand tightly.

Coroner Bearitz slowly opens a vault that is over a large metal table. She reaches inside and pulls out the plastic bag, which was sitting on top of the body bag the Coast Guard brought in earlier that morning. Throwing the bag on the metal table, she then puts on her gloves. "I don't want you touching anything, but I will show you what's here."

Max and Seth, both feeling lightheaded, watch carefully as she slowly places objects on what looks like a piece of wax paper or plastic film. Using tweezers, the coroner slowly and delicately lifts items, one by one, from the bag—a ring; a watch; a neck chain; a card case; a pen; a bloody handkerchief with Logans initials, "L.E.A," mostly obscured by blood; a set of keys with a gold Tiffany ring bearing Logan's initials on it; and a pair of reading glasses, mostly melted with one lens broken.

Max stares intently at the items but says nothing. She examines the items one by one, very slowly. Her eyes are tearing, but she is trying not to cry. Seth put his hand around her waist while he continues to clutch her other hand tightly. Seth is struggling not to pass out.

"They're all his. My husband's. Why didn't you show these to me before?"

Ms. Bearitz takes her gloves off and proceeds to wash her hands without saying anything. She then walks back over to Max and folds her arms. "You think I like showing things like this to someone whose husband is dead or missing? It just adds to the pain. And to be honest, you're still a person of interest to the sheriff. If this ends up being evidence, you've put me in a bad position by showing it to you. That's not good for you, and it certainly isn't good for me."

Max looks at her and says, "I understand. Is this all you have?"

The coroner ignores the question.

"I said, 'Is this all you have?'"

"You wanted to see what was in the bag, and I've shown it to you. That's what you wanted."

"Yes, but do you have anything else?"

"I don't have a body if that's what you're asking."

Max is persistent. "I asked you if you have anything else. Tell me, and I promise we'll go."

"Tissue. Burned human tissue, or at least it looks to be human. A tooth. A … finger. Lots of bloody clothing. I was planning on working on all that tonight before you barged in here."

Max starts to speak, but the coroner cuts her off. "Don't even ask me to show you one more thing, or I'll call the deputies on duty. I'm not about to show you burnt human flesh or body parts before I know if it is in fact human or who it belongs to. The quicker your doctor gets me your husband's medical records and his dentist gets me his dental records, the quicker I can do my job. Now go. I should never have let you in here."

Max goes flush. Seth looks at her and says, "Hey, Maxie, you, okay? Let's get out of here."

Without saying anything, Max leads Seth out by the hand. She stops at the door and looks back at Ms. Bearitz, who is now putting the items back in the plastic bag. "Thank you. I am very grateful."

The coroner doesn't even look up. She waves them out with her hand and says, "Lock the door behind you."

10

Je Deviens Fou! (I'm Going Mad!)

"Why doesn't he answer? *Enfante stupide!*" Viktor is red with anger. He keeps calling his nephew Laurent on his cell phone, but there is no answer. He's been calling since early this morning, to no avail.

Brigitte grabs Viktor's cell phone and pleads, "Viktor, please. Relax. We've all been through a lot. He's probably down in Palm Springs for the weekend. *Se detendre!*"

"Lighten up? My nephew is missing, and you tell me to lighten up?" Viktor is furious. His nephew works at Ethan and Logan's hedge fund. Viktor arranged the job for him. Aside from doing his sister a favor by employing her son, Viktor uses Laurent as his informant about what is going on at the hedge fund. Laurent also looks after Viktor's portion of the hedge fund that he calls his "personal account"— a personal account to the tune of over four hundred million dollars. Logan and Ethan's hedge fund manages over $2.5 billion in assets, of which $1.7 billion represents Viktor's collection of clients. The rest of the assets are evenly divided between Viktor's personal account and the portion belonging to "retail" customers of the fund. The retail customers are mostly long-time friends or clients of Logan's that he brought with him to the fund from his prior investment management business.

Brigitte takes Viktor's hand to calm him down. "Laurent told you he was going away for the weekend. You knew that Viktor.

The boy works hard; leave him alone and let him have some fun. After all, you only have bad news for him, all of which he'll find out tomorrow morning when he gets to work."

Viktor disagrees, "I don't want him to see it on the news or social media. I want to tell him what happened before he sees it on his own." Viktor turns to Brigitte, puts his hand on her knee, then stares out the car window.

"It will be okay. He'll call you back before he speaks with anyone else." Brigitte takes Viktor's hand between both of hers and places them in her lap.

Viktor and Brigitte are in the backseat of the car, and Maria is up front with the driver, Terry. Maria turns to face Viktor and Brigitte. "Viktor, we're almost there. About ten minutes."

"Thank God, mon amie. Is Ethan meeting us?"

Maria is silent for a moment. "Eventually, yes."

"Where is he? I thought he'd be there before us?"

"He's just left the sheriff's office. They're on their way."

By the time they arrive at the Beverly Hills Hotel, it is nearly dark. Brigitte and Viktor go to their respective rooms to freshen up. Maria tells them she will call their rooms when Ethan arrives and then they will have dinner.

The moment he arrives in his room, which is a spacious one-bedroom bungalow in the gardens of the hotel, Viktor places a call to Paris. He is the only one of the group to have kept his cell phone through all the chaos and confusion of the rescue. There is no answer. He then dials another number, but there is no answer there either. He decides to shower and then try his call later. Just as he is entering the shower, his phone rings. He sees the number and quickly answers. "I have it under control. Don't worry."

The voice on the other end of the line is loud and forceful. Viktor keeps shaking his head but says nothing. He just listens to the shouting.

When the shouting stops, Viktor says softly, "I understand. Completely. I will get back to you as soon as I speak with Ethan."

With that, the other party hangs up.

Viktor is sweating, so he wipes his brow. Looking at himself in the mirror he sees that he is flush and shaking. Stepping into the shower, he pounds his fist against the wall.

Ethan and Jaclyn arrive at the hotel and see Maria sitting in the lobby. She runs over to them as soon as she sees them. "He's very agitated. He can't find his nephew, and he was getting nasty calls from Paris while we were in the car on the way up here."

Ethan knows exactly what the calls are about. "Where is he now?"

"In his bungalow. I told him I would call when you were here and ready for dinner."

Ethan shakes his head, "We can't eat here. No privacy. Go to the Polo Lounge and tell Tony to bring dinner to the house. In one hour. He knows what Viktor likes. Tell him the usual lobster salad for me and Jackie. Pick something out for yourself and Brigitte and then meet us at the house."

"What about Viktor?"

"Tell him you'll bring him to our house for dinner. Get Brigitte too. You'll need to keep her occupied while Viktor and I talk privately. Jackie and I want to get cleaned up now. See you at the house in an hour."

"But he'll be upset to not see you right away."

"He will be seeing me. Just tell him we wanted to clean up and have a quiet dinner at the house. The house is ten minutes away; he'll be fine."

Ethan and Jackie drive up Benedict Canyon to their house, which is about a mile up the canyon from the Beverly Hills Hotel. It is a large, sprawling Spanish revival estate that was been built by a silent film star and later owned by a film producer who used it as a party house. Ethan first saw the house when he came to Los Angeles ten years ago. It has an amazing view of the city below.

On most days, you can see the ocean and Catalina Island in the distance. He had dreamed of owning it and restoring it someday. It was empty for years and in a total state of neglect. Five years ago, Ethan bought it from the estate of the film producer and hired Max to oversee the restoration and decoration of the house. It took two years to complete, and he and Jaclyn moved in three years ago.

Walking into the house, Ethan catches his reflection in the hallway mirror. He pauses and stares at the mirror, as if he is seeing someone for the first time. Jaclyn is halfway up the stairs when she glances over her shoulder to see Ethan standing, motionless, in front of the mirror.

"You're still as handsome as ever," she says with a smile.

Ethan seems not to hear her.

"Ethan?"

He looks up at her and smiles. "Tell me I don't look as bad as this mirror shows me."

"I never liked that mirror. Makes everything look distorted. Come on; you'll look better in the shower!" She smiles and hurries up the stairs.

They love to shower together, and doing so is the one thing that truly makes Ethan relax. Jackie knows how to arouse him and please him in the shower. Whatever stress or worries Ethan brings home, Jackie was sure she could fix everything in the shower. This night is no different. The events of the past twenty-four hours seem to fade away, as if they never left the house for that fateful Saturday night on the boat. It is only after the shower, when they are both getting dressed, that Ethan realizes the events of Saturday night and Sunday morning are not a nightmare but are real. Viktor will be there soon, and there is still no word about Logan.

Jackie comes into Ethan's dressing room to say, "We should have stayed in Laguna with Max."

Ethan turns to her. "I thought the same thing. She's all alone down there without Logan. Damn this Viktor thing. We should be down there with her and not here with this snotty little frog."

Jaclyn is startled to hear Ethan agree with her so strongly. "Then let's just leave and be with her."

"I'd love to, but what about Viktor? And I've got to get to the office early tomorrow morning to figure out what's going on."

"What *is* going on, Ethan? Why were the three of you yelling and fighting last night on the boat? Why won't you tell me? I feel like you're lying to Max. Bad enough you lied to the police, but you're lying to Max too. And to me."

Ethan turns to Jackie, who is standing at the door of the dressing room. "Don't ... please don't tell me I'm lying to Max. You don't understand. That argument was between me, Viktor, and Logan. It doesn't concern you or Max. Don't bring it up again. Nothing happened. Period."

Jackie turns away and leaves the dressing room, saying nothing.

Ethan yells to her, "Get dressed! They'll be here soon."

The doorbell rings, and Jackie runs downstairs to greet Viktor, Maria, and Brigitte. Ethan is in the bar fixing himself a drink. At nearly the same time, the catering van from the Beverly Hills Hotel arrives with dinner. Jackie directs them to the kitchen while showing the others into the bar.

The bar is in a beautifully restored art deco room, most of which was recreated from original pictures of the house Max found at the Beverly Hills Historical Society. The silent film star who built the house gave large parties, even during Prohibition. Many of them were beautifully documented in photographs and newspaper stories that told of wild, decadent affairs and police raids.

Descending the steps into the bar, Viktor yells out to Ethan, "I presume you made my drink first, considering all you've put me through, my *borreau*?"

"*Borreau*? What the hell is that?" Ethan is busy shaking a martini.

"Tormentor. Last night and today, you are my tormentor."

"Considering that Logan may be dead, I don't think you have much to complain about, Viktor."

"I should say I do. My nephew is missing, and Logan didn't put through the wire on Friday. Why did he wait until Saturday night to tell us that? And how do we find out what he did, with both him and Laurent missing? Really, Ethan, this is *plus* unacceptable."

"Viktor, can we ditch the French, at least for tonight? I'm sorry if you find this all most unacceptable, but I'm missing my business partner and best friend, your nephew is missing, and we've got your anxious customer looking for a wire tomorrow morning that's not going to show up."

"Exactly. And what are you going to do about it?"

"We're going to the office first thing tomorrow and hope we can figure it out."

"Laurent will figure it out. I'm sure he will be there early."

Ethan looks up at Viktor and says very intently, "And… if he's not?"

Victor looks startled. "What then, mon ami?"

"Then we'll work with Rebecca to log into his computer and take care of the wire ourselves."

"Can we do that? Without Logan?"

"Yes. Yes, we can. We won't have a choice."

"Then what do we have to talk about?"

"You know damn well what we must talk about, Viktor. Let's cut the social curiosity and get to the point."

"And the point is?"

"Are you kidding me, Viktor? Are you feigning ignorance or just testing me?"

Viktor doesn't understand what Ethan is saying.

Ethan hands Viktor his French Martini, and they both sit down at the bar. "I suggest you drink the first one very quickly. That's what *I* intend to do." With that, Ethan downs his gin martini in nearly one gulp.

Viktor hoists his glass with his usual flourish and downs his as well. "There's another where that one came from?"

"Of course." Ethan picks up the martini shaker for Viktor's French martini and pours another round into his glass.

Brigitte and Jaclyn walk into the bar. Before either can say anything, Ethan blurts out, "We aren't finished yet."

Jaclyn smiles and replies, "But can't you at least fix us a wee drinkie?"

"Okay, I'll get you a drink, but then we need a few more minutes alone."

Ethan fixes them both drinks, and Jaclyn says, "Dinner's ready when you are. We'll be out by the pool."

Ethan sits down next to Viktor at the bar and looks at him squarely. "Viktor, your client has made a redemption request that is impossible for us to meet. I want to be sure you understand that we can't liquidate all those holdings in twenty-four hours. It's impossible."

Viktor smiles, "Not my problem."

"Oh, but it is your problem. We'll have to take cash from the retail customers and some from your personal account as a loan until we can liquidate the holdings from your client's account."

"Do what you must with the retail clients. That is not my worry. But you may not touch my personal account."

"Then the wire will be short, Viktor. That's what I want to be sure you understand tonight. Logan couldn't send the wire Friday because he couldn't raise the cash that quickly. The only way we can redeem a billion dollars of your client's money is to borrow some from you and the retail clients. And borrowing from the retail accounts is illegal."

Viktor stares at his drink and says nothing.

"Viktor, tomorrow morning, when you come to the office, we're liquidating most of your account and most of the retail customers to cover the wire to Paris. You know damn well that our fund agreement gives us six months to redeem money from the Global Protocol Hedge Fund. Your client is being unreasonable demanding $1 billion of their $1.7 billion investment, virtually overnight. If I wanted to, I could hold him to that agreement. The Securities and Exchange Commission would back me up on that."

"But a hedge fund is not subject to regulation by the SEC. Even I know that. It's for sophisticated investors."

Ethan nodded. "Exactly. But I think the securities regulators *would* have an interest in a client compelling us to act irresponsibly."

Viktor stares at his drink and speaks slowly, "You know, my friend, that is not an option. Not unless we want to end up like dear Logan. Dead or missing. I am presuming you understand that. *J'ai raison, n'est-ce pas?*"

Ethan knows that statement in French means, 'You know I am right.'

Viktor smiles and hoists his martini.

"Yes, Viktor, you are right about that. Very right. Your client is a nasty man."

"Then Laurent shall prepare for us the wire, tomorrow morning, and all will be *fini*."

Ethan places a fresh drink in front of Viktor and pours another for himself.

"Viktor, I want you to finish that drink and then look at me. And listen carefully."

Raising his eyebrow and his glass, Viktor finishes his third French martini in two gulps. Placing the empty glass down on the bar, he shoves it slowly toward Ethan, who is sitting next to him.

Ethan finishes his third martini and shoves his glass and Viktor's to the side of the bar. He puts his hands together on the bar in front of Viktor, who is staring at him as if expecting a revelation of good news.

"Viktor, in a few minutes, you and I are going out by the pool to have a nice dinner with Jackie, Brigitte, and Maria. We're going to be jovial and happy. After dinner, you will excuse yourself, and Maria will have Terry take you and Brigitte back to the hotel. It's then, and only then, that you will go to your bungalow and have a good cry. You will not cry or be upset in front of Jackie or Brigitte. Or Maria."

"Cry? What do I have to cry about, Ethan? Is there more dour news on Logan?"

Ethan pauses. "No. There's no news about Logan. You will be crying for Laurent."

"What? Laurent? Why should I cry for Laurent?"

"He's dead, Viktor. You will cry for him tonight because he is dead."

Viktor stands up from the bar stool and nearly falls over backward. Ethan catches him.

"Sit down, Viktor. Don't cause a scene. Any of your usual theatrics will upset the girls."

Viktor sits down on his bar stool and takes out his handkerchief to wipe his brow. His lips are quivering, and his eyes are tearing up.

"No tears, Viktor. Not until you get to the hotel."

Viktor starts to say something, and Ethan puts his hand over his mouth.

"Suicide. Friday morning. Laurent never showed up at work on Friday, and when it came time to send the partial wire, Logan said he couldn't do it without the passwords and routing clearances from Laurent. Maria tried to reach Laurent by phone all morning. Logan went to his apartment to get him and found him dead. Overdose of pills and booze."

"*Un accident.*"

"No, Viktor, it was not an accident. It was a suicide."

Viktor holds his head and stares down at the bar.

"Logan had everything cleaned up at his apartment, by a professional. We don't want publicity. Suicide of a staff member would draw attention to the firm that we don't want right now."

"What?" Viktor is clearly startled. "My sister's son is dead, you wait three days to tell me, and you say it's been carefully cleaned up by someone to avoid publicity?"

"That's right, Viktor. And don't pull a guilt trip on any of us. It's your client that has caused all of this. Laurent knew we couldn't meet the wire, and he was going to be shamed in front of his family when they found out why. He also knows the truth about your client—the ugly truth—and he couldn't face it. So, he took his life. Logan showed me the suicide note."

"May I see the—"

Ethan cuts him off. "Not now. I'll show it to you later, Viktor."

"Where … where is he? His body?"

"In a safe place. We have lots to do tomorrow, so tonight you cry for your nephew. But not now. Now we're going out to the pool to have a lovely dinner with three beautiful women, and then you'll leave for the hotel and cry all you want. In your bungalow. That's it for now. Put on your cheerful face."

With that, Ethan holds Viktor by the arm and escorts him out to the pool for dinner.

11

The Red Dragon Appears:
A Sino-French Affair Viewed from Laguna

Seth pulls into the driveway of the Ritz-Carlton Laguna Niguel in Dana Point. As he heads for the valet-parking lane, he looks at Max with a frown. "Y'know, sweets, this maybe wasn't such a good idea."

Max puts her hand on Seth's knee and smiles. "So, the Ritz isn't good enough for Lydia LaFon?"

"Lydia has done the Ritz many times, my dear woman, mostly on her back!"

With that, they both laugh, and Seth stops the car for the valet, who is a different staff member than earlier that morning. "Welcome to the Ritz-Carlton, my name is Jared. Are you checking in?"

"Yes, we are. Seth Boncola and Maxine Aronheart. Two rooms."

Jared smiles, "Please, may I call a bellman to take your luggage to the rooms?"

Max takes the valet's hand and smiles. "Darling, that would be lovely except we don't have any luggage. We're traveling very light!"

With that, they all three laugh, and Seth and Max walk into the lobby. Seth turns to Max and whispers, "Sweetie, are you sure you want to sleep here tonight? This is where your nightmare began early this morning."

"No, honey, that isn't right. My nightmare began when I saw Logan's bloody face and the boat started to sink. That was the nightmare. Nearly drowning at sea was a nightmare—and being abandoned on the beach. Here at the hotel, I was rescued by you. I don't know what would have happened if I hadn't seen you sprint into the lobby early this morning. So, this is a happy place for me. And I know Logan is still here, somewhere, not far away. Please, I really want to stay here tonight."

"You sure?"

"More than sure. This place makes me think of Logan. I feel like he's just up in the room."

"Whoa, sweetie, are you delusional? It's been a long day."

"You forget. Logan and I were just here, a month ago. The wedding for Logan's cousin and her fiancé, they had it here, over-looking the ocean at Sunset. Logan and I spent the night here."

Seth is relieved. He puts his arm around her, and they approach the front desk to check in. They are both surprised to see Chad still on duty at 5 p.m. this evening. He was the night front desk clerk on staff when Max made her surprise appearance in the lobby at 3 a.m. earlier that same day.

Seth frowns, "Chad, it's great to see you but don't tell me you've been at the front desk all morning and afternoon since we last saw you in the wee hours this morning?"

"Well, yes sir, it's unusual to work the afternoon/evening shift the same day we work the late night/early morning shift."

Max and Seth look at each other but say nothing.

Chad, sensing their unease, speaks up, "Let me explain."

Seth smiles, "No explanation necessary, we just want to check into our rooms and get some rest. It's been a hellacious day. I'm sure you understand."

Chad purses his lips and shakes his head. "Sure, yes, of course. Mr. Engel, the Night Manager, has upgraded you both to a junior suite. Unfortunately, they aren't adjoining rooms but are directly across the hall from each other."

Max pulls her hair from her eyes and places her hands on the desk. "Is Mr. Engel here, so we may thank him? That is very kind."

"No, Ms. Aronheart, he's not here, but he asked me to be the one to check you in tonight, and to let him know you're safely here. That's why I'm working a double shift. He couldn't be here, so he asked me to take care of you. Since I know you both. That's the reason I'm here." And, well, there's one more thing."

Seth frowns. "Something more? Like what?"

"Well, let me look at my notes one more time." Chad pulls a piece of paper from his jacket pocket, and reads it, mumbling his words to himself. "Well, see, we are checking you in under different names. And your bill has been taken care of."

Max steps back from the desk and shakes her head. "What? Our rooms have been paid for, but we must check in under different names."

Chad nods his head, "Yes, Ms. Aronheart."

Seth and Max look at each other, confused. Seth asks Max, "Should we leave?"

Chad interrupts, "No, please don't leave. Mr. Engel wants you to stay, please. I don't know what's going on, but Mr. Engel was emphatic that you are our guests tonight, you will be safe, and he will speak with you in the morning before you depart. I have two lovely junior suites for you. Please, enjoy them. Don't get me in trouble. Please stay so Mr. Engel may speak with you in the morning."

Max takes a deep breath and exhales. "Ok then. Thank you, Chad." Looking at Seth, she goes on, "Sweetie, let's get some rest. Can this day get any stranger? Let's get some sleep and deal with all this in the morning."

Seth says nothing, but nods in agreement.

As they walk down the lobby corridor to the elevators, Max glances over her shoulder and waves to Chad. "Well, that was certainly a different reception than last night."

Seth pulls her shoulder closer to his. "Well, it makes a huge difference when you arrive in a BMW with a great-looking guy instead of dragging your sandy, wet ass in sweatpants into the lobby of the Ritz at three in the morning! Speaking of which, we've got to get you some clothes, Max. I mean, really, I never thought I'd see you wearing a jogging suit for a whole day, let alone checking into the Ritz!"

They both laugh.

Max looks down at her jogging suit and then up at Seth. "I can't believe I've been wearing this all day. Let's see if the shops are still open. We could both use a clean outfit for tomorrow."

Seth agrees. "And some toiletries!"

"Let's try the shop down the hallway and then hit the spa, where I'm sure we can get some essentials for tonight."

The hotel gift shop has a nice collection of *resort wear*. While neither Seth nor Max is crazy about the selection, it is better than what they both had worn all day. After Seth pays for a couple of items for them both, they visit the spa for some toiletry essentials, have a quick bite at the grill, and head to their rooms.

As they walk down the hallway to their rooms, Seth takes Max's hand and looks at her. "Well, are we going to talk about it? Or not?"

Max stops walking and turns to face Seth. "The free rooms, different names? That?"

Seth laughs, "Well, yes...! What the f...?"

"I don't know sweetheart. Too much to digest while we're tired. Let's get some sleep and talk with Mr. Engel in the morning. He seemed like a good guy. Let's give him the benefit of the doubt and see what he tells us before we leave."

Seth nods in agreement, hugs Max, and escorts her to her room.

"Hey, gorgeous, sleep tight!" Seth gives Max a kiss on the cheek. "I'm right across the hall if you need me."

"You're always everywhere when I need you. Thanks for all you did today."

Seth smiles at Max and winks. "Someday, I hope we'll look back on all this and laugh. With Logan."

"Me too. I haven't given up on him, Seth."

"Me either. Don't say another word."

They hug again, and Seth walks toward his door across the hall.

Max winks, "Seven okay to meet for breakfast?"

"Sounds perfect. Sleep tight. I love you, Max!"

Max peeks out from her door. "I love you more!"

Hours later, Max can't sleep so she gets out of bed at four in the morning, puts on her clothes, and steps into the hallway of the hotel to go for a walk. Across the hall, she notices light coming from under the door of Seth's room. She knocks quietly on the door.

"Hey, honey, you up? It's Max."

Seth opens the door. He looks wide awake, as if he hasn't slept a wink.

"You look dazed, sweetheart. You watch an old movie on TV?"

Without saying a word, he takes Max by the hand and pulls her inside his room. After closing the door, he turns to her and asks that she sit on the bed and look at the TV.

Max stares at the TV and then moves closer to turn up the volume. She is silent for almost a minute. "Oh my God. My God! How long have you been watching this?"

"About an hour. I didn't want to wake you. You seemed so tired. I just sat here mesmerized by what I was seeing. I woke up about an hour ago, turned on the TV to help me fall back asleep, and when I flipped the channel to CNN, this was the lead story."

A grainy black-and-white security camera in a parking garage in Paris captures an attractive Asian woman being abducted by four men in a van. The van pulls up behind her, the doors open, and four men grab the woman. She struggles, but they put something over her nose and mouth to subdue her. Within seconds, she goes limp, and the four men throw her into the van and take off. The lady loses a shoe and some beads from what appears to be a silver cocktail dress. The tagline on the story reads, "Prominent French Chinese Businesswoman Abducted in Paris." One of the CNN commentators identifies the woman as Bao Lucienne, a native of Shanghai and owner of several businesses in France. They keep running the clip about every twenty minutes.

Seth turns the volume down and asks Max, "She's Viktor's wife? Why would someone kidnap Viktor's wife, and why is it on CNN? I thought she was just his wife, not an international businesswoman. Why is she being kidnapped? Max, it's scary. What's going on?"

Max is confused. "Baby, you really don't know. Logan never told you who Viktor's wife is?"

"Maybe he did. I never cared. I was surprised to learn he was married in the first place. He's so annoying. Is she a celebrity in France?"

"Well, I'm not sure *celebrity* is the right word. Perhaps *notorious* is a better description. She's a cousin of the Chinese president, the general secretary of the Chinese Communist Party." With a smile that is more of a smirk, Max goes on to say, "You've perhaps heard of him?"

Seth is stunned. "No shit. You're kidding me?"

"No, honey, I wish I was. Her married name is Bao Lucienne, but her maiden name was Bao Tse. She went by Bao Chia, which is, I'm told, sort of a derivative of Tse. Anyway, she's part of the family of the Chinese president, and she has a lot of money and influence."

"But why would she be with Viktor? What would someone that powerful see in him? He's a snotty little Frenchman."

"Viktor comes from a prominent French family. Lots of connections to the French government and businesses. Though the Lucienne family fell on hard times financially, they remain politically well connected. If you're from China and you want a French husband who can get you in all the doors at the Élysée Palace and help you meet prominent French businessmen at the Paris Club, then Viktor Lucienne looks very attractive. And, after four years of marriage to your French husband, you can become a French citizen. You bypass all the French immigration restrictions. You get it?"

"I guess so." Seth is silent for a moment, then asks, "So, the money. The money Viktor invests for his clients in France. Is she part of it?"

"Logan asked that question many times, and Viktor always says no. He claims the money is from a collection of other investors, but not his wife's money. Viktor is a financial adviser for many French businessmen who want to invest in the United States. The funds that Ethan and Logan manage are just a part of what he represents."

"Do you think Viktor knows she's been kidnapped? Should we call him? Or Ethan?"

"It's already 1:00 p.m. Monday in Paris so I'm sure someone from Paris called Viktor hours ago. If not, he'll certainly see it on TV in a couple of hours when he gets up." Max stands up from the bed and holds Seth in her arms. "Honey, we're going to have to get out of here."

"Why? We just checked in late last night, and neither one of us has gotten much sleep."

"I know, sweetheart. I thought spending the night back here at the Ritz would be a good idea since we'd be closer to the sheriff and Coast Guard crew looking for Logan. Or at least I felt we'd be closer. But something's up and I'm sure it's related to Logan. The yelling on the boat, the gash on Logan's head, and now Viktor's wife is abducted in Paris. Something's going on at the firm, so we need to go to the office—before Ethan and Viktor get there. I want to see what's in Logan's office."

"So, just like that we leave Logan out there in the ocean or a burned corpse stolen by someone. You want to leave before we know what happened to him? I'm shocked."

"Sitting in a hotel room isn't going to help find Logan. Something is going on at the firm. Something that may be very bad. And Dr. Dorsett promised me he would send a courier down to the coroner's office this morning with the medical records for Logan. I need to know if there's a match with what Coroner Bearitz has in that awful bag of flesh and teeth."

"Crap, you sound like Perry Mason. I felt better when you were crying on my shoulder."

"I can't sit here and think about Logan being gone. He'd understand that and want us to try to find out what's going on at his firm. Get showered, and let's leave in forty-five minutes."

12

Wake-Up Call Paris Time

Ethan and Jaclyn are sound asleep when the borrowed cell phone from Maria begins to ring just after 4:00 a.m. Monday morning. Ethan picks up the phone from the nightstand. "Maria?"

"Yes, it's Maria. I'm sorry to call so early, Ethan. It's Viktor. He's hysterical. He called me from the hotel. Bao has been abducted in Paris."

"What? Bao, abducted? When did this happen?"

"I don't know. He got a call from his sister in Paris. Said she saw it on the news. He's a mess. I'm sorry, Ethan, but he's on his way to your house."

"Oh, no. At 4 a.m.? How's he getting here?"

"A bellman from the hotel is driving him up there in the house car. I'm sorry. He's just hysterical so I thought we should get him out of the hotel."

"Okay, okay, don't worry. I'll go downstairs to meet him. Maria, let's meet at the office by 7:00 a.m. I'll bring Viktor with me."

"Okay, meet you there. I've got your new cell phone being delivered to your office first thing."

"Great, thanks. Oh, and were you able to reach Rebecca to ask her to get to the office early?"

"Yes, she said she was going in by 5 a.m. to get ready to prepare your wire to Paris later this morning."

"Good work. See you there."

Ethan no sooner hangs up with Maria when the doorbell begins to ring. Viktor is hitting it repeatedly, and now Jaclyn is up and asking Ethan what's going on. They both run downstairs and open the door for Viktor, who is drenched in sweat. Without saying anything, Viktor grabs Ethan around the shoulders.

"Ma vie est terminee, Ethan! *Terminee!*"

"Your life is not over, Viktor. Everything will be fine. Come in; we'll make you some coffee and breakfast. Then we'll go down to the office and speak to the authorities in Paris about Bao."

"I've already spoken to the police commissioner and chief inspector. They'll never find her. She's likely not even in France."

"How can you say that? When did all this happen?"

"Last night when she was coming back to our flat in Paris after a reception. It's all over the news. Four men in a van kidnapped her. Right in our parking garage."

"Ransom? Have they contacted you about a ransom?"

"There's no ransom for *Shuanggui*, Ethan. Only death or prison."

"What the hell are you saying, Viktor? What is that word anyway?"

"*Shuanggui.* You pronounce it 'schwang-grei.' It's an old Soviet style of torture, to get a confession from someone. Whether you're innocent or guilty, the Party, the Communist Party, has fingered you for corruption and wants a confession from you—and a return of property they believe belongs to the state."

"Has she been charged with anything?"

"There are no public charges for shuanggui. The trial, if there is one, will be in China and closed to the public."

"Viktor, you'd better come clean with me on this. Why would your wife be abducted by her own government? Why are you saying these things about torture and confession?"

"Bao called me Saturday afternoon, just before we were leaving to head to the harbor for the cruise. She said she received a surprise formal visit by two men from the Chinese embassy in Paris, advising her that she and her family members in Shanghai were under investigation by the Party for misuse of public funds.

They told her to prepare to go with them to China for questioning right away. She refused. She said she was a French citizen and if anyone in China wanted to question her, they could do it at the embassy or elsewhere in Paris. She told them she would not go to China. The visitor reminded here that she had many family members in China who could be hurt if she didn't cooperate."

"Hurt? As in physically harmed if you don't cooperate?"

"Oui, mon ami. They threatened her family if she did not cooperate and go to China to be questioned. But she knew it would be her last trip anywhere if she voluntarily went to China. And if they had fingered Bao, then her other family members were likely already in custody or confinement. That's how things work in China. By the time they come for you, they've already visited your family."

"What happened then? How did she leave things with the visitors from the embassy? Were they even legit? Did she check them out?"

"When she refused to leave with them, they said they would be in touch. As soon as they left, she called her sister and brother in Shanghai, but their phones had been disconnected. She then called her nephew in Beijing, and he hung up on her."

"My God, Viktor, this all unbelievable."

"I told her to go stay with my uncle in Brittany who used to work for the DGSE—the French agency called the General Director for External Security. Sort of the French version of the CIA. I told her she'd be safe with him, and to go right away."

"But she was abducted in Paris, right?"

"Yes. *Merde.* Big mistake for her. She decided to go to a reception Sunday night hosted by two big fashion houses that are buying a new design space from her and her real estate partner. She planned to leave that night, after the reception. When she went home to change her clothes and drive to Brittany, the men in the van kidnapped her from the garage."

"Viktor, what can we do? Are the French authorities not able to do anything? Did they get a lead on the van or who the men were?"

"The van was found outside Paris, burned. No sign of the men or Bao. They likely took her into Switzerland or Germany on a private jet and are certainly on their way to China by now."

Ethan turns to look at Jaclyn, who is horrified at what Viktor has said and is shaking her head. He then holds Viktor by the shoulders and looks into his eyes. "I don't think you're telling me the whole story. Is there something more you should tell me, Viktor?"

"Mon ami, I have been married to a Chinese Communist Party member for fourteen years. I've met her family in China and in Europe. I know the Chinese Communists well and how they operate. This is a pattern I have seen before, but I never thought it would come to us. We were always very careful."

Jaclyn stands by Ethan, holding his arm and wiping tears from her face. She says nothing.

Letting go of his shoulders, Ethan tells Viktor to come sit down at the table. "We'll have some coffee, and then we need to get you cleaned up and go to the office."

As they are walking to the kitchen, Viktor turns to Ethan and whispers, "First Laurent, and now Bao. I'm not sure I can make it through this, Ethan."

Jaclyn keeps walking to the kitchen, but Ethan holds Viktor back and speaks to him softly. "Viktor, I feel terrible about Laurent, and God knows I'm praying for Bao to be okay. But you need to tell me if this Bao abduction has anything whatsoever to do with the fund redemption your largest client asked us to wire to them."

Viktor looks down at the floor but remains silent.

Ethan grabs hold of Viktor's arm. "Viktor. Viktor! You need to come clean with me. Your nephew is dead. Your wife was abducted and is likely in grave danger. Does *any* of this have to do with the demand of your largest client to send a one-bil-lion-dollar redemption to them today? Which, of course, they thought went out on Friday?"

Viktor remains silent.

Ethan pulls Viktor toward the kitchen and sits him down on a stool at the table. Jaclyn has already set the table and is scooping fruit and yogurt into bowls. She asks Viktor if he would like some coffee.

"Latte, si vous plait."

Ethan sits down next to Viktor at the breakfast table. "Viktor, we must go to the office shortly and hope that we can assemble the funds to send to your client. Is there anything you want to tell me? No, wait, is there anything you *should* tell me before we send the wire?"

Jaclyn brings a latte to Viktor and black coffee to Ethan. "Eggs? *Oeufs*, Viktor?"

Ethan and Viktor both nod yes to Jaclyn.

Ethan stares at Viktor as he is momentarily lost in his latte. "You need to come clean, Viktor, before we get to the office. Who is this client, and why do we have to liquidate a billion dollars in a couple of days? And what does your wife or her family have to do with all of this?"

Viktor puts sugar in his latte. He stirs it for a moment and then looks up at Ethan. "Mon ami. My friend, Ethan. I am sorry that our relationship is coming to an end."

Ethan doesn't say anything. He takes a drink of his coffee as Viktor gathers his thoughts to continue.

"My client. There are many, of course, but my main client with you, he is a cousin to Bao. He is an advisor to government officials in China who want to invest their money outside of China."

Ethan perks up. "Invest it, or hide it?"

Viktor is startled. "Invest. Invest it for the future and for their families. Relatives."

"Bullshit, Viktor. China has a growing economy. Growing faster than here or in Europe, God knows. Why invest in my hedge fund in the US when you can invest in growth in China?"

Viktor looks up at Ethan. "*Securite*. Security. Safety from repatriation by the government."

"And why would the Chinese government take money from their own officials?"

"*Merde*! You really must ask me that, Ethan? Are you an idiot? You've known the source of these funds from the beginning."

"True. You said it was an adviser to government officials who wanted to diversify their holdings. Diversify. That's a big difference from hiding money."

"Enough, Ethan! Governments come and go in China. They are all Communist. They are all corrupt. When one regime takes over, they purge the old regime—officials, family members, and their money. It's okay to be corrupt and take money when you are in power. But, when that regime ends and a new regime takes over, everything in the old regime is taken. Not just the money, but lives. Souls. Relatives. Bao and I thought we would stay ahead of the changes and not be affected. We were wrong."

"But the money in our fund is not regulated by China. We are a United States hedge fund. Screw the Communists in China."

"Be careful, mon ami. The reach of the Communist Party in China is far and wide. The shroud of the red dragon, as I call it. Money from the 'red nobility.' Ironic, isn't it? Communists who own billions of dollars from capital ventures. Or, more likely, corruption. Graft. If we don't redeem the $1.7 billion from Bao's family members, they will come after me. And you and your family, Ethan."

"One point seven billion? They asked for one billion last week, and even that will be a struggle. You know that."

"*Oui.* But they told Bao they want everything. Now. All funds returned to the Party in Beijing. That is what she told me Saturday, in our phone call. New leadership coming in and Bao's family is out. Her cousin, the president, has been removed. A new president and general secretary of the Chinese Communist Party will be announced soon. His ultimatum to us: return the money and you live as peasants. Don't return it and everyone in the family dies—right away or a long and painful death in prison. That includes French husbands too, by the way."

"You can't be serious? They want their whole 1.7 billion dollars back. How soon?"

"This morning. On the wire we are sending today. All of it."

"And what happens if we need three to six months to sell the assets to raise the money?"

"*Mort*. Death. That is what it means, Ethan. They view this money as stolen from government coffers. And it was. And the next regime will steal it again. Each one thinking they will be the last. No more regimes change, and everyone keeps their billions hidden overseas. But it never lasts." Viktor puts down his coffee cup and holds his head in his hands. He begins to sob. Ethan and Jaclyn put their arms around his shoulders, and Jaclyn dabs his eyes and nose with a handkerchief.

"Viktor, if what you are telling me is true, we will all go to jail. If I redeem all the funds we have, including your money and our retail clients, the SEC will come after us. The SEC *does* regulate the retail fund, the Aronheart Fund that Logan manages. If we touch a penny of that money illegally, we could all go to jail. We'll end up serving time for fraud and a host of other charges. And we won't be able to get our hands on the full 1.7 billion dollars of your client's money that is in the hedge fund. You know that. Some of those properties are going to take months to liquidate. And there's no guarantee we'll get full value liquidating everything at once."

"Then we all die, Ethan."

"This sounds like a cheap spy novel, Viktor. There aren't Chinese agents running around Beverly Hills looking to kill investment managers."

"Are you so sure of that, Ethan? Remember the carjacking and murder of that real estate agent, Lyon Dejean, last October in Brentwood? The unsolved mystery, as the police call it. She worked for the Chinese real estate investment syndicate that purchased the two large hotels."

Ethan raises his voice, "They went bankrupt. The hotel operators couldn't turn a profit if they had to pay the royalty fees to the property owners. It was a ridiculous deal. Bankruptcy was no surprise."

"Apparently that's what Ms. Dejean thought before her Bentley was carjacked and she ended up strangled in the trunk. She and the car were incinerated, as you may recall. She was dealing with the red nobility too. The shroud of the red dragon reaches far and wide. Chinese agents operating here in the United States tracked her down and killed her."

"Okay, Viktor, so what are you saying? We'll end up car-jacked and torched if we can't raise the funds today for the wire to your client in Paris?"

"Why is Logan not here, Ethan? We've been avoiding this discussion since the fire on the yacht, but why didn't Logan send the wire Friday as he was supposed to, and where is he? Are you hiding him? Have you two conspired to take the money from my client?"

"What the hell are you saying, Viktor? Are you mad?"

"Where is Logan, and why didn't he send the wire on Friday? And why did it take until Saturday night, on the boat, for him to tell us the wire did not go out?"

"He told you, Viktor. He couldn't liquidate the funds quickly enough to send the wire Friday. There wasn't enough money."

"A partial wire would have sufficed. But he sent nothing. You caused this to happen, Ethan. Or you and Logan."

"Bullshit. Viktor, finish your eggs. I'll drop you back at the hotel. Shower and get dressed and I'll pick you up at 6:30. We'll get to the office and assemble as much cash as we can. We will discuss this then."

"And you killed my nephew. Or did Logan kill Laurent?"

Jackie gasps when she hears what Viktor said. "Laurent, dead? Oh my God, what happened? Why didn't you tell me?"

"Damn it Viktor, I told you not to say anything."

Jackie is sick to her stomach and runs to the kitchen sink, where she hunches over as if she is going to vomit. Ethan leaps from his chair and puts his arms around her. She is gagging and sweating. "What's going on, Ethan? What's happening? Logan, then Bao, and now you tell me Laurent is dead?"

"Killed himself. Sorry to put it that way, Jackie, but Logan found him Friday. At his apartment. There was a note. I'll tell you more later. But now we all need to get cleaned up and Viktor and I need to get to the office."

Jaclyn wipes her face with a dishtowel and looks up at Ethan and Viktor. "And me? I'm to sit here alone while all this is going on. Where's Max now? Or is she dead too?"

Ethan takes Jaclyn in his arms and tells her to get cleaned up and they will all go to the office together. "And, Viktor, you're going to get your client on the phone, and we will all have a discussion. No more mystery. I want to speak with your client in Paris."

"C'est impossible."

"Bullshit, Viktor. If you don't want to end up like Laurent, you'd better make it possible by the time we get to the office."

13

Early Day at the Office

Seth and Max pull into the parking garage just before 6 a.m. Monday morning. The offices of Global Protocol Investment Strategies (GPIS), Ethan and Logan's firm, are in a stylish building on Wilshire Boulevard in Beverly Hills. As with Ethan's home, and her own, Max designed and decorated the offices of the firm. She knows all the staff, which includes forty people. In addition to Ethan and Logan, there are several traders and investment analysts, along with fund accounting, clerical, and administrative staff. The legal department includes several lawyers who assist in the acquisition and disposal of real estate for the fund, as well as personnel who work on compliance issues with the regulatory authorities. In the hedge fund business, the firm is well regarded as a high-caliber boutique investment shop and has a clean record with the regulators.

Seth and Max enter the elevator from the parking garage and ascend to the lobby of the building. Seth looks at Max and smiles. "We aren't exactly dressed for showing up at the office, are we? Hopefully no one will be in. This resort wear makes us look like tourists!"

"Honey, most everyone *will* be in. First, the stock market opens at nine-thirty Eastern time, which is six-thirty here in La La Land. So, all the traders will be in the office. Most of the clerical and other staff will be trickling in shortly thereafter.

Hopefully, Ethan isn't here yet or at least won't be until we get a look at Logan's office."

"How can you be sure? Wouldn't he be here early too?"

Max laughs. "Are you kidding? Most days he's home nursing a hangover before coming to work. He knows Logan will always be in before the traders start their work. On most days, Logan holds a 'stand-up' meeting with the traders before the market opens. He goes over the latest news and events that may affect trading that day. Ethan, on the other hand, usually schedules his first appointment as a luncheon with a client or prospective client. Logan would often rush from the office to join them for lunch after the market closes at 1 p.m., Pacific time."

"Wow sounds like an easy life for Ethan. Logan does all the work."

Max smiles. "It's a blessing for Logan. Ethan is a tyrant in the office if he comes in early. It's easier on Logan and the staff if Ethan comes in after lunch. The market is closed and there's a more relaxed attitude in the office, especially on the trading floor."

"You have a key to Logan's office?"

"No. Not with me. But if Maria or Donna are in, they'll let us into his office."

The elevator door opens, and they walk to the security desk in the building lobby to sign in. The guard on duty is startled to see Max. "Mrs. Aronheart! Are you okay? I didn't expect to see you here today! Any word on Mr. Aronheart?"

"Hi, Stuart. No, no word yet. I still have hope. We need to get up to the office. Can you sign us in and send the elevator for us?"

Stuart is confused. "Mr. Chandler isn't in yet."

Max pauses. "No matter. He's expecting us. We'll wait for him in the office."

"Okay, Mrs. Aronheart. And your guest?"

"This is my assistant, Seth Boncola. He's on the permanent sign-in list. You'll see his name."

"Thanks, ma'am."

They step in the elevator and take it to the fifteenth floor, both uncertain what they will find in the office.

Max holds Seth's arm. "I'm not sure what to expect. Not even sure what I'm looking for."

The elevator door opens and reveals the receptionist speaking with a red-haired woman sitting in the lobby. She appears to be sobbing and very upset. Max recognizes her. "My God, that's Rebecca."

Seth looks at both women and says, "Who's Rebecca?"

Max whispers, "CFO. Chief Financial Officer for the firm."

Both women look up as Max and Seth approach the lobby from the elevator. They are both surprised to see Max.

Rebecca jumps from the chair, her face wet and makeup running down her cheeks. She gives Max a clammy hug. Mascara, tears, and sweat cover Max's neck where Rebecca is clinging to her. "My God, Max, what happened out there?"

"We don't know yet. It's been a nightmare."

Rebecca grabs Max by her shoulders. "Max, you've to get out of here!"

"What? We just got here. I want to see Logan's office."

"You can't be here when Ethan and Mr. Lucienne arrive. Maria just called, and they're on their way here."

"Why? Why do we have to leave? What's wrong, Rebecca?"

"It's gone. Logan wired it out Friday. All of it. Ethan will be furious."

"What are you talking about?"

"The wire. To Paris."

Max frowns. "I thought the wire to Paris couldn't go out on Friday."

"It didn't. There wasn't enough liquid cash to send anything close to a billion dollars."

"Then what are you talking about, Rebecca?"

"The retail accounts. The individual investors who have money with the firm. The Aronheart Fund, the one Logan manages for retail customers. We call it the A Fund. Assets of over half a billion dollars. All of it was wired to a Swiss clearinghouse in Zurich. They're acting as custodian issuing checks to all the individual investors. Over fourteen hundred individual investors will be getting a check for their account balances."

"What? Why? Why would Logan do that? Why would he liquidate a fund he has managed for years?"

Rebecca stands silently, wiping her face. The only other person in the lobby is the receptionist, who is horrified at overhearing the conversation. She stands by the reception desk with her hands over her mouth. Two of the clerical staff behind the reception desk are now taking notice of the discussion.

Max takes a stack of files out of Rebecca's hands. "Honey, let's get your face cleaned up and go into Logan's office where we can talk about this in private."

Rebecca shakes her head in agreement.

As they walk to the ladies' room, Max introduces Seth to Rebecca. She then tells the receptionist they will be in Logan's office, and they should let Ethan know that when he arrives. She asks the receptionist to get Logan's assistant, Donna, and have her bring the key to Logan's office to Seth.

Seth stands outside the ladies' room waiting for Donna to show up with the key. Inside, Max cleans Rebecca's face with cold water and paper towels.

Rebecca thanks her but keeps sobbing. "It's all over, Max. You need to get out of here. Logan left me a note. He voluntarily liquidated all the holdings in the individual accounts three days ago. When the cash settled Friday, he wired it to a custodian in Zurich who has instructions on how much money is owed each investor. The checks go out today from their affiliate in San Francisco. There's a letter to each investor telling them that he acted as an emergency fiduciary to liquidate their funds before they could be misused. Oh my God, Ethan will be furious. He'll blame me for being duped."

"What? Logan liquidated a half billion dollars in assets for fourteen hundred investors without their knowledge or approval. Oh my God. Isn't that illegal?"

"Yes, and when the Securities and Exchange Commission hears of it, that will be the end. But not as terrible as what Ethan and Mr. Lucienne will do when they get here."

"Look, Rebecca, let's get to Logan's office where we can discuss this privately. And I need Seth to hear this."

Outside the ladies' room, Seth and Donna, Logan's secretary, are standing by the door. Donna is holding the key to Logan's office but refusing to give it to Seth.

When the door to the ladies' room opens, Donna sees Max and Rebecca. "Max! It *is* you! I've been trying to reach you and … and Logan ever since yesterday afternoon when I heard the news. What's going on? Any word on Logan?"

"Donna, we don't have much time. We need to get into Logan's office. Right now."

Donna pauses for a moment and then replies, "Well, okay, then come with me."

They go down the hall and to the other side of the floor where Logan has a beautiful corner office. It looks west toward the ocean and north to the Hollywood Hills. Max pauses for a moment. The office smells of Logan—his cologne and the sandalwood air sanitizer he has in the corner. It takes her breath away.

Seth closes the door, and he, Max, Rebecca, and Donna sit down at the conference table in Logan's office. The office is neat and tidy, as is his desk. Logan is meticulous and believes a cluttered desk reflects a cluttered mind. Donna goes to Logan's desk and surveys it but finds nothing out of place. She then opens his top right drawer and frowns when she looks inside.

Max watches her curiously. "Anything wrong, Donna? What's in the drawer?"

Donna looks up. "Nothing. It's empty. That's where Logan keeps his inbox—things he will be working on for the day. He doesn't like a stack of papers on his desk, so he keeps the stack in here and works on them one item at a time. His daily schedule is usually right on top. Nothing. Nothing here."

Max stands up and walks toward Donna, who is still standing near the desk. "Did he leave you a voicemail or a note or anything?"

"No. Nothing."

Rebecca becomes very agitated and asks Max and Donna to return to their seats at the conference table right away. Looking at Max and Seth, she says sternly, "Look. You two have got to get out of here now. Right now."

Max sits back in her chair, looking at Rebecca. "We aren't going anywhere until you clarify for us why exactly why we have to leave."

Rebecca clears her throat and opens her file to a page with a lot of numbers on it. "Global Protocol manages a total of about $2.8 billion in assets. Of that amount, $1.7 billion belongs to Mr. Lucienne's clients in Paris. Another half billion belongs to the individual clients. Most of those clients were from Logan's former business, clients whom he brought to the firm when he and Ethan started Global Protocol ten years ago. Mr. Lucienne has a personal account worth about $.4 billion. There's another couple hundred million from some pension funds and a Russian investor with the last name of Barinsky."

Seth is writing the figures down as Rebecca speaks. He looks up at her and says, "So what's the problem? I don't get it."

Rebecca rubs her hands across her dress to clear the sweat from the palm of her hands. "We're short. It's that simple. Logan managed the Aronheart Fund, what we call 'Fund A,' for all the ten years this firm has been in existence and for eight years prior to that at his old firm. This fund invests in stocks and bonds. Those holdings are valued every day and easily bought and sold on the exchanges. You know the names, New York Stock Exchange, the NASDAQ, the foreign exchanges too. It's a registered mutual fund, open to individual investors."

Max nods. "Yes, of course I know that. The A Fund has been Logan's baby for years. He has solid returns, and the fund is used by a lot of retirees."

Rebecca shakes her head. "Exactly. And all the other investors are in the Global Protocol Hedge Fund. We call it the B Fund, which has some holdings in stocks and bonds, but the bulk is in real estate and private placements. Luxury homes and condos, office buildings, mortgages, personal notes, commercial property. Things that can't be sold overnight. This fund is a hedge fund and can't be sold to regular investors. It's only available to educated investors, and it's not traded on the exchanges."

Seth speaks up. "And that's the fund where Viktor's big client in Paris has his money, right?"

Rebecca points to Seth. "You got it. In fact, Viktor's Paris client is the *only* investor in the Global Protocol Hedge Fund. Logan and Ethan and their team of managers manage that fund *exclusively* for Viktor's client."

Max shakes her head. "Of course, and we know that, so what's the issue?"

"Well, the client wants $1 billion of his $1.7 billion right away. Wants it in cash, wired to his account in Paris. Last Friday, actually. We don't have that kind of cash on hand. That's why Logan couldn't send the wire to Paris on Friday. We need time to sell holdings in the B Fund to raise the cash. Could take weeks, even months to liquidate all the holdings. Especially the real estate."

Max shrugs. "No big deal. You know that the hedge fund agreements for clients like Viktor's give the fund months to liquidate. Investors must file their intention to leave, and the fund can take sometimes up to a year to pay out all the assets to investors wanting their cash. So what?"

Rebecca shakes her head. "Viktor said his client demanded the money immediately. Ethan and Viktor agreed to redeem a billion dollars of the $1.7 billion investment. They told Logan to take the cash from the individual investors and they would put it back later. That fund, the A Fund trades on the exchanges; those stocks and bonds could be liquidated in one day, and the cash would be available in three days when the trades settle. In other words, Ethan and Viktor wanted to liquidate the individual investor holdings and give that money to Viktor's client, plus whatever other cash we could raise to come close to the one billion dollars. It was impossible to wire a billion dollars to Paris, without taking the money from the individual investors. Logan knew that. He was afraid the individual investors would never get their money back if Ethan and Viktor got their hand on those funds. So, Logan wired the funds out so the individual investors would get their money back right away. He tricked Ethan and Viktor to save the assets of the individual investors from being misused by them. Or lost."

Max puts her hand on her chin. "But in doing that, he broke the law."

"Yes, Max. He did. Investors in retail funds like the Aronheart Fund must ask for their assets to be redeemed. We can't just do it at our discretion. But Logan knew there wasn't time to contact all fourteen hundred individual investors and seek their approval to liquidate. So, to protect the individual investors, he did an automatic, unauthorized redemption. He invoked an obscure clause in the fund agreement permitting the fund manager to take actions necessary in a 'financial emergency' to protect the best interests of the investors. That's a stretch since there was no market or financial emergency, in the traditional sense. That's probably why he chose a custodian in Switzerland. They don't ask questions. They're happy to take the money, and for a handsome fee, they send it out as you instruct."

Max speaks up. "But Logan takes the fall for all of this. Even though he prevented Ethan and Viktor from misusing investor funds, he's the one they'll blame."

Seth is confused. "What do you mean takes the blame? Sounds to me like Logan is a hero."

Max disagrees. "Logan knew that Ethan and Viktor were going to use individual investor funds to pay Viktor's client in Paris for an early liquidation. I'm sure Ethan and Viktor will deny that and say Logan panicked and possibly harmed the firm and thousands of investors in doing so. They'll make Logan out to be the villain."

Rebecca nods her head. "Exactly. Now we have an illegal redemption for fourteen hundred people and a large investor in Paris fuming that his wire never showed up. And Logan is missing or dead, which makes things even worse ... Oh, Max, I'm sorry. That was careless of me."

"I understand, Rebecca. Go on."

"And our chief financial analyst, Laurent, didn't show up for work Friday. Or this morning. At least not so far. That's why you must get out of here, Max. We'll have to report this to the SEC as soon as Ethan gets here. He'll be furious. The SEC will want to speak with you, and God knows what Ethan will do. And then there will be the police. If we suspect theft, we're obligated to inform the police. This day will get even uglier. You need to get out of here until we know what's happening."

There is a knock on the office door. Without asking who it is, Donna tells the person to go away, that this is an important meeting. The door opens, and an older woman with gray hair says, "I'm sorry, Donna, but this is an emergency. I have the Beverly Hills Police on the phone, and they say the Aronheart residence has been broken into and they're looking for Mr. or Mrs. Aronheart." The woman then stares over at Max. "I'm sorry, Mrs. Aronheart. What should I tell them?"

Max is speechless.

Seth stands up. "Tell them we are on our way to the house now. Come on, Max; we need to get out of here."

14

Il se Tourne vers la Merde
(Everything Turns to Shit)

Ethan and Jaclyn retrieve Viktor from the Beverly Hills Hotel at about six forty-five a.m. and head straight to the office. Viktor is dressed to the nines, as if he is going out for the evening—black suit, yellow shirt, lavender bow tie, diamond fleur-de-lis cuff links and a matching diamond lapel pin.

Ethan opens the door for Viktor and does a double take on his attire. "My God, Viktor. We're going to the office, not a cocktail party."

"You pick me up in a new Bentley Mulsanne that cost a half million dollars, and you think I am overdressed?"

"For the office, yes. We don't want the staff to feel uncomfortable."

"Uncomfortable? Imagine how uncomfortable they are going to feel when their largest client can't get their money back."

"Enough, Viktor. Enough."

Viktor's face is swollen, and his eyes are puffy, likely from crying or heavy drinking the night before—or both. There is not another word said among the three of them on the ride to the office.

The parking valet at the building takes Ethan's car, and he, Jaclyn, and Viktor go up to the office. It is almost seven thirty a.m. when they walk in, which is very early for Ethan.

The receptionist stands up as they arrive. "Maria is in your office, Mr. Chandler."

"Thank you. No calls or visitors this morning."

Ethan's office is the mirror image of Logan's, at the other end of the building facing north and east. They pass by the trading floor on the way to Ethan's office and nearly every eye turns toward them as they walk by. Maria steps out of Ethan's office and walks down the hall to greet them.

"Good morning! Here's your new phone. All set. Same number as before. Your directory and everything are loaded up, or at least it should be. It was backed up on your computer, and I just synched it for you."

"Thanks, Maria. Here's your mother's phone. Is Rebecca here?"

"Yes, yes, she's in your office, but I'm afraid she is most upset, and she has some very unsettling news."

Ethan says nothing but frowns at Maria.

When they all four enter Ethan's office, Rebecca is sitting at Ethan's conference table, staring out the window. As they walk in, she turns and stands up slowly.

Ethan, startled at how Rebecca looks, snaps at her. "You look like shit!"

Rebecca agrees, "Yes, sir, Ethan, I do look like shit. And soon you may look the same way."

"What are you talking about? We don't have time for jokes."

"Oh, it's no joke, sir. There's just no other way to say it. All the individual investor money in the Aronheart Fund, the A Fund, is gone."

Ethan is visibly stunned. "Are you shitting me? Gone? Where? How?"

"Wired out Friday afternoon. Just over a half a billion dollars."

Viktor is elated at the news. "Merci, merci, so the wire *did* go to my client in Paris, at least a partial one! We are saved Ethan, we are saved!"

Rebecca interrupts, "No Viktor, you don't understand. The wire didn't go to your client in Paris. It was sent to a custodian bank in Zurich, Switzerland. The wire was not for your client in Paris."

Viktor falls to his knees and grasps for the edge of the conference table as he hits the floor. Jaclyn tries to catch him, but it us too late, and he drags her to the floor with him.

As he reaches down to help both up from the floor, Ethan's face is bright red with anger. He pulls Jackie up first and helps her to the sofa near his desk. He then struggles to get Viktor off the floor. Viktor is as white as a ghost and perspiring. His legs are like jelly, and Ethan can barely get him to the sofa.

Maria asks Ethan if they should call a doctor. "No, not yet. Viktor, can you compose yourself long enough to let Rebecca finish? I can call a paramedic if you want."

Viktor begins wiping his face with a handkerchief, and waves his hand, as if to say, "Go on."

Ethan pulls up a chair next to Rebecca, who is by now nearly hyperventilating. "Tell me, slowly, what happened, Rebecca, and when did you find out?"

"This morning. I got to the office about five thirty a.m. and was hoping Laurent would be here to help me prepare the funds for the wire to Paris, just as Maria asked me to do yesterday evening. I got here early to get everything prepared. It's not easy to send a wire in that amount. I assumed Logan liquidated the funds from the A Fund Tuesday or Wednesday, so they would be sitting in the disbursement account this morning to wire to Viktor's client in Paris."

"And? Then what?"

"The disbursement account has only a few dollars in it. I was shocked to see that, so I thought perhaps someone already sent the wire."

"Someone? Someone who?"

"Laurent. Logan. You. I don't know. I saw no redemptions from the Global Protocol Fund, which is where Viktor's client has his money. I then looked for a wire receipt in the wire account. And then I saw it."

"Saw what, Rebecca? Damn it, can you get to the point?"

"I'm trying to get to the point, Ethan! There was an outgoing wire Friday after the market closed. Logan apparently did it himself."

"That's impossible. It takes three of us to send a wire over a million dollars."

Rebecca is silent.

"Well, so how did he do it? How did he wire a half a billion dollars, and where did it go?"

"He signed for you, for Laurent, and for himself. He used our electronic codes with the bank. He had them, and he used them to have the bank make the wire. They phoned for verification, and Logan verified it with the verbal password. It's all right here. I've written it down. I have a call in to Vanessa at the bank."

"Who the hell is she?"

"Our business banker. For the firm. I suspect Logan spoke with her. She won't be at work until the bank opens, but I left her a voice mail."

"Holy Shit! We must get the money back!"

Rebecca shakes her head. "That won't be possible. I already called the bank in Switzerland. It's the custodian division at UBT in Zurich. It's a 'one-way' custodial trust account. Disbursements to clients only. We can't ask for the money back. Logan authorized a formal distribution order as trustee and fiduciary, as if the fund had closed and distributed all the assets. The custodian is following those protocols, which they are obligated to do."

"Good God, setting all that up that takes days, or weeks."

Rebecca is trembling so badly she takes her hands off the desk and places them in her lap. "I know. It seems he's been working on this for at least a week or more. He sold all the shares in his fund, the 'A' Fund, last Tuesday. He told the traders there was a portfolio rebalancing that he was handling himself so no trades in the fund, except through him. He locked out all the screens for the traders in the 'A' Fund."

"That's impossible Rebecca. *You* had to be involved."

"Ethan, I wasn't. You know that Logan was the primary manager of the A Fund. He and the trading team always handled the rebalancing in that fund. You both co-manage the B Fund, but

Logan was the exclusive manager of the A Fund. The Aronheart Fund has always been his baby, and Logan is the sole manager. None of the traders likely suspected a thing. Rebalancing the fund and locking the traders out for a couple days was done three or four times a year by Logan. He's done the rebalancing personally for years. None of us, including me and the traders, would have thought that unusual."

"Do the traders know that the money in the A Fund is gone?"

"They know something is up. I suspect they're just confused. Logan left a small balance in the A Fund, so the system is still calculating a daily share price, and the inter-day trades were showing on the trading screens last week. They are probably showing now, but the traders don't know there's only a few thousand dollars in the fund instead of over a half billion. They're seeing the individual share *values*, but not the *number of shares*, which would be normal for them when the fund is in a rebalancing mode. They're following share prices today, but they won't see volume numbers until the end of the day, when the rebalancing period ends. That's when they'll see that the money is gone. When the market closes, the computer system values the fund and sets the closing share price. The total asset value of the entire fund will show on the trading screens, and then, well, it will no longer be a secret."

Viktor grabs his stomach and bends over. Jaclyn kneels beside him on the floor next to the sofa. "Viktor, are you alright? Do you want us to call a paramedic or take you to the emergency room?"

He looks up, ashen in color, and asks, "My God, what are we to do?"

Ethan stands up, goes over to Viktor, and tells him to stay calm. He assures him they will figure it out, but in the meantime, Viktor will need to tell his client that they don't have the cash.

"Tell your client we are working on it, but we need more time to liquidate the assets."

Viktor shakes his head. "He won't want to wait. Do we have any cash to send him? Can I tell him we are at least doing a partial liquidation?"

Ethan looks at Rebecca. "What cash do we have? What's on hand in the trading account or the cash account in the B Fund? Or in the union pension fund or the Barinsky account?"

Rebecca pulls out several pieces of paper from her file folder. "I looked at that this morning. We have, probably, fifteen to twenty million, if we borrow from our capital account, which technically is illegal. And we have Viktor's personal account. If those bonds are trading at book on the Paris market, then we'd have about $380 to $400 million more. So, at most, about $450 million, if we borrow from the capital account and from Viktor."

Viktor stands up, goes over to the window, and leans against the windowsill. Behind him, the Hollywood Hills look like a backdrop on a movie set—sun rising in the east and the silhouette of the mountains behind him. It is a beautiful scene for what is a dismal morning for everyone in the room. "I'm afraid my account won't be of much help."

Ethan shoots back. "Of course, it will. It will help us send almost half what your client is asking for."

"The Paris LVK bonds are not liquid. They are private placements. The bonds pay interest from the borrower, but each bond is really a personal note. A debt. I'd have to find buyers for the notes if you want me to redeem them."

Ethan walks slowly to Viktor. As he reaches the window, he puts his hands on Viktor's shoulders. "Logan and I always let you do what you wanted with your personal account. It is, after all, your money. You made the investments. We knew they were private placement bonds, but you told us they were corporate borrowers. You now say they are *personal* debts. And, Viktor, you have an eighteen-million-dollar loan from our firm, secured by your personal account as collateral. So, the first eighteen million dollars in proceeds from your account go to the firm. We're carrying that loan as part of our required capital for the regulators. But now that we know what type of investment it is, it won't qualify as acceptable capital. So, we're going to be short in our capital account until you give us eighteen million in cash."

"*Oui.* I understand. I am only telling you the truth. I can't liquidate those bonds today, this week, or even this month. Or maybe ever."

The room falls silent. Ethan returns to his desk and says, "Listen carefully, each of you. Here's what we're going to do. I'm going to call the SEC and tell them that one of our partners in the firm committed fraud and illegally closed and redeemed a fund for over 1,400 investors without our knowledge. That's the truth. Are we clear on that part?"

Everyone nods in agreement, except Rebecca, who is biting her lip and sitting stoically.

"Next, we'll report to the police and SEC that not only is Logan missing, which everyone knows about, but so is our senior accountant, Laurent Latour, and that as far as we know, Logan is the last person to see Laurent. Rebecca, you will need to back us up. You know that Logan went looking for Laurent at his apartment on Friday morning."

Rebecca nods her head and whispers, "Okay."

"Viktor, you're going to call your client and tell him all that just happened. That my fellow partner has wired out a half-billion dollars without our approval and gone missing. You will need to call your sister and tell her Laurent is missing. You then need to tell your client the same thing. It will add to our credibility if he knows that you are personally affected by all of this. And, finally, tell him we will begin liquidating the properties and other assets in the B Fund forthwith. We will begin wiring him the proceeds as soon as we get them. As a show of good faith, we will liquidate the pension holdings and those of the Raminsky family and send him two hundred million dollars by Wednesday."

Rebecca and Maria both gasp. Jackie stands up and shakes her head. "It's one thing to blame all of this on Logan and perhaps that will stick and perhaps it might even be true, but if you liquidate pension funds and money from Lev Raminsky, you'll go to jail or be dead, Ethan! You can't do that. He's killed other people. You steal his money, and he'll likely kill all of us."

"They won't know. I'll handle the liquidation, and we'll keep posting returns to their assets, just as if they were never liquidated. We will track them meticulously. Then, as soon as we have enough money from the B Fund to repay the pension and Raminsky account in full, we will. No one will be the wiser."

Rebecca throws up her hands. "No one will be the wiser. Ethan, I'm a CPA. This will cost me my license if this is ever discovered, or we don't get the money back. And we will all go to jail. It's fraud covering up fraud!"

Ethan puts his hand up. "Stop, all of you. I understand the ramifications. I promise to make it worth your while, financially, to see this through. There is no other alternative. If we tell the truth now, we're *all* sunk."

Rebecca shouts back, "That's not true, Ethan. We should come clean now with what has happened. Just the facts to the SEC. We don't add to the problem by making more illegal redemptions and illegal loans from customer accounts."

Ethan shakes his head. "We're sunk in the retail mutual fund business. Once those checks start showing up, some investors will be angry that we redeemed their funds without their approval. We can blame it all on Logan, but we won't be able to be in the retail investment business anymore. Personally, I don't care. Never liked all those individual whiny investors anyway. They were Logan's 'little people.' The mom-and-pop investors. But that still leaves some money in private investments from Viktor's clients and the Raminsky family and the two pension funds. That's where we make our money anyway. If we can't contain this issue to the retail investors, we *are* ruined. The fund is ruined. The firm will close, and you are all out of a job. Being honest just puts us out of business. No one needs to know all this ever happened. Once we raise all the cash, we move on. No one knows any differently. We can stay in business, but we will need new hedge fund clients, the private institutions, and we can survive this if we can buy some time. Besides, no one knows any of this except the five of us in this room."

"Yes, they do," Rebecca says. "They do, and you can't control them."

Ethan stands up from his chair and puts his face right next to Rebecca's. "Who? Who knows, and who can't we control?"

"Max. And her friend—that's who."

"We don't tell them."

"It's too late. They know."

"How the hell could they know?"

"They were here, this morning, about a half hour before you arrived."

"What the hell? When were you all planning on telling me that? Max and her drag queen friend were here and they both know about the A Fund redemption? About what Logan did?"

Maria and Rebecca shake their heads.

"Damn it, Maria, why didn't you tell me?"

"I was waiting to get you alone. I just learned they left about ten minutes before we all arrived."

Ethan lets out a huge breath of air and falls into his chair. "Where were they going?"

Rebecca speaks softly. "Home. Max and Logan's house was broken into. They left to go there."

Ethan walks over to Rebecca. "I need you to go quietly to your desk and do everything you can to stay calm. Look for as much money as you can find from whatever accounts you can. Say nothing to anyone, and don't go anywhere from your desk until I come get you. You can leave my office now."

Rebecca objects. "Max will never let you pin all of this on Logan. Especially if you make it worse by piling on all these other illegal actions."

"Enough, Rebecca. Enough. You've said your piece. Now get to work as I asked you."

As soon as Rebecca leaves, Ethan closes the door. "Jackie, I need for you to go home. And stay there. Speak with no one. No one, until I come home."

Jackie begins to say something, but Ethan points toward the door. "Go. Now."

When Jackie leaves the room, Ethan tells Maria they need to find Max and Seth and keep them quiet until this all blows over. Maria starts to speak but Ethan cuts her off.

Viktor stands up and walks over to Ethan's desk. "I'll take care of keeping them quiet. I just need Maria to help me with some information on both Max and her assistant."

Ethan looks at Maria and says, "Go with Viktor. Do what he tells you. Oh, and, Maria, keep an eye on Rebecca. Listen to her phone, and don't let her leave the floor. Not even for lunch. She can't leave until I tell you personally."

15

Uninvited Guests

As they get into the car to leave the parking garage, Seth pulls his cell phone from his pocket and throws it in the console. "Shit! I'm sorry, Max—I've got a voice-mail message that came in this morning when we were driving up from Laguna. I'll bet it's your alarm company." He picks up the phone, dials his voice mail, and listens to the header of the message. "Crap, it *is* from your alarm company. They called at five twenty-three a.m. I turned off my ringer last night to go to sleep, and in all the commotion this morning, I forgot to turn it on."

Max reaches over to pat his shoulder. "Don't worry, honey. We've had a lot going on."

Seth is driving out of the parking structure at the firm when he sees Ethan drive by in his new Bentley. "Wow, that was close. He's just getting here. Looks like Jackie in the front seat and someone in back. Probably Viktor?"

Max tries to see, but the car is already at the valet stand. "I'm sure it's Viktor. God knows what's going to happen up there when he finds out what Logan did. Poor Rebecca. I could just cry. Logan loved working with her. I can't believe he'd leave this mess for her to find. It doesn't add up, Seth. Just doesn't add up. And Laurent not showing up for work, even though his uncle Viktor is in town. That's also very strange."

Seth thinks for a moment and then turns to Max. "Wouldn't

surprise me if Viktor and Laurent conspired in some way to cause this whole mess."

"I thought about that. Something isn't right with this whole Viktor thing and his wife being abducted and Laurent missing. And Logan. Dear God, what is happening?"

🔥

Seth drives quickly down Wilshire Boulevard in the direction of Logan and Max's home in Beverly Hills. He looks over at Max, who is staring out the passenger window, as if she is studying something in the distance. Seth taps her on the shoulder. "Hello! Anybody in there?"

Max turns toward him with a smile. "Of course, silly you! I'm just trying to get this all figured out or at least the part about Logan and the money. And if that's maybe what they were all yelling about on the boat. Before the explosion and fire."

"And, um, you aren't even worried that we're rushing to your house that was just broken into?"

Max takes a breath and cups her hands over her mouth. "You know, sweetie, for some reason, I am just not even worried about the house. It's as if it no longer matters. There's nothing for me there without Logan. I feel like we're driving to some stranger's house. Not mine. Isn't that funny?"

"Well, yeah, I'd say that is more than a little bit funny. Did it occur to you that the break-in might be related to what's going on?"

"I did think of that, for a moment. But there's nothing there that would have anything to do with what happened on the boat. At least that I'm aware of."

"All the same, I'm surprised how calm you are. You love that house. You've got your heart and soul in it."

"Not without Logan. I did it all for Logan. I always told him it's our sanctuary, but it's nothing without him. If he doesn't come back, I can't bear to live there. But enough. Let's see what the circumstances are when we arrive. It wouldn't be the first time we had a false alarm; God knows. I just want to get back to looking for Logan."

Seth looks over and winks at her. "And by the way, aren't you going to ask me to get you a new cell phone today? Has that occurred to you yet? And shouldn't we check in with the office voice mail?"

"I don't need to think about those things!"

"Oh, and why not?"

"Because I have you! And *you* think of those things!"

They both laugh, and Seth turns up Rodeo Drive toward Sunset Boulevard. Max and Logan live very close to Ethan and Jaclyn, just off Benedict Canyon. As they pass Sunset Boulevard and head up Benedict Canyon, they both have trepidations. Their laughter moments ago was an avoidance of what both know could be a strange scene at the house. Though she laughed it off, Seth knows that Max is probably frightened more now than she has been since the disappearance of Logan. Logan's actions at the office the day before the cruise made it obvious that the events on the boat were not unrelated. And, in a few minutes, Max will have to confront the fact that someone broke into her home in the early hours this morning. Though she made light of it, Seth is certain she is worried that any break-in is part of whatever terrible story is still unfolding.

Seth sees the gates to the house up the road as they turn off Benedict Canyon. "Two cop cars and two cars from the security company. That looks serious."

Max waves her hand. "It's Beverly Hills. Not much exciting happens, so a break-in is a big deal. The neighbors will be peeing their pants to find out what happened."

Two police officers and a private security guard approach the car as they park in the motor court. The shorter police officer asks, "Mrs. Aronheart?"

"Yes, I'm Max Aronheart. This is my business associate Seth Boncola. What happened?"

"I'm Officer Dauton, and this is my patrol partner Officer Weston. The other two officers are inside with a photographer from the department taking pictures."

The private security guard steps forward. "Don Beich, with BHB Patrol. I was the first one here. When the command center couldn't reach you, your husband, or your alternate contact, I was dispatched to investigate."

Max puts out her hand to Mr. Beich. "Thank you. I'm sorry you couldn't reach us. What will I find inside?"

"A big mess. Every door, cupboard, and closet in the place opened. They were obviously looking for a safe room or a hiding place. There had to be at least three or four of them because every cabinet and drawer has been opened, but when I arrived, there was no one here. I got here within sixteen minutes of the alarm going off and—"

Max interrupts. "Whoa, wait a minute. Sixteen minutes? That seems a long time for a patrol service to respond."

"The dispatcher spent about five minutes trying to reach you before sending me out to respond. Most alarm activations are false alarms, so I don't get dispatched unless the command center can't reach any of the primary and secondary contacts. When I got the call, I was up on Mulholland Drive, so it took me almost ten minutes to get here. I'm sorry."

"Okay, go on. So, what were they looking for?"

Before Security Patrolman Beich could answer, Officer Dauton speaks up. "Not what, *who*. We'll need you to confirm it, but they didn't seem to take anything of value. Your safe is unopened; there's jewelry on your nightstand and in your closet—watches, cuff links, and what appears to be a cocktail ring. All left untouched. You've got some expensive artwork and collectibles in there. Nothing even taken from the shelves, near as we can tell. Looks like they ran from room to room looking for someone. They even opened all the doors and trunks of the two cars in the garage. But they left the cars, even though you had the keys in both. When they couldn't find who they were looking for, they apparently just left."

Max gets goosebumps from that last sentence, and Seth gives her a haunting stare. She looks back at Seth, smiles, and pulls her hair back with both of her hands. "Okay then, that sounds odd. Let's go inside."

Max and Seth stand in the entry to the house. From there, they can see that every door and window is open, both inside and out. How ever many intruders there were, they had run through the house looking in every room, closet, and storage space.

When they go upstairs into the master bedroom, there are scrape marks and dents along the molding on the bedroom walls. The same marks are in the hall closets and in the bathroom.

"What in the world are these?" Max rubs her hands along the scrape marks and dents. Pointing to her jewelry box on the bathroom counter, which is full of earrings and necklaces, she asks, "Why were these things left here, but they banged up the walls?"

The security patrolman, Mr. Beich, rubs his hands across the wall. "Because they were looking for a hidden door. A door to a safe room or a hiding place. They were banging on the walls and molding trying to find an opening or a concealed door. They did the same thing to your study downstairs. That beautiful wood paneling—they pried a lot of it away. I'm sorry. That room looks very torn up."

Max takes Seth's hand in hers and looks at him. Seth knows she is now frightened to death.

Officer Dauton speaks up. "Don't tell me where it is, but do you have a safe room here?"

Max chuckles nervously. "No. Isn't that silly? It never occurred to me that we would need one. I've heard about them of course, and I've worked for clients who have them in their homes."

Office Dauton asks her what type of work she does.

"Designer. I'm an interior designer."

No one says a word for a few moments, but they are all thinking the same thing. The intruders were obviously looking for Max. Perhaps Logan too, but since it was well known that Logan Aronheart is missing, the intruders were likely planning on finding Max at home in the wee hours of Monday morning, when she would likely be in bed.

Officer Dauton clears his throat and steps closer to Max. "Do you know of anyone who would want to harm you? Or your husband? Anything you want to tell me?"

Max looks up, smiles at the officer, and says softly, "Have you read the papers in the last day or so?"

"I don't read the papers, but I'm aware of the fact you've had a rough twenty-four hours. I'm sorry I had to ask you that, but it's standard procedure when there's a break-in that appears to have been motivated by a possible …"

Max frowns. "What? Possible what?"

"Kidnapping, I'm sorry."

"Don't be. I get it."

"I know this is not the time or place, but at some point, we'll need for you to come to the station and help us file a full report on the incident."

"Of course. Of course, we'll do that. But not now, as I am sure you understand."

"Oh, oh, yes, certainly."

Max squeezes the officer's arm. "Not that it matters much at this point, but will you lock up the house when your photographer is done inside?"

Patrolman Beich speaks up before Officer Dauton can answer. "I'll do it. I'll check every door and window and have the central station reset your alarm. That is, if they can. Looks like some of the alarm wires and contacts may have been damaged. We may need one of our installers to come here to repair the damage. And, um, many of the doors and windows may need to be fixed first."

Max turns to Seth and points to his phone. "Honey, would you please call Andre and ask him to come up here right away and repair the doors and windows, at least enough for Mr. Beich here to have his installers repair the alarm?"

Patrolman Beich asks, "Who's Andre?"

Seth speaks up as he is looking for Andre's number on his phone. "Our door and window guy. He installed all of them here at the house, and we use him for other jobs. He'll know what to do so you can get the alarm connections repaired."

Patrolman Beich pulls out a card and gives it to Seth. "Please have him call me when he's ready for us to come up and patch things together for the alarm system."

Max extends her hand to patrolman Beich. "Thank you. Thank you ever so much. I truly appreciate it."

Patrolman Beich motions toward the closet in the master bedroom. "Would you like to take some things while you're here? Before you leave?"

Max looks around the bedroom, puts her hands on her hips, and turns toward Seth. "No. Nothing. We'll go now and come back if we need something."

Seth grins and says, "Really? Max, you can trade in that resort wear for some of your own things. You don't look all that great in those clothes. Just sayin' …"

Max smiles. "Have you looked at yourself in the mirror this morning? I think we both need a shower and change of clothes."

"I quite agree!"

"But not here. We'll go now and come back later if we need something."

Seth is startled. He senses that Max has absolutely no intention of ever coming back—not without Logan. He glances at Max and holds up his hands. "So, we're leaving. Just like that?"

"Yes, just like that."

16

Paris Is Burning

"Oui, oui. I understand. Completely. It will be done." Viktor puts his phone down and wipes his face with a handkerchief. He is sweating so badly that his shirt is damp, as if he'd been in a sauna.

Maria sits across the desk from him. "What did he say, Viktor?"

Viktor takes two deep breaths and then a drink of water. He stares out the window and will not look directly at Maria. "The president wants his money. All of it."

"How soon?"

"Yesterday."

"That's impossible; you know that. What about the $250 million we can wire from the Barinsky account and the union pension fund?"

"A down payment that he will accept but with collateral."

Maria frowns. "He has collateral. Those buildings and other assets can be sold. The fund owns them. He'll get his money."

"My dear, we are dealing with the Chinese Communist Party. He's talking human collateral, as if your little Mexican mind wouldn't know that already."

Maria stands up and puts her hands on the desk. She leans in slowly toward Viktor and whispers to him, "Listen, Señor Viktor the *Frenchman*, I don't care who you are, but I won't tolerate belittling comments." She then leans in further, inches from his face. "You lied to my boss about the source of these funds, and now we're all in trouble as a result."

Viktor laughs, almost uncontrollably. He leans forward in his chair, even closer to Maria, who is still leaning into his ear across the desk. "Your boss knows *exactly* where this money comes from. He simply miscalculated how soon the next president of China would purge the former regime. He thought he, or we, had several years. *Mauvais choix*, as we say in French. *Bad choice*. With every regime change in China comes a purging of the old. Charges of corruption by the old, only to be trumped by corruption of the new. It's such a lethal combination, this merging of Communism and Capitalism. Une comparaison faite par le diable." And with a flourish of the hand, Viktor says it again, "Une comparaison faite par le diable!"

Maria sits back in her chair and folds her arms. "Translation please?"

"*A match made by the devil*. Communism and capitalism. It's perfect! The Communist Party provides the corruption, and our capitalists provide more money. It really is perfect, isn't it? Communist countries used to be Socialists. The automatic road to ruin. The economy deteriorates under Socialism and the Communist Party eventually starves itself. Only after starving its people, of course. Then the country collapses. But now, we have the perfect economic solution! Communist dictators fed by the ever-flowing money of capitalism. It really *is* perfect, isn't it? Corruption has never been easier. If only Lenin had figured that part out. *C'est le vie!*"

Maria stands up, stares at Viktor for a moment, and then leans against the window, facing Viktor at the desk. She crosses her arms and her legs, both of which Viktor is admiring. "I don't need a lecture in political science, Viktor. In fact, the last thing I need is a *Frenchman* lecturing me about economics. My job is to help save the firm and save Ethan. Your client is thousands of miles away. I say screw him. He'll get his money as we liquidate the funds. That's it. We'll find new clients to replace him."

Viktor sits back in his chair and purses his lips. "And what of my wife? She is the cousin of my client. And she's missing."

"Not our problem. You made this mess. Your wife is obviously a huge part of it. If she's being held somewhere, that's your problem. I'm going to advise Ethan that we proceed with an orderly liquidation of the B Fund, and your little emperor of China will just have to wait in due course for his money."

Maria gathers her file and briefcase and starts toward the door.

Viktor stands up and walks to the door with Maria. As he opens the door for her, he clears his throat and puts his hand on her shoulder. "I think we will both be giving our recommendations to Ethan. Separately."

In a feigned bow, Maria replies, "As you wish. It's always nice to have two options, isn't it?" And with that, she waves her hand gesturing that Viktor precede her out of the office.

They both enter Ethan's office to see he is speaking on the phone with the Orange County Sheriff's Office. "It's Goddamn ridiculous. No body has been found, and yet you've stopped the search. So, we just sit and wait? As if a dead body is just going to show up in your office someday?" He slams the phone down. "Incredible. The Coast Guard has stopped searching, and the sheriff has listed Logan as a missing person."

Maria is surprised. "What about the coroner? Has she determined whose body was in the bag before it disappeared?"

Ethan shakes his head. "No. She's expecting the dental and medical records this morning. But so, what? Whether she determines that it was or was not Logan in that bag, he's still missing. If he's not dead, I could kill him myself now that I've seen what he did here. Almost half a billion dollars, gone!"

Maria sits down, but Viktor keeps standing and moves closer to Ethan. Viktor stares down at Ethan. "We knew this Saturday night. He told us he wouldn't do the redemption. We should have figured out that he had already made the retail funds unavailable to us."

Ethan is silent for a moment. "But by then there was nothing we could have done, Viktor. He sent the wire Friday."

Maria looks at them both and says, "So that's what the fight was about on the boat?"

"What fight?" Ethan snaps.

"The fight that Max says she heard. You two said there wasn't a fight, but she said Logan was bleeding and she heard fighting on the deck before the explosion. Why was he bleeding? Did one of you hit him?"

"Enough, Maria. We can get back to the fairy tales on the boat later. Viktor, what did our client say?"

Viktor takes out his handkerchief, wipes the seat of a chair that faces Ethan's desk, and sits down. Maria is already sitting in the adjacent chair.

Ethan throws up his hands. "For cripes sake, Viktor. You afraid of catching something in my office?"

"Bad habit, mon ami."

Viktor places his elbows on the arms of the chair and puts his hands together in a prayer position. He looks at Maria and then at Ethan. "I'm afraid the president, the secretary, is not exercising any patience in this matter. He is demanding a very expeditious return of his money. And demands collateral, until all his funds have been returned."

Ethan looks at Viktor. "Collateral? What the hell do you mean, Viktor?"

Leaning over in his chair, hands still folded in the prayer position, Viktor whispers, "Perhaps the better term for it is … *insurance*. Yes, that's the best English word. *Insurance*. Insurance that you will … perform accordingly."

Ethan stands up from his chair and leans over his desk. "What the hell are you talking about, Viktor? We aren't in the insurance business. We're in the investment business. Investing funds for your clients. Or, as it's turned out, your *client*. Singular. Which is a surprise to me."

"Oh, no, mon ami. It is not just the secretary, or should I say, soon to be former secretary, who is my client. He represents many other, shall I say, *associates*. He is their advocate. Their representative."

"But you take your orders from him."

"Oui. And so do *you*."

Maria stands up and takes out a notepad from her briefcase. "Viktor, we will begin liquidating the fund immediately. But you know it takes time to sell real estate and the other assets in the B Fund. Your own client hand-picked some of the properties we acquired with the fund, especially the properties in New York— the townhomes, condominiums, nail salons. He certainly knows we can't sell these properties overnight."

Viktor nods his head. "Yes, of course, and in some of those properties, you have leases with tenants that the secretary brought to you."

Maria and Ethan look at each other, saying nothing but thinking the same thing. Ethan speaks up. "Viktor, when we sell those properties, the new owner must assume the leases, but as you know, they will not be bound by them after they expire."

Viktor nods his head. "Yes, yes, a matter for the secretary to be aware of."

Ethan and Maria shrug their shoulders, being very confused by Viktor's comment.

Maria gives a thick file to Ethan. "I had Rebecca print out the statistics on the primary real estate holdings of the fund. I thought we could start there. We'll deal with the other assets later. Most of the properties are in New York and Los Angeles. We have our real estate broker and appraisers in both cities. Mark already has relationships with them. We simply bring him in here and tell him to advise the brokers and appraisers of our plans to liquidate the properties."

Viktor perks up. "Who is Mark?"

Maria replies, "Mark. Mark Grossman. You've met him. He's the assistant fund manager of the B Fund. He has an excellent relationship with the brokers in New York and LA who buy and sell these properties for us.

Viktor shakes his head.

Ethan jumps in. "No, no we aren't using Mark's two primary brokers. Not for all of it. These are trophy properties. Properties that are expensive and well known to the local real estate community. We can't put them all on the market at once. And not with the same broker."

Maria is confused. "But why? We bought these properties through these two brokers. Wouldn't they be the best ones to sell them?"

Ethan takes the file back from Maria. "One by one, yes. All at once, no. It will raise questions about why we're putting a billion dollars of real estate properties up for sale, all at once. All of which are owned by our firm. Too many questions. Bargain hunters will appear overnight. They'll smell blood. No, we must do these piecemeal. Slowly. A couple at a time, through different brokers. And appraisers. In the perfect world, we change the title of these properties to different entities. All controlled by our firm but under different names. That's how we maximize the value and avoid the appearance of panic selling."

As Ethan is looking over the asset summary Maria provided, Viktor says, "Ethan, how much longer will that take. To get the money, I mean. If you do what you are saying, it could take weeks, months, or longer to liquidate all the properties."

"Of course, but that's how you maximize the value. That's the whole point. We don't want a fire sale. Legally, our master fund agreement gives us up to a year to liquidate the fund. Longer if we can prove it is in the best interests of the shareholders of the hedge fund."

Viktor bites his lip, stands up, and picks up a picture of Jaclyn in a frame on Ethan's desk. He stares at it for a moment before handing it to Ethan. "I wouldn't think you'd want a year without seeing your dear wife, my friend."

Ethan sets the frame down on his desk, sends a confused look to Maria, and then turns to Viktor, who is standing over his desk. "I'm confused, Viktor. Jaclyn has nothing to do with this."

"Oh no, mon ami, I'm terribly afraid she does. She has a lot do to with this. And so does your friend Max. And my dear sweet Bao. You see, they all have this one thing in common."

"What thing? What the hell are you talking about?"

Ethan and Maria both stand up from their chairs and move toward Viktor.

Viktor looks at both, speaking slowly and choosing his words carefully. "The insurance. That you will perform. You see, the secretary may live in Beijing, but he has a long reach. Jaclyn did not return home when she left here a couple of hours ago. Just as my Bao did not return to our apartment in Paris. I would hope that Jaclyn was retrieved in a less dramatic fashion than my Bao."

Ethan's face turns red, and he grabs Viktor by the shoulders. "If you harm my wife, I will fucking kill you, Viktor. Where is she?"

Maria is stunned. "We need to call the police."

"Oh, if you want to see Jaclyn or Max ever again, I wouldn't do that, mon ami. Your little firm here will come to an end, as will our loved ones and surely us as well before it's all over. You need to return the funds to my client quickly. By whatever means you can. The secretary will become angrier the longer his funds are … unavailable to him."

"Jaclyn. And Max? You have them both?"

"I don't have anyone. I was told on the phone call that they would both be taken for insurance that you will perform. They are in the custody of individuals employed by the chairman. As is my dear Bao."

Ethan takes out his cell phone and calls Jaclyn. It is picked up on the first ring. The person answering the phone is a woman but not Jaclyn. "Good morning, Mr. Chandler. I would think you should be spending your time raising money for your clients instead of making telephone calls."

"Who is this, and where is my wife? Who is this?"

"We will be in touch, Mr. Chandler. I suggest you get to work."

17

The Sum, or Some, of the Parts

A courier with a large leather bag arrives at the office of the Orange County Coroner shortly after 11 a.m. Monday morning. The bag contains medical records and DNA information from Logan Aronheart's doctor and dental records from his dentist. Coroner Bearitz and Catherine, her medical examiner, began working on the items as soon as they arrive.

After closely examining the records for about an hour, the coroner and her staff have a conference call with Dr. Dorsett, Logan's doctor, and then subsequently with his dentist, Dr. Duane Elliott.

As soon as she ends her conference calls with Logan's doctor and dentist, Coroner Bearitz and her medical examiner return to the examination room. After pulling the tissues, teeth, and other items from the bag, the coroner examines them again with a magnifying glass. Without looking up, she places a tong around the larger tooth and gives it to her medical examiner. "One more time."

"But I've done it twice, so—"

The coroner cuts her off. "Catherine, I said one more time."

"Okay, then." Catherine takes the tooth and places it under the microscope. She studies it closely, moving the tooth around with a pair of tongs. "Am I supposed to arrive at a different conclusion?"

Coroner Bearitz clears her throat and says, "What then is your conclusion?"

"Just what I told you before. It's a match. Tooth 16, third molar. Porcelain filling. Filled by Dr. Elliott in March of 2013. Replaced a silver filling approximately sixteen years old. This is Mr. Aronheart's tooth."

The coroner turns, removes her glasses, and folds her arms. "Method of extraction?"

"Unknown. Recently extracted, possibly voluntarily or by force. Torn root fragments still pliable, so a recent extraction."

"That is your only conclusion?"

"How many times are you going to ask me that? Without having the rest of the body or at least the head, I can't determine how or why the tooth was removed from his mouth."

"Those scrape marks on the side. They don't lead you to conclude the tooth was extracted by an instrument and not by an accident?"

"I'd have to see the adjoining molar and the cheek. The records from Dr. Elliott indicate that Mr. Aronheart has enamel deterioration on several teeth and that he has bonded four of them. In two of them, the erosion exposed the underlying dentin of the tooth. He has soft or deteriorating enamel. These abrasions could be from regular wear and tear or from an instrument. I can't tell."

Coroner Bearitz is skeptical. "You think a molar at the back upper left of your mouth, the last one, just pops out when you're on a sinking ship?"

Catherine folds her arms and frowns. "Aren't you simplifying the events a little too much? There was an explosion on the ship. His wife says that Mr. Aronheart had a gash in his face and was bleeding profusely after the explosion. If there was facial trauma then yes, it's very possible the tooth was forced out. And, another thing, what if the facial trauma resulted in the loss of several teeth? We have only one tooth here. That doesn't mean it's the only one he lost in the trauma event. It's possible he suffered substantial head or facial trauma."

The coroner let's out a sigh and shakes her head. "Well, an active imagination doesn't help determine whether Mr. Aronheart's body was in that bag or not."

"You know that's not my job. I'm the medical examiner, not the coroner. I can establish that this is, in fact, Logan Aronheart's third molar, tooth number 16. The blood inside the tooth is also a match. It's not my job to determine the cause of death, if he is dead, or the way he died or was injured. That's your job. You're the coroner. Do I need to remind you that California law requires the coroner to determine the identity of the victim and whether the cause of death is the result of homicide, suicide, or accident? Or undetermined, which somehow, I think you are reluctant to declare."

Coroner Bearitz puts her hands on the table and leans in toward Catherine. "Thank you for the refresher on my duties. I don't think I need reminding after thirty-five years."

Catherine turns off the light in the microscope and places the tooth back in the bag. "And I'm sure the tissue inside the tooth will be a blood match with the other sample we have from the blood stains on the clothes."

"Same blood type but not a DNA match."

"Not yet. DNA preliminary results tomorrow morning. I'd be surprised if there's not a DNA match, but I won't speculate. Do you need anything else?"

"Holy crap, Catherine. I don't know if you're a robot or a person."

"Is that another swipe at my Asian composure?"

"Catherine Honda is Asian?" The coroner laughs; Catherine smiles.

As they walk from the examination room, the coroner puts her hand on Catherine's shoulder. "Nice job. You know I enjoy testing your steady composure!"

"And you're stumped."

"What?"

"I'm not emotional about this case, but you are. And you're stumped. I get it."

The coroner stops and turns to face Catherine. "What's with the attitude?"

"It's not an attitude. It's an opinion. An observation if you will."

"How so?"

"You have no body, just body parts. A finger, a tooth, some tissue, hair, and a lot of blood. All quite certainly belonging to Mr. Aronheart. But the rest of the body is missing. These tiny bits of his worldly being don't conclude that they were life-ending. Lots of people walk around without teeth or limbs."

"Of course, so what's your point, Catherine?"

"You like certainty. A dead body and a cause of death. Case closed. Next body, please."

"The two years you've worked with me and that's all you think of my abilities. Really? Three years out of medical school and you're an expert on my thirty-five-year career?"

Catherine looks at her but doesn't say anything.

"Yes, I like things tight and buttoned-up. Of course. But the last two years you've had with me certainly don't mirror the hundreds of other professional decisions I've had to arrive at over thirty-five years."

"But other bodies didn't walk away from your morgue, like this one."

"I beg your pardon, Catherine! Who says a body walked away from my morgue?"

"You don't read the papers?"

"Oh, okay, now I get it. Now I get the attitude. You're embarrassed. You work for me, and our illustrious Orange County paper says a body has gone missing from my morgue. Is that it? You're being embarrassed? Ridiculed? A few snarky comments from your young friends at the bar or UC Irvine? If your skin is that thin, you won't have a future as a medical examiner. You know damn well that the Coast Guard delivered a body bag here without a body. It never went missing. It simply was not in the bag when it arrived."

"But the Orange County—"

The coroner cuts her off. "Yes, that rag of a newspaper speculates that I'm somehow involved in the fact that 99.9 percent of the body is missing. I know. It's not the worst they've said about me. It sells papers. And Captain Westmore is so charming and good-looking that of course no one believes that he or anyone in the Coast Guard made a mistake."

"But he said he saw it. Or at least his sailors saw it. And they put it in the bag."

"Catherine, *who* saw *what*?"

"Captain Westmore. His crew plucked the burned body from the sea. It was dead and burned. A whole body. And they put it in the body bag, and then it was delivered to you. To us, I mean. Here, at the morgue."

"Were you here when the body bag arrived?"

Catherine is silent.

"Well, were you? Were you here early Sunday morning when the body bag was delivered, and the deputies put it in the cooler?"

"No."

"Well, I wasn't either. You know that. They called me at home, woke me up to tell me a body was delivered from a yachting accident. They thought more bodies might be coming so I decided to come in. I got here as soon as I could, and when I removed the bag from the cooler, it contained only the items you've been examining. You know that."

"Well, it just—"

Cutting her off again, the coroner finishes her sentence. "It just means you do your job and leave the rest to me. Your findings won't be questioned if that's what you're worried about."

"I'm sorry."

The coroner turns away and heads toward her office. As she is walking away, she looks over her shoulder at Catherine. "No time for sorry. Get those DNA results and come get me the moment you have them."

Back in her office, the coroner sits down in her chair and looks at her cluttered desk. Her nameplate on her desk reads, "Elizabeth Bearitz, County Coroner." She stares at her first name, Elizabeth, as if it belongs to another person. Though she's had a distinguished career, it has never been easy. Women are not well-accepted as coroners, particularly by the cops, who joke about her large size, masculine demeanor, and rough appearance. When she reaches conclusions that do not agree with law enforcement's, her life can be tough. She has been threatened with death on several occasions over the past thirty-five years. Families of criminals, crime victims, and even the cops who didn't like her findings have threatened to kill her. She was once attacked in a parking lot after her testimony that the death of an inmate was a murder, not a suicide, as had been claimed by the prison guards. Gang members tried to attack her in her home when she concluded that the cause of death of a young gang recruit was murder by his fellow gang members and not the cops. As a large and overweight woman with short hair, she is often described as "manly" or otherwise. In truth, she is a soft and understanding woman but with a very tough exterior. It is simply what the job requires. She never married and has no children; her job is everything. Now, nearing retirement, she is realizing that she has few interests or activities outside of her work. Retirement means more of an end than a beginning for her. And now, with all the publicity about a missing hedge fund genius from Beverly Hills, the press coverage borders between satire and comedy. She is in an open dispute over the missing body with the United States Coast Guard, the good-looking heroes who handle search and rescues at sea. It's a battle she knows she can never win—at least not in the court of public opinion.

At her press conference in the hot and crowded media room yesterday, reporters snapped at her like alligators, with all manner of allegations and questions about the missing body. At Captain Westmore's news conference later that afternoon, the atmosphere was quiet and composed. He is a striking man in uniform, well-spoken, flanked by four of his senior officers—nice, neat, tidy, and all very handsome. The questions from the press were orderly and neat, just like a military man would require.

So, here she sits, with newspaper articles lamenting the missing Beverly Hills aristocrat who was carefully placed in a Coast Guard body bag and then deposited in the county morgue, only to be found "all gone" as one headline put it. Later tomorrow, she will face another press conference, and this one will likely be uglier than the first.

She pulls her pen and paper from the drawer and begins to write her opening comments for the press conference tomorrow. Though she doesn't have the DNA evidence yet, she knows that it will confirm a blood match for Logan Aronheart on the tooth, finger, tissues, and blood found in the body bag. Her initial conclusions will be:

1. The third molar, tooth 16, does in fact belong to the body of Logan Aronheart.

2. The fingerprint on the (detached) right-hand pinky finger in the body bag matches the right-hand pinky fingerprint on Logan Aronheart's fingerprint records for his securities licenses.

3. The blood and tissue in the body bag are a DNA match for Logan Aronheart.

4. No determination can be made if Mr. Aronheart is alive or dead from these items.

5. The whereabouts of the rest of Mr. Aronheart's natural body, alive or dead, is unknown.

It sounds very tidy, except that Captain Westmore and three of his sailors are insisting they put a dead, burned body in that bag and that it was then handed over to a representative of the coroner's office. The body parts and tissue in the bag clearly belong to Logan Aronheart. The body that was in the bag was burned beyond recognition, but it is now missing. She knows the press conference will be a nightmare. Someone was dead and in that bag. The only tissue and items in the bag belong to Logan Aronheart. Yet she knows there can be no cause of death determined if there is not a corpse to examine. On the other hand, if it is just a missing person, the coroner has no role to play. A missing person is a matter for the sheriff's department. And that was what she writes at the end of her prepared remarks:

> The coroner can make no determination about the tissues and body parts in the bag, other than to conclude that they are associated with Mr. Logan Aronheart. However, since there is no body associated with these items and tissues, the coroner concludes that this is a "missing person" issue for the Orange County Sheriff's Department. The office of the county coroner has no further involvement in this case until a body is produced.

She knows that the "no further involvement" statement is a pipe dream. The Coast Guard, or perhaps even the Orange County District Attorney's Office, will likely call for a full investigation of the circumstances, all of which would certainly focus on alleged mishandling by the coroner's office. Though her instincts tell her that this was a kidnapping or stolen body that was in some way associated with the sinking of the yacht, she has no leads to follow for either hunch.

There will be pressure for her to more closely investigate the actions and background of her intern who retrieved the body bag from the port agent. The young and naive intern has already been interviewed twice by Detective Carter, who is handling the investigation of all events surrounding the sinking of *Copious*. The press will no doubt start to finger him and the coroner as the sloppy handlers who botched the fine job done by the United States Coast Guard.

In any case, the press conference will be a nightmare. And what to tell Ms. Aronheart? No doubt she will call today, or worse, show up in person.

The coroner opens the file, looks up the number, and places a call to Seth Boncola's cell phone.

18

We Can't Be Us

Seth drives only a few blocks down the street after leaving Max and Logan's house when his cell phone rings.

"Ciao. Hey, Phyl. Yep, I know, it's terrible about Logan. Max? She's here, with me. Do you want to speak with her? … What?" As the person on the other end of the line is speaking, Seth turns to Max and silently whispers, "Oh My God!"

Max looks at Seth, confused by his expression. "What is it, honey? Is that Phyllis from the office?"

Seth, still listening, looks at Max and nods his head slowly. "Oh My God, Phyl, call the police, stay out of the office, and lock your door. We'll be there shortly. Do *not* open the door until we or the police get there." He hangs up and speeds down Benedict Canyon.

Max grabs Seth's knee. "Honey, what is it? Is she okay?"

"She's okay, but our office isn't."

"What? They've been there too?"

"Apparently. She got to her office a few minutes ago and noticed that the door to our office was open. Smashed open, she says. It's a mess inside."

Phyllis is a sales representative for a line of high-end fabrics used by interior designers and custom furniture makers. Her tiny office is across the hall from Max's design studio. They share a small, two-story brick building on a little street named La Peer in West Hollywood, just outside Beverly Hills. Max and Seth have a sunny design studio on the top floor, and Phyllis has a small office across the hall. Most of the downstairs of the building is a showroom for the fabric lines that Phyllis represents.

Seth is driving fast down Benedict Canyon and is almost to Sunset Boulevard. The office is only about fifteen minutes from there. Max turns to Seth and says, "Don't turn on Sunset Boulevard. Pull over."

"Why? Did you change your mind and want to get some clothes back at the house?"

"Not quite."

"What then?"

"Honey, just pull over."

With no place to pull over on narrow Benedict Canyon, Seth veers into a driveway and stops the car. "Okay, what's up?"

Max smiles and gives Seth a big hug. She whispers into his ear, "This is where you leave me, dear one!"

"What? What are you saying? Who's leaving?"

"You leave me here, and you get out of town for a while. Go to Palm Springs. No, farther than that. Go somewhere that you'll be safe."

"What? What are you saying? I'm not leaving you."

"Honey, they're looking for me. You saw the house. Now the office. I don't want to endanger you. Until I figure out what's going on, I want you to be far, far away from me."

"No way. No way."

"Yes, Seth. I can disappear. And that's what I intend to do until I figure out what's going on."

"Well, I'd say you're pretty much invisible now. No cell phone, no house, no office. Where, exactly, do you plan to go?"

"Don't worry about that. What we need to figure out is how we communicate. You need to ditch that phone, Seth."

"What? Really?"

"Yes, what, really! Figure it out. You're my best bud. Whoever is doing all of this has probably figured that out by now. If they've been to the office, they likely know you're my business partner. Worse, they could know that you're the one who picked me up Sunday morning and that I might still be with you. So, please ditch that phone and let's get two prepaid cell phones. You leave town, and we'll stay in touch that way!"

Max no sooner finishes her sentence when Seth's cell phone rings.

Seth sees the caller ID pop up. "Damn! It's Patrick. From the club. I just remembered I didn't show up at the brunch show yesterday, on Sunday."

"You were rescuing me in Dana Point, remember?"

Seth picks up his phone. "Hey, Patrick, I'm so sorry … You've seen the news? That's why I didn't perform at the Sunday brunch show. … You cool? … I'm so sorry."

Seth listens as Patrick speaks on the other end. "Shit, I'm sorry." Patrick keeps talking, and Seth wipes his face with his hand. "Oh my God, how could they do that?" Seth keeps listening, shaking his head, as Patrick continues to speak. "Patrick, I'm gone. I'm sorry. Forget about me. Don't try to reach me."

Seth throws the cell phone on the floor and clasps his hands over his face.

Max puts her arms around him. "So, they *are* looking for you, too! At the club?"

Seth is sobbing, wiping his eyes, and reaching for something on which to blow his nose.

With no purse, Max searches Seth's car for a tissue or napkin—something to wipe his face. In his glove box, she finds some napkins from In-N-Out, a popular burger chain in Southern California. "You kidding me? With that figure, you eat at In-N-Out? Really?"

Seth laughs and covers his face, as if he is blushing.

Max laughs and says, "I love the double-double. My fav. Would never admit I go there, but I love 'em!"

Seth hugs her and wipes his nose and eyes with the napkin. "My showbiz days are finished, at least at the Queen of Hearts."

"What? Why? Because you didn't show for the Sunday brunch performance?"

"No, I wish that were the case. Patrick wasn't upset that I didn't headline the Sunday brunch drag show."

"Okay, good, then what's the problem?"

"I would say a broken nose is the problem, apparently."

"On no!"

"Yep."

"Oh, honey, I'm sorry. What happened?"

"The brunch went fine. Even though I didn't show for my numbers, the human petri dish took over, and the crowd forgot all about me. A smash the night before, and a distant memory the following morning. That's me, I guess."

"Oh, sweetheart, I'm sorry. It's all my fault."

"Patrick said that several of the patrons *did* ask for me and were upset that I wasn't there to perform."

"No surprise! So why is Patrick upset?"

"Well, because early this morning when he went to the club to have a meeting with the chef, a couple of, well, let's see how he said it, 'Chinatown thugs' accosted him at the door."

"What?"

"I know. Sounds odd. But apparently two Asian men, one very tall and one very short, asked for me. Patrick said he hadn't seen me since Saturday night. They asked for my address, which, thankfully, Patrick doesn't know. They then asked for my phone number, which, God bless him, Patrick gave them, but with two digits intentionally wrong. When they called that phone number, they got a voice mail and hung up. That was just before they punched Patrick in the nose and fled."

"Oh my God, that's awful."

"Yep, that's awful, but I hope to God they don't trace that phone number to some poor unsuspecting soul, thinking it's me."

Max pulls her hair back and clears her throat. "Babe, we've got to get out of sight. You and me. At first, I thought it would be just me. But now, it must be the two of us. We need to give ourselves some space to figure all of this out. We've got to find out what's going on at the firm, how we find Logan, if he's alive, and do all of that without being targets ourselves.

Seth sniffles. "I get it."

"Okay, then here's what we do. First, we get two prepaid phones, one for you and one for me. Ditch yours, Seth. And we need to ditch this car."

"Oh, no! I love my phone, and I love this car! I just got it, er, leased it last month!"

"Sweetheart, I know it. This is all temporary. Ditch your car wherever you want, but odds are they'll find it. When this is all over, I'll buy you a new one. Same on the phone."

"Okay. I get it."

"So, let's get the phones, and then we ditch the car."

"Cool, but what about money? Can't use our credit cards, right?"

"Right."

"So, what do we do for money?"

Max takes a deep breath and points toward the steering wheel. "Aim that in the direction of my jeweler, Julian. You remember where he is?"

Seth pauses. "I do, I think, remember where he is, but how does that help us?"

"Julian always buys back his jewelry. Not, mind you, at what you paid for it, but at some *fair value* he determines."

"Are we going back to your house to get some jewelry to hawk?"

"Well, no, that wouldn't be too safe, would it?"

"Okay, then what? You're flat busted, no purse, no cell phone, no jewelry, so what do you have to hawk."

Max winks at Seth and reaches inside her blouse for the necklace Logan gave her on Saturday night, in the limousine on the way to the fateful voyage on *Copious*. She dangles it in front of Seth and says, "This is the most recent creation of my friend Julian, and I'm sure he'll give us some cash and hold it for me until I can redeem it when my fortunes are better."

"That's the pendant Logan gave you on the way down to the cruise on Saturday night?"

"Yes, sweetheart. The last piece of jewelry my dear Logan had made for me. And I hope to reunite them both when Logan is found."

Seth says nothing. He's beginning to feel that Max is delusional about Logan still being alive.

"Well, do you know the way to Julian's shop, or need I direct you?"

"The side street by the Beverly Wilshire Hotel. Right? Or is he in the Hollywood Cemetery by now?"

Max frowns. "Okay, ha ha! Let's not make cracks about Julian's age. He's been making jewelry for my family for over sixty years. And unless you've stashed some cash at Queen of Hearts, he's our only option for cash at this point. We'll get the cash and ditch your car right afterwards but far enough away from Julian's that he won't be in danger."

"Are you sure we aren't putting him in danger by going to see him?"

Max shakes her head. "I've thought of that. I really have. Unless we're being followed, there's not an easy connection to Julian. But we need to make the visit quick. Very quick."

"And then?"

"And then we disappear."

19

Black Monday, *de Nouveau* (Once Again)

Ethan holds his head in his hands as his face turns beet red. He just hung up with the woman that answered Jackie's cell phone. She told him to get to work and that they would be in touch about his wife.

Maria stands up from her chair and heads to the door of Ethan's office. "I'll call the police."

Viktor leaps up from his chair and reaches the door before Maria. He stands in front of the door, blocking her exit. "I don't think that's wise, mon amie."

"God damn you Viktor, get out of my way!"

Ethan points toward Viktor and yells, "Get away from that door before I come over there and push you away from it myself!"

Viktor puts up his hand. "You won't get your dear Jackie back that way, Ethan. You call the police, and she dies. We all die."

Ethan gets out of his chair, and shoves Viktor against the door. "Exactly how much do you know, Viktor? Who has Jackie, and why are you protecting them? I'll kill you before I let anything happen to her."

"Killing me won't stop them from killing Jackie. Or Max. Or my dear Bao. You need to get that money to my client. That is the only way Jackie will be safe—that everyone will be safe."

Ethan lets out a sigh and looks at Maria, who is shaking and perspiring. "Let's sit down. For just a moment. We can't go out on the trading floor like this. Look at the three of us; we'll scare the hell out of the staff."

Ethan sits down on his sofa while Viktor and Maria sit across from him in chairs. "Let's remember the plan. We need to stick to it. Maria, after you compose yourself, you go tell Rebecca that I am phoning the SEC to inform them that we just learned of the involuntary closure of the A Fund for retail investors. She should be prepared to meet with me in my office when the SEC wants more details."

"Okay. I'm ready. Let me go to the ladies' room and fix my makeup, and I'll inform Rebecca."

"Good. Then as soon as I phone the SEC, you call the Beverly Hills PD and tell them we are concerned for the safety of Max Aronheart now that we know what Logan did."

"And what of Jackie? Won't you report her missing?"

"*No!* Between the three of us, we don't know about that."

Maria objects. "Ethan, are you crazy? Your wife is missing, abducted. You aren't going to tell them that?"

"We can't tell them what we aren't supposed to know. I love Jackie, and I'm sick she's been taken, but if we let on that we believe one of our clients is responsible, then everything is over."

Maria is taken aback at Ethan's attitude about his recently abducted wife. She looks at Ethan stoically and nods her head in feigned agreement.

"After those two calls, I'll convene the staff on the trading floor when the market closes at 1 p.m. I'll inform them of what Logan has done, that we have reported it to the SEC, and that the B Fund and other clients are not affected. I can mention that we will be selling some assets of the B Fund, but I'll say that was planned well before Logan's action to liquidate the A Fund. I'll assure the staff that the firm will continue to prosper, and there is no cause for concern. Individual investors are getting their money back, and we will now focus on growing our private, institutional business."

Maria stands up and straightens her jacket around her waist. She goes to the window and gazes out for a moment before speaking. "Sounds okay, Ethan. Especially the part about Logan and reporting his actions to the SEC. But if I go to Curtis on the trading floor and tell him to redeem the Barinsky funds and that we are selling, over time, some of the B Funds, it just smells funny. At least it does to me. Curtis is head of the trading floor, he's been here a long time, and he'll be surprised if we don't give him an explanation."

"Stick with the plan, Maria. We have full discretion over the 'B' fund, the union fund, and the Barinsky account. Bad timing, I agree, but we need to convince the staff that the redemption of the A Fund by Logan and the repositioning of the B Fund and other accounts is unrelated."

Maria folds her arms and gazes at Ethan. "A stretch. At best, it's a stretch. I don't think Curtis will buy in without asking a lot of questions about making those trades."

"And you have a better plan?"

Maria shakes her head. "No. No, I don't."

"Okay, then. Go tell Rebecca I'm placing the call to the SEC shortly. Tell the staff we have a meeting on the trading floor at five minutes after one p.m. today. Then go to Curtis and tell him to convert the Barinsky account and the union fund to cash before day's end. Tell him we will explain more later, during the staff meeting. Stick with the story."

Maria walks from the window toward the door. Before she opens it, she looks at Viktor and Ethan. "God help us if any of this goes wrong."

Ethan frowns, and waves her out of his office to do her task.

Once the door to his office is closed, Ethan goes to Viktor, who is still sitting in his chair with his hands in his lap. He looks almost despondent. Ethan sits in the chair beside him. "Viktor, you've got to buck up and call your client. Tell him we'll be sending about $200 million to his account by week's end. Assuming all the trades clear today, he'll have a nice deposit in his account by close of business Friday."

"Oui, I will tell him."

"And that's not all. You get his agreement that he will release Jackie when the $200 million clears his account Friday."

Viktor looks at him and frowns.

"Don't frown at me, Viktor. You tell him that. No Jackie, no $200 million. I mean it."

"And what of my dear Bao? What of her?"

"I'm glad you asked that. Because you tell him that Jackie gets released with the first $200 million. Bao gets released with the next $200 million. From assets we liquidate in the B Fund."

"But when will that be?"

"Depends on how long it takes to liquidate $200 million of assets in the fund. Weeks. Months, maybe. We'll return the whole $1.7 billion, but it will take time. But we want Jackie and Bao released sooner."

"And what of Max?"

"Do they have Max too? Are you sure?"

"Oui."

"Viktor, she was just here, in the office this morning, before we got here. You're telling me that both she and Jackie have been taken hostage? Really?"

Viktor nods his head slowly.

"We'll deal with that later. I want Jackie free first. With the first $200 million. Go. Make your call."

"But my dear Bao—"

"Shut up, Viktor. You've got $400 million of some shit investments in your personal account. And I've just begun to figure out why your little stash is so illiquid." Ethan goes to his desk and pulls some papers from the file Rebecca gave him earlier.

Viktor squirms in his chair. "Whatever do you mean?"

"You know exactly what I mean. Rebecca pulled a few of the holdings of your personal account. Just a few in New York."

"That is not her business. Those are my personal assets."

"You've got an $18 million loan from the firm against those assets. So, if you owe the firm a penny, I have every right to know what you've posted as collateral, if you can call it that. Ethan throws one of the papers on the coffee table. Viktor leans over to glance at it and then sits back in his chair without reading it. "Seems you've been running a nice little EB-5 green card business. That should be the name of what you call your 'personal account,' Viktor."

"They are legitimate investments. Perfectly legal."

"Perhaps legal, but hard to classify as an investment."

"How so?"

"Viktor don't be coy with me. You know that someone who wants to live in the United States can apply for an EB-5 green card, which lets them remain in the country so long as they have invested at least $500,000 in a legitimate business. A business that is supposed to create ten or more jobs."

Viktor says nothing. He is still sitting back in his chair, refusing to look at the paper on the coffee table in more detail.

"So, here we have a nice tidy little package. Two nail salons in New York City. One on Fifty-Seventh Street and the other on Sixty-Fifth. Two crappy little buildings for which you provided $7.8 million from your personal fund to purchase. The salons are owned by Mrs. Daiyu Jung. Mrs. Jung no doubt applied for and received a green card, did she not? She has invested over $7 millions of someone's money to get a green card and stay in the US. That's very nice for her, isn't it, Viktor? She gets to live in New York, have a green card, and her name is on at least $7 million in properties and businesses."

Viktor remains silent.

"Here's an interesting link, Viktor. In the B Fund, we have a loan to Mrs. Daiyu Jung, who also appears as Jade Emery, wherever that name came from, on a nice condominium on Fifty-Eighth Street, for which we put out $2.6 million. Between your 'loans' to Ms. Jung from your personal account and our mortgage on her condominium, I'd say we have Mrs. Jung financed quite nicely. Almost ten million dollars in total. Am I right? I can imagine this little link repeats itself over and over if we take a closer look at a lot of the holdings in the B Fund. Chinese nationals get and EB-5 green card, a business that they own, and a condominium to live in. The funding comes from our fund, so it looks like a legitimate investment, with some financing from your personal account."

Viktor clears his throat. "This is a good investment then, no? Seems of excellent quality to me. A business and a condo, both of which are likely worth more than I, or we, invested in them."

"Whose money is this, Viktor?"

"What?"

"Viktor don't bullshit me. This isn't *your* money. It belongs to someone else. Probably a lot of other people."

"I am earning a healthy return, so what concern is that?"

"Viktor, cut the crap. The payments into your personal account are a couple million a year. A $400 million portfolio investing in properties and businesses in New York and Los Angeles would be returning $40 to $50 million a year. You're getting chump change. Because you're the chump who funnels money from Chinese politicians and wealthy Chinese businesspeople to the United States for hiding their investments. You always told me and Logan this was family money, as in the *Lucienne* family. Of France, not China! It's family money all right, but not your family's. Lots of Chinese families. Who are these people, Viktor? Who are we dealing with, and why are people dying and being kidnapped?"

Viktor is silent, staring out the window.

Ethan gets up from his chair, pulls Viktor out of his seat and slams him against the window, ripping off part of Viktor's lapel in the process. As Viktor's head smashes against the glass, he lets out a cry, so Ethan covers his mouth.

"It's over, Viktor. I know what's going on. Logan's clients were the only legitimate investment business we had at the firm. With that gone, we're only a conduit for the Chinese Communist Party to hide money for their elites in the United States, far away from the reach of the Chinese government. Not only is the money safer here, but so are the Chinese officials and relatives who have obtained these green cards. The US *doesn't* have an extradition treaty with China. It's very hard for the Chinese government to reach the money or their citizens who are living here legally. This scheme provides them with a very safe haven – for hiding their assets and family members. And our firm is the conduit to make this happen. It's a Chinese laundry. A *money* laundry machine, that is. I can't believe we were this stupid."

"You got rich, mon ami. Very rich. You have been more than amply paid by the hefty management fees you take out of the fund every quarter. Release me and get to work liquidating the money."

Ethan lets loose of Viktor, who wipes the sweat from his forehead and turns away.

"Go make your call, Viktor. Make it clear that Jackie must be released when the first installment appears in your client's account in Paris. As for Bao, you raise your own funds from your little pisspot of blood money."

"Ethan—"

"Go! Get out of my sight, Viktor. Make your call. Oh, and one more thing. If anything happens to Jackie, you're dead, Viktor. I mean it. I'll kill you with my own two hands."

Viktor says nothing and leaves the office.

Ethan takes off his shirt so it can dry out. It is soaked with sweat, and he will need to look composed when he has his staff meeting. He then glances at the clock. He will wait for about an hour and then place a call to the regional SEC office to report what Logan has done. That will permit time for Maria to tell Curtis to begin liquidating the Barinsky account and the union fund, so that will all be done before close of market and the 1:05 staff meeting on the trading floor.

As Ethan sits down at his desk to begin looking over the figures Rebecca provided to him, the door to his office bursts open. Maria rushes in, closes the door, and shouts, "She's gone! Rebecca's gone!"

20

Not Exactly Breakfast at Tiffany's

Seth pulls up in front of Julian's jewelry studio on North Rodeo Drive, just across and up the street from the Beverly Wilshire Hotel. The studio is marked with a simple "J" above the door, which has identified the discreet location for over seventy years. Julian's father, a Jewish immigrant from Poland, started the jewelry studio in the 1940s, and his son by the same name still operates the business. In the '70s and '80s, Julian was *the* jewelry designer in Beverly Hills. As time wore on and big-name fashion houses overtook Rodeo Drive, Julian became even more exclusive, making custom jewelry for celebrities and wealthy referrals on an invitation-only basis. But as Julian aged, so did his clientele. Now at eighty years of age, Julian finds his clientele greatly diminished, and he is now a one-off specialty jeweler, making a dozen or so pieces a year for old—and some very old—clientele. Among them are older celebrities, wealthy Iranians who came to Beverly Hills after the shah was deposed, and some wealthy Jewish families like Max's, who have patronized him for decades.

Seth waits in the car as Max rings the buzzer on the door. There is no response at first. She buzzes again. A fragile, small voice comes over the intercom. "Who is calling?"

"Julian, it's Max."

After a brief pause and no response, the buzzer sounds, and Max opens the door. The scent takes her breath away. Since she was a small child of seven years old, she remembers her father taking her to Julian's shop to buy items for her mother and grandmother. The smell was the same. It was hard to pin down, but it is the smell of an old jewelry shop—jewelry cleaners and polish, canvas, and the leather chairs clients sit in while trying on custom jewelry.

A tall but now hunched-over man with long blond (gray but dyed-blond) hair comes toward her. He stretches out his arms and gives her a tender hug. "Oh, my dear Maxine, you look divine."

Max smiles but says nothing. *Has he read the papers? Does he know that Logan is missing?* She opts for silence, save to say, "You look marvelous, Julian. How I have missed you."

He looks at her, holding her hand and glancing up and down, smiling. "I am so pleased to see you, but I must say, I'm surprised you're here."

Max sighs. "So, then you know?"

"About dear Logan? Yes. I'm sorry. Mrs. Levine phoned me this morning after she saw the news. I don't know everything, but I hope he is found."

"That's sort of why I'm here, Julian."

"You want me to help you find dear Logan?"

"Well, not exactly, but I do need your help."

"Anything, my dear, anything."

Max holds up the pendant from her neck. "I love this. Logan gave it to me Saturday night, on our way to our fateful cruise."

Julian stares at her and at the pendant. He holds the pendant in his hand, studying it closely. "Stunning. You love art deco. That's what the design is, right? Art deco? Wherever did you get it?"

Max takes a deep breath. She lets him continue to examine it. "It's lovely, Julian. I adore it. When did Logan order it?"

Julian is confused. He asks her to take it off.

Max gently removes the pendant and hands it to Julian.

He stares at it, inspecting the back and the front, and then takes it to the counter and turns on a magnified jewelry light. Julian continues to examine it for what seems an eternity to Max. She finally sits down in a chair across the counter from him.

"Julian? Julian? It's beautiful. Thank you for making it. I need your help. Can you take it back, for some cash, for just a few weeks, at the most?"

Julian is clearly puzzled. "My dear Max, that is two questions. Did I make it, and can I loan you some money? Am I right?"

Max is silent for a moment. She rises from her chair and moves closer to Julian at the counter.

"Yes, I would like to leave this with you, pawn it temporarily, but you know I'm good for it."

"Oh, no doubt, of course, I can give you what you need. How much?"

"That's up to you, Julian. What did Logan pay for it?"

Julian is stumped. He doesn't say anything, but sits down in his chair behind the counter, still admiring the pendant. "It is beautiful. Who designed it?"

Max doesn't know what to say. Surely Julian did not become senile in a week. If Logan presented this to her last Saturday night, he must have picked it up from Julian a few days before.

"Stunning, I love it. But very heavy. Is it solid gold, no, looks like platinum. Yes, I'm sure it is platinum."

Max picks up the pendant from Julian's hand. "Julian, do you not recognize this? Really? Logan just gave it to me Saturday night, and he said you made it."

Julian stands up, and leans across the counter to face Max. "My dear Max. How long have you known me? I know I've slipped a bit, or more than a bit, but you don't think I would recognize a piece I created. I know all my children. All of them. I wish I created this, but I didn't. This is not mine, though I wish it were."

Max is speechless.

"Why do you think this is my creation?"

"Because Logan told me you made it."

Julian picks up the piece again. "No, I wish I had. But this is not mine. And it is so ... so *thick*. What's inside here?" He holds it up, as if to shake it.

"What do you mean, what's inside?"

"It's very thick for a pendant. I believe it is hollow or at least not solid platinum." He again places it under the magnifying glass and light, noticing that there are six tiny screws on the back plate. "May I open it?"

"Why? What's the point of opening it, Julian?"

"A jeweler's curiosity, I guess. There's no reason to have a back plate on a piece like this. It should be solid. I promise you I won't harm it."

Max raises her eyebrows and holds out her hands in a "Why not?" gesture.

Julian carefully removes each of the six tiny screws with a jeweler's screwdriver. He looks as if he is repairing a watch, carefully placing each of the screws on a piece of black felt. With all the screws removed, he gently lifts off the back plate with a jeweler's cloth. "Oh, my. Look at that," he says very quietly. He then looks up at Max but does not speak.

"What is it?" Max leans over the counter, and Julian tilts the magnifying glass toward her. She squints, adjusts the magnifying glass higher, and then looks more closely. "My God, Julian, what is it?"

They both look at each other and are silent for a moment.

Julian clears his throat. "Well, I made something like this once, but it didn't look quite as elaborate."

"What do you mean? Something like this? What is it?"

"I believe it's a tracking device, a transmitter, if you will. Do you see this small battery, and the two little wires that look like antennae? Can you see this tiny light that flashes every fifteen seconds or so, on this silver cylinder? It's probably a transponder. Certainly, much smaller than the one I installed."

"You installed one, but why? Why would a piece of jewelry have a transmitter?"

At first, Julian doesn't respond. He then turns to Max and sits down on his stool behind the counter. "Well, I would never admit it to anyone, my dear Max, but in view of the circumstances, I must say that I did it for a great deal of money for a gentleman, well, that's a poor choice of words ... a man who wanted to keep tabs on his mistress. I so regret doing it. He eventually killed her, and I'm always haunted about whether my beautiful creation led him to find her in a situation that resulted in the end of her life." He looks at the floor and then up at Max.

"Oh my God, Julian. That's terrible. But certainly, that's not the case here? Why would Logan want to keep tabs on me?" She no sooner said those words than she puts her hands to her mouth and exhales loudly.

"My dear Max, are you okay? What's the matter?" Julian comes around to the other side of the counter and puts his hands on Max's shoulders.

"Julian, how much do you know about Logan's disappearance and the yacht sinking last Saturday night?"

"My dear, I know only what Mrs. Levine told me this morning, when she called. I'm very confused, but I know you appeared mysteriously while separated from the others on the yacht. I know dear Logan is missing, or … well, I know how awful this must be for you."

Max shakes her head and looks up at the ceiling, pulling her hair back from her face. "This explains so much. I need to drink it in for a moment."

"Whatever do you mean?"

"The transponder you made for your client was used to keep track of someone. It seems that mine was perhaps to find me, floating around in the ocean." She sighs with relief that perhaps Logan, by tossing her into the sea, was trying to save her and that the pendant was the device the men in the boat used to locate her. But if that is the case, then Logan planned all this well before the night of the cruise. But why? What was to happen on *Copious* that night for Logan to plan to throw her into the sea? Fighting back tears, she is happy and sad at the same time. She is relieved to discover that Logan was likely trying to save her, but worried something had unfolded on the yacht that evening which was planned by Logan in advance. But that means he lied to her about several things that evening. They never lied to each other.

Why did he tell her Julian made this piece? She asks Julian for a tissue or handkerchief.

"Maxine. Maxine. You all, right?"

She shakes her head to get back into the moment and leave her thoughts for the time being. "Julian, how much money can you loan me?"

"What? You're making me worried! Are you running from Logan or someone else?"

"Julian, I can't explain now, but I promise you that I will repay you every dollar you can lend me. And I'll need for you to keep this quiet, and for your own protection, don't tell anyone that I was here today. Please. Or you might be harmed."

Julian moves slowly to the back of the shop and motions for Max to follow him. He pulls back a curtain and points to the safe. It is electronic, and Max is quite surprised that dear old Julian would have something so current.

"Wow, an electronic safe. I'm surprised to see that in your studio!"

"Don't be. The insurance company insisted on putting it in. They think I'm too old to be in this business, so this new safe is the only way I could keep my insurance. I must tell you that motion around the safe is linked to a camera, so you need to stand back toward the counter. I don't want you to be in sight of the camera when I open the safe. I can't access this camera; only the insurance company can."

Max moves back as she watches Julian grab a large black bag, as if he were putting something *in* the safe rather than taking something out. He punches in a code and then places his hand on a scanner, and the safe pops open. Julian places the bag in the safe and then turns his back toward Max while he closes the door. He walks back slowly, and when out of sight of the camera, he motions her to the front of the shop, behind a wall that hides part of his workbench. He pushes an envelope into her hand. "Should be about thirty thousand dollars, give or take."

Max places the envelope in the pants of her sweat suit.

"Thank you, my sweet friend. I promise you will have this all back, with interest."

"No interest and no worries. I don't care about the money, but I'm very concerned about what's going on with you. Are you in trouble? Do you know where your husband is? What's going on?"

"Julian, I must go. Please promise me that you'll erase the camera record when I leave. She points to the camera at the front door and the one above the counter."

"Oh, I can easily do that. You know how many times I must remove celebrity images from visits to my store. I can't modify the camera over the safe, but I can erase these two. Go. I'll do that now, and please take care of yourself."

"Thank you. You are my lifesaver, Julian. And remember, don't tell anyone you've seen me."

"Wait. You must take this." Julian hands her the pendant.

"No, that's your collateral."

"He laughs softly. I don't need collateral from you. But *if* you are right and Logan had this made to keep track of you, you had better take it with you and wear it. If he's not dead, it may be the only way he can find you."

Max thinks for a moment. "Well, in any event, if it is someone else tracking me, I certainly don't want the trail to end at your shop. Thank you, dear friend."

She looks outside the door to be sure no one is on the sidewalk, and then makes a beeline for Seth's car. She closes the door and says, "Hit it, honey."

"What took so long? I was getting worried."

"Seth, just drive."

As they drive away, Seth's cell phone rings. They both look at each other. The caller ID says "E. Bearitz."

21

Involuntary Exits and Sudden Arrivals

Maria stands at the door to Ethan's office, breathless. "Gone, her purse and everything. Even the two pictures on her desk. Gone."

"Damn it, Maria! I told you to keep an eye on her. You weren't supposed to let Rebecca out of your sight."

"She must have fled immediately after leaving your office, while you and Viktor and I were talking."

"The front desk, did they see her leave?"

"No. Rebecca called Evelyn, the receptionist, to come back to her desk. Seems it was a ruse. Evelyn left the front desk to go to Rebecca's office, and Rebecca apparently slipped out of the lobby and into the elevator while no one was there."

"Damn it. God damn it! Go get Viktor and bring him in here."

Viktor and Maria enter Ethan's office. They close the door and sit in chairs at Ethan's desk. Ethan looks remarkably relaxed, considering what just occurred. "This is a gift. A true gift."

Maria leans over Ethan's desk. "What? Are you crazy? This screws up the plan before it's even begun!"

"Not at all. Not at all. If I could have scripted this, it's perfect. Rebecca is on the run. She was conspiring with Logan, and we caught her at it. We informed her that we were going to call the SEC today and that she would have to explain what happened last Friday. We told her to stay at her desk until we came to get her, and she bolted. She called the receptionist to get her away from the front desk, and she fled. It's perfect. Evelyn at the front desk will verify that Rebecca snuck out, because we caught her in cahoots with Logan. The three of us will stick to that story. Now I can not only make the call to the SEC, but I'll tell them that it seems Rebecca conspired with Logan and that her guilt made her flee before we called the authorities. This is perfect! It deflects attention away from us." Ethan is grinning. He looks like a heavy load has been lifted from his shoulders. Viktor sighs and makes a "that's it" flourish with his hand.

Maria, however, isn't convinced that Rebecca's disappearance is a good thing. "It's too convenient. Why wouldn't she want to stick around to vindicate herself? She'll lose her CPA license if she's linked to the illegal redemption, and attempting to flee makes it even worse for her. I'm suspicious, Ethan."

"Don't be. This makes it easier for us. Having Rebecca in here blubbering and crying in front of the SEC would have been a distraction. Now it's clear. She was in on it and ran to save her skin. It's almost eleven, so I should make the call."

"Who are you calling at the SEC?"

"The SEC Regional Office on Flower Street. I'll ask for the director's office and tell him what's happened. They will of course open an investigation. I'll announce that to the staff at the meeting this afternoon."

Suddenly, there's a loud knock at Ethan's door. Ethan looks up. "Come in."

It's Donna, Logan's assistant. "There's a Detective Carter on the phone from the Orange County Sheriff's Office. Says it is urgent and he wants to speak with you and Mr. Lucienne."

"Is it about Logan? Have they found him?"

"He didn't say. Just said to interrupt you; it's urgent."

"Put him through."

Ethan answers the call and clicks on the speakerphone. "Good morning, Detective Carter. I have you on the speakerphone."

"Is Mr. Lucienne with you?"

"Yes, yes, he is."

"Anyone else?"

"No, just the two of us." Maria puts her hands up as if to question why Ethan doesn't say she is in the room as well. Ethan puts his finger over his mouth to let her know to keep quiet.

Detective Carter begins to speak, "I'm afraid I have some bad news."

"About Logan? You've found his body? I hope that's not it."

"No, Mr. Chandler, that's not it. It's your captain. Mr. Grays. He passed away in the hospital last night."

Ethan is stunned. "What? How can that be? I know he was unconscious, but were his injuries that serious?"

"No, actually, they weren't."

"Then what happened? Oh my God, poor Clint."

"We're hoping the coroner can tell us that. But the nurse and doctor on duty last night said it looked like he was poisoned in the hospital, Sunday night. They said the poisoning symptoms were obvious, but they couldn't save him."

Ethan turns white. "What? How does that happen in a hospital, and why?"

Viktor says nothing; he is staring out the window as if ignoring the conversation. Ethan snaps his fingers to get his attention. Viktor turns to look at Ethan but stays silent.

Detective Carter goes on, "I'm told that as Mr. Lucienne was leaving the hospital Sunday afternoon, he stopped by the intensive care unit to inquire about the condition of Mr. Grays."

Ethan looks at Viktor and mouths in silence, "Well?" He was prodding Viktor to respond to the detective.

Detective Carter asks, "Is Mr. Lucienne still there, and did he hear what I just said?"

Ethan motions for Viktor to speak up.

"Oui, Detective Carter, I am here."

"Did you visit Mr. Grays before you left the hospital yesterday afternoon?"

"Oui, I stopped in to check on him before we were taken to the hotel."

"Was anyone with you when you went to see Mr. Grays?"

"No. Just me."

"How long were you with him before the nurse came in and asked what you were doing there?"

"I had just gotten there. He was unconscious, and she told me to leave. Which I did."

Detective Carter is silent for a moment and then can be heard speaking with someone in his office.

Ethan asks, "You still there, Detective?"

"Yes. I am. I'll need for you and Mr. Lucienne to come here for questioning before the end of the day."

"What? That's impossible. You know what we're dealing with here. First day back at work after what happened. We have a senior partner of the firm missing, and we've discovered some financial issues we are discussing with the SEC in just a moment. We can't get there today."

"Okay, then we'll come to you. We'll be there in a couple of hours. Don't leave the office until we get there."

Ethan throws up his hands and mouths, "Shit," in silence to Maria and Viktor. "Can we at least meet you somewhere outside the office so the staff is not more upset than they already are?"

"Tell you what. We'll be at your office at 6 p.m. tonight. Be sure your staff has all gone home. That way, no one gets upset."

Ethan sighs. "Okay, we'll see you then." He turns off the speakerphone and stands up from his desk. He walks over to Viktor, who is still sitting silently in his chair. Maria is glaring at him, but also silent. Ethan puts his hand on Viktor's left shoulder and speaks to him from behind. "Viktor, did you do anything to harm Clint?"

"And why would I want to harm dear Clint?"

"I didn't ask you *why*. I asked you if you *did* anything to harm him. You didn't tell me you went to see him in the intensive care unit before you left the hospital last night."

Viktor turns to Maria, as if he is afraid to speak with her there. She looks back at him and leans forward. "Go on, Viktor, tell us what happened. When I picked you up, I asked you if you'd seen Clint or Rick and you said no. Now we find out you paid Clint a visit in ICU before we left."

"He called me a liar. Said he'd be sure I paid."

Maria and Ethan look stunned.

Ethan puts his hand on Viktor's chin and makes him turn his face toward his. "My God, Viktor, what are you saying? When did Clint tell you that?"

"After the argument on the yacht. The first explosion, when Logan ran away to get Max. Clint turned toward me and told me I would pay for what I did and that I was a liar. He then ran to the front of the ship, and there was the second explosion. I didn't see him again until we were at the hospital."

"So, you killed him for that?"

"He heard the argument. Saw me strike Logan with the bottle. He could have exposed the whole … problem."

Ethan lets go of Viktor's chin. "My God, Viktor. What did you do to poor Clint?"

"My little pill. The one I always carry if I must end my misery. I gave it to Clint."

"To end your misery? What are you saying?"

"I always carry a cyanide capsule just in case I am ever in a situation where I need to end my life. My father taught me. When he was in the French resistance against the Nazis, he always had a pill to be sure his life ended on his terms and not the Nazis'. I've carried one most of my life. This is the only time I've used it. Bad timing. I am sorry."

Ethan goes silent and looks at the floor. Maria goes to Ethan and puts her hand on his shoulder. "It's time you tell me about the last conversation on the boat. Clint is dead because of it, Logan is missing, and so is Jaclyn. And Bao. Tell me what happened."

Ethan stands up, clears his throat, and wipes his eyes. "Viktor arrived two weeks ago with the news that his largest client—or as it turns out, his *only* client for our firm—wants most of his money back, $1.7 million out of the $2 billion or so we manage for him. Instantly. He will not honor our agreement to liquidate his holdings in the fund over a period of twelve months. You know by now who Viktor's client is? Him and his family members?"

"Yes, I do."

"Well, at the time, Logan and I had no idea, though we certainly should have. Anyway, Viktor and I agreed to use the retail client's money in the 'A' fund to get a down payment to Viktor's client so we could have time to raise the rest from the B Fund. Logan objected to what Viktor, and I wanted to do. He said it was illegal, and morally wrong. He wasn't going to ruin his reputation to satisfy a greedy client. We argued. To my surprise, Logan ultimately backed down and said he would agree to the transaction. Apparently, he was fooling us and had no intention of selling the retail fund assets to make a payment to Viktor's client. In retrospect, he was just diverting us to buy some time for him to do what you learned about this morning.

Maria doesn't understand. "What do you mean?"

"Logan was to liquidate all the holdings for the individual investors and wire the cash to Viktor's client's account in Paris. Assets in the retail fund are traded on the exchanges, so they could all be sold, and the funds would settle, or be available, in three days. He was to establish a set of 'shadow' books on the computer that would make it look like the assets in the Aronheart Fund were still there. We would execute trades and handle redemptions and deposits as usual. We would replace the money taken from the individual investors with proceeds from the B Fund as we sold off the assets in that fund. It was like a loan from one fund to the other. It was to be very quiet, very simple. Borrow from the A Fund to pay Viktor's client part of what he is owed and use the B Fund proceeds to repay the A fund, over time. It would all be secret, of course."

Maria interrupts. "But that's illegal. You can't liquidate a client's funds without their approval."

Ethan points his finger at Maria, "Depends on your perspective, Maria."

"How so?"

"Logan is the sole manager of the Aronheart Fund, the A fund. He has full discretion to buy and sell securities in that mutual fund anytime he chooses. So, one way of looking at this is that Logan would use his discretion to liquidate the funds and buy them back later."

Maria disagrees, "If the funds stayed in the account, then yes, I could see your point. But when you redeem them and pay them to someone else, another party that the funds don't belong to, that's fraud. Come on Ethan, you and Viktor were asking Logan to break several laws. The redemption is clearly illegal."

Ethan nods. "Yes, quite illegal. But the assets in the A Fund are traded on the exchanges and we can cash them in *immediately*. The assets in the B Fund are invested in real estate, mortgages, and private placements that take time to sell. So, we wanted to sell the assets in the A fund and make a partial payment to Viktor's client. In simple terms, it was to be a loan. But yes, redeeming retail investor funds without their approval is, technically, illegal. *If* anyone ever found out about it..."

Maria shakes her head. "Go on."

"It would look like the money was still in the Aronheart Fund, the A Fund, but it would mostly be gone. The wire was to have gone out last Friday, the day before the cruise. Logan not only did not send the wire to Viktor's client's account in Paris, but he began a process to liquidate the individual shareholders' money and send it to *them*, as you heard Rebecca describe this morning."

Maria nods. "Logan wanted to be sure the individual investors got their money back before you and Viktor got your hands on it."

Ethan shakes his head. "That's right. On Saturday night he told us he did not send the wire to Paris on Friday because he couldn't raise the cash quickly enough from the sale of assets in the A fund. That's all he told us, that the wire did not go out Friday, but he'd handle it Monday. But in fact, he had already liquidated the A Fund and returned all the money to individual investors on

Friday. He did send a wire, but to a custodian in Zurich instead of Viktor's client in Paris. We didn't know that part of the story until Rebecca discovered it early this morning."

"So, you only found out about him *not* sending the money to Paris on the boat that night, just before the explosion?"

"Yes, but there's a bit more to the story than that. When Max went below to get her wrap, Jackie did the same. It was just me, Viktor, and Logan on the deck, having champagne. Viktor asked if the wire had gone out okay on Friday. Logan said it had not gone out because he had a question for Viktor. Viktor wasn't happy to hear that but asked him for the question."

"And the question was?"

Viktor speaks up before Ethan can respond. "He asked me when I was going to tell him and Ethan that my client was the head of the Chinese Communist Party. He asked me when I was planning on telling them that."

Maria looks at Ethan and then back at Viktor. "And what did you tell him?"

"I told him that was none of his business. I am the only client that matters, and it is of no concern to Ethan or Logan who my client or clients are."

Everyone is silent for a moment, and then Maria asks, "What did Logan say?"

Ethan stands up. "I'll tell you what Logan said. He said that he doesn't invest laundered cash, and he certainly never would have taken Viktor's money had he known he was abetting the Chinese Communist Party by hiding money for government officials and their families in the United States. He said he was through with Viktor's money and that he wouldn't touch any of it. He told Viktor to find a new home for his business, like a trash dump in New Jersey."

Maria blinks. "That doesn't sound like Logan."

Ethan nods in agreement. "Viktor, obviously offended, threw his glass of champagne in Logan's face. He then grabbed the champagne bottle from the bucket, probably to hit Logan, but it dropped on the deck, breaking into two pieces. Logan and

Viktor both looked at the larger, jagged piece of the bottle on the deck and reached down to retrieve it. Viktor grabbed it first, and with Logan's face only a few inches from his, Viktor swiped it across Logan's brow. Hence the bleeding face."

Maria looks at Viktor, who is now staring at the floor. "So that's what Max heard, and when she got up to the salon, the first explosion happens. Logan then comes in having just had his face slashed by Viktor."

Ethan nods in agreement. "And Clint apparently saw it all, at least the final bits of the conversation."

Maria stands up and puts her hand on her chin. "But how did Logan find out? How did he know all of this about the real identity of Viktor's client before you did, Ethan?"

Ethan is quiet for a moment and then looks at Viktor, who also seems anxious for the answer. Ethan says softly, "Laurent."

"What?" Viktor is incensed. *"Ce n'est pas possible."*

"Yes, Viktor, it *is* possible. Your nephew Laurent figured it out weeks ago. Seems he met a very wealthy Chinese boy at a gay bar here in LA. One thing led to another, and when the young Chinese boy learned who Laurent worked for, he told him he was managing money 'for dogs' or some Mandarin slang for handling dirty money. Seems he was schooled in France, knew of Viktor's family and his wife. That's what Logan told me when he said he had a question for Viktor. The rest you know."

Maria takes a deep breath. "Well, then. So now we have it. I see why you didn't answer the detective's questions about the last fifteen minutes on the boat."

Viktor is starting to speak when there's a knock at Ethan's door. Donna opens the door and bursts in before Ethan can even respond.

"Good God, Donna, why are you just barging in here?"

"There are four men in the lobby. They want to see you right away."

"Not today, we're busy. Have them make an appointment with Maria for later in the week."

Donna smiles coyly. "Oh, I don't think they're the type who need appointments. Two are from the FBI, and two are with the regional office of the SEC."

Ethan looks at Maria. "Oh, dear God."

22

When Dead Is Not Dead

Seth picks up his cell phone as he drives away from Julian's shop. Since the caller ID says "E. Bearitz," he hands it to Max before he says a word.

Max anxiously takes the phone from Seth. "This is Max Aronheart. Is this Coroner Bearitz?"

"Yep, Ms. Aronheart, this is Betty. I'm glad I could reach you. I'm holding a press conference this evening, and I wanted to give you a … well, a bit of a preview of my findings."

"Oh, please yes. Is there anything encouraging? We've not heard from the Coast Guard, the sheriff, no one."

"Well, I'm afraid I don't have anything definitive, Ms. Aronheart. I can confirm that the tissues, body parts, dental samples, and blood are a match for your husband. I'm expecting the DNA results any minute, but I'm certain they'll also verify a match."

"Oh, no! So, what does that mean? Is he likely dead?"

"Well, that's why I'm calling you. At this point, I am referring the case of your husband back to the sheriff's department as a missing person."

"Oh, that's wonderful news! From what you found in the bag; do you think he could still be alive?"

"Whoa, just a minute, Ms. Aronheart. I'm saying that I don't have enough of anything to determine *if* whoever was in that bag is dead or alive. The whole body is missing, but the burned tissue

I do have, well, it ... it would be hard to have a live body if the rest of the body was as badly burned as these tissue samples."

"I see." Max was hoping for better news. "What happens now?"

"You pray that this is a hoax."

"What? A hoax?"

"Sorry to be blunt, but *if* your husband's body was in that bag, he is most surely dead. On the other hand, if only parts of his body were placed in this bag, the parts I have, excuse me, aren't enough to say he couldn't be walking around without a finger, some burned skin, and a few missing teeth, if you know what I mean."

Max is taken aback by the blunt comments from the coroner. She puts the phone on speaker so Seth can now hear the conversation. "You're saying Logan could be alive but badly burned. Or he's dead and someone took the body."

"Exactly. There are other possibilities, but those two are at the top of my list. He's dead and someone is trying to hide it. Or he's not dead and someone's trying to make it look like he's dead."

"But why?"

"That's exactly what I want to ask you, Ms. Aronheart. Anyone you know that wants your husband dead? Or to appear to be dead? Any reason everyone survived the sinking but him?"

Max is silent. She looks at Seth, who mouths in silence, "Ethan?"

"No, no that would make no sense."

"What? What makes no sense, Ms. Aronheart?"

"Um, my associate here, he said Ethan, but I'm not sure why."

"He's referring to Mr. Chandler?"

"Yes, but I have to ask him why."

Seth pulls the car over to the side of the road, puts it in park, and takes the phone from Max. "Ethan wouldn't want Logan dead, even if he were."

The coroner is silent for a moment and then asks, "Say again?"

"Logan's the brains of the operation. Ethan is nothing without Logan. Everyone knows that. If Logan *is* dead, Ethan wouldn't want that to get out. At least not for a while. That's just my theory. I haven't mentioned it to Max until now."

The coroner is silent.

Max asks, "You still there, Ms. Bearitz?"

"Yep, still here. Let me ask you this then …"

Seth looks at Max. Both are puzzled. "Go on."

"Any reason to be concerned about another missing person here in this whole yachting affair? Or a dead one?"

Seth and Max are both confused by the question. They look at each other, hoping the other will speak first.

"You both still there? Hello?"

Max speaks up. "Yes, we're still here, but confused. What are you saying?"

The coroner clears her throat. "You know nothing of Ms. Chandler or Mr. Grays?"

Seth and Max stare at the phone and then look up at each other. They say nothing.

"Is that a reply or are you thinking about it?"

Max leans into the phone and says, "It sounds like you have something to tell us, Ms. Bearitz."

"You've not heard from Mr. or Mrs. Chandler?"

"Obviously not. What are you getting at? I thought you called me to talk about my husband."

"I did, yes. But there are two other topics which will likely come up at my press conference."

"And those would be?"

"Mr. Grays died in the hospital last night."

Max and Seth look at each other and shake their heads.

"No response? Is this news to you or do you simply not want to reply?"

Max speaks up. "This *is* news to us. We thought the captain was okay and recovering in the hospital."

"Yep, that's right, Ms. Aronheart. At least he was until they wheeled his body in here to my morgue this morning."

Max looks at the phone and then at Seth. "That's very odd.

I didn't see him after the sinking, but I didn't think his injuries were serious."

"Exactly. So why does his body appear in my morgue this morning with symptoms of poisoning?"

Seth is silent. Max takes the question literally. "You're asking me? How would I know?"

"I didn't mean that the way it sounded. The press got wind of it from the hospital staff, so now I've got another dead body to deal with, aside from the one that's 'gone missing,' as they say. I just wanted to talk with you before the press conference and tell you that my office won't be dealing any further with your husband's case until a body is found. Dead or alive. Uh, I could have worded that better. Sorry."

"It's ok. I understand what you're saying. In that case, may we retrieve his personal items from you?"

The coroner hesitates. "I'm sorry, I can't do that. I need to keep those items until we have a more definitive answer on your husband. Once I release the items to you, I can no longer use them as evidence, if that situation arises."

Max nods her head. "Understood. I'll speak with the sheriff's office and Captain Westmore at the Coast Guard to see what we do from here. It's just so frustrating. I shouldn't have gotten my hopes up."

"I know how you feel. This is a very frustrating case. For all of us. Oh, I have one more thing, as I mentioned. Have you spoken with Ms. Chandler since yesterday?"

"No. Why?"

"Do you know where she might be?"

Seth and Max are both silent, not sure if they should say they saw her arriving at the office early this morning with Ethan and Viktor.

"Did you hear my question?"

Max purses her lips and then looks up at Seth, who is waving his hand in front of her and mouthing, "No, no." Max nods at Seth. "No, we don't know where she is. At her home, I would guess."

"You haven't spoken with her since your tearful reunion here in my office yesterday afternoon?"

"No. Why? Is everything okay?"

"Don't know. A reporter called my office to ask if I had any comment on the carjacking of Jackie Chandler and if I thought it could be related to the disappearance of Mr. Aronheart."

Max is shocked. "What? Carjacking? When? Is she okay?"

"You two don't watch the news? Where are you anyway?"

Seth and Max look at each other in disbelief. Seth shakes his head, and Max's eyes began to tear up.

"You two still there? Are you okay? I'm sorry. Only wanted to know if you had heard from her since yesterday."

Max wipes her eyes as Seth searches for a tissue or a napkin. "No, we haven't seen the news. Please tell me what you know."

"That's it, pretty much. Detective Carter heard from Beverly Hills PD this morning. They called him because they knew her husband worked with yours and that Detective Carter is working on the yacht sinking case. Seems she was driving home, and a car forced her to the side of the road. A guy walking his dog said two men jumped out, forced her out of her car and into theirs, and they sped away. Torched the car, I guess. Right in her own neighborhood."

Max turns to look at Seth. "Oh my God, this is getting crazy."

"I quite agree, Ms. Aronheart. Are you sure you aren't in any danger?"

Max takes the phone off speaker and places it in her hand. She tells Seth to start driving. "We're fine, Ms. Bearitz. Thank you so much for calling us about Logan and filling us in on the others. Please let me know whenever you have anything more on my husband. Please."

Max hangs up before the coroner can even reply. "Honey, we've got to get moving. Now. Turn around. Go back to Sunset Boulevard, and head west. Turn south on San Vicente."

"The London Hotel? We're going there. Why?"

"Start driving, and then I'll share my plan with you. But first, let me tell you about my visit with Julian."

"Did he loan you the money?"

"Oh yes, but that's not the surprising part." She holds up the pendant around her neck and looks at Seth. "Julian didn't make this. Someone else did."

"What? Well then why did we go to see Julian? I thought Logan had it made for you."

"He apparently did but not by Julian. And that's not all. It has a transmitter in it."

"What the hell? A transmitter? You kidding me? Why?"

"I'm not sure, but I think it was so Logan, or someone else, could keep track of me after *Copious* sank. At least, that's what I'd like to believe."

Seth looks over at Max, who is still holding the pendant. "If that's a transmitter, you might be on to something. But how can you be sure it's Logan, that's tracking you? It could be someone else. And - was it used just so the guys in the fishing boat could find you, or is it still tracking you now?"

"Exactly what I'm thinking. Was this for the sole purpose of being sure I was rescued if Logan and the others died in the sinking? Or is it also to keep tabs on me after the sinking. Or both."

"Yep, but what if it isn't Logan keeping track of you? What if it's someone else?"

"I thought of that too. But Logan gave it to me on the way down to the boat. Those two men did appear out of nowhere to rescue me and take me to the beach. We were a long way out there, almost to Catalina, so what are the odds two fishermen just happen to be nearby when *Copious* blows up?"

"Right. Makes sense. But what's the purpose of it now?"

"That's the question. Julian said the blinking lights mean it's still transmitting. That's why I didn't leave it with him. In case someone is following me for the wrong reasons, I don't want the trail to end with Julian."

"Well, I hardly think Julian is a techno-expert, is he? Are you sure he's right about all this?"

"Don't know, but he took the back off and showed me a battery, two small antennae, and a cylinder with a small blinking light.

Not really a light. More of a glow every fifteen seconds or so."

"Geez, you don't think it's a bomb, do you?"

"This small? Doubt it. Besides, if Logan wanted me dead, he'd have let me drown."

"Maybe you shouldn't be wearing it. Just in case."

"It's a risk, but then if Logan *is* alive and trying to keep track of me, then it could be important. Either way, we've got to flush out whoever is on the other end of this transmitter, Logan or not. And we've got to disappear in case we're next on the list behind Bao, Jackie, and poor Captain Grays."

"Couldn't agree more. Plus, I'm hungry!"

Max laughs and puts her hand on Seth's shoulder. "Keep driving, stay under the speed limit so we stay out of trouble, and in a few minutes, we'll be on our way to a bath, food, and a little Hollywood disappearing act."

As they drive west on Sunset Boulevard, Seth asks, "Left on San Vicente? The London Hotel?"

Max lifts her sunglasses from her nose and replies, "You'll see."

"Well, if we aren't checking in to the London hotel, where are we going?"

"Stick with me, and please just do what I tell you. The next couple of hours will be very busy, and I'll need your help to pull it off."

"Of course, you don't even need to tell me that."

"I know, honey, but before all of that, we have a stop to make that might be, well, a little uncomfortable, but he's the only one I can trust. At least right now."

Seth is confused but says nothing. They turn left on San Vicente Boulevard and drive past the London Hotel, a school yard, and down the street.

"There, sweetie, on the right, pull over."

Seth stops the car in front of a driveway with a metal gate and tall hedges on both sides. There is a call box by the gate, partially obscured by ivy growing on the wall.

"Let me see if he's here. If he is, come in with me. This will be the last you see of the car. Oh, and bring your phone." Max gets out of the car, goes up to the call box, and pushes the buzzer. Seth can see her speaking with someone on the intercom. She then turns to Seth and waves for him to follow her. The large metal gate opens slowly to reveal a circular driveway and a small but tidy English cottage at the end. Max motions for Seth to move the car off the street and into the driveway behind the opening gate.

Seth parks the car in the circular driveway, gets out, and takes Max by the hand. "Who lives here? Seth is becoming suspicious and uncomfortable, but he doesn't know why.

"Sweetie, this is where Alton lives. Well, he doesn't live here, but this is his office."

Seth stops in his tracks and lets go of Max's hand. "You kidding me? Alton? Alton Price? We're here to see that nasty prick?"

"Hey, honey, I know. I know. But he's the only one who can help us now. He's the best crisis coach in LA. And discreet. You know that."

Seth looks down. Max can see sweat forming on his brow as he wipes his eyes. The name *Alton Price* is a terrible reminder of Seth's past, the low point of his life, when he was addicted to crystal meth. Logan and Max tried to help Seth kick his habit, first on their own, then with the help of several rehab programs. None of them worked. Seth would be fine for a while, and then he'd be back at it and in for another futile trip to a rehab clinic. Nothing worked, and Seth was slowly dying.

Out of desperation, Max and Logan called Alton Price, the man known in the business as the most expensive *crisis manager* in Hollywood. He specializes in cleaning up after misdeeds or unfortunate events that befall the rich and famous—messy affairs, domestic violence, an accidental overdose here or there, misbehavior of all types by corporate executives. He's the best "fixer" in Hollywood, hands down. Alton cleans up the mess, diverts the press, and gets the *proper* story out instead of the real one. If there are victims, he will quietly take care of them, and ensure that the celebrity perpetrator is sanitized from any nasty publicity or police involvement. Not all his clients are celebrities. There are businessmen and politicians, and the occasional clergy, who get themselves in nasty situations or sexually related incidents that need to be covered up, as if nothing happened. He is the make-it-go-away expert in Los Angeles.

Alton's assignment for Seth was messy and heartbreaking, but it worked. After Max and Logan hired him, Alton abducted Seth from a West Hollywood gay bar one night while he was on the verge of prostituting himself for a supply of meth. Alton took him from the club, drove to Rancho Mirage, near Palm Springs, and checked him into the Betty Ford Clinic. That was the easy part. Most people go to the Betty Ford Clinic voluntarily. It's not a place for forced treatment or internment. In Seth's case, Alton had to make him *willing* to check in. That involved beating him up, so he was in no position to fight back. When he was checked in, he was exhausted, badly bruised, and bloody. The clinic was told he was beaten up in the club after a meth deal had gone bad. Alton made sure there were no police and no questions asked, and he stationed a nurse, undercover, to keep tabs on Seth for weeks while he was being treated at the clinic. He made sure that Seth never left the facility until the day Max and Logan drove out to get him and take him to their home.

It was a grueling course of treatment for Seth. Meth addicts have about a 95 percent relapse rate, and the "cure" rate is only about 10 to 20 percent. Nearly half of admissions for drug treatment in the United States are related to crystal meth.

When Max and Logan picked him up from the clinic, Seth was a different person. He hated both Max and Logan for having him kidnapped and admitted against his will, but he knew it had saved his life. No one else was there for Seth. His family, upon learning he was gay, had disowned him years ago. Even when Max phoned to ask them to visit Seth during recovery at Betty Ford, they refused. They said he was "already dead" in their eyes. After a few months living with Max and Logan, Seth joined Max in her design business, and he never looked back. Thus far, he is still one of the small percentages of meth-heads to kick the habit. Friends often said that Seth viewed himself as an abandoned puppy rescued at the pound by Max and Logan, just before he was to be euthanized. They are his only family and his best friends. Max and Logan view him as a son, and the three of them are inseparable.

"Honey, it'll be okay. I promise. This time, Alton's helping *me*. I need him, and you'll see why. Please come in with me. I promise to make it quick."

Seth shakes his head, wipes his eyes, and takes Max by the hand. The metal gate at the driveway closes behind them.

At the end of the circular driveway stands Mr. Alton Price. Tall and slender with a dark complexion and thin dark beard, Alton stands in the doorway to the cottage, with his hands in his pockets. He's wearing a dark suit, impeccably tailored, with a white shirt and turquoise tie. He looks at Seth and Max walking toward him and gives them a steely gaze. He has a rather dark grin on his face, but then he half-smiles as they draw closer, and he begins to speak. "What the hell took you so long? I thought you'd be here early this morning. I wasted a whole day sitting here waiting for you two to show up."

23

Parking Garage Exit

Ethan gets up from his chair and tells Donna to inform the gentlemen from the FBI and the SEC that he will be right with them.

Donna smiles. "They seem quite anxious. Won't even sit down. They're standing just down the hallway."

Ethan waves her out of his office. "Fine, take them to the conference room—the one adjoining Logan's office. There's no window to the hallway there so we won't alarm the staff."

"I'm afraid the staff is already alarmed, Ethan. They know something's up. Logan's disappearance is all over the news."

"Okay, okay, I know, Donna. Please take them to the conference room, and we'll be right down."

As Donna leaves and closes the door, Ethan puts on his tie, adjusts his shirt, and grabs his jacket. "You two wait here. If I need you, I'll come get you. But don't leave my office. Either of you." He picks up the file Rebecca gave him earlier in the day and goes toward the door.

Maria objects. "Ethan, you should have me join you. You know you aren't great at details. You need me there."

"I need you to be certain Viktor stays here, and hopefully, they won't want to talk with either of you. At least not now."

"Wishful thinking, Ethan."

"Maria, you aren't an officer of the company. You're my assistant. I don't want you implicated in any of this."

"And Viktor?"

"Viktor? Viktor is a client. He doesn't work for the firm. They have no business talking with him."

Viktor perks up and raises his finger at Ethan. "Oh, no, mon ami, I don't work for the company, but I am a *victim*."

"Victim? You're saying that you're a victim? On the contrary, I think the *firm* is a victim of your unscrupulous client."

"Mon ami, what are you going to tell them? About my client, I mean?"

"Nothing, Viktor. I'm sure they're here about the redemption of the A Fund. Let's hope the issues with your client don't even come up. You two stay here. Don't leave."

Ethan walks down the hall and turns the corner toward Logan's office. He enters the conference room that adjoins Logan's office and sees four men sitting around the table.

"Good morning. I'm Ethan Chandler."

"Mr. Chandler, I'm Ted Ravens, assistant director of the SEC Regional Office, and this is Erwin Jakowsky, an examiner from our office."

Ethan shakes their hands, and then looks at the other two gentlemen. Both gentlemen stand up, and each presents his FBI badge before saying anything. "Special Agent Henry Winters. This is my associate Special Agent Marcello Ritacca. We're both from the LA FBI field office."

After shaking their hands, Ethan pulls out a chair at the table and is seated. "I don't know if Donna told you, but ironically, we were just about to call your office, Mr. Ravens."

Raising his eyebrows, Ravens asks, "Really, why would that be?"

"This morning, we discovered that my partner, Logan Aronheart, redeemed all the shares of our A Fund, the fund used by our retail investors. Its registered name is the Aronheart Fund, and he executed the redemptions last week. The proceeds were sent to a bank in Switzerland, and the checks to the investors are being sent out today by a third-party custodian."

The four men look at each other, and then Mr. Ravens says, "Go on."

Ethan hesitates for a moment. He's inclined to only discuss the Aronheart Fund redemption and not disclose anything about Viktor's client, the incident on the yacht, or anything else. The FBI involvement makes him uncomfortable, since he doesn't know why they're accompanying the men from the SEC. "We just discovered this redemption this morning and are still attempting to get all the facts. However, this is something we obviously would have to report to you, although I don't know all the details at this point."

Assistant Director Ravens clears his throat and says, "Exactly how may we obtain all the details of what occurred? Who advised you of this, and who has all the details of the transactions?"

Ethan sits forward in his chair and looks at Mr. Ravens. "I was told about all of this when I got to the office this morning. Rebecca, the CFO for our firm, told me this morning when I got to work. She saw the outgoing wire from last Thursday and tracked down the recipient, which a bank in Switzerland. They received the funds and have checks going out today from their correspondent bank in San Francisco. Here's the file she gave me. This is the only detail I have from Rebecca."

Ravens takes the file, opens it, and without even looking up, asks, "May we speak with Rebecca?"

"I'm afraid she has left the office. I told her to remain at her desk since we'd need her to give the SEC details of what she found. About an hour ago, I was told she slipped out. She called the receptionist to come back to her desk, and while the receptionist was back at Rebecca's desk, she apparently slipped away without anyone seeing her."

"You have no idea where she is?"

"No. We've tried her cell phone, her home. No answer anywhere."

"What is her last name?"

"Walsh. Rebecca Walsh."

"Any reason she would leave?"

Ethan hesitates for a moment. He then speaks up, slowly, "I … I think that perhaps she was in on it."

Ravens frowns, "In on what?"

"The redemption. She told me she just discovered it this morning, but after I told her we'd have to report this, she vanishes."

None of the other men say anything. Ravens continues to look through the papers Rebecca gave to Ethan.

Ethan is curious why individuals from the SEC and FBI arrived in his office without notice. "May I ask how you gentlemen came to be here this morning?"

Ravens leans back in his chair and closes the file. "A tip. Someone reported that an illegal redemption of millions of dollars was taking place. Examiner Jakowsky here looked up the information on your firm when the tip came in, and we noted that coincidentally, one of your principals is dead from a yachting accident this weekend."

Jakowsky interrupts Ravens as he's speaking. "Not exactly, sir. Mr. Aronheart is *missing. Presumed* dead but missing. At least that's the latest we have."

Ravens puts up his hand. "My mistake, yes. Sorry. In any event, since there's a death or potential death or missing person along with the missing money, we called the FBI. This is routine procedure in a situation like this where money is missing, along with a person who is also missing. I'm sure you get it, Mr. Chandler."

"I understand. You've been in contact with the Orange County Sheriff's Department, I presume?" Ethan had no sooner said that than he regretted it, remembering that Detective Carter is coming up to the office that night to inquire about the death of Captain Grays. They wanted to speak with Viktor in particular.

Special Agent Winters nods his head. "Yes, we've been in touch."

Ravens looked at Ethan and then at the others as he pulls out a document from his briefcase. "Mr. Chandler, in view of the circumstances, I'm afraid the SEC regional director, my boss, has issued an inspection notice." He pushes a piece of paper across the table to Ethan.

"Shit, you're going to raid my office?"

"Well, we don't like to call it a raid if you're going to cooperate, Mr. Chandler."

"Of course, we'll cooperate. Just tell me what you want to do."

At that moment, Donna opens the door to the conference room and looks at Ethan. "Good God, Donna, every time I see you this morning, you're busting in a door! Now what?"

"I'm so sorry, Ethan, but it's your car. In the garage. The valet backed another car into your new Bentley as they were moving it to be washed. The garage manager wants to see you before they call the insurance company."

"God, can this day get any worse? Tell them I'll be down later."

"They're frantic. The two cars are blocking the ramp, and they won't move either of them until you come down and be there for the pictures to be taken. Said it would take just a minute. I've been begging them to let it go, but they're insisting. The building manager just called too."

"Okay, okay. Donna, these gentlemen are to have full access to anything they want. And anyone. I'll get Maria and have her come up here to show them around."

Ravens speaks up. "Who's Maria?"

"She's, my assistant. I'll get her now, and you can tell her everything you need. I'll have to say something to the staff, of course."

Ethan walks down the hall and into his office. As he passes the trading floor, he can see the staff is already aware that something is wrong. Instead of working at their monitors, they're standing around in small groups, talking. He opens the door to his office to find Maria and Viktor arguing. "What's going on? Sounds like you're shouting."

Maria turns away from Viktor and says, "Nothing. Nothing important."

"Well, this *is* important. We're being raided by the SEC."

Maria and Viktor are startled. They both stand up. Maria speaks before. "Oh my God, Ethan, what does that mean?"

"It means we need to be cooperative and show them everything. But only everything related to the A Fund. Try to avoid any discussion about the B Fund. Maria, come with me. I want you to start showing them the office and find out what files or other documents they want. I've got to run down to the parking garage, and I'll be right back up."

"What? Why?"

"Maria, just do what I ask. The valet backed another car into mine as they were moving it to be washed. They want to see me before they can move both vehicles. Go down the hall, introduce yourself, and get started with what they want. Don't mention a thing about the B Fund. Viktor, you keep your mouth shut and stay here in the office until I get back."

Viktor sits back down slowly. He nods his head. "Oui."

Donna comes to the door, and Maria follows her down to the conference room. Ethan walks quickly around the trading floor and past the reception desk to the elevator.

Donna takes Maria to the conference room, where the four visitors are all now standing up. "Hello. I'm Maria. Maria Salinas, executive assistant to Mr. Chandler."

Each of the men introduces himself, and then Mr. Ravens asks, "Where is Mr. Chandler?"

"He'll be right back. He had to go to the parking garage for a moment, but he asked me to get you started with whatever documents you might need."

Ravens frowns and looks at FBI Special Agent Winters. "Shouldn't one of you go down there with him?"

Before Agent Winters can respond, Maria assures them that Ethan will be right back and that they can begin by telling her how this will be handled and what they want to start with.

Winters ignores her and motions for Special Agent Ritacca to go accompany Ethan to the parking garage.

Ravens shows Maria a copy of the inspection notice and asks her if she was present earlier this morning when the missing funds were discovered. She says she was, so Ravens replies that they will begin by taking her statement, and then they want to see the bank wire records and all the activity undertaken last week to liquidate the fund.

Maria nods, "Let's begin by going to Rebecca's desk. I'll log you in, and you can see all the fund transactions last week and the banking transactions she showed us this morning. I can give you our contact at the bank too. We've spoken to them several times this morning."

As Maria is opening the door to take the men to Rebecca's desk, Ravens grabs her by the arm. "Before we do that, Ms. Salinas, we need to gather your employees together and inform them that they are not to tamper with or modify any records, documents, or e-mails. It's a lockdown order, so they need to be informed that any modification or concealment of records will result in prosecution."

Maria goes flush and is taken aback by the seriousness of what she just heard. "So, this can't be done quietly? You're going to tell the whole staff before we start?"

"I'm afraid so. It's a requirement that they be informed about what will be happening. And, later in the day, we'll have several of our staff members here to box up items we need, including computers, if necessary."

Maria closes the door. "Okay, well, then if that's the case, Mr. Chandler should be here to make that announcement to the staff with you."

"Fine. Let's go out to the lobby and wait for him and Special Agent Ritacca to come up the elevator from the garage. We can speak with him then and convene your staff. No one should leave before we have the meeting. We also need the names and contact information of all your employees."

Maria shakes her head, shows them out the door, and escorts them to the lobby.

Downstairs, Ethan has arrived at the parking garage. When the elevator door opens, he turns left toward the valet stand, but as he exits the elevator, two men grab him by the arms, one on each side, and they tell him to be quiet or his wife will die. They take him out of the parking garage to a black Chevrolet Suburban parked at the curb, where they open the door and place him in the backseat. One of the men sits in the back with Ethan, while the other takes the wheel and then slowly pulls the Suburban away from the curb.

A few minutes later, Special Agent Ritacca arrives by the same elevator at the parking garage and immediately goes to the valet stand. A young man looks up from the desk. "Do you have your ticket, sir?"

"I'm looking for Mr. Chandler and your garage manager."

"I haven't seen Mr. Chandler, but the garage manager is over there." He points to a booth with a glass window where the parking cashier is seated. Special Agent Ritacca runs over to the window and asks to see the garage manager. The woman gets up from her chair at the cashier's window and goes to a side door to summon the manager.

A short Hispanic man comes out of the cashier's booth toward Special Agent Ritacca. "You asked for me, sir?"

"Yes, I understand you called Mr. Chandler to come down here about his car."

The garage manager is confused. "Does Mr. Chandler want his car?"

"No, I understood there was an accident with his car, and you called him to come down to see it."

The garage manager is surprised and goes over to the valet stand. "Is there something wrong with Mr. Chandler's car? His new Bentley?"

The valet points to where the car is parked, right up front in a space with Mr. Chandler's name on it.

"Did you call for Mr. Chandler to come see his car?"

The valet shakes his head, no.

The garage manager goes back to Special Agent Ritacca. "There must be some confusion. That's Mr. Chandler's car over there. Who, may I ask, are you?"

Special Agent Ritacca flashes his badge at the garage manager. "FBI."

"Oh, what's wrong with Mr. Chandler's car?"

"You didn't call for Mr. Chandler to come down here to see his car?"

"No, sir. I haven't seen him since he arrived this morning. That's his car right over there."

"May I see it?"

"Yes, of course." The garage manager has the valet take the keys to the car and escort Special Agent Ritacca to where it is parked. He opens the car and inspects the interior and the trunk.

"If you see Mr. Chandler, call me on my cell phone right away." He hands the garage manager a card. "Don't, under any circumstances, let Mr. Chandler or anyone else leave with that car."

"Yes, sir. Is something wrong?"

"Just do as I ask. I'll be back shortly." Ritacca pulls his cell phone from his pocket and dials Ravens. "He's not here. Garage manager said he never called. I just inspected his car, and it's fine. No accident. It's a ruse. Looks like Chandler has fled."

"Shit!" Ravens turns toward Maria and says, "Get that woman who told us the garage manager wanted Mr. Chandler."

Maria goes to the reception desk and tells the receptionist to page Donna. She then goes back to Ravens and asks what's wrong.

"It seems Mr. Chandler has fled. The garage manager didn't call for him to come down."

Maria shakes her head and sits down on the sofa in the lobby. She puts her head in her hands and says, "Oh my God, Ethan, don't leave me alone with this. Please."

24

In the Lair of the Villain

Max and Seth follow Alton into the storybook English cottage he uses as his office and part time residence. It is immaculately kept and larger than it looks from the outside. To Seth's surprise, the interior is modern and open. Alton removed most of the interior walls, so it's like a loft inside. An open-beamed ceiling follows the line of the roof where an attic had once been. The ceiling, beams, and walls are all painted white but in different shades and finishes. Only a designer or someone with a keen sense of color and texture would even notice the subtle difference. Of course, Seth and Max notice immediately. The white terrazzo floor has accents of silver and black, and the baseboards are trimmed in stainless steel.

Alton's office is to the left of the entry, separated by a pair of sleek French doors. A hidden panel behind Alton's desk hides his bedroom. Another room to the right of the entryway has all manner of computer equipment, including an impressive wall of monitors, some of which are on. A kitchen and large table are at the back of the house, which opens to a small but lush yard with a pool. Seth is impressed. "I like your digs, Mr. Price. Who knew such a nasty man would have such a beautiful office?"

Alton laughs and invites them to sit on a large red sofa looking out to the pool. "Don't the nasty villains in the movies always have the coolest lairs, Mr. Boncola?"

Seth grins and looks at Max, who is amused by the banter.

Alton gestures to Seth, "By the way, your singing has gotten so much better."

Seth isn't sure what he heard Alton say. "Excuse me?"

"I said your singing has gotten much better. Oh, pardon me, that's not right. I should have said that Lydia LaFon's singing has gotten much better."

Seth looks over at Max and then back at Alton. "How would you know? Don't tell me you've heard Lydia sing? In person?"

Alton gets up from the sofa and goes to the kitchen counter. "May I serve you some coffee or tea? Something more exciting like a cocktail or wine? I have a wonderful bar out by the pool."

Ignoring what Alton just said, Seth scoots forward on the sofa and asks, "Exactly when did you start seeing my shows?"

Alton doesn't say anything at first but walks over to his desk and picks up a cell phone. He turns it on and scrolls over to a playlist titled "Cardio Workout." He shows the screen to Seth as he scrolls down the song playlist. Max looks over to see what Alton is showing Seth.

"You kidding me? You beat me up, throw me in rehab, I go through weeks of withdrawal and therapy, then you follow me around for a year making sure I don't relapse, and suddenly, you're a Lydia LaFon fan?" Seth looks over to Max, while pointing at Alton. "He's still on your payroll? Checking up on me?" Before Max can answer, Seth leaps up from the sofa and goes to the sliding doors that look out to the pool. He opens the door to step outside.

Max is surprised. "No, sweetheart! This is all news to me. Alton, what's up? Why are you spying on Seth?"

Alton slowly put his hands up, motioning for to Seth and Max to calm down. "Seth, I've not been on your case or paid by anyone to look after you for years. I do, however, take an ongoing interest in my clients. Well, some of them."

Seth is standing by the sliding door, halfway in, halfway out. "I was *never* your client. I was your victim. Max and Logan were your clients. And to them, I am grateful, forever. They're my family. But I am *not* your client."

Alton walks over to Seth and stands next to him as they both look out at the pool. "Of course, I understand. Please know that I come to the club to listen to you because I enjoy your performances. And I'm proud of you. Truth be told, most of my drug rehab assignments don't end well."

Seth shakes his head. "Isn't that the truth. Saw your latest notable accomplishment. Seems your little blonde pop star died in the bathtub from an overdose just after you picked her up from rehab last week. That was a waste of money for your client, wasn't it?"

Alton purses his lips and nods. "As I said, most of my drug assignments don't end well."

Max is still sitting on the sofa watching the nasty exchange between Alton and Seth. She stands up from the sofa and walks over to them. "Well, I'd love to stand here and watch this bitch fest go on, but I have a husband to find, if the two of you don't mind."

Seth and Alton turn to Max and are embarrassed to be carrying on as they were. Seth reaches out to Max, gives her a hug, and whispers, "I'm sorry. You saved my life, and here I am bitching about it. That's bad enough, but I know we're here to help Logan. I'm sorry. Just a lot of emotion at seeing Alton after all these years." He then turns to Alton, puts out his hand, and says, "I'm truly sorry, Alton."

"No apology necessary. I'm used to it. Wouldn't be in this business if I had thin skin. I was going to approach you last winter when I saw you at the Cabana."

"Palm Springs? You caught my weekend run at the Cabana in Palm Springs? You've seen my show in Palm Springs *and* here at the Queen of Hearts?"

Max interrupts. "Well, I knew it. I always told Logan you were gay, Alton. I can sense these things."

Alton turns to her and smiles. "Now, now Max, just because I go to watch someone perform at a gay club, doesn't mean I'm gay."

Max laughs. "True, but my intuition is still gay, or at least bisexual."

Alton smiles, "Well, how about *sexually ambiguous*?"

Max shakes her head and waves her arm across the room, "What straight man decorates his office like this? Not that I care, really, because the most important person in the world to me, next to Logan, is this boy standing right there." She points to Seth. "Sexuality doesn't make any difference to me. Wait—actually, I guess it does. I rather prefer the company of gay men. No guessing about their motives."

Seth smiles. "Can't argue with that!"

Max puts her hands together, in prayer fashion. "We can continue this conversation about sexual orientation and exploration under happier circumstances, if that's okay with you, Alton. But now, I need your help. Desperately."

Alton motions them back over to the sofa, and he sits down next to them. He has an iPad on the coffee table, which he turns on, and slides over to Max. "Why the hell didn't you call me yesterday, when all this was unfolding?"

Max is surprised. "Why should I? You working for Logan? You involved in what's going on here? Do you know where he is?"

Alton scrolls the iPad screen over to a front-page article in the *Los Angeles Times* this morning. The headline says, "Beverly Hills Investment Manager Missing in Yachting Accident." Underneath the headline, it reads, "Badly burned body recovered, now missing. Wife mysteriously appears unharmed but miles away from incident." Neither Max nor Seth had bothered to look at the papers that morning. They are both taken aback to see the incident described that way for millions of readers. Alton looks up at the two of them. "The tabloid headlines are even worse."

Max shakes her head. "I can imagine."

Alton pulls the iPad back away from them before they can finish reading. "I'm not that sloppy, Max. You know that. Would that be the headline if your husband hired me to make him disappear?"

Max shakes her head, and Seth puts his arm around her.

"Worst part is that it implicates you. Have the police been to see you? None of my jobs are that sloppy, unless of course a client like Logan *wants* to implicate his wife."

Max looks at Alton and puts her hands on the table. "Well, we certainly know that's *not* the case, is it?"

Alton raises his eyebrows, "Unless he hired someone else."

"What are you saying? Does this look like the work of one of your competitors?"

"I don't have any competitors."

"Fair enough, Alton. Your ego aside, I'm here because I need your help. Can you help me, or do you have a conflict in this situation?"

"Conflict? You think I would have answered my door and let you in if I had a client involved in this mess?"

"Okay then, let's get going. Someone is out for us. They've ransacked my home and now the office. Logan's missing, and now Jackie's been carjacked. The captain of *Copious* has been murdered, and two thugs beat up the club manager at Queen of Hearts while looking for Seth. Until we can figure out what's going on, Seth and I both need prepaid phones that can't be traced. Outgoing and incoming calls. We need clothes and basic toiletries. Place to hide out, and—"

Alton cuts her off. "Max, I know *exactly* what you need. You don't have to rattle it off. In fact, I know more of what you need than you do. That's my business. That's why you're here, and I've been wasting my time all day yesterday and today waiting for you to finally arrive."

"Really? Well, then why am I wasting my breath?"

"I know what you need. What I want to know is *why* you need it."

"Are you kidding me? You show me the headlines, know my house and office have been broken into, say I should have contacted you yesterday, and now you ask *why* I need your help?"

"Exactly. You're telling me you and your buddy here want to disappear. To hide. From *what and from whom*?"

Max frowns, looks at Seth and then back at Alton. "It's not obvious to you that someone is trying to kidnap us, or worse. You've seen what's going on!"

Alton sits forward on the sofa, clears his throat, and looks intently at them both. "Max, this is my job. I know exactly what's been happening. Who's missing, who's dead, your house ransacked. All that. I know. What I'm asking you is *why*? *Why* is this happening? You know how I work. I can't, won't, help you if you don't tell me everything. Right now."

Seth speaks up first. "Makes sense. How can he help us if he doesn't know what's happening at the firm. How I found you. All that."

Max nods in agreement, "Okay, I'll start at the beginning."

For the next hour, Max tells Alton everything, including what they learned at the firm earlier that morning. Alton asks many questions and is most interested in the pendant and the visit to Julian. He goes to the computer room and looks up what he can find on the Orange County Sheriff's reports and what the Beverly Hills PD and the media have on the kidnapping of Jackie Chandler. As Alton is wrapping up his questioning with Max, he goes to the kitchen to prepare some sushi, hummus with chips, and fresh fruit. He brings it back to the coffee table with a bottle of wine and some sparkling water.

"Please, help yourself. I'm going to call someone I know at the FBI about this Bao Lucienne kidnapping in Paris. I know everything going on here in my town, but that part of your story in Paris needs a little investigating. If everything you're telling me is true, then some of our Feds might already be involved, in at least part of this case."

Alton excuses himself to the computer room, where he closes the door. Seth and Max are a bit concerned but help themselves to the food and drinks. They haven't eaten much since their long day began at the Ritz-Carlton, and now they're famished.

Seth looks over at the closed door to the computer room and then back at Max. "What's so secret that he can't make that call in front of us?"

Max chews on a piece of sushi and then takes a sip of her wine. "Alton has friends in, well let's just say, *sensitive* positions.

His contact at the FBI is likely someone very high up, who can't be known to have any contact with someone on the fringe like Alton."

"Probably saved their ass in some torrid affair?"

Max shakes her head and hoists her wineglass, "That wouldn't surprise me a bit."

Moments later, the door to the computer room opens. Alton bolts out and sits down on the sofa. "You've got it wrong. Very wrong."

Max and Seth put down their plates and look up at Alton. Before either can say anything, Alton goes on, "You don't need to hide or disappear. You need to be out in the open and *in their face.*"

Max is startled by his statement. "What? Do you want to get us killed?" Max looks over at Seth, who is nodding in agreement. "How can you say that?"

"Because the FBI is raiding the offices of the firm today. They've been tipped off, by someone, to what Logan did and the fact the CFO disappeared too."

"Rebecca? She's gone? We just saw her hours ago."

"He didn't give me the name, but yes, it's the woman CFO. She's runoff."

"My God, what happened to Rebecca?"

"No idea. She's just disappeared."

"Why do we need to be out in the open?"

"First of all, you're implicated. They're curious how you were rescued and why the call came in for Seth here to come get you even *before* the boat sank. And, well, this is sticky, but the Chinese embassy in Washington is raising a stink. They want this all kept quiet, and the State Department is pressuring law enforcement not to make this an 'international incident' relating to Chinese families or some such bullshit. They want to make this appear to be a case of good old American greed. Fraud, if you will. They don't want the nefarious clients of Ethan and Logan's business exposed, at least not in a way connected to the new, incoming Chinese government."

Max is in disbelief. "You mean this has come to the attention of the Chinese government? That quickly? Hard to believe that is true."

Alton throws up his hands. "You kidding me? The firm's biggest client is—*was* the general secretary of the Chinese Communist Party and you're stunned the Chinese government is aware of it? The former secretary demanding his money back, members of his family arrested, and you don't think the Chinese embassy hasn't got their nose in it? Unfortunately, Ethan and Logan are dealing with what's called the 'Red Nobility.' Very senior members of the Chinese Communist Party who have socked away billions of dollars abroad in the names of various family members and associates. You can bet that, by now, the outgoing *and* incoming general secretaries know all about you. And so do their agents working on their behalf here in the United States."

Max now realizes she's been in denial of the obvious. "You're right. I guess I'm being naive. Or I'm in denial that Logan and Ethan's little firm could be involved in such an international incident."

Raising his eyebrows, Alton chuckles. "Little firm? I hardly think a firm managing over three billion dollars is a 'little firm.'"

Max takes another sip of wine, wipes her mouth with a napkin, and looks over at Alton. "So why should we be out in the open?"

Alton is silent for a moment. "Because, frankly, it will be easier for them to kill you and the others if you *are* in hiding. Like Logan. He may never appear, body or otherwise. They don't want you arrested because you'll talk. You'll spill the beans, as they say. They likely want you dead but not in a way that would implicate whoever is behind all of this. Remember this - they would prefer you to just be *missing, rather than be found dead.* They don't want you to talk, but they don't want a dead body leading down a trail to where they could be implicated. That's why Jackie was kidnapped and there's no body, even if she's dead. And, well, and Logan. Hate to say it, but first there was a dead body, and now there isn't. Fits the pattern. Do you understand what I'm saying?"

Max flinches at how blunt Alton is about Logan's possible fate, but she knows Alton doesn't mince words. He isn't in the business of soothing souls. "Exactly, we get it. But wouldn't it be easier for them to kidnap us if we're out in the open?"

"Not if you're staying at your favorite bungalow at the Beverly Hills Hotel, surrounded by reporters and all manner of humanity. If you go missing while you're in hiding, nobody knows. But if you're staying at one of the swankiest spots in town, with people and paparazzi all around, how could the thugs working for the Red Nobility carry out a discreet kidnapping? They don't want publicity, and they don't want to be implicated. A public kidnapping would be out of the question."

Max seems let down, since this wasn't what she had planned. "But … but how will that help us find Logan?"

"It won't. He'll have to find *you*. *If* he's alive. That thing around your neck was put there to save you from drowning, apparently. Now, the question is if it has another purpose. Or not."

"What?"

"If Logan's hiding, then that thing will help him find you. Unless of course he's dead and it's being used by someone else. If you're in hiding, you'll be an easier target. Believe me, Max; this is the *only* way. It will bring all of this to an end much quicker. We can flush out Logan, *if* he's alive, and your Chinese pursuers. Or both."

"Okay, what if you're right. What do we do if our pursuers show themselves? Then what?"

"Leave that to me. If the Chinese government is involved and the US State Department is putting heat on the FBI to keep this quiet, we'll have to deal with your pursuers in a very special way."

"Special?" Seth perks up, frowns, and looks at Alton. "That sounds sort of ominous—'special.'"

Alton smiles. "All my jobs are special."

Max shakes her head and grins.

Seth looks over at Alton. "So, we're going to the Beverly Hills Hotel?"

After downing a piece of sushi and gulping a glass of wine, Alton points at Seth. "Sort of. *You're* checking into the Beverly Hills Hotel, and Max here will be hiding out up the street at the London Hotel."

Seth looks at Max, who is also very confused, and says, "What the crap are you saying, Alton?"

"Seth, how quickly can you make yourself up to look like Max? At least enough to slide past some hotel staff and maybe a few reporters, while covering your face?"

Max and Seth are silent. They don't understand what Alton is asking.

"Oh, and Seth, you also need to make Max up here like a boy, or a man. She's checking into the London posing as a man, here on movie business. I'll have the clothes and makeup here in about forty-five minutes, so start thinking creatively."

25

Requiem in Palm Springs

The sun is just coming up in the east, and Tahquitz Canyon is awash in a red glow. The San Jacinto Mountains on the west side of Palm Springs are an impressive sight, rising to over eight thousand feet above the valley floor. Nestled behind one of the mountains closest to town is a steep and beautiful canyon named Tahquitz.

Tahquitz Canyon has been inhabited for over two thousand years by Native Americans, some of whom are descendants belonging to tribes that inhabit the region today. The canyon is steeped in legend and myth. Some Indians regard Tahquitz as a powerful *nukatam*, or shaman, who was created by *Mukat*, the creator of the world. Others shun the Native American folklore and simply view it as a magical, spiritual place. One legend says that the spirit of Tahquitz, once a mortal inhabitant of the canyon, lives on as a spiritual caretaker of the canyon. Some believe this spirit can be welcoming and empowering to visitors. Others believe in a less friendly spirit, one who steals the souls of those who venture too far into the canyon at night. Some hikers claim to have seen visions or strange glows in the canyon, which they attribute to the spirit of Tahquitz. But, to the tens of thousands who hike this canyon every year, it is simply a glorious and challenging climb. The canyon is incredibly beautiful and has a waterfall that can be quite spectacular during the spring runoff from the mountains above. It has been the setting for many movies, including the original *Lost Horizon* and countless western movies and television shows. Though a popular hiking spot, it is best for experienced hikers since it can be a difficult climb. It remains a sacred place for many and not just Native Americans. Many who have hiked these trails have also felt the spirit of the canyon, from whoever or whatever it may be that resides there.

This October morning, the air is crisp and cool. The fall sky is bright blue, and the western canyon walls glow red from the rising sun. The eastern walls of the canyon are still in the early morning shadows and will not see daylight for another hour or more.

Four figures come up the canyon trail, two of which are carrying a black bag, about six feet long, on their shoulders. They walk silently up the narrow trail, ascending over two hundred feet from the canyon floor. After a long climb, the foursome arrive at Tahquitz Falls, which is but a trickle this October day. Beyond the pool of water, above the base of the falls, is a small perch, barely big enough for two people to stand on. A long and narrow trench has been freshly dug, probably in the dark the night before. The two figures gently place the black bag in the narrow trench, where it barely fits. As the two men step away, the tall man in a suit comes forward and kneels beside the trench. He slowly opens the bag, and the two men who had carried it up the canyon turn away. Inside the bag is a badly burned corpse, decomposed so severely that it is not fully evident it had been a living soul. The trench has now become a grave. The fourth man, dressed in colorful Indian ceremonial attire, kneels alongside the man in the dark suit who opened the bag. Together, they hold a satchel containing a sparkling powder substance and sprinkled it on the corpse inside the open bag. The man in the ceremonial attire recites a Native American chant in a low but steady voice. It is beautiful and melodic, subtle yet powerful. Toward the end of the chant, he raises his voice and his hands upward, and the final chant can be heard echoing in the canyon below.

The two men kneeling at the grave stand up and step back, as the other two men begin to cover the grave with the dirt from the trench. The tall man in the suit puts his hand on the shoulder of the man in the ceremonial garb, who is much shorter and quite old. "Thank you, my friend. I will never forget your kindness in letting this sweet soul rest here with the spirits in your sacred sanctuary forever."

The older man in the ceremonial garb looks up slowly to the tall man in the dark suit. "I hope his soul finds peace here. You made an unusual request. This place, not for burial, especially for someone of his … ancestry. You must never tell anyone there is a body buried here. Even so, Tahquitz may reject him. His soul may not rest here if Tahquitz wishes to expel him as an intruder. Over that, I have no control."

The tall man in the suit is silent for a moment. "He told me that a voice in this canyon invited him to die and to be buried here, that his soul would be at peace, forever, in this place he loved. This was his favorite place on earth. He hiked and meditated here hundreds of times. He slept here overnight quite often lately, though it's against the park rules. Told me he camped out here for a week before he made his decision. After he got the spirit message, he begged me to promise he would be buried here."

The older man shakes his head. "The spirits speak to whom they choose. It is not for me to judge. I know he was a regular visitor here. We all knew him. The tribal ranger knew he stayed here for days, against park rules, but he left him alone and said nothing."

"Does the tribal ranger know we're here, doing this?"

"He chose this day to come in late. He also told the park patrol to stay away from Tahquitz and to go up to Indian Canyons instead until 9:00 this morning. No one is here until then. The tribal ranger can say he has seen nothing."

The tall man shakes his head. "Thank you, my friend."

The older man points to the two men with shovels, covering up the grave. "Can you trust them?"

The tall man nods his head. "Yes."

With the grave covered, the four men start their way down the trail to the canyon floor. No one speaks a word until they get to the bottom of the canyon, where there is a modern visitors' center and parking lot. The tall man hugs the older short man, and then he and the other two men walk to a black SUV in the parking lot and drive away. The older short man in the ceremonial attire knells, faces the canyon, and chants again for a few minutes. He then stands up and begins his walk down the road to town.

26

A Forced Reunion

The black SUV makes its way from Palm Springs back to Los Angeles in about two hours. It turns off the freeway in Studio City and up Laurel Canyon to Mulholland Drive. About a half mile off Mulholland Drive, the black SUV turns onto a street that leads to a narrow road lined with eucalyptus and palm trees. It is wide enough for only one car. At the end of the road is a large aluminum gate. Stopping momentarily, the gate opens, and the SUV and its occupants arrive at a modern home cantilevered out over the hillside, with a spectacular view of the San Fernando Valley below. The house has two levels and is built mostly of glass and steel beams. The large, cantilevered deck has an infinity pool suspended over the hillside below.

The two men dropped off the tall man in the dark suit, and the black SUV leaves through the gates, in a hurry. Inside the house, the tall man in a suit goes to a large bedroom upstairs and takes off his clothes. He looks at himself in the mirror. Still stunning, even though he is no longer a young man, he's tall, slim, and firmly toned. Slipping into the shower, he turns on the water, and leans against the wall as the warm water soothes his back. Letting out a cry, he weeps for the soul he has just buried in Palm Springs, for the young life unlived, the way he died, and the lonely graveside service. *To die young and be buried alone is a hard way for a soul to begin its journey,* he thinks to himself. But he did exactly what was asked of him, and that gives him some solace. His sweet soul was laid to rest exactly as he wished, at the exact moment of the canyon sunrise he specified.

Showered and cleaned, the tall man takes a towel from the bathroom to wrap around himself. He combs his hair and goes to the kitchen. His cell phone rings. The caller informs him they will be there in an hour. He tells them he will be ready. Going outside onto the deck, he removes his towel, and sits on his favorite corner of the deck, unclothed, looking out over the valley below. It is a bright October morning in LA, but cooler than Palm Springs. He sits at the edge of the cantilevered deck, folding his legs under him, closes his eyes, and meditates for almost an hour.

The silence of his meditation is broken by the sound of the gate at the driveway. Taking his towel, he goes inside and upstairs to the bedroom, where he puts on another dark suit, white shirt, and teal-blue tie with matching teal cuff links made of stone. He walks down the half-circular black marble staircase to the living room, where there are two men seated, waiting for him. They look up as he comes down the staircase.

One of the men stands up to speak but waits for the man in the suit to arrive at the bottom of the stairs. "They're on to us, sir, but we were able to outrun them. At least for now."

The tall man shakes his head. "Took them longer than I thought, but we knew they were watching the office. They hoped not to miss nabbing Ethan after screwing up on Jackie."

"Exactly."

"Where did you lose them?"

"Below Sunset Boulevard. We turned up Alpine Drive, then down an alley, and, well, through someone's yard under renovation."

"Any damage?"

"Yes, but no one was hurt. Just a setback for their pool construction. They didn't have the construction fence up in the alley. Bad mistake on their part. They'll be fined if they report the incursion since the fence should have been there."

"You lost the pursuers there?"

"Ah, yes, sir, after their Escalade slammed into a garage on the corner. Looked a bit nasty. But they've seen our vehicle and maybe the license plate, so we'll swap it out tonight."

"Good idea. We don't have much time, but soon this will all be over, one way or the other. Is our captive guest downstairs?"

"Yep. He's none too happy, though."

"I imagine so. He's been under a lot of stress. Probably thinks we're going to kill him."

"No doubt. Should we set things in motion?"

"Yes, let's get started."

The three men go down a wide stairway that curves slowly to a lower level of the house. Lighted panels on the side walls glow eerily, and there is a lobby area at the bottom of the stairs. It resembles the lobby of an intimate theater, with vintage movie posters and a half-circle bar trimmed in black marble and white leather. The top of the bar is an amber stone, which is lighted from underneath. To the left of the bar are two large doors that lead to a theater, which seats twenty-two people in large, leather reclining chairs. It's inside the theater that the captive guest, Mr. Ethan Chandler, has been left, handcuffed to one of the chairs. The three men enter the theater, but the taller one in the suit stays in the back, hidden in the darkness. The other two men come forward to Ethan, who is trying to stand up from the chair, but handcuffs prevent him from doing so.

"Who are you, and what do you want from me? What the fuck is going on here?"

One of the two men says, "Please be seated, Mr. Chandler, and face the screen. Don't look over your shoulder, or you won't like what happens. You won't be harmed if you cooperate and listen."

Ethan is sweating and nervous, but he sits down in the chair. A light shines on the curtain at the front of the theater, but it's dim enough for Ethan only to see he's in a theater, albeit a small and very ornate one. The two men are seated directly behind him.

The curtain slowly pulls back, and when the projector comes on, it's a picture of Ethan and Jaclyn at their wedding. Ethan begins to weep when he sees the picture. At first, there is silence, but then a voice begins to speak. Ethan doesn't recognize the voice. "Ethan, you will make an important choice today. You can return to the firm and suffer the consequences of what has unfolded. That means years in jail, unless your largest client kills you first, which is a strong possibility. You have no hope of retrieving the secretary's money in time, so they're going to kill you and Jackie and make it look like you worked for the mob and that you stole their money from Chinese immigrants—Chinese immigrants who are here trying to make a living. You'll have no way to implicate the head of the Chinese Communist Party. And the State Department won't let you do that anyway, even if you *do* survive. In fact, they'll try to avoid embarrassing the new Chinese regime that is now in power. You know that. There are simply too many billions of dollars in business between the United States and China to let a little graft and corruption by Communist Party officials get in the way. If you return, which you can do, then your life is over. At least your life as you knew it."

Ethan is confused. Who is speaking, and what, exactly, is he offering? "What choice do I have? And where is my wife?"

The voice responds, "Your wife is safe. She has the same choice as you, but you must make your choice together."

"Thank God she's alive." Ethan shakes his head. "And what is that choice?"

"This is your choice." As soon as those words are spoken, a picture of two people flash on the screen. A frontal face shot is followed by a side shot and then top, bottom, chin, and forehead shots, all appearing for about five seconds before changing.

Ethan squints and focuses on each changing picture. His current picture appears, and then it morphs into the other picture. The same is done for Jackie's picture. The message is obvious. He and Jackie will change their appearance, through plastic surgery. They will become someone else. He sits in silence while he takes it all in.

"What happens to Ethan and Jackie Chandler?"

"They disappear, never to be seen or heard from again. That will make the American and Chinese governments both very happy. You just disappear, so there's no witness to the billions they've hidden away from their constituents. But there's no coming back, even if you change your mind. You'll put others in danger if you ever return and you'll face prison time. This is an irrevocable decision."

"Where will we live? What will we do for money?"

"Italy or Switzerland. And for the first five years, you can't leave either. Afterward, you can travel and lead a normal life under your new identities. You'll have enough money in an Italian or Swiss account to live comfortably. The account will be replenished every few months, so long as you abide by the arrangement. But you can't come back to the United States or travel to China. Ever."

Ethan is silent again for a few minutes. "And what of Jackie? Is she safe? When do I see her?"

"She is safe. You're going to see her in just a few minutes. We'll take your handcuffs off, and you and Jackie can discuss your choices."

"Thank God. Thank you."

The voice does not respond, so Ethan tries to turn around, but one of the men behind him pushes his head back to the front of the theater.

Ethan asks, "Does she know all of this? Have you told Jackie what you've just told me?"

"Yes, she's seen the same movie as you."

Ethan isn't sure if this is his salvation or a trick. After all, it's the Chinese who kidnapped Jackie, so if she's here, then this is likely a trap. "Who are you? How do I know this isn't a trap, just to get rid of me and my wife?"

"You don't. But at this point you don't have much choice. However, if you and your wife want to go back and resume your life, your life at the firm and all that is unfolding, you have my word we'll return you to the office tonight. You can tell them the truth—that you were kidnapped, and you got away. We will then leave you alone, but your choice is irrevocable."

One of the two men seated behind Ethan gets up and walks to a side door in the small theater. He opens it, and in a few moments, he returns with Jackie Chandler on his arm. She is dressed nicely, has her hair done, and seems relaxed. She runs to Ethan as soon as she sees him.

"Oh my God, Ethan, it *is* you. I didn't know if it was a trick or what. Thank God, you're safe!"

They hug and kiss, and both are crying. Ethan whispers in Jackie's ear, "Did the Chinese kidnap you? Is this who we're dealing with?"

Jackie shakes her head, no. "I was taken by these guys just moments before the Chinese agents were to ambush me at home. These guys made it look like a carjacking, but it wasn't."

The voice comes on again, and the two men go to the back of the theater. "We're going to leave you alone. You must decide what you wish to do in the next thirty minutes. Your decision is irrevocable."

Ethan looks to the back of the room, only to see the two men standing there, and a light now shining in his face. He raises his hand to shield his eyes from the light. "But how do I know if I can trust you? Who are you, and why are you doing this?"

The voice from the back of the room hesitates for a moment and then speaks softly. "A leap of faith on your part. Your situation at the office is hopeless. Your nice Beverly Hills life is over, either way you choose. Make a wise choice. Not just for you, but for your wife."

"Okay, but why are you helping me? Can I at least know who you are?"

There is silence.

Jackie takes Ethan's arm and turns him to face her. "Should we ask if Max will have the same choice? And Logan if he is found? What about them?"

Ethan takes a deep breath and nods in agreement. He turns

to the back of the room, shielding his eyes again. "Did you hear my wife?"

"Yes. Would it be important for Logan and Max to have the same option as you?"

"Yes, yes, of course it would. I'm responsible for this mess, but you probably already know that. Logan and Max are our best friends, and he's saved my butt more than once. Now, here we are with this choice, and I don't even know if Logan and Max are alive." Ethan is weeping, and Jackie is hugging him from behind.

"Would it be important for you to see them before you begin your new life, if that is your choice?"

Jackie speaks first. "Yes, yes of course it would be. Please, can that happen? And will we ever be able to be together again? I mean, after a time, can we be known to each other, to Max and Logan, or are we exiled forever?"

Before the voice responds, Ethan asks, "Do you know where Logan is? Is he alive or dead, and Max, is she ok? Can you tell us anything before we make our decision?"

There is silence. The two men at the back of the theater slip out the door, and the other figure, the one doing the speaking, steps out of the darkness at the back of the theater. Ethan and Jackie squint to make out the figure as it walks down the aisle of the theater toward them. It is clearly a man, tall, slender, wearing a suit. The light shining in Ethan's face fades out, and as the figure approaches, the lights of the theater come up slowly.

Jackie shrieks and puts her hands to her mouth. "Oh my God! Oh my God!"

Ethan steps forward. "Logan! It is you! Oh my God, can you ever forgive me?" Ethan's knees are weak, and he becomes flush and breaks out in a sweat. Jackie lunges forward toward him, and both she and Ethan hug Logan. He feels different to them, smells different. It is him, but he is thinner, and something is not the same. He's more rigid and not as affectionate as he usually was when they greeted each other. Instead of hugging them back, his arms hang limply at his sides. Jackie notices the pinky finger of his right hand is missing and crudely bandaged. She cringes for a moment but says nothing.

Logan gently pushes back from them both, and with a serious expression, he asks, "Have you made your choice, then?"

27

From Russia with Love

A van pulls into the driveway of Alton's English cottage office, and out pops an older, wiry woman with gray curly hair and a flowing kaftan in red and white horizontal stripes. She's wearing a yellow scarf around her neck and a matching headband that keeps her hair piled on top of her head like a huge bag of curly fries.

She flings open the side door of the van and pulls out a rolling wardrobe rack filled with clothes and bags of wigs, shoes, and jewelry. The sign on the side of the van reads, "Bagley Studio Rentals, Serving Hollywood for over 70 years."

Alton opens the front door, and the woman barges in like a fireman on the way to a fire. Without saying anything to anyone, she goes to Alton's office, pushes on a panel in the corner, and goes through an automatic door that opens to what is obviously Alton's hidden bedroom.

Alton yells out, "For cripes' sake, Ruthie, that door's hidden for a reason! You don't just open it in front of anyone!"

"They're not just anyone. It's Max Aronheart, I know that. I know you love having secrets from everyone, Alton, but really, there are no secrets, are there? Your life's a bore, Alton; you just don't admit it! And if anyone *doesn't* need a secret bedroom, it's you! If you're really getting laid, you're surprising everyone!"

Alton laughs and folds his arms in front of him. "Are those insults included in your bill, or am I paying extra?"

"Altie, my dear, you always pay extra. You want everything yesterday, so you must pay like it's tomorrow!" After wheeling the wardrobe cart into the bedroom and throwing the bags on the bed, Ruthie put her hands on her hips and turns to face Alton, Seth, and Max, who are now standing in the small, but expensively furnished bedroom. "You need my help with makeup or clothes? I think not—with a drag queen and a Beverly Hills Jewish princess, I'll bet you don't need much of anything to whip up a disguise. Am I right?"

Seth and Max are a little stunned at her brashness, but they both let out a laugh. Seth puts his hand on his chin and looks over at Ruthie. "So which one of us is the drag queen?"

She laughs. "Well, let's see, it's either you or Alton, so I could toss a coin."

Alton smiles and then protests. "Ruthie, please, you'll ruin my image!"

Everyone laughs, and as Ruthie is making her way out the door, she turns to Seth. "You're great. Don't know why you're wasting your time working as a decorator."

"Say what?" Seth isn't sure he heard what she said.

"Seen your show. More than once. Altie here's afraid to go to a gay club alone, so he needs a beard. Sometimes that's me, but then I hate being asked by patrons if he's my grandson, so I don't always go along. But you're good. Damn good. I'm eighty-two, and I've seen drag queens come and go. You've got a voice. Keep it up. Oh, and don't get killed in this whole *megillah*. Ironically, someone always dies in Altie's 'lifesaver' projects!"

Ruthie rushes out the front door, slams the side door of the van to close it, and opens the driver's door.

Alton yells out to her, "I'll let you know when to come back for a pickup."

Ruthie looks at Alton, gets out of the van, and walks back to the porch of the cottage. "Altie, you know I can never take back what you rent from me. If I took anything back, I could be implicated in some dead celebrity case or some torrid affair cover-up. Half the stuff you rent from me comes back with blood on it or something worse! Tonight, these items will be listed as missing from a film shoot in Malibu. That's it. I'll pick up the check in a few days, just like usual."

With that, she drives the van out of the driveway and waves to Alton as the gate closes behind her.

When Alton comes back inside, Seth asks him a question. "She's a thief? She steals from her employer and pockets the money?"

Alton purses his lips. "Well, not exactly. Yes, she steals these old items from her wardrobe company, but no, she doesn't pocket the money. I make the check payable to the Motion Picture and Television Country House, and Ruthie hand delivers it to them."

"Why? Why there? Is that where she lives?"

Alton shakes his head but doesn't answer at first. After a few moments, he replies, "No, she doesn't live there, but someone very special to her does. I can't tell you anything more detailed, but it's an old man who was a famous child star that became ill and penniless. They were, well, I'll tell you another time. Ruthie is very protective; let's just leave it at that. And I do send the costume company a nice envelope of cash a few weeks after Ruthie makes me a 'delivery'. I'm not in the business of stealing."

Max was curiously studying Ruthie the whole time she was there. While she found her entertaining, there was something familiar, yet intriguing about her, but Max couldn't make sense of it. Alton was about to say something, but Max interrupts. "Something about her. Have we met before, Alton? I'm searching for something in my mind, but I can't get hold of it. She looks familiar."

Alton begins shaking his head before Max even finishes her question. "Another time, Max. Another time. I know why you're getting that feeling, but let's stay focused, okay?"

Alton surveys the bedroom and the items Ruthie brought. "Let's get on with it. Seth, can you get made up for an 8:00 p.m. check-in tonight at the Beverly Hills Hotel? Max, I've got a car service coming for you at 7:30. They'll take you up the street to the London. You'll check in, go right to your room, and stay there until I come for you—or better yet, until Logan shows."

Max steps forward before Seth can speak. "Alton, please tell me why we're doing this? Why is Seth putting his life at risk posing as me, and why am I hiding out as a man at the London Hotel? How will this help us find Logan? You really think Logan's going to show up at either hotel?"

Alton rubs his left hand across his neatly trimmed beard and shakes his head. "I know it sounds odd, but it's the only way to flush out Logan, *if* he's alive. And I'm sure your Chinese pursuers, or whoever is working for them, will reveal something to us. I can help you both survive and be safe, but I need to know who, or what, we're dealing with. I've known Logan a long time. This missing or dead thing is just odd. If he's behind it, I'm sure there's a good reason, but we need to know for sure. If he's not alive, well, then our plan will be quite different. Either way, we've got to flush out your pursuers, which hopefully includes Logan. And yes, if this involves only you Max, then I need to get Seth out of the way and be sure he's not collateral damage. Believe me. I know what I'm doing. This will all be over by tomorrow morning if you just do what I ask."

Max goes to Alton and holds his hand. "You're mad Logan didn't come to you to help him with whatever is going on, aren't you? Admit it."

"Of course. I'm pissed, and I'm hurt. But that's not clouding my judgment in what's best for you and Seth. I can only imagine that Logan didn't want to drag me into something he thought was too threatening. Or worse, that he was caught by surprise and had no time to plan. That's what really worries me."

Seth speaks up right after Alton finishes. "The fact he didn't come to you before or after the yacht sinking is scary. Maybe he couldn't."

Alton lets loose of Max's hands and looks at them both. "You're both right. And by tomorrow, we'll know the answers. Good or bad."

Max pulls on Alton's arm to get his attention. "You know Viktor Lucienne and his assistant are at the Beverly Hills Hotel?"

Alton nods. "I do. He's in a bungalow, one pathway down from the bungalow I booked for you, and Brigitte is in a room in the main hotel."

"I don't get it. Why run the risk of him seeing Seth dressed as me? He'll never fall for it, and the jig's up before it starts."

"Leave it to me, Max. I need to keep an eye on him too, and this is the easiest way. From what you've told me, I don't trust him, and we've got to keep him close at hand as our little plot unfolds tonight. I've uncovered some facts about Viktor we can discuss later."

Max shakes her head, looks at Seth, and says, "I'm all yours."

Seth takes his time going through all the clothes Ruthie brought and then carefully arranges the makeup and wigs in the adjoining bathroom. "Pretty amazing stuff. Professional makeup artist kit, wow! And all this foam and putty! I'm in heaven! Max, we'll do you first." Seth carefully surveys Max and holds up some of the male clothes. "Hmmm. Biggest problem is your chest."

Max perks up. "That's a problem? Thought they were two of my best assets!"

"I'm quite sure Logan agrees with that! Problem is, to give you the physique of a man, I'd have to pull your boobs in so much it would be uncomfortable."

"Ok, what's plan B?"

"It's plan F, for fat. If we can't restrain your chest, we'll have to give you a big belly to make them look smaller. Sort of the sagging man-boob look."

"Oh no, so I have to be a fat man?"

"'Fraid so, sweetie. You're checking into the London as Fatmax, but we'll try to make you as stylish a fat man as possible."

The men's clothing from Ruthie is quite slim, so Seth rips open the back of a shirt and sews in a strip of cloth so it will accommodate the large tummy he's making for Max. "You can't take off your jacket until you get to the room. The back of the shirt will look like crap, so don't draw attention by taking off the jacket."

"Got it."

About an hour later, Seth has Max fully outfitted as a rotund businessman, but not so obviously out of character that he would draw attention. He's outfitted in a suit, shoes, shirt, and tie, loosely tied of course, and a small suitcase with a leather briefcase that Seth is borrowing from Alton. Seth adds some stubble to Max's chin and jaw so she looks like a businessman would checking in after a long day traveling. Seth opens the door to the bedroom and asks Alton in.

Alton smiles, "Impressive! You make a nice fat man, Max! Just don't let anyone focus on your looks too long. Check in, go to your room, and don't leave until I tell you."

Seth is already at work making himself up as Max. Since he is taller than Max, he's challenged in lopping off a few inches, so he won't appear taller than Max, even at a distance. He cuts the heels down on the pair of shoes he decides to wear. Ruthie certainly did her homework. She brought two wigs that are a close match for Max's hair. Alton had sent pictures of Max to Ruthie, so she had an idea what to bring. The two wigs and dresses are a close match for what Max might wear for an evening out. Seth thinks the outfits are bit formal for a woman focused on finding her husband, but he'll make it work.

Alton knocks on the door to the bedroom. "Hey, you two, we've got to get going. I've got a friend at the *LA Times* who's going to photograph Max as she enters the lobby in the hotel. It'll be part of a follow-up story on Max's home and business being ransacked earlier this morning. We've got to be there in about thirty minutes."

The door to the bedroom opens, and there stands Max, albeit the Seth version of Max. "Ms. Aronheart is ready for her ride to the hotel, Mr. Price!"

"Damn! That really looks like you, Max!"

Max, in her man costume, stands beside Seth and shakes her head. "I wish I really did look like that. Seth's ass is much smaller than mine!"

Seth looks over his shoulder. "Crap, you noticed. I already put some padding there to make my skinny ass look bigger."

They all laugh, and Alton goes to the hallway to show Seth the luggage he arranged for his appearance as Max—three matching silver Rimowa bags, two filled with clothes, one with toiletries and cosmetics. "Max, you wait here. The car is on the way. Driver's name is Jimmy. He'll get you up the street to the hotel … Oh, and one more thing. Seth, this is the necklace you'll be wearing. It has a tracker in it, so I'll know where you are. Whatever you do, don't take this off."

Max is confused. "Wait a minute, Alton; if Seth is me, then shouldn't he be wearing the pendant transmitter Logan had made for me?"

Alton shakes his head, no. "That's part of the trap. The papers and TV cameras will show *you*, Max Aronheart, checking into the Beverly Hills hotel. A bereaved wife with a missing or dead husband, forced out of her own home by intruders. But the pendant Max would be wearing is now on the neck of the businessman checking into the London Hotel. *If* Logan is indeed the one tracking you, then he may be confused for a moment, but I'm betting he then figures out what's happening. This will be his chance to retrieve you, subtly, from the London Hotel while Seth here has all the attention at the Beverly Hills Hotel. *If* he's alive, then this will be the safest way to retrieve you discreetly while everyone is focused on Max at the Beverly Hills Hotel. Get it? That's part one of the trap."

"And if you're wrong and it's not Logan, that's tracking me?"

Alton raises his eyebrows. "Then it gets interesting."

Seth speaks up. "How interesting? Like people get killed – that kind of interesting?"

Alton looks at Seth for a moment, still marveling at how much he looks like Max. "Don't worry. I'll have you covered. My associate will be helping me keep an eye on you. We've got your bungalow wired every which way from Sunday, if you know what I mean, so no one is getting in there without us seeing it."

"But I *am* the bait?"

"Yes, dear, you *are* the bait. At least for all the paparazzi to see."

"Who is your associate?"

"You've never met her, but Max knows her. Her name in Russian is Оксана. You would pronounce it Oksana in English."

Max interrupts before Alton finishes the name. "No, no, Alton. She's a bitch. An absolute bitch. A killer. A killing bitch."

Seth is startled. "Really? Is that a good thing or a bad thing?"

Alton puts his hands up to calm them both down. "She's worse than a bitch. And yes, she's a killer. Former KGB agent. She got traded for a US spy during the Cold War years. Both were traitors against their government. She was captured by the Russian KGB while working as a double agent for the CIA. She switched teams, as they say. The American spy was working for the CIA but became a double agent for the KGB during Vladimir Putin's days there, to be exact. He sold out for a lot of money, but the CIA caught on to it. Hence the trade. Two traitors, swapped in a single deal. She's bitter, angry, and just the type I need when I'm worried, we might be dealing with killers from the Chinese Communist Party. This is her turf. Plus, if she kills someone and gets caught, the CIA will likely get her released. Long story, but she sort of has a lifetime pass."

Seth is impressed. "That shit really happens?"

"Yes, it does, Seth. But these are nasty, angry people we're dealing with. I use people like Oksana only when I really need them. She got burned by a Chinese agent in Russia years ago. That's who exposed her cover, so she's motivated to be sure your life is protected from the Chinese Communists who are after Max and maybe you."

"Is she pretty?"

"What do you care? You're gay!"

"Just curious. Will I be guarded by a beautiful Russian spy who looks like Ursula Andress?"

Alton rubs his beard and grins. "Well, let's just say she used to have that kind of body. But now she's packed on a few pounds, and the years haven't been very kind to her. A life of fistfights, a few gunshot wounds, and a stabbing here and there takes its toll. You'll see her in the lobby when we get there. Think of a very tall Mamma Cass Elliott with long blond hair. That's her look.

Unless she's gotten a makeover lately, that's how I would describe her to you. But she'll be dressed like a million bucks, and she's a great shot, if we need it. Let's get moving. We're late."

Max gives Seth a big hug and a kiss. "Be safe, sweetheart. We'll be celebrating happier times soon."

Seth shakes his head and wipes a tear from his eye. "I know. Be safe, Max. I love you."

"I love you, too."

28

A Midnight Swim, Interrupted

Special Agent Ravens gathers the employees of the firm on the trading floor at 4:00 p.m. The meeting gets off to a very late start, thanks to the unexpected disappearance of Ethan. Ravens explains what will happen later that afternoon and evening. Every employee will be interviewed and formally checked out before they can go home. Everyone will need to provide their log-in credentials and work IDs to the examiners, who are arriving shortly.

As Ravens is speaking to the startled and frightened staff, Viktor, and Maria watch from behind a glass partition that separates the trading floor from the hallway. Viktor is ashen white and keeps wiping his brow. Maria thinks he might have a fever or very high blood pressure. "Viktor, you all, right? You going to make it through this?"

"No, mon amie, I am not. Brigitte is on her way to retrieve me. She will be here any minute."

"You crazy? You think they'll let you leave?"

"I am a client. I don't work for the firm. I've spoken with my attorney, and he is coming with Brigitte in case there is any trouble. You are all subject to the jurisdiction of the SEC. You have securities licenses. I don't. I am a member of the public. They have no reason to detain me."

"But what about Detective Carter? He'll be here tonight to interview you."

"Did you tell the FBI about that? Did you tell them?"

"No, of course not. But surely, they know, or will know, when Carter shows up here at 6:00 p.m. and sees what's going on."

"Don't say anything. You can act surprised."

"Viktor, I was in the office when Detective Carter told Ethan they're coming up to speak with you about the poisoning of Mr. Grays."

"Oui, but they don't know that. Ethan told you to be silent, so they thought it was only me and Ethan on the phone, in the office. They don't know you were listening."

Maria folds her arms and shakes her head. "I'll be here left alone to deal with this mess."

Viktor nods, "I am sorry, mon amie."

"I'm not your friend, Viktor. In fairness to Ethan, I won't make things worse by ratting on you. But I won't help you. Once Brigitte gets here, I'll disappear into my office and whatever you do will be out of my sight."

Viktor sees Brigitte and his attorney arrive at the reception desk. Viktor's Beverly Hills attorney is a correspondent of Viktor's main law firm in Paris. He's met this attorney, Sheldon Ayres, only once before. But his attorney in Paris assures him he is in good hands and that Mr. Ayres will get him released from the office. The main worry for Viktor, at this point, is if he can leave the United States and, if so, where he will go. With Logan still missing, Ethan now gone, and the firm being raided by the FBI and the SEC, Viktor knows there is now little chance of getting the money to his client, at least not quickly, or if ever. But where will he go? France isn't safe since Bao's kidnappers will surely be waiting for him. The secretary will soon learn what is going on at the firm and that will be very bad for Viktor. He needs someplace safe to go, but he doesn't know where.

Viktor walks toward the reception desk, where Mr. Ayres, Brigitte, and the receptionist are talking. He sees the receptionist go through a glass door on the trading floor and speak with Special Agent Ritacca. Ritacca then follows the receptionist out of the trading floor and into the reception area, where Viktor is now just arriving.

Brigitte runs over to Viktor and asks him if he's all right. Viktor nods and asks if they can leave.

Brigitte tells him, in French, that the attorney is discussing it with the FBI agent.

As Brigitte and Viktor stand at the reception desk, Mr. Ayres and Special Agent Ritacca are seen talking in the corner of the reception area. A few minutes later, Agent Ritacca goes back into the trading floor and begins speaking with Special Agent Winters.

Mr. Ayres comes over to speak with Viktor and Brigitte. "Good afternoon, Mr. Lucienne. I'm Sheldon Ayres. I believe we met a couple of years ago?"

"Oui. Good to see you again. Are we going to be able to leave?"

"I think so, but you'll likely be confined to your hotel until the SEC and the FBI question you."

"But why? I am just a client. Why do they want to speak with me?"

"Because you are an investor."

"But I am not an investor in the fund that has been liquidated."

"I understand that Mr. Lucienne. But at this point I'm not sure they've distinguished how your relationship is different from the other investors."

Viktor shakes his head, thinking he will worry about that later, just so long as he can get out of there now. As Viktor is about to sit down, Special Agent Ritacca comes out from the trading floor and summons Mr. Ayres to speak privately with him. They go back to a corner in the reception area, speak briefly, and then shake hands. Agent Ritacca then returns to the meeting taking place on the trading floor. He doesn't say a word or even acknowledge the presence of Brigitte and Viktor across the room.

Mr. Ayres walks over to Viktor and put his hand on his shoulder. "You and Brigitte may go now."

Viktor lets out a sigh and whispers, "*Merci. Merci!*"

"But I'm afraid I'll need to meet you at the hotel and take your passport, Mr. Lucienne."

"What? Why?"

"Because they want to speak with you tomorrow. If everything is okay following your discussion, they'll return your passport to you after your meeting."

"Then I can give them my passport tomorrow, no?"

"No, I'm afraid not. The main condition of your release tonight is that I vouch for you, as your legal counsel, and agreed to personally deliver your passport to the FBI this evening. Otherwise, they want you to wait here and will talk with you later tonight. It's up to you."

"*Oui*, let's go. I will give you my passport at the hotel."

"I'll follow you. Where are you staying?"

Brigitte speaks up as she takes Viktor by the arm. "The Beverly Hills Hotel."

Mr. Ayres nods, "I'll follow you there and meet you in the lobby."

🔥

Brigitte and Viktor get in the backseat of the limousine Brigitte has arranged, and they head off to the hotel, with Mr. Ayres following in his car.

Viktor's cell phone keeps ringing. The caller ID is the same each time—the outgoing general secretary's personal cell phone. Again and again, the phone keeps ringing, until Viktor finally answers it.

Brigitte can hear yelling on the other end of the line. She knows who it is.

Viktor listens in silence as the outgoing secretary threatens him with death if his money is not returned quickly. "Oui, oui. But killing me and the others won't get your money back, Mr. Secretary. You must also remember that the funding mechanism for your family members and friends here in the US and in Europe depend on continuation of the firm. If Mr. Chandler and Mr. Aronheart are dead, the firm will not survive. How will we the get money to your associates? To members of your family?"

Viktor listens to the secretary intently as he gives Viktor his instructions. He begins to sweat and wipes his brow with the back of his hand. Brigitte takes a handkerchief from her bag and gives it to him.

"Yes, sir. Yes, sir. Your information is correct. I had not informed you earlier because we just left the office and the SEC and FBI had only then arrived."

There is more yelling on the other end of the phone as Viktor shakes his head. He looks over at Brigitte, ends the call and turns off his phone.

After Viktor places his phone in his pocket, Brigitte grabs his hand and holds it between both of hers. She gazes over to Viktor, who is staring straight ahead. "What did he tell you? What does he want you to do?"

"To die, actually."

Brigitte is startled. "What? You can't be serious?"

"Oh, he's quite serious. But I believe that is the last we will hear from him."

"Why? Why won't he be calling again?"

"Since the money can't be returned immediately, he will have to admit shame, plead guilty to graft and corruption. Aside from the humiliation, he will be locked away forever. Which, I'm sure, the new secretary general *wants* to happen."

"But wasn't that going to happen anyway? Don't all the leaders of the former regime get swept aside when a new general secretary of the party comes in?"

"Mostly, yes. But sometimes there is a reprieve for all or some of his immediate family. Returning the money, giving it to the new general secretary discreetly would have saved some family members. Even mine, perhaps."

"Bao. You mean Bao? You think she won't be safe from her kidnappers?"

Viktor shakes his head. "She knows too much. Even if she promises to remain silent about all the money hidden overseas, they won't trust her."

"What of us? What of you? If the outgoing secretary is locked away, we will be safe, no?"

"No."

"Why? Why not? If he's gone and the money can't be liquidated, what would they want with us?"

"The confession by the outgoing general secretary won't be heard here—or anywhere. It will be done in a secret court. He will have to answer to the charges from the CCDI—Central Commission for Discipline Inspection. To avoid embarrassment to the Party, it will be done in secret. You see, the goal of Chinese security is *weiwen*, 'stability maintenance,' another way of saying 'maintaining party rule.' It could lead to social unrest if the masses see the corruption of their wealthy and privileged Communist Party leaders. That's why this will all be done in secret."

"But that is good news for us, no?"

"No. And this have been my fear all along, *mon coeur*. With our client, or former client, out of the way, the new general secretary will claim that the assets in the B Fund belong to ordinary Chinese businesspeople who were cheated by American investors. They will paint themselves as victims of a couple of greedy Americans and make no admission of who owns the money and what it was really used for."

"That is good. Good for us. They sweep it under the carpet, and we go on as if it never happened."

"If this were a fairy tale, that's how it would end, *chere*. But no. They will not want any witnesses who know the real story. All of us who know the source and history of these billions of dollars are at risk of being killed. So, instead of getting the money back now, they will focus on silencing any of us who know its origins. The new secretary can get his hands on the money over time. He can be patient, whereas our client, the former secretary can't."

Brigitte says nothing but squeezes Viktor's hand tighter. "You know too much? That's why you're worried?"

Viktor nods his head and strokes Brigitte's cheek with his finger. He begins to sob, almost uncontrollably.

Brigitte is trying to get Viktor to calm down, but he is sweating and sobbing. "Viktor, *sang-froid*. Calm down, calm, please!"

"What am I to do, my dear Brigitte? They are desperate to silence me. You are in danger, too."

"Viktor, when we get to the hotel, we'll call the spa and get you a massage and a hot bath. You will relax tonight. Tomorrow will be better."

Viktor shakes his head. "No, no. They will be coming to find me."

"Not until tomorrow. You heard Mr. Ayres."

"Not them, Detective Carter."

"Who?"

"The police. Police in Orange County. They want to speak with me about the death of Mr. Grays."

"What? When did that happen, and why do they want to speak with you?"

"Later, I will tell you later. Here is what you do. When we get to the hotel, you take my passport to Mr. Ayres. Tell him I will be available tomorrow at any time for the interview with the FBI and SEC. They need only to call you to arrange the time."

"Okay. I will do this, Viktor. May we have dinner, later? May I arrange a massage?"

Viktor is silent, deep in his own thoughts.

They arrive at the Beverly Hills Hotel shortly after 6:00 p.m., and there is much commotion in the lobby. Paparazzi and reporters are lined up behind a rope, and several hotel security men are in the motor court and in the lobby.

Brigitte helps Viktor out of the car, and a security officer asks if they are hotel guests. Brigitte says yes, and he asks to see their room keys before letting them into the lobby.

Brigitte asked, "Who is arriving, a celebrity?"

The security officer says nothing and waves them into the lobby.

Viktor and Brigitte walk through the crowd in the lobby and outside the door that leads to the bungalows in the back of the main hotel.

When they arrive at Viktor's bungalow, he opens the safe, retrieves his French passport and hands it to Brigitte, who is standing at the door. "Take this to Mr. Ayres. I assume he is in the lobby or stuck in the motor court. I will call you in your room later." Viktor closes the door to his bungalow and immediately places a call to the private aircraft charter service he uses in the United States when traveling domestically. "Good evening, this is Viktor Lucienne. May I speak with Ms. Posten?" He is on hold for a short time when his regular contact at the charter company, Sherry Posten, comes on the line.

"Bonsoir, Ms. Posten! This is Viktor! I need a transport this evening, as soon as possible, to Washington DC."

"Good to hear from you, Mr. Lucienne. Let me see what I have. What time do you want to leave?"

"As soon as possible. I can be there in two hours."

"Oh my, that's soon. It's also getting quite late. Please hold for a moment and let me see what I can do. How many of you are there? What size aircraft do you need?"

"Just me. Any size you have. I'll take whatever you have so long as we go tonight."

"Okay, then, may I ask you to hold?"

"Oui, I mean yes, please."

Viktor holds for what seems a long time, and then Ms. Posten comes back on the line. "Mr. Lucienne, I have a small Lear coming in from Vegas at 10:30 p.m. tonight. We need a crew change, but I have two pilots who can be here by midnight if that's not too late. I realize it will be an overnight flight, but we can get you to DC by 9:00 a.m. tomorrow morning, if that will work."

"I will take it. See you tonight. I will arrive early."

"Very good then. Should I make the usual arrangements for transportation to the airport with Brigitte?"

"No. No, I will make those myself. I am giving Brigitte a couple of days off, and I don't want to disturb her. I will handle this myself. You have my cell number if you need me?"

"Yes, of course Mr. Lucienne."

"*Bon*. I will see you tonight."

"Well, I won't be here, but Monica will be at the desk, and you will be all set. Billing as usual?"

"Oui. And, Ms. Posten, this is a matter of government business. French government business, so please let the pilots know this is a confidential trip."

Ms. Posten is silent for a moment because she is confused by the desire for secrecy. "Of course. Of course, Mr. Lucienne. Safe travels."

Viktor surveys the room to take stock of what he will need. While he can't travel overseas without his passport, he can travel domestically on a private plane. He still has his French driver's license for identification, if needed. His plan is to go to the French embassy in Washington, where he has a close friend in the ambassador's office. He'll be safe there from any US law enforcement, for the time being. It will also be a safe refuge from his client and the new general secretary of the party. There is a French consulate in Los Angeles, but the consul general there hates Viktor. Their families are adversaries back home. The Lucienne's are viewed as selling their name for favor and patronage in a variety of business ventures. The consul general in Los Angeles comes from a family steeped in decades of public service to the French Republic. Besides, the protection at the consulate would not be the same as at the French Embassy in Washington DC. His good friend Guillame at the embassy in Washington will see that he is looked after and protected while Viktor sorts out his many problems.

Viktor decides to pack, take a nap, and call for a cab to take him from the hotel to the charter terminal at LAX at 9:00 p.m. that night. Brigitte keeps calling, so to keep her at bay, he tells her he will nap until 10:00 p.m. and they will take a late supper in the Polo Lounge at 11:00 p.m. She agrees, and the calls stop. Viktor knows her life will be in danger if they stay together, so he decides to leave her. He pens a note explaining his decision and puts it in an envelope with twenty thousand dollars in cash. The note says he is sorry to leave, but her safety is the most important thing right now. She is not known to the client, and she would be viewed as an insignificant player if discovered. If that were not the case, he would never leave her. He advises her to take a flight back home to Paris and wait there for him. The note goes on to say he will be in touch in twenty-four hours. He seals the envelope and plans to leave it at the front desk when he departs later tonight.

Viktor awakens from his nap about 8:00 p.m., takes a shower, and gets dressed. He grabs his bag and picks up the phone to call the doorman for a cab to LAX. There is no dial tone. He goes to the phone in the living room of his bungalow, and it is dead too. No matter, he will just walk to the lobby and have the doorman hail a cab from there.

When he opens the door to his bungalow, two men push him back slowly, with one covering his mouth. Two more men came in the back door, which adjoins a small kitchen at the back of the bungalow. All four men are Chinese, and he recognized one of them, a very short man who accompanied the secretary's assistant on a trip to Paris. Two of the men walk through the bungalow, checking the closets and drawers. One of them takes Viktor's bag and begins unpacking his clothes.

"What are you doing? I have a flight to catch."

None of the men say anything. Two of them keep holding him, very tightly, and then the one places his hand back over Viktor's mouth, so he cannot speak.

After his clothes are put away and his bag placed back in the closet, one of the men asks if he has a bathing suit. Viktor shakes his head, no.

"Well, you're going for a swim, so let's see what you have here that would pass as a bathing suit." The shorter man rummages through the clothes he had just placed in the drawers and comes upon a pair of boxer shorts.

"This will do."

The two men holding him begin to take his clothes off, carefully, so not to indicate a struggle in the bungalow. They want it to appear to be a suicide and not a murder. Being a slight man, Viktor is no match for the two of them. Once he is naked, they slip the boxer shorts on, grab the robe in the closet, two towels, and slippers. They wrap the robe around him, put the slippers on his feet and open the door.

"We're going to take a nice trip down to the pool. If you say anything or try to draw any attention to yourself, you're dead."

"But I am dead anyway, no?"

The short man replies, "Not if you are a very strong swimmer, Mr. Lucienne!" All four of the men laugh, and Viktor pleads with them to spare his life.

To keep Viktor quiet, the tall man stuffs a sock in Viktor's mouth. He shoves it so far back that Viktor can hardly breathe.

The four men and frail little Viktor step outside into the darkness and down the winding path from the bungalows to the pool.

29

Too Obvious Even for Beverly Hills?

Alton pushes Seth, dressed as Max, through the crowd in the lobby of the Beverly Hills Hotel and past the front desk.

"Aren't we stopping to register?"

"You're kidding me, right?" Alton tugs harder on Seth's arm and keeps pushing him through the crowd. They navigate through a throng of photographers and reporters who are roped off past the front desk. Despite the ropes put up by the hotel, reporters shove microphones and cameras in their faces as they make their way to the door. Reporters are yelling out questions for Max.

"What did you think of the coroner's press conference?"

"Any word on your husband?"

"How long you are staying at the hotel?"

"Who were your mysterious rescuers?"

"How did you get to the Ritz-Carlton while the others ended up in the hospital?"

They finally make their way out the door from the lobby to the pathway leading to the bungalows in the back of the hotel. Once on the pathway, the hotel security staff holds back the reporters and tells them they can go no further. As they walk down the pathway to the bungalow that Alton booked, Seth seems overcome by all the commotion in the lobby.

Alton ushers him down the pathway. "You did well, very well. I'm proud of you. Max would be too."

"Did we fool anyone? A couple reporters got close. If those pictures are in focus, it might give us away."

Alton chuckles and guides Seth up the doorway to the bungalow. "The two big guys in your face work for me. The legit reporters were several feet away. They might get suspicious later tonight, if they examine their photos closely, but by then, it won't matter."

Seth smiles, "Because I'll be dead?"

"That's not the plan, Ms. Aronheart!" Alton opens the door to the bungalow and quickly checks out the kitchen, bathroom, and bedroom, to be sure they're alone. He tells Seth to go into the bedroom until the luggage arrives. A few moments later, two bellmen arrive at the door with the luggage. Alton shows them where to place the bags, and then he dismisses them.

Seth pokes his head out from the bedroom. "Nice digs! Can we order room service?"

"Don't get too comfy, because you won't be here long."

"They'll kill me before dinner?"

Before Alton can answer, his cell phone rings. The caller ID says 'Ruthie'. He isn't expecting to hear from her tonight. "Hey, Ruthie, what's up? I'm sort of occupied here."

Ruthie's voice sounds strange, as if she's spooked or unnerved. "Altie, I'm not sure what just happened, but when I left your place, I noticed a car following me. Thought it might be my imagination, so I ignored it. By the time I got to Malibu for the film shoot, I forgot about it."

Alton, not seriously listening, says, "Okay, then, all is cool? You're, okay?"

"No, not really. When the shoot ended and I was collecting wardrobe items from the costumer, I noticed the same black car was sitting in the parking lot, across from my van."

"Go on."

"At first, I ignored them, but when the camera crew turned off the lights on the beach and the film trucks started moving out, two men from the car approached me. Showed me FBI badges."

"Did you see the names?"

"Hey, babe, I'm eighty-two. I'm lucky if I remember my own name every day. No, sorry."

"Too bad. Okay, sweetheart, go on."

"Asked me questions about my stop at your place. Who was there, what I was delivering, that sort of thing."

"What'd you tell 'em?"

"Nothing. Just went about my business. Told them they could call my attorney if they had questions."

"You have an attorney?"

"Shit no. But you'll get me one if I need it, right?"

Alton chuckles. "Good girl."

"One more thing, Altie. They asked me who the man was that was picked up at your place by the limo that went up the street to the London Hotel. Wanted to know who would be that important that they needed a ride to a hotel just up the street."

"What'd you say?"

"Said it had to be you. You were the only man I saw when I paid you a social call, purely a social call, and it was just you and me."

"How'd that go over?"

"Like a piece of gum stuck to your shoe! How'd you think it went over?"

"Got it."

"They leave you alone?"

"Yep, yep, they did Altie. But one more thing. They asked me if I knew the whereabouts of Maxine Aronheart."

Alton is silent.

"Don't worry. I told them I never met a man with that name."

"Good answer."

"Didn't fool 'em. They were trying to throw me off."

"Then what?"

"That's it. But now I'm worried, Altie. Asking about Max and who was that man going to the London. Get it?"

"I do."

"Are we wired? This call being listened to?"

"Not on my end."

"You little shit."

"Just teasing, Ruthie. Don't worry. Go home. And stay out of sight until I call you tomorrow, okay?"

"Want me to swing by the London and see if she's, okay?"

"*No*, no, absolutely not. That's what they're hoping you'll do. Go home and watch a movie. I'll call you tomorrow."

Before Ruthie can say good-bye, Alton hangs up.

Alton takes a deep breath, lets out a sigh, and then tells Seth to sit down on the bed and get serious for a moment, which of course is hard for Seth to do.

"Who was that? Everything okay? Sounded odd."

Alton says, "Forget it. Not related to this episode. Let's have a chat."

"Gee, I'm a married woman. I shouldn't be sitting here on this bed with you, Mr. Price."

"You're safe as in the hands of Jesus, Ms. Aronheart."

"Because you're gay?"

"Let's just say you're not my type!"

They both laugh, and then Alton waves his hand as if to say, "get serious."

"We're going to make a little switch here, Seth. To get you out of harm's way."

"What? I thought I was the bait."

"Oh, you are. You are the bait. We're just going to make a small change in the lineup." Alton turns on his phone to read a text message. He then turns to Seth and motions toward the door. "In about five minutes, two maintenance men are going to appear at that door with a television. They're going to say they're here to replace the TV in the bedroom. They'll both come in, and you will swap outfits with the large, burly guy. So, take off these clothes and throw them in this bag. Everything except the wig. Put that on the bed. Quickly." Alton goes to one of the suitcases and pulls out a foam-rubber-padded stomach and foam-rubber butt cushion, which will make Seth look portlier under the maintenance man's outfit.

"Oh, crap, I have to be a fat man like Max?"

Alton looks at Seth. "Did you get a look at the big gal standing near the stairway as we went outside the lobby to the pathway?"

"Yep, and I can guess that's your Russian killer-Bambi, right?"

"You got it, but when she gets here, she's dressed as the maintenance man you'll be swapping outfits with."

"Okay, I get it, but she's huge! She can't pass for Max."

"She doesn't need to. I just need a way to get her in here and you out. We can never get her to pass for Max in the light, but fortunately you did that, and you did it well. By now, everyone, including our Chinese pursuers, thinks Ms. Maxine Aronheart is checked into this bungalow. You've done your job, and now the objective is to get you *out of here* safely."

"You think whoever is after Max will come here to get her?"

"That's what I'm counting on."

"And you really think Logan will show, if he's alive?"

Alton nods his head. "Hopefully not here, but at the London. I'm betting he's wise to the switch."

"But why now? *If* he's the one on the other end of the tracking pendant, why didn't he come for Max before? Why would he come to get her now?"

"Because now he'll know that Max isn't hiding and that she could be in danger here in the open. He knows our little Commies could be coming for her."

Seth is silent.

Alton raises his head and looks over at Seth. "You don't think I'm right, do you?"

"Logan's very smart. I don't think he'd fall for a trick like that."

"Maybe not, but it could still flush him out—*if* he's alive."

"How so?"

"He obviously knows what, or who, he's dealing with. They're ruthless. They've ruined his business. He likely wouldn't take a chance that this was a setup if there was even a remote possibility that Max is in danger. He'd be curious where Max is, even if he thinks you're a decoy. If he's the one with the tracking pendant, he'll see where Max *really* is, and he'll go get her there. At least, that's what I'm planning."

Seth isn't so sure. "Someone's going to get killed, no?"

"No, hopefully not."

"But what then?"

"Just leave that to me. Now start taking your makeup and clothes off. You'll have only about ten minutes or so to make yourself look like the large maintenance man. When you leave, just stick close to Scotty."

"Who's Scotty?"

"He's the other maintenance man, but he really does work here. He'll take you down to the maintenance room and keep you out of sight until I come get you."

There's a knock on the door, and one of the men yells out, "Maintenance here. TV replacement you requested."

The voice is so loud Alton thinks it a little too obvious they're making their presence known to anyone watching the bungalow. Alton opens the door and motions them both in. He points to the right of the door. "Broken TV is in the bedroom."

Both men go into the bedroom, and the smaller one begins to disconnect the TV on the stand across from the bed. He pretends not to notice Seth, who is standing in the back of the dimly lit bedroom in a robe. The larger figure enters the bedroom quickly, immediately takes off all their clothes, and throws them on the floor. Standing there naked, Oksana, the former KGB agent, puts her hands on her hips and looks over at Seth, who is startled to see her standing there naked before they have even been introduced. Oksana grabs the bra and underpants Alton laid out on the bed and begins to get dressed. Seeing that Seth is still standing there, she picks up the clothes off the floor and kicks them over to him.

"Qvickly. Get moving, my little *shlyuka!*" Fortunately, Seth doesn't know that *shlyuka* is Russian for whore.

Seth puts out his hand to Oksana. "My name is Seth."

Oksana, now wearing the large bra and panties Alton brought for her, knells down on one knee, takes Seth's hand, kisses it, and then slapped it hard before pushing it away.

"Ouch, that hurt!"

"No time for formalities, my little ugly twin, so get dressed. You are leaving qvickly!"

Alton stands at the doorway, watching all the commotion but says nothing. Seth grabs the foam-rubber butt and tummy and straps them on, making a rather a big deal about it so Oksana can see that he is fattening up before putting on the maintenance man outfit she had just worn.

Oksana, while ignoring Seth, finishes dressing in the larger Max outfit so quickly that Seth can hardly believe it. She grabs the makeup case and wig and goes into the adjoining bathroom.

Alton looks at Seth and points to his watch. "It's time for you to leave, and you're not dressed yet. Snap it up, maintenance man!"

Seth zips up the one-piece outfit, which is more like a dark-green khaki jumpsuit. It has a single zipper from his navel to his neck. "All set. Gee, I'm sorry to leave before saying good-bye to Miss Personality in the bathroom."

The other maintenance man grabs the TV he replaced and motions Seth toward the door. "Put this cap on and pull it down tightly around your head. Like mine."

As they're heading for the door, Seth hears a voice from behind him in the bedroom doorway. "Good luck, my little comrade! I likely save your life tonight."

Oksana is standing in the doorway, all made up as "large Max." Seth is impressed. "Damn, you're good." He looks over at Alton. "You sure she's not a drag queen? I mean, really, take a look at—"

Oksana cuts him off. "No drag. Everything you see here is real, my little pushkie." She smiles and winks at Seth and then blows him a kiss.

Seth is taken aback. Looking at her face and her eyes, he can see that she was probably stunning, years ago. Though she's overweight and very tall for a woman, she is still striking. Her face is beautiful and still captivating. He looks at Alton and points to the pendant around his neck. "Should I give her the pendant, the one you gave me?"

Oksana looks over at Seth to see the pendant on his neck. "Ah, yes, the target. The walking bull's-eye, no?"

Seth smiles and nods.

Alton shakes his head. "That's for me to keep track of *you, Seth*. I know where Oksana will be."

Oksana smiles and comes over to kiss Seth on the cheek. Speechless, Seth stands there just looking at her.

Alton taps Seth on the shoulder. "Time to get moving. You can ogle at Oksana later."

Seth nods and follows the other man out the door. He turns to Alton to ask a question before he leaves the bungalow. Alton puts his finger to his mouth and whispers, "Keep quiet for now."

Seth and the other man walk down the steps from the front door of the bungalow and down the pathway back to the main hotel. As they come to a point where two paths met, just outside the back door of the main hotel, Seth and the maintenance man see four dark figures escorting a man in a robe down a path toward the pool. One of them looks over his shoulder and catches Seth's gaze. A shiver goes up his spine, but he doesn't know why. The maintenance man takes Seth's arm. "Come on; we have to get going."

Seth is momentarily startled but follows Scotty down the steps to the maintenance office while the other five figures vanish down the dark pathway to the pool.

30

When Discovery Is Its Own Shame

Ethan and Jaclyn follow Logan and the two men up the marble stairs from the theater into the living room. A large half-round sofa faces a curved wall of glass doors which are open to reveal the cantilevered deck, pool, and the valley below. It's now dark, and the lights of the San Fernando Valley look like a huge lighted carpet below them. Logan is standing behind a sunken cocktail bar in front of the sofa. He motions for Ethan and Jaclyn to be seated on stools at the bar. "Cocktail time. May I offer you two a cocktail before I go on my last errand?"

Ethan takes Jackie's hand and looks up at Logan. "Hardly seems a proper time to have cocktails. Not the time I mean, but the circumstances. You haven't told us about Max."

Logan doesn't acknowledge Ethan's question. He stands behind the bar, looking out at the lights in the valley below. "I buried Laurent this morning. Just so you know."

Ethan lets go of Jackie's hand, stands up, and goes to where Logan is standing behind the bar. "Where? Where did you bury him?"

"Tahquitz Canyon. Palm Springs. Exact spot he picked out."

"The hiking canyon? There's a cemetery there?"

"No, of course not. You're not allowed to bury people there."

Ethan is confused and tries to get Logan to look at him, but his gaze is fixed solidly on the valley lights below. He doesn't move. Ethan goes back to Jackie and sits on the bar stool next to her.

Logan turns away from gazing at the view and now faces Ethan and Jackie seated at the bar. "He was a brave little Frenchman. We killed him. But thank God we didn't kill his spirit."

Ethan is frustrated. "Logan, what are you saying? You're talking in riddles."

"Did you ever get to know Laurent?"

Ethan is silent.

"Well, let me tell you, he was one amazing young man. He discovered everything his Uncle Viktor was up to, months ago."

Ethan frowns, "How could he figure it out before we did?"

"Through an odd coincidence, he met a young Chinese boy who studied in France at the Sorbonne and is now working in the investment business here in LA, as an intern."

Ethan perks up. "What firm? Do we know them?"

"Pan-Asia Strategic Partners. It's that joint venture between that CTC Hong Kong bank and Varex mutual funds. In downtown LA. You've met a couple of their principals."

Ethan nods in agreement.

"Anyway, they met at a gay bar and then again at a night class at UCLA that teaches foreigners better English and American customs for use in the business world. They went to dinner a couple of times, and Laurent thought it might get romantic. One thing led to another, and when the Chinese boy learned of Laurent's mother's family, the Lucienne's back in France, he told Laurent he was working for Chinese pigs, or some derogatory slang word in Chinese that I can't recall. He said he didn't want to see Laurent again and that he should be ashamed. Laurent was upset and confused. He asked his Uncle Viktor about the comment, and Viktor waved it off. Told him to find a nice French or American boy and stay away from the Chinese. Laurent wasn't satisfied with that response and was curious to know the truth. So, he stayed after work, almost every day, for months. He also came in on some weekends and poured through the investment holdings in the B Fund. He went through public records to find out who was occupying the buildings, what businesses were there, and who owns them. He then matched up mortgages held

by the B fund, with businesses records for owners of those businesses—and what links there were to Viktor's 'personal' account.
That's something we should have been doing all along. Ethan, we
never did the due diligence we should have. We relied too much
on Viktor's lies. After a few months of research, Laurent finally
discovered the whole visa program, the laundered money hidden
in our investments, everything. He was ashamed. He felt used by
his Uncle Viktor and that he had shamed us as well."

"Why didn't he come to us?"

"Oh, he did, eventually. Problem is, he went to Viktor first."

"Why?"

"Isn't it obvious? Because he's family. He's the son of Viktor's
sister, Ells. Viktor got him the job with our firm. Viktor was the
link to the client, the secretary general of the Chinese Communist
Party and his associates and family members."

"And?"

"And Viktor threatened him. Told him he'd ruin the family
name if he said anything, and he'd tell his family he was gay if
he exposed his little Chinese investment scheme to anyone. So
aside from the humiliation of working for a firm that is investing
illegal money for the Chinese Communist Party and sullying the
Lucienne name, he'd be outed to his family."

"But being gay is not a big deal in France."

"Not by itself, no. But when it comes with the revelation that
the Lucienne family has ties to the Chinese Communist Party,
and is laundering money and investments for them, it would be
ruinous to the family name. Even if he was just the whistleblower,
Laurent's career would be ruined in France. His mother would be
humiliated to learn what her brother was doing. The Lucienne
family traffics on their name and business and political connections. Once the name is sullied, that's all worthless. And Laurent
would be hated for exposing it all and bringing the family down.
He could keep quiet and become part of the whole scheme, as
Viktor wanted him to. Or he could expose it, and the world comes
crashing down for everyone at the firm and his family."

"So, what then?"

"Then? Then he came to me. About two months ago. In a tearful session at his apartment, he showed me everything. It was devastating, Ethan. It was like everything we worked for was a sham. We were used. We should have known better. Viktor's little flamboyant French persona hides an ugly truth. A murderous, vindictive bunch of thugs in China working for the senior leaders of the Chinese Communist Party, the CCP. And, to make it worse, we're working for the *former* leadership that is being thrown out of power. Hundreds of family members and others will be imprisoned. Or worse. The new leader is accusing the old regime of corruption. And there we are, with about two billion dollars of their money, already loaned out to their own families and friends living here in the US."

"Logan, I know all that now. I'm sorry."

"Laurent educated me. Showed me where everything was, who was owed what, who had the business visas, the shell companies, everything."

"Why didn't you tell me earlier, Logan? Why did you keep it from me?"

"Because you'd have reacted the way you did on the yacht last Saturday night. You'd want the easy way out, Ethan. That was always your answer to a problem. You couldn't envision an end to your way of life."

Ethan doesn't reply.

"So, dear Laurent began a spiritual journey to decide what to do. He loved the desert. Spent much of his free time out there. He did a lot of soul-searching; all the while Viktor was breathing down his neck to keep his mouth shut and 'don't rock the boat.'"

Ethan is surprised. "Thought he went there, to the desert, to party and have a good time. Some of those Monday mornings he looked like he'd had a heavy party weekend."

"Maybe at first, but he found something spiritual there that, I must admit, I don't fully understand. I don't think I ever will."

"Did you kill him, Logan?"

"I guess, in a way, I did."

Jackie gasps and starts to cry.

"He came to me one day to tell me he decided to end his life. I tried desperately to talk him out of it. But he insisted he was at peace; the spirits were guiding him away from this world, that he was going home. All he asked is that I bury him in this special place, in the canyon, where there is no cemetery. I thought it impossible, but I made it happen."

"How?"

"A tribal elder and an old medicine man made it possible. I met the tribal chief at the Palm Springs Film Festival a few years ago. You might remember that I got his daughter, who was gravely ill, into Cedars-Sinai hospital through Dr. Snell, one of my clients. A client in the A Fund, Ethan. One of the people you wanted to steal from. Wanted *me* to steal from."

Ethan shakes his head and looks at the floor.

"When I explained what was happening, the tribal elder introduced me to the ranger who oversees the canyon, hiking trail, and visitor center. As it turns out, the ranger had seen Laurent there many times, camping overnight, which is not permitted. They knew he was in touch with something there. They left him alone. So, our brave little Frenchman is buried in his special place. And he left me a detailed dossier with all the facts on our illustrious clients, the Red Nobility."

Ethan and Jackie are wiping their eyes. Jackie stands up and goes to Logan. "I don't know what to say, Logan. It all seems so worthless, doesn't it? Sweet little Laurent."

"Oh, and one other thing. Laurent made one more sacrifice for me. I burned his body."

Jackie asks, "Like cremation?"

"No, not exactly."

"Well, what then? What do you mean?"

"When it became apparent our business, or the bulk of it, was a dark money operation to hide illicit assets, I knew we'd forever be a target of the CCP, and they have a lot of agents operating here in the US. I'm sure you've read about their activities. Even if we could eventually sell all the assets in time to appease them, they'd never let us go free because now we know too much. And there's the friends and family members with the businesses and EB-1 visas permitting them to live and work in the US. Thanks to Laurent, we have a full dossier with all the details on this web of dark money and illegal business activity, financed by illicit funds from a foreign government."

Ethan interrupts, "But why did you have to fake your death when *Copious* sank? Why didn't we just all head out of the country and be done with it?"

"Because Viktor knows about the dossier, and he told his client about it. That's why, Ethan. Before we even sailed on *Copious* last Saturday night, I knew were targets for kidnapping or death even if we could get all the money to Viktor's client. That's why Viktor and I had such an argument before he slashed my face with the champagne bottle before the first explosion. He told Laurent he informed his client about the dossier, and that Laurent had shared it with me. I knew we were all targets to be kidnapped or killed the moment *Copious* would return to Dana Point harbor. Sinking *Copious* made it impossible for any agents of the CCP to harm the four of us with so much activity going on. That's why they started to come after us one by one. My original plan was to fake my own death, take the blame for what happened, and that would be it. You two and Max would be free to go on with your lives. But once I learned that Viktor told his client about the dossier, I knew they'd come for all of us to keep their secret, and the money, hidden."

Jackie asks, "So is that why your burned Laurent's body? To make everyone think you were dead?"

"Yes. I needed to make it look like I was dead, burned in the explosion. I needed a burned body. After Laurent hung himself in his apartment, I carefully took him down and cleaned up his apartment." Logan then motions to the two men in dark suits at the other end of the living room. "I had my two associates here, these two who retrieved you, burn his body and place it in the sea, near *Copious*, just before they retrieved Max. They made sure the Coast Guard found the body when they scooped up the rest of you."

"Why didn't you let the Coast Guard rescue Max with the rest of us? Why did you throw her overboard and have her rescued by your two mysterious men?"

"I separated us as a backup plan. I could only use Laurent's body as a temporary diversion. After the Coast Guard crew put his burned body in their body bag, my men removed it before the coroner's assistant came to pick it up from the port agent. They put in my finger and my tooth and the other tissue to be certain the DNA would match mine. We'd never be able to produce a full body to prove I was dead, so we used Laurent's for a visual, then we took him to Palm Springs for the burial. That little charade bought us some time to pull all this off, but it was only temporary. I wanted Max separated from you two in case we had to, well, leave on our own. If I couldn't arrange the Swiss visas for all four of us, Max and I would disappear together without being able to take both of you. I know that sounds harsh, but that's the honest answer."

Ethan is unsure about the visas, "Well, do you in fact have it worked out? For all four of us?"

"Yes, Ethan. I don't need the backup plan. As you'll learn later, our escape plan is very complicated, and it cost a fortune. But I've got everything set for the four of us. I just got the last details this morning."

Ethan stands up and walks slowly to Logan. He reaches out his hand to put on Logan's shoulder. Logan pulls back, without saying anything. He doesn't want Ethan to touch him. Ethan pulls his hand back. "Logan, what about Viktor?"

Logan doesn't answer but walks over to the open sliding door leading to the pool. He stares out at the view, hands back in his pockets. "I'm afraid I can't help Viktor."

Ethan waits for a moment and then asks, "What does that mean? You *can't* help him, or you *won't* help him?"

"It's the same thing."

"What? Surely you can make him part of this plan, your plan, to save our skins?"

Logan turns to face Ethan. His face is pained, and he frowns as he responds. "You still don't listen well, do you, Ethan? Viktor is a liar. He betrayed his own nephew and would have gladly sacrificed the lives of all four of us if it would have saved him from the secretary's rage. You know that. He wanted us to use other people's money to save his own skin. He was pressuring us to steal from others, and he knew that you and I would likely go to jail as a result. All to save his skin and his money—his client's money. I can't believe you would even ask me to save him. It'll be hard enough to save the four of us without risking harm by trying to save Viktor as well."

"You just let them find him? Abandon him?"

Logan shakes his head. "Don't make me regret saving you, Ethan. Truth be told, I felt Jackie needed saving because she and Max had nothing to do with any of this. You and I are the guilty ones. But I knew I couldn't just save Jackie without having you join her. It wouldn't be fair to her. I know you and Viktor go way back to your New York days, but he ruined our business, our lives. He used us. He used you. Most of all, he used you because he knew you were easily swayed by … money. Do I need to make it any blunter than that?"

Jackie speaks up before Ethan answers. "He's right. Ethan, he's right. We don't owe Viktor a thing. He made fools out of all of us. He knew you and Logan were running a front for him and his Chinese Communist Party buddies so they could hide their assets overseas. You just can't admit when you've been scammed, can you?"

Logan nods in agreement with Jackie. "And karma is something you can't avoid, Ethan. I always tried to tell you that."

Ethan becomes agitated and asks Logan what he means by that statement.

"You screwed people in New York and came to Los Angeles for a second chance. Ironically, you're on the other end this time, and you got screwed by someone you trusted. Sort of a turnabout, wouldn't you say?"

Ethan nods in agreement, moves closer to Logan and speaks directly to him, only inches from his face. "Okay, dear friend, okay, but then why were you taken down with me? What did you do to be the recipient of this karmic boomerang? Why are you ruined too?"

"I've been asking myself that question since the day Laurent told me what a sham of a business we were running. I don't have an answer for you. But I've done something, obviously, so we're joined in the same fate."

Just as Jackie is about to say something, one of the men in the dark suits at the other end of the living room runs over to Logan and pulls him aside. He shows him something on his cell phone. Logan stares at it intently, motioning to the other man in the dark suit to turn on the television in the den, which is down the hall from where they are standing in the living room. Logan turns to Ethan and Jackie and says, "Stay here. Make yourself a drink, but don't leave this room."

Jackie grabs Ethan's hand and asks, "What's wrong? What happened?"

Logan says nothing and runs down the hallway to see what's on the television in the den. It's one of those 'film at eleven' news trailers with a short clip about the lead story on the local 11:00 p.m. news later tonight. The clip shows a throng of reporters and onlookers at the Beverly Hills Hotel as Ms. Maxine Aronheart is being escorted from the motor court and into the hotel lobby. She's lost in a sea of reporters and flashing bulbs, and she has a purple gauze scarf wrapped over her head, partially obscuring her face. Logan and the two men in the dark suits stare closely at the television screen. Logan steps closer to the television and asks in a quiet voice, "You recorded this?"

One of the men answers, "Yes, sir. And on the other channels too."

A voice from the doorway interrupts the silence. "My God, is that Max? What is she doing there?"

Logan and the two men in dark suits turn away from the screen to see Ethan and Jackie standing in the doorway of the den.

"I told you to wait in the living room."

Ethan pleads, "Logan, please don't shut us out. Let us help. What are you doing to get Max? Why didn't you get her first?"

Logan is silent. He motions for them to be quiet and sit down on the sofa by the door to the den. He turns the volume down on the television and rewinds the recording to the opening shot of the news teaser. It's a short clip, only about fifteen seconds long. He stares closely at the screen and then turns to look at the two men in the dark suits. "So, he's finally emerged. Wonder what took him so long. Thought he would have done that last night. Now he's messed up our retrieval plan. God damn Alton."

Both men shake their heads.

Logan whispers, "God bless Seth, we have to get him before our gaggle of Chinese Commies get hold of him first."

Ethan and Jackie look at each other. Ethan stands up and moves closer to the screen. "Seth? What about Max? She'll be a sitting duck at the hotel. That's where Viktor and Brigitte are staying—Viktor's client and his buddies know that. What the hell is she doing there, and why are you concerned about Seth?" Ethan and Jackie clearly don't know that it's Seth, posing as Max, in the news clip they just watched. Logan knows it's not his wife, so he surmises that it's Seth, put up to this by Alton Price, whom he recognized instantly.

Logan says nothing and goes to a computer monitor at a desk in the den. He opens a screen and motions to both men in the dark suits to come over. He points to something on the screen, and the three of them watch closely for about a minute. Logan then turns the screen off, and both men shake their heads. One of the men gently grabs Ethan's arm and the other man holds on to Jackie.

Logan speaks quickly. "Sorry for the interruption, but we'll need to lock the two of you up until we get back."

Ethan and Jackie both protest, but the two men in dark suits have them handcuffed to the railing in the hallway before either can figure out what's going on.

Ethan is furious, "God damn it, Logan! First you tell us you're saving our butts, and now you lock us up. Why?"

"Can't have you wandering about, unsupervised. Thought I had only one more retrieval to make tonight, but now it's two. Don't have much time. You should've taken me up on that cocktail."

With Ethan and Jackie handcuffed to the stair railing, Logan and the two men retrieve three large bags by the front door and run outside to the SUV.

Just as Logan is closing the front door to the house, he stops for a moment and yells out at Ethan. "While you're sitting there for the next couple of hours, you can work on your apology to Rebecca."

Ethan looks confused and frowns. "What the hell does she have to do with this?"

"She's starting a new life too, Ethan. But before she leaves tonight, you're going to apologize to her and ask for her forgiveness. Work on that until I get back."

With that, Logan closes the door and he and the two men jump in the black SUV, and speed down the driveway.

31

(The) London Calling

Jimmy drops Max, dressed as a man, at the London Hotel on San Vicente Boulevard. He waits outside the main entrance to the lobby until he sees Max at the reception desk. There is some brief chatter between Max and the young girl at the reception desk checking her in, who thinks he is a man from New York in the movie business. It's clear that Max is striving to make it a brief conversation, despite offers from the receptionist for restaurants, club passes, or other perks that the hotel is so gracious to offer its guests.

Once Jimmy sees Max shake hands with the young woman at the desk and proceed to the elevators, he thinks Max is safely delivered and he can proceed to his next pickup.

As he's returning to his car, Jimmy notices two other men, quite young and in dark suits, also watching Max. He sees the two men enter the lobby and speak with the woman at the front desk who just checked in Max. Jimmy continues watching the conversation from his car. It looks like the two men are questioning the young woman after showing her some identification. Watching intently, he's startled when one of the valets taps on his windshield to get his attention. Jimmy rolls down the window. "May I help you?"

"Yes, sir, do you mind moving your car? We have a guest arriving, and he has well, what should I say, a motorcade of five cars. I need the room, sir."

Jimmy replies cheerfully, "Oh, yes, of course. On my way."

He pulls out of the motor court of the London Hotel and backs up the street to the parking lot behind the Viper Room, a popular club on the Sunset Strip. The entrance is on a side street named Larrabee, and Jimmy often brings celebrities and out-of-town visitors in the music business to the club. He knows the parking attendants well. As he pulls his limousine into the entrance to the parking lot, the attendant on duty, an older Greek man, recognizes him and immediately proceeds to open the back door for Jimmy's passengers.

Before Jimmy can say anything, the attendant puts his hands up. "You lose your passengers tonight, Mr. Jimmy?"

"No, I actually just dropped him off at the London."

"Oh no, not that nasty New York Russian you bring here last week. He was a nightmare."

"No, no, don't worry, Mr. Vasilakas. Not the same client. But may I ask you to leave my car here, for just a few minutes? I promise to be right back."

"Of course. Put it over there. Will be empty for another hour."

"Oh, I'll be back long before that." Jimmy waves to Mr. Vasilakas and walks quickly to the back driveway of the London Hotel. He places a call to Alton.

"Hey, boss, it's Jimmy."

"Hey, bud. You deliver the goods to the London?"

"Yes, sir. No problem. Client checked in." Jimmy knows to never use the name of the client when working for Alton just in case someone is listening to their conversation on the phone or nearby in person.

"Cool, thanks for letting me know."

"No, wait! Don't hang up. After I dropped off the client, I noticed two men who were also watching the client check in at the front desk. After the client went to the elevators, the two men went to the front desk to speak with the young woman who checked in the client. They showed some identification and seemed to be asking questions, sir."

Alton is silent for a moment. "Okay, thanks for letting me know, Jimmy. Where are you parked now?"

"Parking lot at the Viper Room."

"Okay, cool. Jimmy, what's your next pickup?"

"LAX, that woman singer you know. You hate her, client of yours from England. I don't want to say the name."

"Good boy. No need to. I knew she was coming in tonight."

"Okay, good, then I can leave, but I wanted you to know it looked strange here. That's all."

"Jimmy, would you do me a huge favor? I promise you won't regret it."

Jimmy hesitates for a moment because he knows Alton's assignments are never easy, but they pay well. "Yes, sir, what may I do for you?"

"Stay there. Or, better yet, leave the lot and go down Larrabee Street and find a place to park and wait. It could be five minutes, it could be all night, but find a good spot, leave your phone on, and wait. I'll make it worth your while."

"Yes, sir, but what about my picking up the British diva?"

"Don't worry; I'll take care of it."

"You won't make me look bad? She's a nasty woman, but she pays me well."

"Jimmy, I'll make you look like a hero; don't worry."

"Okay, boss. I'll wait for you to call. I'll be here all night if you need me."

Alton rubs his eyebrows and reflects on his conversation with Ruthie and now Jimmy. He mumbles to himself, "Shit, we're being watched. Damn. Should have known better."

Alton surmises that the FBI had his place under surveillance because of his past connection with Logan and Max. They may suspect he was involved somehow, either in Logan's disappearance or helping retrieve Max. But why didn't his contact at the FBI tell him that when he spoke to him earlier in the day? He tipped him off about the State Department involvement but not that his own agents are observing him. Doesn't make sense, but a change of plans is in order.

Alton calls Jimmy back. He answers immediately. "Hey, boss."

"Jimmy, I need you to listen carefully. Leave your car parked on the street. Go into the hotel and take the elevator to the room number I'm going to text you. That's the room where the client is staying."

"Yes, sir."

"When you get there, knock on the door, and tell her it's you. Hopefully she'll open the door. Go in quietly and tell her that they're on to us. She should take off the disguise and walk out as a woman, with you."

"Yes, sir."

"And leave everything in the room. The bags, clothes, everything. I don't want whoever is watching downstairs to make a connection between the two of you. Did those two men or the front desk lady get a look at you when you dropped the client off?"

"Don't think so. I opened the door to the car for the client, and the bellman took care of him from there. I never went in. Just watched from outside the lobby, and then from my car."

"Okay, that's good. Put the client in your car and just drive around until I call you. It might be a couple of hours so don't stop anywhere you might be seen. Just drive around, in another neighborhood, but not West Hollywood. Got it?"

"Yes, sir."

"Call me or text me only if you do *not* make the pickup. Otherwise, I'll assume it went well, and I'll call you later with more instructions. Tell the client not to call me from their phone until I reach out. I'm not sure who we're dealing with just yet."

"Yes, sir. I will take good care of the client."

"I know you will. Thanks, Jimmy."

As soon as Alton hangs up with Jimmy, he places another call.

"Hey, Mitch, how you are doing?"

"Well, Mr. Price. How good to hear from you?"

"You busy?"

"Yes, very busy."

"Have time for a little diversion in your schedule? For the right price?"

"For you, and for the right price, of course."

"Cool. Can you get to LAX for a 9:00 p.m. pickup from British Airways, Flight 4337? It's a connecting flight from London via Dallas."

"Oh. Would this be your big British client, Ms.—"

"Don't say it. Remember our rules. No names in phone conversations. I'll text you if you need a reminder, but don't say it."

"I don't need a reminder, Alton. I can never forget that…person."

"I figured so. Here's the assignment. You tell her you pushed Jimmy aside, over his objections, because you wanted to pick her up and show her a good time before her big screen test tomorrow. It's a part she's just begging for."

"Umm, okay, but will she go for that? Our last encounter was, well, not the best."

"It wasn't the best because she was all screwed up on disco biscuits. Quaaludes. She was completely shit-faced. Believe me, she won't remember. She loves you. Fantasizes about you. Take her wherever you want; show her a good time. And show yourself a good time. *But* you must get her to the Peninsula Hotel by six tomorrow morning. Earlier, if you must, but keep her out as late as you can. Just be sure she's there when the studio car comes to get her at six."

"Mr. Price, if she has a screen test tomorrow, do you really want me to have her out all night and not get her to the hotel until 6:00 a.m.?"

"Yes, that would be perfect. Not a minute sooner if you can avoid it."

Mitch laughs. "Okay, I get it. This is a sabotage assignment."

"I wouldn't call it that, Mitch."

"But that's what it is, right?"

"Yes, but let's not call it that. It sounds so, devious, and we're not devious, are we?"

They both laugh.

"Mitch, you'll be well taken care of. Just be sure she knows you threw Jimmy under the bus so you could pick her up and show her a good time."

"Of course. It'll be perfect, Mr. Price."

"For you, I hope perfect; for her, I hope she looks like Godzilla for the screen test."

"No worries, Mr. Price. A happy ending for me and an ugly one for her."

"Music to my ears. Thanks, Mitch."

Alton is worried about who might be following Max and how they could possibly be interested in a character just created for the evening. The man Max is pretending to be doesn't exist. Everything is made up, so it's impossible for someone to be there waiting to observe him checking in, unless they were followed from the pickup at Alton's. That would mean his office is under surveillance. By someone.

Alton feels better having Jimmy retrieve Max and keep her moving around until after the events of the evening at the Beverly Hills Hotel. The problem now is that Logan will not find her at the hotel. She's now a moving target in Jimmy's limousine. But Logan is a bright man. *If he's alive and if he wants his wife, he can track down the limo thanks to the pendant on her neck.* The main event this evening is at the Beverly Hills Hotel, and that's what Alton will focus on.

Besides, he thinks to himself, this turn of events is an unexpected gift. Alton suddenly has the opportunity to make things a bit rough for his British diva. He saved her reputation and cleaned up for her after she attacked her boyfriend, a well-known Hollywood celebrity, with a curling iron. A curling iron attack would not have been a big deal, except the boyfriend was in the bathtub, and the diva threw the curling iron into the tub, while it was still plugged in. Fortunately for the boyfriend, the diva isn't very smart, and the circuit breaker prevented him from being electrocuted. He was, however, shocked for a couple of seconds, before the circuit breaker tripped. When the power went out, she then assailed him on the head with the butt of the curling iron, and then began to choke him with the cord, at which time he pulls her into the tub and holds her underwater. She would have drowned, but a hotel guest next door, hearing the commotion earlier, called security, who arrived in the bathroom just in time to rescue the diva from the clutches of her boyfriend. Alton arrived moments later and paid the security staff handsomely to avoid calling the police because they had just witnessed a 'rehearsal' for a movie part. He assured them it was not a crime. It's funny how wads of cash can change your perspective on just about anything.

It was a messy scene and a potentially embarrassing situation for both the diva and the local golden boy celebrity. Alton patched everything up at the hotel, and then staged a minor car accident as an excuse for both the diva and the golden boy being badly bruised from the fight, and the boy having stitches. He made a hero out of both spoiled celebrities, saying they had to swerve to avoid a child running in the street, causing the car to hit a tree. Alton, being the perfect crisis manager he is, also produced an actual little girl who hugged and kissed both her saviors for the reporters and paparazzi. Of course, he whisked her away before there could be too many questions. As a reward to her and her cooperative parents, the little tike now has a groovy gig in a toilet paper commercial, thanks to Alton. The whole affair cost the diva and her boyfriend a fortune in fees from Alton, but they emerged as heroes rather than the spoiled, self-absorbed narcissists they are. Alton often says his career wasn't built on helping nice people. Instead, he hides the sins of the rich and famous.

After such a stellar cleanup and turning a tragedy into a positive publicity event, Alton expected a gracious 'thank-you.' While he did get paid handsomely by both the diva and the golden boy, the diva snubbed Alton at the Oscars last year. The golden boy was gushing in his gratitude to Alton and paraded him around the Governor's Ball to meet a host of other celebrities, some of which will no doubt be future clients for Alton. The diva, on the other hand, pretended she had never met Alton, or heard of him. The snub embarrassed Alton in front of his companion, a beautiful actress who asked him to escort her to the Oscars.

Alton feels a glow of satisfaction. Jimmy, a loyal and competent driver, will retrieve Max and take good care of her. As for the diva, he's certain that Mitch, a much-sought-after rent boy/limo driver, will be sure the diva looks like a train wreck for her screen test in the morning. Alton smiles, and then his phone alarm goes off. With Seth safely away from the bungalow, it's time to get on with the evening.

32

A Premature Farewell

As they near the entrance to the pool, which is now closed for the night, Viktor begins to struggle and tries to scream, but the sock in his mouth muffles the sound. As one of the men strikes him in the back of the head, the cell phone in the pocket of the shortest man rings. He answers the phone and has a brief conversation in Chinese with the caller. When the call ends, he's angry, and whispers something in Chinese to the other three men, who then also become agitated. The tall man begins to argue with the short man who took the call, both now yelling at each other.

Viktor, still nearly choking, thinks they might have decided to just shoot him instead of drowning or waterboarding him in the pool. The tall man and the short man continue to argue, but in a whisper. As soon as the arguing stops, one of the men picks up Viktor's feet and the other two men hold him by the arms, quickly taking him toward the pool.

They hurriedly open the locked gate with a key, and the tall man goes into the pool area first to be sure no one is there. He comes back in about a minute and waves the rest of them in.

Viktor keeps making muffled sounds and struggling, but he is no match for his captors. They take him to a cabana at the far corner of the pool. Inside the cabana is a chain, rope, and what looks like a large kettle bell, something you'd find in a gym. Two of the men hold Viktor while the tall man chains him to a concrete pillar holding up the awning. The short man watches with an angry expression. He then looks at his watch and waves for the three of them to come with him. Viktor is momentarily relieved, thinking his drowning has been put off by something more urgent. At least, that was what he thought until he sees the tall man reach inside a bag at the back of the cabana and pull out a large assault rifle. Viktor's momentary relief turns to sheer terror.

♨

As Viktor's nightmare is unfolding hundreds of yards away at the pool, Alton and Oksana are still in the bungalow. Alton finished his call with Jimmy and Mitch and is preparing to leave the bungalow.

Oksana comes into the living room and gives Alton a big hug. "So, my bubee, vhat you have for me?"

Alton reaches into a suitcase he brought with him and pulls out a Taser and two handguns. He gives one of the guns to Oksana, who carefully inspects it. "Good. Dis is good."

Alton motions for her to go into the bedroom. "As we rehearsed, you stay in there. Whoever is coming, Logan or our Chinese friends, they're here to kidnap you, not to kill you. They think you're Max. Don't use that gun unless you absolutely must. I'm not expecting them to harm you, at least not here, and not right away."

Oksana smiles. "Is dat a guarantee?"

"I can only guarantee it will be exciting."

She smiles and nods her head. "As it always is with you. Always is."

"I'm going out the front door, so it looks like I've left you here alone. I'm going over to check out Viktor Lucienne's bungalow. From what Max and Seth told me, I don't know if he's a pursuer or is being pursued."

"Vhy you do not know?"

"He's the link to the client, the secretary. But with the firm being raided today by the SEC and the FBI and with Logan, and now Ethan, missing, likely kidnapped, Mr. Lucienne is either on the list to be kidnapped, like his wife, or *he's* behind what's happening. Either way, he's still registered here, and I'm going to pay him a visit. I want to see if he's alone or has some of the secretary's goons with him. When I'm done in his bungalow, I'll come back here through the bedroom window, which I've left open, and I've taken the screen off. You stay in the bedroom, and I'll go into the living room, behind the bar. You close and lock the bedroom window as soon as I come in. Then stay here, sitting on the bed."

"Vhat if they get past you?"

"They won't."

"No worry. I know vhat to do."

Oksana shakes her head and goes into the bedroom.

Alton grabs the Taser and the other gun and puts them both in holsters around his waist. He then carefully put his suit jacket on and prepares to leave. He hides a strobe light on the top of the bar in the living room and brings a smaller portable strobe in his jacket pocket. As he steps out the front door of the bungalow, he hesitates for a moment to survey the pathway to the left and right. No one is there, but Alton suspects the bungalow is being watched.

He walks down the pathway and comes to a place near the back door of the hotel where three paths came together. The path he is on leads to four bungalows, one of which is where Oksana is waiting. The other path leads to the pool and tennis courts on the other side of the hotel, and the third path leads to another set of bungalows, among them, the one where Viktor Lucienne is registered. Alton turns down the path to Viktor's bungalow, and it is the first one he comes to. One light is on in the living room, but the lights in the kitchen and bedroom are dark.

From his cell phone, he calls the hotel switchboard. "May I speak with Mr. Lucienne in Bungalow C-2 please?"

The operator obliges, but Alton hears nothing—no ringing, no voice mail. He calls the switchboard again. "I'm trying to reach Mr. Lucienne in Bungalow C-2, but when I was transferred, there was no ringing, no answer, no voice mail."

The operator asks him to hold while she tries to ring the bungalow. A few moments later, she comes back on the line. "I'm sorry, sir, but that line isn't going through. Would you like me to send a bellman to the bungalow with a message from you?"

Alton declines and hangs up, since he thinks the phone line might have been disconnected, which is worrisome. He goes to the front door of the bungalow and rings the bell. He then hides across the pathway near the side of another bungalow. No one comes to the door. He rings again and then knocks on the door. No answer. He tries the doorknob, but it's locked. After pulling a clip from his pocket, Alton trips the lock on the front door and goes in. He yells out for Mr. Lucienne, but no one is there. He quickly checks the bedroom and kitchen. Viktor's belongings are still there, so it's obvious Mr. Lucienne is still in residence. The only light left on in the bungalow is a table lamp on the desk. Underneath the light, there is an envelope and some cuff links, a watch, some loose change, and a room key. It looks a bit obvious to Alton. If Viktor left the room, why leave a room key and a light on with his jewelry on the desk?

The envelope on the desk is unsealed and simply says, "*A Ma Famille*" on the outside. Alton doesn't speak French, but he presumes it means "to my family" or "for my family." Is it a gift? He opens the flap, and inside is a card with a message handwritten in French:

Pardonnez-moi ma honte et de prier pour mon âme d'être avec Bao.
Viktor

"Shit. Goddamn French." Alton pulls out his phone and goes to a translation app he often uses with his foreign clients. He finds the French-to-English tab, and types in the words from the note. While missing some of the punctuation, it translates, "Forgive me my shame and pray for me to join my Bao." He knows Bao is Mr. Lucienne's wife and that she has been kidnapped or is dead. "Suicide note? Shit." He quickly checks the kitchen, bathtub, and shower. No one is there, dead, or alive. He wants to go check the bedroom and closets more closely, since he had only poked his head in when entering the bungalow. As he walks into the darkened bedroom, he hears the front door of the bungalow open, very loudly. Peering around the corner from the darkened bedroom he sees the commotion in the living room. Four figures charge in, one of them barking orders to the others in Chinese. One is on his cell phone, and the others are retrieving some items from a bag they brought in with them. One man has something wrapped in a towel, about the length of a rifle. Alton can't understand a word they're saying, but he knows these guys either work for Mr. Lucienne, who isn't there, or they have done something that's related to the suicide note, if that is what it is. In any event, he must get back to Oksana without the men seeing him leave.

The layout of Viktor's bungalow is similar to, but smaller than, the one Oksana is in. Alton opens the bedroom window quietly, removes the screen, and leaps out the window to the garden below. He runs quickly around the back of Viktor's bungalow to the other pathway leading to the bungalow where he left Oksana.

33

Hotel Hopping

Jimmy leaves his car and walks slowly up the back driveway to the lobby of the London hotel. He walks in and goes directly to the elevators in the back of the lobby.

Arriving on the twelfth floor, he must decide between two hallways. The one on the left will take him to the room number Alton gave him. As he turns the corner down the hallway, he sees a woman walking toward him. He wants to avoid eye contact, and apparently so does she. They're going to pass quietly in the hallway like two ships in the night. Suddenly, as they're passing, they both recognize each other and yell out each other's name.

"Shhh!" Max covers Jimmy's mouth before he can speak another word. She points down the hall to the room with the ice machine. They both walk quietly down the hall, open the door, and begin whispering.

"Where are you going? Mr. Price sent me to get you!"

"Great timing, Jimmy. The girl at the front desk who checked me in, called me shortly after I got to the room to tell me that there were two men from the FBI asking about me. Said she told them they would have to speak with the manager, but he wasn't available. They kept asking questions anyway. She said she told them nothing, but they said they'd be back. For all I know, they might still be in the lobby or watching somewhere. That's why I took the costume off, so I wouldn't be recognized."

"That's what Mr. Price said, and he wanted you to walk out as you are now, no costume."

"Perfect. Let's get moving. Where's your car?"

"Larrabee Street, just behind the hotel."

"Okay, let's go to the elevator, walk casually out the lobby and down to the car."

"I can't believe that girl called your room."

"Oh, she's looking to get into acting, and when I told her what I did for a living, or what the little fat man did for a living, she was just gushing, of course."

"Did she have a crush on you?"

"Oh, Jimmy, in this town, who knows? A young girl like that who just moved here from Indiana and wants to get into the movies probably would do just about anything, if it got her a connection in the business. Do I need to tell you that? I hope not!"

Jimmy shakes his head, and they both enter the elevator.

The trip in the elevator and out the lobby is uneventful. The lobby is busy with all sorts of activity. The celebrity guest with the motorcade had arrived, and there's a lot of commotion in the lobby, including some reporters and paparazzi. Jimmy and Max stare straight ahead and go out the front door and down the back driveway to the car. No one even glanced at them.

Arriving at the car, Jimmy puts Max in the backseat. Before he can say anything, Max says, "Jimmy, you're taking me to Alton at the Beverly Hills Hotel, right?"

"Uh, no, Ms. Aronheart, Mr. Price wants me to drive you around until he calls me. Wants us to keep moving so we can't be located easily."

"Located? By whom? We were hoping Logan would find me. Now we're going to make it difficult for him?"

"Mr. Price, he's afraid of those two men who were asking about you, I mean the man checking in."

"Yeah, that's odd. I've been wondering about that too, but at this point, I want to be with Seth and Alton at the hotel." She holds up the pendant around her neck. "If this thing's still working and Logan is on the other end, he'll find me as easily at the Beverly Hills Hotel as he would here in the car."

"But Max Aronheart has already checked in to the Beverly Hills hotel. Mr. Price has his plan. People know you there. You'll be recognized."

"Got it, Jimmy. I'm aware of that. You're going to drop me off at the corner of North Beverly Drive and Sunset Boulevard. It's dark. I'll walk in through the back garden."

"Oh, I will be in trouble with Mr. Price if I do that. He never hires you again if you don't follow instructions. He's a good client for me. He pays well. You don't want me to lose his business, do you?"

Max thinks for a minute. "I don't like to see anyone lose their job, but under the circumstances I hardly think Alton will fire you. But let's do this. He told you to drive me around, so drive me around the Beverly Hills Hotel. I'll get out; you keep driving around and give me time to check out what's happening there. I'll be discreet. I promise. You give me your cell number, and I'll call you when I'm ready to be picked up, and then we'll keep driving around until Alton calls you."

Jimmy doesn't like the sound of it. "If something happens to you, I'll be responsible."

"Nothing will happen. Jimmy, either we do this, and you trust me, or I bounce out of here now and call a cab. Now that would really make Alton angry."

"Oh, man, why do I always get stuck with strong women for clients? Same for my dating. Where are the subservient women?"

Max laughs. "Jimmy, this *isn't* the town for subservient women. Maybe you need to go back to India?"

"Oh no, my mother is there, and she is the strongest woman I know. It's just my karmic journey, I guess."

"Speaking of journeys let's press on to the hotel, Jimmy. It's getting late, and I want to see what's happening there. I'm worried about Seth."

The Beverly Hills Hotel is only a short drive down Sunset Boulevard, so they arrive there in about ten minutes. Jimmy stops the car on the corner and turns to Max in the backseat. "I have a bad feeling about this."

"Well, I have a good feeling about this, so we're even!"

"Do you even have a phone?"

"Yes, I do. Alton gave it to me. Here's the number. Please dial it now so I have your number for my phone."

Jimmy dials Max's temporary phone so his number will appear on it. She hadn't called anyone with the phone since Alton gave it to her, so Jimmy's number is the only one on it.

As Max is getting out of the car, she leans in and smiles at Jimmy. "Don't worry. This will be fine. Alton will be thrilled at how well you did tonight. I promise. Keep an eye on that phone. I'll call you."

Max walks up the side of the hotel, across the lawn, and back to the part of the property where the bungalows are. There is a fence, and lots of hedges and security cameras, but she knows the grounds well. Her family stayed there on special occasions when she was growing up, and she and Logan frequently entertain there. They also stayed in a bungalow for four and a half months when they were waiting for the renovations on their house to be done two years ago. She knows that Alton arranged for the same bungalow they always preferred, both for them and for guests of Ethan and Logan's firm who would come to town. She knows it well and how to get to it discreetly. She also knows which bungalow Viktor prefers. After dodging a room service golf cart and a few guests, she comes upon the bungalow where Alton and Seth are staying—or where she assumes Seth still is. She quietly settles in across the pathway from the bungalow, behind a large Ficus hedge separating another bungalow from the pathway.

The bungalow is well lit. The lights in the living room, kitchen, and bedroom are all on. Yet, it's quiet. Too quiet, perhaps. She thinks this might be a good time to take a closer look through the windows and then go to Viktor's bungalow to see what's going on there. Just as she is stepping out from behind the hedge, she hears something above her. It's a whirring sound but fading in and out. She can't see what it is, but something is

buzzing overhead. A moment later, the front door of the bungalow across the pathway opens. A figure steps out and looks up
and down the pathway. It's Alton, but where is he going? For a
moment, she thinks of greeting him on the pathway but opts to
remain behind the Ficus hedge. Until she knows what is going
on, she decides to wait and observe.

Alton closes the door and goes down the pathway toward the
back of the hotel. Should she try to reach Seth inside the bungalow?
Then she hears it again. The whirring sound. She looks up and sees
something moving in the darkness. The object is following Alton
down the pathway, about fifty feet above him. Her thoughts flash
momentarily to Logan. How he loves to play with drones.

34

The Strong Arm of the ...

The picture from the drone is nice and clear. The night-vision camera on the drone can clearly see the bungalow, the walkways in front and back, and the tall figure in a dark suit leaving the front door of the bungalow. When the drone scans the pathway from the bungalow, his face is clearly visible. There is a breeze, so the image from the camera is a bit wobbly, but the breeze helps rustle the trees and muffle the sound of the drone's propellers.

"Alton, damn it. It's Alton Price. He's baiting the kidnappers. Or someone. Seth is obviously the bait."

One of the dark-suited men looks at Logan and whispers, "But what if we're wrong and that really is Max in there? They've been to see the jeweler. They could be on to the transmitter."

Logan shakes his head. "You think I can't recognize my wife from my own son?" Though Seth is not, in fact, Logan's biological son, he loves him as his own son.

Both men looked confused.

"Seth. He's like my son. I'd know his walk anywhere. They've dressed him up like Max, but that's not the way she walks. And he's too tall. They'll all figure it out soon, but it's not Max inside that bungalow. It's Seth. Alton must be using him to trap the secretary's henchmen."

The taller man says, "Or you, sir."

"I've thought of that, but I'm betting Max still has her pendant on, and she's out of harm's way hanging out at the London

Hotel. That's where we tracked her just a couple hours ago."

"But why, sir? And why don't we get her now?"

"If Alton has Seth, he's likely looking after Max too because they're inseparable. You know we've tracked them together all day. Alton split them up for a reason. But we must get both Max, and Seth. First Seth, then over to the London for Max, then we finish our business, albeit a few hours later than we had planned."

Logan is guiding the drone from behind a large hedge at the very far end of the bungalow pathway. He hands the drone controller and screen to one of the two men and motions for both to follow him to the bungalow. "Tommy, you keep the drone over the bungalow. Jared, you knock on the front door. Keep knocking until whoever is in there comes out. If they don't come out, keep knocking until I come in the back door."

"Yes, sir."

Jared goes to the front door of the bungalow, knocks, and then rings the bell. Logan goes around to the back door in the kitchen and slides a metal card down the side of the lock. The door opens. He quietly goes into the kitchen and keeps his eye on the front door. Jared keeps knocking and saying, "Room service," but whoever is in the bedroom isn't answering, or coming out.

From across the pathway, Max is watching all of this unfold on the doorstep of the bungalow. The man on the doorstep has no tray, no cart, and is wearing a dark suit, certainly not the outfit of a waiter from the restaurant. Who is he? Will Seth answer?

Logan, inside the bungalow and now crouching down in the dark kitchen, waits to see if his entry had been detected. He's certain that Seth is in the bedroom, but there's no sound. Maybe he didn't hear Logan break into the kitchen, but certainly he hears the knocking on the door. Logan decides to remain silent for few minutes more, hoping there will at least be a sound from the bedroom.

Across the pathway, Max doesn't know what to make of the man on the bungalow doorstep who will just not go away.

Logan, still inside in the kitchen, decides that Jared pounding on the front door isn't going to entice anyone out from the bedroom, if anyone is there. He begins to think that no one is there, but he must find out before he gives up and leaves the bungalow. He grabs the ice bucket from the kitchen counter and throws it into the living room where it lands with a crash, and he immediately hears some motion in the bedroom. Alas, someone *is* there. The person in the bedroom moves slowly, as the wooden floors creak underneath the footsteps. Whoever it is must be disturbed at the sound of the crashing ice bucket, even though they ignored the knocks at the door. A shadow now looms across the living room floor from the bedroom. It's a large shadow, certainly not slim like Seth. The light from the bedroom is weak, like a night-light. Suddenly, the bedroom light switches off, and now there is no shadow, only darkness. Logan is certain that the figure in the bedroom is not Seth. But he knows Seth arrived earlier that evening, dressed as Max and escorted by Alton. This *is* the bungalow registered to Ms. Maxine Aronheart, so who's in there? Could Seth be tied up in the bedroom? Has he left and this is someone else? Why did they move but not say anything? There is just silence, but he knows someone is only steps away, near the door of the bedroom which leads to the kitchen.

Across the path, Max hears the crash of the ice bucket. While she doesn't know what it was, it made the man on the porch stop knocking on the door. He now has his ear pressed closely to the door, but he's no longer knocking. It's now very silent, and there's no light from inside the bungalow.

Back inside, Logan prepares to toss a glass from the kitchen to the living room, hoping to trigger more movement in the bedroom. Just as he has the glass in his hand, a long arm comes around the corner of the kitchen door, and he is suddenly in a headlock with a large person, whom he cannot see. The long, strong arm smells of heavy perfume. He knows it can't be Seth, but he yells out his name anyway. "Seth, it's Logan. Logan!"

The grip tightens around his neck, and he grabs at the arm, to no avail. The arm pulls him more tightly, up and around what seems to be a breast, a very large breast, but he thinks this grip is too strong for a woman. The more he grabs at the arm, the tighter the grip. He now knows he's misjudged the whole situation. This obviously isn't Seth. It isn't Alton either. He may have fallen into a trap, but he still has the glass in his hand. He smashes it against the floor and jams the sharp, broken stem into the arm that is strangling him.

35

Flash Mob Bungalow Party

Logan is still in a headlock. The grip on his neck is tight, and he's struggling to breathe. The broken glass he jammed into the arm of his pursuer has loosened the grip, but only slightly.

It's still dark, and the assailant is frantic to see what the stinging is in her arm. A light switches on in the kitchen. Oksana still has Logan in a headlock, but her arm is bleeding, badly. The broken glass slit her forearm, but she quickly surmises that her captive was unwise in not slitting her vein on the underside of her wrist. Since she now knows it's Logan, she's relieved. She knows she won't die from this wound. Though there is a lot of blood, it is a minor injury. Several stitches, at most. That's how Oksana thinks. Logically, no panic.

With the lights now on, Logan is startled by the dress and the wig and not sure who it is. Yet something is familiar. The blood from the arm holding him is dripping down his neck and onto his shirt.

With her poor English and heavy Russian accent, Oksana speaks to Logan, "Oh, boobie, vhy you be hiding so long? Vhy you hack me wit that glass? Bad boy! You don't know how to use broken glass. Someday, I teach you. Vhy you come to Oksana? You should be vit your vife. You not supposed to be here. Alton be pissed at you, Mr. Logan."

Logan lets out a sigh of relief, although Oksana still holds him tightly. Initially, he forgot her name, but he remembered

Oksana as soon as she said her name. He'd met her through Alton, only once, but she's hard to forget.

"Are you going to keep choking me, or will you tell me where Seth is? Where's Alton? Certainly, he's close by?"

"He be here soon. Who was doing that annoying knocking at the door? I should shoot them."

Logan yells out, "Jared, it's okay. You still out there? One of Alton's people is in here."

Across the pathway, Max is stunned. She hears the voice that just yelled out to Jared, which must be the name of the guy standing by the door of the bungalow across the pathway. The voice yelling out to him is muffled, yet it makes her tingle. She heard commotion just seconds before, and the man on the doorstep put his ear against the door and twisted the doorknob to try to get in. He was obviously agitated but didn't know what to do. *Was that Logan's voice, or was she imagining it?*

Jared yells out, asking to be let in. Max can now hear that clearly.

Oksana yells back, "Stay there! I let you in when I'm ready."

Max grins. She knows that voice, even through a door. When she met Oksana years ago, she told Alton that her voice sounded like Natasha Fatale, the companion to Boris Madenov, the spies from Pottsylvania in the Rocky and Bullwinkle cartoon. At the time, Alton looked at Max like she was from another planet. He had no idea about Boris and Natasha. Days later, Max found a Rocky and Bullwinkle cartoon clip and showed it to Alton. He roared when he heard the Natasha character speak. He then showed it to Oksana.

She wasn't amused, "Dis like the millionth time someone show me this silly American cartoon. Not funny first time. Not funny now."

Max knew Oksana was helping Alton tonight, so if she is in there, is Seth in the bungalow too? And where is Alton? Maybe that was Alton's voice she just heard?

Back inside, Logan is still in a headlock with Oksana's blood now all over his shirt and jacket. It's puddling on the floor.

"Oksana, I'm only here to get Seth. I know he came in here with Alton earlier this evening. Where is he?"

"Vait for Mr. Price."

"Oksana, we really can't wait. First, I need to get Seth out of here. Secondly, I've got to get my wife, and I know where Alton has put her. Thirdly, there's some very nasty people who are here, somewhere on the property, maybe even just outside this bungalow. They almost got my men earlier today. If you're the bait, I hope you have a lot of reinforcements because they've moved from kidnapping to killing. And we've got to get your arm patched up."

Oksana is about to respond to Logan when there is suddenly a noise in the bedroom. Alton comes bolting out to the living room after entering the bungalow through the bedroom window. He looks at Oksana, who is still holding Logan. "Holy shit, what happened to your arm?" Before Oksana can respond, he notices Logan in Oksana's headlock and covered with blood. "Well, I knew it! You're very much alive, but shit, Logan, you fucked up. You're supposed to be rescuing your wife at the hotel. Why are you here?"

"To get Seth. I need to get him out of here, Alton, and then get Max. And you must be expecting some nasty company if you've got Oksana here as the Max-bait."

"You're right. I was just in Mr. Lucienne's bungalow, looking at a suicide note, when four of them burst in. I think they've taken the bait, and they'll be here for Max any minute."

"I've got to get Seth."

"He's safe; trust me. But I can't let you step outside. They're coming here. Lights off! Logan, you go behind the bar; Oksana, you in the corner of the living room. Whether they come from the bedroom, kitchen, or the front door, we'll be able to see them."

Logan says, "I have my man Jared outside, on the doorstep."

"Shit, get him out of here."

Logan yells out at Jared, who is still on the doorstep outside. "Jared, everything's okay. You've got to get back across the path with Tommy. I may need you, so keep your guns ready. But don't do anything until I ask."

There is a muffled "Yes, sir" on the other side of the door.

Outside, Max hears noises coming up the pathway to the bungalow. She sees four men, running. Three go around the back of Oksana's bungalow, and one starts coming to the front. The guy on the front doorstep, Jared, who was just told to leave, hears them too. He bolts across the pathway into the bushes right next to Max. He's breathing heavily, and focused on the door of the bungalow, or he certainly would notice Max standing just feet away, behind an adjacent Ficus hedge.

Logan is upset, "Alton, you can't just shoot four men at the Beverly Hills Hotel and get away with it."

"O ye of little faith! I don't believe you just said that! Who do you think you're dealing with?"

"Alton, be smart. We're trying to get away, to disappear before these goons kill us. We can't be arrested by the police and still disappear tonight. And you need to stay out of it, so you aren't a target too."

"There will be a lot of people disappearing tonight, Logan. Just sit tight and do exactly as I tell you. Oksana, there are four of them. One very short, he's in charge; a big, tall one who is the most threatening; and two smaller guys. We'll strobe them when they come in. I'll Taser the first two, whoever they are, so no shots. If the other two won't put their hands up after we get the first two, you do what you need to do. Logan, you stay here, behind the bar unless I call for you."

With the lights out, the three of them sit in silence. Seconds later, they hear footsteps and bushes rustling at the back of the bungalow. Then, there's a knock at the front door.

"Ms. Aronheart, we are here to deliver a message to you from your husband. It's urgent that we speak with you."

No one inside says anything.

Max shivers when she hears the man on the doorstep call out her name. They're looking for her, and they think she's in there.

She's frightened—not for herself, but for Oksana and the others in the bungalow. She prays that Seth is not in there, too.

Another knock is followed by a twist of the front door handle, but it's locked.

Alton feels two short vibrations on his back. One of the sensors he installed has just gone off. He wired the bungalow with silent alarms that send a message to a small receiver on his back. The number of vibrations tells him which door or window someone has passed through. Three quick vibrations tell him that someone just came through the bedroom window. It buzzes again. That means two of them. Alton stands by the wall between the bedroom door and the bar. He kneels, pulls out the strobe light from his pocket, and with two bright strobe flashes, he blinds the two men just coming around the bed to the doorway. He leaps up, using the Taser to stun them both while they're momentarily blinded.

As soon as Alton encounters the two men in the bedroom, Logan texts Jared from his phone. "If there's a man knocking on the front door, take him out." About fifteen seconds later, there's a thud on the door, as if someone has slammed into it.

Across the pathway, Max sees the flash of the strobe through the windows of the bungalow. Moments later, her companion in the bushes to her right looks at his phone and then bolts across the pathway to the doorstep of the other bungalow. He body-slams the man so his head violently strikes the door, and then his limp body lands on the doorstep with a thud.

Alton is startled when he hears the thud and looks to the door. Logan puts his finger over his mouth, points to his phone, and waves his hand. Alton looks pissed.

There's still a fourth man somewhere, but total silence inside and outside the bungalow. Logan texts Jared again. "Drone. Can you see a man outside?"

No response from Jared, but just then, the kitchen door bursts open and the big, tall man comes in. It's still dark in the bungalow, so Alton rounds the corner to the kitchen in the hopes of blinding the intruder with a strobe flash. But this time, the intruder is too quick, and he swipes the side of Alton's face with his rifle. Alton falls back into the dark living room and lands on the floor. The intruder blindly fires two shots into the living room. Fortunately for Alton, he is on the floor and the bullets fly over his head into the wall behind him. Oksana, on the floor in the opposite corner of the living room, sits silently until the gunman enters the living room from the kitchen. He's groping for a light switch when Alton leaps up off the floor and through the door to the bedroom. With perfect timing, Oksana fires her muzzled gun, hitting the tall man in the left shoulder as he turns to pursue Alton. He falls back into the kitchen, and Logan comes out from behind the bar and jumps on him. A struggle ensues. Oksana joins in and so does Alton. Within seconds, the three of them have the tall man pinned down. Alton uses the Taser to keep him quiet, turns on the kitchen light and motions to Logan to open the front door. Logan opens it carefully. The little, short man is unconscious, lying on the doorstep, his head against the door. Logan isn't certain he's alive. Jared and Tommy both rush in. "Everything okay, boss?"

Alton cocks his head toward Jared and Tommy, asking Logan, "They with you?"

Logan smiles, "Yep, they're with me."

"Good, then you leave with them. Go get Max and get the hell out of here. You don't want to know what happens from here."

"Seth. I want to take Seth with me."

Alton is hesitant. "You think these are all the goons we're going to see tonight? Your guys see anyone else lurking about?"

Logan looks over at Jared and Tommy. "You see anyone else out there?"

Jared shakes his head. "No, sir. And that tall guy there was driving the Escalade that chased us earlier today when we retrieved Mr. Chandler. I'm sure it's him."

"Do you recognize these other guys?"

Jared and Tommy both shake their heads, no.

Logan puts his hand on Alton's shoulder. "Seth will be safe with me. Please let me take him, and then I'll get Max."

Alton asks, sadly, "Will I ever see you and Max and Seth again?"

Logan shakes his head, no. "But, Alton, I do want to thank you for what you did. For Max and Seth. I was really hoping to retrieve them before they had to come to you for help. I didn't think things would unfold so quickly at the firm this morning. Thought we could get Seth and Max before Jackie and Ethan. Turns out we had to get Jackie and Ethan first, or we might not have gotten them at all."

Alton nods his head. He is getting teary-eyed.

Logan looks closely at Alton. "You, okay? Something wrong?"

"I don't like good-byes."

Logan shakes his head. "Me either."

Alton leans in to hug Logan good-bye, when he notices Logan's right pinky finger is missing and the base stitched up in a rather messy way. "God damn, you did cut it off, didn't you? To throw it in with your teeth and part of that burned body in the now-infamous body bag. Shit, I never thought you had it in you, Logan. I really didn't. But when I heard it was your right pinky finger, I thought you might have staged all of this. You're left-handed. So, if you're going to butcher one of your hands, might as well be the right one, no?"

Logan nods. "I never thought I'd fool you. Just needed to fool the others for a while."

Alton pulls his phone from his pocket and sends a text to the maintenance man looking after Seth. He then puts his phone in his pocket and looks up at Logan. "Seth will be waiting for you at the end of the pathway. He's dressed in a maintenance man outfit. Please tell him I said good-bye."

"You can come tell him yourself, before we leave."

Alton takes a deep breath. "Logan, I have a lot to do here. It's going to get messy, and we've got to get you out of here. And I still need to see if Mr. Lucienne is alive or dead somewhere on the hotel grounds."

Logan looks surprised. "What? Viktor's still here? Ethan's gone and the firm raided by the SEC and FBI, and Viktor is hanging around?"

"His things are still in bungalow C-2, but I found a note. Reads like a suicide note. Either he escaped or killed himself before these goons found him. Or the goons killed him and faked the note. My guess is the latter, but there's no body. I need to know for sure."

"That's very likely, Alton. Viktor knows more about all of this than anyone, so if they want to hide what's gone on, Victor has got to be silenced. That's why I was certain the little coward was already gone."

Alton winks, "I'll take care of it. If you want to know what happens, you know where to reach me. Oh, and, Logan, I'm sure you know that the way this will all unfold in public is not in any way related to the truth."

Logan nods his head. "I know that. At first, I wanted justice, but I know that exposing all of this is not something the government, our government, will want to happen. We have too many business ties with China, and they aren't going to let my little firm embarrass the outgoing and incoming leaders of the Chinese Communist Party. But, Alton, I won't give up. Once we're all safe, I'd like the truth to come out. Eventually."

Alton smirks, "Good luck with that, buddy. You know who've I've spoken to, and the shroud is already being lowered on this whole deal. I can promise you that the SEC and FBI will finger you and good ol' Ethan as the villains. Greedy American fraudsters taking advantage of poor Chinese immigrants. That's how they'll frame it."

Logan shrugs his shoulders. "Maybe, Alton. Maybe."

Those words are no sooner spoken than Jared looks up from a device he retrieves from his pocket. He looks at it twice and then up at Logan. "Oh my God, she's here."

Alton asks, "Who? Who's here?"

Jared doesn't answer Alton but looks over at Logan and shows him the screen of the device. The little beeping blue dot is right there, where they're all standing.

Logan says slowly and quietly, "Max, she's here, right here."

Alton speaks right up. "That's impossible. She's with Jimmy, and if we're sure there's no more of these guys following her, I can have him bring her here."

Logan is confused. "She was at the London. We were going to get her there. With all the commotion going on here, she must've left and we didn't notice it on the tracker."

Logan walks to the front door, and slowly steps outside onto the doorstep.

Standing across the way, behind the Ficus bushes, Max sees a figure come out of the bungalow across the pathway. She squints and looks more closely through the bushes. *Oh my God, it's him! He's not dead. That was his voice!*

Logan walks off the doorstep and onto the pathway, looking left, right, and across the pathway. He calls out her name softly. And then he sees it. Straight across from him, across the pathway, and on the side of the other bungalow, a figure is emerging from the hedges. *It's her!*

Without either one saying a word, they run to each other, meeting in the middle of the pathway. They both sob, hug, and kiss one another passionately. Still, not a word is said.

Alton steps outside to see the two of them embracing. "Well, I'll be damned."

Oksana, Jared, and Tommy come out behind Alton, watching the two figures embrace. It's as if everything is frozen in slow motion.

Alton, worried that he has bodies to dispose of and lots to clean up in the bungalow, starts walking toward Logan and Max. Oksana grabs his arm. "Vait. Let them love a moment longer."

Alton nods his head and waits a few moments, as if he's counting the seconds. He then gently removes Oksana's hand from his arm and walks over to Logan and Max. "Hey, kids. I hate to be the spoiler, but you're now on borrowed time. Seth is waiting for you at the end of the pathway. You need to get Seth and get out of here. I've got a lot to do here to make sure this ends in a way that lets you disappear easily. Go. God, I hate to say it, but go. Go get Seth and get out of here."

Max starts to speak, but Logan puts his finger to her lips. "Later, Maxy. I know you have a million questions, but we have a *lifetime* for me to answer them. For now, let's get Seth and get out of here. We have a busy evening."

Max shakes her head, looking over at Alton. "What can I say, Alton? What can I say?"

Alton, his eyes welling up with tears, looks away and says, "Please go. I love you both so much, but please you must go. Now."

Logan takes Max by the arm, and they walk down the pathway with Jared and Tommy following behind. They go only a few more steps, where the pathway turns toward the back entrance of the hotel. There's a light where the paths came together. Seth is standing in the shadow under the light, hands in his pockets, staring down the other pathway, watching in anticipation. The maintenance man had simply told him to go there and wait.

Seth hears someone coming down the pathway to his right. He turns and sees four figures. He glances away, assuming it's a group of guests going into the main hotel building. But as soon as he turns away, they all stop, a few feet from him. A voice says, subtly, "Hey there, my son; it's time to go home."

Seth knows the voice immediately. Turning towards them, he sees Max and Logan, and embraces Logan so hard it almost knocks him over. Logan and Seth are both crying, as is Max. "Oh, thank God, Logan! Thank God you're here. And, Max, you, okay? Everything went all right?"

Max nods, and she smiles.

Logan tells Seth they have to go. He knows there are many questions, all of which he will answer tonight, but they need to go. Now.

Seth shakes his head, wipes his eyes and his nose, and hugs both Logan and Max.

Logan nods his head to Jared and Tommy. "Let's get to the car."

They both nod in agreement. Tommy pulls out a flashlight, and they walk across the lawn behind the bungalows to where they parked the Suburban.

36

Kettlebell Water Aerobics

Alton watches the reunion of Seth, Max, and Logan from the bend in the pathway. He stands there, heartened by what he sees. Oh, how he will miss them. And they have so much ahead of them that will be troublesome. He wipes his eyes, turns around, and runs into Oksana, who is also watching and standing right behind him. She pulls out a tissue and leans down to wipe Alton's eyes. "You are not such big tough guy after all. You are *too* sentimental."

Alton nods his head and whispers, "Now we've got to finish up."

They walk back to the bungalow and see three men waiting outside. Oksana stops and holds Alton back from walking further.

Alton smiles, "No worries, they're with me. Helping me clean up. They have a van back by the tennis courts to get all of this out of here."

Alton directs the three of them in cleaning up the mess in the bungalow. He wants no evidence Logan has been there, so they wipe everything clean—the blood, fingerprints, everything. They pack up the clothes for Seth and Oksana, and everything is taken to the van.

Three of the Chinese men are handcuffed, and one of Alton's men bandages the tall man's shoulder where he was shot. They blindfold all three of them. The little, short man on the door-step is conscious and becomes very agitated. Alton asks him if he speaks English. At first, he says nothing. Alton tells him he will shoot all of them if he doesn't speak up. He points to the tall man, who the short man could see is already shot. "I know who you work for and what you were doing here tonight. Ms. Aronheart is safe. The police and the FBI will be here in about ten minutes. Before they get here, I want you to tell me about Viktor Lucienne. You're working for him too?"

The short man says nothing.

"Okay, well, I found this little note in Mr. Lucienne's bungalow. It looks like a suicide note. The four of you came busting into the bungalow and retrieved a bag. You clearly had been there before. Your prints are all over the place. So, here's the deal. You tell me where Mr. Lucienne is, and I say nothing to the FBI about this note or that you have been in his bungalow. They'll search everywhere, and he'll turn up, dead or alive, and you'll be charged with kidnapping, or murder. Tell me where he is, dead or alive. You have two seconds to tell me."

The short man grunts, "Pool."

Alton asks, "He's *at* the pool or *in* the pool?"

"At pool."

Alton shakes his head.

Just a few minutes after the cleanup crew leaves the bungalow and goes back to the van, two Beverly Hills Police (BHPD) officers run up to the door of the bungalow, accompanied by a woman who says she's the assistant manager of the hotel. Following behind her are two men with a stretcher.

Alton arranged for all of them to show up, but only when he was ready. The FBI will be there soon, along with ICE, the US Immigration and Customs Enforcement Agency. Alton knows the State Department will not permit the four Chinese men to be prosecuted, but nonetheless, he wants to provide a big smoke-screen to be certain the events of the past day won't focus any attention on him, Logan, or Max.

One of the BHPD officers asks, "What the hell happened here?"

Alton points to the four Chinese men, handcuffed and blind-folded. "These four men burst in here tonight to kidnap Ms. Maxine Aronheart. Fortunately, I was here with Ms. Aronheart, as was my associate there …" He points to Oksana, who is now wearing a nice black pantsuit. "When these four men barged in, I was able to detain three of them, but Ms. Valkassa had to defend herself from this tall man here, who shot at her with his rifle. The two bullets are there, in the wall. He also slashed her arm with a broken piece of glass."

"Where is Ms. Aronheart?"

"Frankly, I was going to ask that of you. Isn't she the one who called you? She used that phone right there."

"We didn't speak with her directly. Dispatch said Ms. Aronheart phoned, frantic that men had just attacked her in her bungalow."

"Yes, and then she ran into the hotel to get some help because she saw that Ms. Valkassa here was bleeding profusely."

"Didn't she come back?"

"No, no, she hasn't. Probably very angry at me. Here I was, hired to protect her after her home and business were ransacked earlier today. We come here, her favorite spot and her favorite bungalow, thinking she'd be safe, and it ends up she's nearly killed by these four guys. She'll probably fire me."

"We have other officers coming. We'll search for her."

Alton interrupts, "I'm going to check the lobby right now, just to be sure she's not sitting up there, frantic. Oksana, come with me."

Alton and Oksana leave the bungalow and immediately run down to the pool. The gate is locked, so Alton uses his clip to jimmy it open. They both run in, surveying the area. Alton has a pocket light, which he gives to Oksana. "You go around the pool that way, and I'll go this way."

The light is on in the pool, and Alton doesn't see a body in it. He uses his cell phone for light and walks around the other side of the pool. At the very end of the rows of cabanas on his side of the pool, Alton hears something, a muffled, gagging sound. He shines his phone light in the back of the last cabana, and there is a thin figure chained to a pillar. It's Viktor, still alive. Alton smiles and thinks to himself, *this is going to be interesting.*

Alton takes the sock from Viktor's mouth. He's nearly out of breath and his mouth is so dry he can barely speak.

"Calm down, Mr. Lucienne."

Oksana arrives at where Alton is standing, overlooking Viktor. She looks down at him and frowns. "Scrawny little frog."

"Let's get him some water, get these chains off of him."

Oksana shakes her head and rummages around to see what the Chinese men have left with Viktor. Alton and Oksana both eye the kettlebell, which most certainly was going to be tied to Viktor's feet and then tossed into the pool, dragging Viktor down to the bottom. *Simple suicide, tying your own feet up to a thirty-pound kettlebell. Not that much weight really, but when you tie your feet together, even a small weight is enough to do the trick*, Alton thinks to himself.

As Oksana is working to get the chains off, Alton holds Viktor by the chin to get his attention. "Mr. Lucienne, we're going to have a little chat, after which you need to make a very quick decision."

"A decision, now? *Mon Dieu!*"

Alton gives Viktor some water and asks Oksana to go stand by the gate to the pool, so no one will enter. He's worried a hotel security guard, or the police will show up any minute.

"Mr. Lucienne, I assume you know what was going to happen here. Your killers were interrupted from their task, but you know what it was."

"Oui and thank you for saving me. Who are you, monsieur?"

"I'm with the FBI, and so is my associate over there, the woman. We came here to your bungalow to speak with you, found the suicide note, and began to look for you."

Viktor shakes his head. "Merci. What of the men who tried to kill me?"

"They're in custody. We have all four of them."

"Oh, thank God."

Alton asks, "Who are those men, and why do they want to kill you?"

Viktor shakes his head and puts up his hands as if to say, "Who knows?"

"Does it have anything to do with your client, who has invested money in the firm run by your friends Ethan Chandler and Logan Aronheart?"

"They are not my friends. They have stolen my money. I am a victim of their firm, like so many others."

"A victim? Really? I thought that your client, the former general secretary of the Chinese Communist Party was trying to kill you."

Viktor is startled and waves his hand, almost violently. "*Merde! Merde!* That is a lie! I work for investors in France and for others. Not the Chinese."

Alton is quiet for a moment. "So, that's your official answer to the FBI? You won't tell the truth about your client and where this money came from?"

"Why did you come to speak with me?"

"We're looking into the missing money at the firm, where you have your client's money invested."

Viktor objects, "I am telling you the truth. I do not know who those men were or why they were trying to kill me. I know nothing of any Chinese client."

"That's your official answer? You'll have to attest to that in a sworn statement. What about your friendship with Ethan and Logan?"

"They are no friends of mine. A bad business relationship. They invested the money in poor investments that they can't sell. They are involved in loaning the money of my clients to questionable illegal immigrants, for unscrupulous investment."

Alton gets up and runs over to Oksana, who is across the pool by the gate. Viktor yells out for him not to leave. "I'll be right back, Mr. Lucienne."

Oksana is staring down the pathway, expecting others to show up any minute. She turns to see Alton run up to her.

Alton tells her, "Denies everything, throws Ethan and Logan to the sharks. He's lying to save his own skin."

"I know dat. Could tell by looking at him. Lying leetle frog. You take care of him, no?"

"I am taking care of him right now. You wait about ten minutes, and then you run back to the bungalow and tell them we arrived just as Viktor jumped into the pool. We heard a splash. I rushed in to get him, and you ran for help. If they show up before ten minutes, run out like you were just leaving."

"I know vhat to do. No vorry. Go!"

Alton runs back to Viktor, who is feeling well enough to start walking back to his bungalow. Alton scoops him up in his arms and places him at the edge of the pool. He puts a chaise lounge on his torso, so he'll struggle a bit to get back up. Viktor is yelling profanities in French.

Alton grabs the chains and the kettlebell. He runs back to Viktor, loops the chain through the kettlebell, and begins to tie the chain around Viktor's feet. He tosses aside the chaise and kneels on Viktor's torso, facing his feet, as he ties up the chains around them. He wants it to appear the chains were put on by Viktor himself and not someone standing below his feet. He ties the chains loosely and sloppily, since Viktor is a slight man with little strength. Alton doesn't want it to appear the chains were tied by someone else.

Viktor is struggling, screaming, and beating Alton on his back as he finishes tying up the chains. Alton swings Viktor around, throws his feet and kettlebell into the water, and watches the little man slip off the pool deck, arms flailing, and sink to the bottom of the pool. He slides down the side of the pool just as if he had scooted himself in from the deck. Viktor, in only four feet of water, is looking up at Alton as he holds his breath and shakes his head. Bubbles then start to come from Viktor's mouth. Alton stands there, watching the last of the bubbles come to the surface. This means his natural body reflexes will soon kick in, and he will inhale water. Rigors will set in, and he'll flail around for about five to ten seconds. Viktor's eyes are open, and his arms reaching up to the surface. It will take only three to five minutes for his brain to die of asphyxiation. *Does he really think I'm going to change my mind and jump in to save him?* Alton keeps an eye on his watch. *After five minutes, I'll jump in, for appearance purposes.*

Only seconds later, he hears Oksana yell out, open the gate, and begin running down the pathway screaming in Russian. *Shit, they must be here right now.* Alton wants to wait another minute or two, but he sees three men come in the gate, so he jumps in the pool. *I'll take my time, drag him to the shallow end, and struggle to get him out. That should buy enough time for the little frog to be dead.*

Alton is underwater, dragging Viktor, under his arms, along the bottom of the pool, slowly toward the shallower end where he can stand up. Suddenly, a man jumps in, swims to Viktor's feet, lifts the kettlebell, and begins pulling in the same direction as Alton. This moves Viktor's body much faster, and as soon as the other man can stand, he reaches toward Alton to grab Viktor's head to lift him out of the pool. Alton has no choice but to aggressively do the same. Within moments, Viktor's head is above water, but he remains motionless.

They drag his limp body to the edge, where two paramedics lift Viktor's upper body out of the pool. They begin performing CPR even before Alton and the other man can lift his feet and kettlebell out of the pool. Alton glances at his watch. *Four minutes. Shit, was that enough time?*

The two paramedics work furiously on little Viktor's limp body. Oksana and Alton watch intently from several feet away. Alton is nervous but trying not to show it.

Oksana whispers to Alton, "How long?"

"Four minutes."

Oksana nods her head. "For leetle man like dat, not in good shape, four should be fine."

She no sooner said that than one of the paramedics yells out, "Pulse! I've got a pulse!"

Oksana puts her long arm on Alton's shoulder and whispers into his ear, "You lose your touch, bubee! You get old and soft." She then smiles and gives him a kiss on the cheek.

37

Reality Ends with Perception

Logan and Max get in the backseat of the Suburban, along with Seth, whom they put in the middle between them. Jared is up front with Tommy, who is driving.

Logan looks at both Seth and Max and says, "I really don't know where to start, except to say we need to talk about what's happening tonight, first. I can fill you in on everything else after that."

Max holds up the pendant.

"I know, sweetheart. I know. Believe me; I would never have let you drown. Don't you recognize your rescuers?"

Max is confused. Logan points to the front seat.

Jared turns around from the front seat, "We just gots *you*, ma'am."

Max's eyes get huge, and she puts her hand to her mouth. "Oh my God, you two are the ones who fished me out of the ocean and took me to Salt Creek Beach?"

Jared nods. "Yes, Mrs. Aronheart, and sorry for the fake hillbilly accent."

Tommy, driving rather fast down Sunset Boulevard, shakes his head and reaches his hand back to Max. She grabs his hand, and Tommy says, "I'm sorry that we terrorized you. Tried to be gentle but if we were too nice, you'd have been suspicious."

Jared goes on, "Yes, that was a harrowing night. Mr. Aronheart here, he gave us a logistically tough assignment. First, retrieve you which he said was job number one, then place the burned dead body in the ocean, be sure the Coast Guard sees it, that's job number two, and then retrieve him, which he said was job number three."

Seth shakes his head. "Crap, I don't believe it. Logan, you were bobbing around out there until these guys came back to get you after Max?"

Logan nods. "But I had a raft. Biggest problem was staying close enough behind Jared and Tommy's boat but far enough out for the Coast Guard to *not* see me first. After Jared and Tommy dropped Max at Salt Creek Beach, they used a different transmitter on my raft to find me before the Coast Guard could."

Max, wiping her eyes, releases Tommy's hand and says, "Thank you. To both of you."

Logan puts up his hand. "All of that later, and more detail, but let me tell you what's going to unfold at the house. We'll be there shortly."

Logan leans over, across Seth, to clasp Max's hand. He uses his other hand to grab Seth's hand. "To be blunt, you know our lives here are over. Seth, you have a choice, which we'll discuss in a minute. But for me and Max, the only choice is a new life, away from here."

Seth is surprised, and objects loudly. "No, no, that can't be. You can't leave. Why? Why would you have to leave? It's over. The people chasing us are caught. The SEC and FBI are investigating, so why wouldn't you just go back and help them sort things out at your company?"

Logan shakes his head, lets go of Max's hand, and hugs Seth with both arms. He then looks at both Seth and Max and clears his throat. "First of all, I liquidated the A Fund illegally. I knew I had to get that money away from Viktor and Ethan, who were intent on cashing out those securities to raise money for the secretary's investments in the B Fund. I had to do it. I had to be sure that all the retail investors got their money back before the secretary could get his hands on it."

Seth agrees. "Yes, that's right, but you're a hero. You saved those people from losing their savings. When everyone knows the facts, they'll thank you."

"Possibly, but any vindication could take years. I'll have to fight to prove what I did was right and hope that the SEC and FBI agree. That's a big risk, because when these things happen, everyone involved looks for someone else to blame."

"So do it! We're with you!"

"It's more complicated than that, Seth. Besides the issue of the A Fund, there's the B Fund. And that's going be the killer, so to speak. You know what it is. It's money that's been stolen through bribes, kickbacks, and political favors. And it belongs to the outgoing general secretary of the Chinese Communist Party, who stole it from others and his own people."

"But he's gone; he's out. Alton said there will be a trial in private and he'll be locked away for the rest of his life."

"That's probably how they will deal with him in China. And his family and perhaps Viktor too, since he couldn't get the money to the former chairman in time for him to vindicate himself."

"Would that have worked?"

"Absolutely not. There's a new general secretary, and he's begun a purge of everyone associated with his predecessor. Even if we could have returned all the money in cash, it wouldn't have saved anyone."

"Why? Why not?"

"First of all, the Chinese government will never admit that this money belonged to the former secretary. It would be embarrassing. And it would show the link between that money and many of the investments we have in the B Fund. The 'opportunities' Viktor steered us to are, in many situations, just family businesses set up by the chairman's friends so they could hide money here in the United States and get their visas. It's all a sham. But since China and the United States don't have an extradition treaty, it's difficult, almost impossible, for the Chinese government to reach all those friends and family of the former secretary who are living here in the US with stolen money. Laundered money. And, of course, the new secretary will want as much of those two billion dollars given to him, now or over time. He'll claim it for himself, one way or the other, and the process of corruption repeats itself."

Seth is in disbelief, "Can't you put up a fight?"

"Yes, yes, we can. But I can't fight the Chinese government *and my own government too.*"

"What? Why would you have to fight our government?"

Max, listening intently to all of this and nodding her head in agreement with Logan, speaks up. "Honey, the United States does a lot of business with China. A lot. Millions of people's jobs, in China and the US, depend on that business relationship. Lots of rich people, in both countries, depend on that relationship. Though the senior levels of our government certainly know what is going on, hiding Chinese, Russian, and other money in our country, they're not going to cause an international incident to embarrass the Chinese government. I hate to say it, but business and politics trump ethics. And the law."

Seth leans back in his seat, frowns, and is silent for a moment. He shakes his head. "You mean to tell me this will all be shoved under the rug, just as Alton said?"

Logan nods. "Alton's right. The State Department won't want me and Ethan telling our story about the B Fund, our relationship with Viktor, or how we learned what happened. They don't want publicity about people being murdered and kidnapped by the Chinese government over this money. They don't want that sort of publicity to damage their relationship with China."

"So, they get away with it."

"Yes, they get away with it. And we have two choices. We can stay here and suffer the humiliation of being blamed for losing their money, making bad investments, and endangering the savings of hardworking Chinese immigrants, business owners, and entrepreneurs, all working to have the American dream. With stolen money, of course. Ethan and I become just another couple of unscrupulous hedge fund managers who harmed all these helpless investors. We're the scapegoats."

"And the other choice? That's obviously the one you've made."

"The other choice is that Max and I and Ethan and Jaclyn vanish. Whether people think we fled the country, were killed by the Chinese, or a little of both, we're gone. We will be vilified in the press just as we would have been if we stayed. But at least we'll have a life. A life as four people with new identities. We live out the rest of our lives as people who never existed, and the four lives we had, our real lives up until today, will end. End as greedy American investors who ripped off our clients and then fled or were killed. No one will ever know. But we *will* have a life."

"And maybe avoid prison, too?"

"Yes, that's a consideration, of course. If they really want a scapegoat, the Chinese government could press for prosecution of me and Ethan, at least, and perhaps even some of our employees. Maybe even our wives. We just don't know. So, we must disappear, Seth. Tonight."

"You have a plan?"

"Yes, we have a plan. And you, my son, have a choice."

38

Somewhat Shaken, but Not Stirred

The Suburban turns off Mulholland Drive and heads down the narrow street leading to the modern steel-and-glass house overlooking the San Fernando Valley. They stop at the big metal gate as it is opening.

Max looks over at Logan. "Our new digs?"

"Just for a few hours. Don't get too comfy!"

Seth leans forward to see the home through the front windows. "Wow, it's beautiful. And all lit up like a Christmas tree. Whose house?"

"One of the glamorous holdings of the B Fund. Paid for with our money … er, the secretary's money. We acquired it as an investment a year or so ago. We were renting it out for a princely sum to a French film director who was living here while making a movie. The shoot's over, he went back to France, and the property's been empty for a couple of months. I had the property manager hold it back from the rental market when I cooked up my little scheme. I knew we'd need a place to operate from that would be difficult to trace. The home's owned by a partnership set up by a member of the secretary's family, and the B Fund acquired controlling stake in the partnership."

"Who's the minority owner in the partnership?"

"One guess. Owned through a Los Angeles shipping company controlled by the Chinese government. But, at the top, it's all the same; the secretary and family members. Viktor identified this particular property to the firm as a good mortgage investment, with a year of prepaid rent from the French film director, whom Viktor knew. The property was bundled with some mortgages on other properties and the B Fund bought the whole package. I didn't know any details about this particular property until Laurent told me about it. Our analysts looked at the whole package, gave the thumbs-up, so we bought it."

Max asks if all the properties in that package are owned by Chinese, or friends of the secretary of the CCP.

"Not that I know of. The fact that Viktor was making individual recommendations on certain properties wasn't known to me until Laurent told me. Ethan knew, but I was never told about it. Anyway, we'll be leaving it early tomorrow morning, but let's go in and I can tell you the rest."

Logan taps Jared on the shoulder. "Would you please take our two guests in the living room down to the guesthouse? Make them comfortable and tell them we'll be with them in an hour. I don't want them to see Seth and Max just yet." What Logan really thinks is that he doesn't want *Seth* to see Jaclyn and Ethan just yet. If Seth decides to stay behind and not go with Max and Logan, he wants him to be able to pass a lie detector test, if need be, that he never saw Jackie or Ethan after hearing about the sinking of *Copious*. He doesn't want Seth implicated in any way with their disappearance.

Jared nods. "Yes, sir."

Seth is very curious. "Who are you hiding in there? Who don't you want us to see? I can guess."

"Well, don't guess. It's not important. Not right now."

Jared and Tommy go in ahead of Max, Logan, and Seth, so they can properly take care of Jackie and Ethan, who are still chained to the stair rail. *Or at least they're hopefully still there*, Logan thinks.

A few minutes later, Tommy appears at the front door and waves the three of them in.

Seth enters the front door and sees the expansive living room, marble stairs, and the walls of glass doors overlooking the cantilevered pool and the valley lights below. "Cool digs! Love it!"

Max nods in agreement. "So, sweetheart, is this where you've been hanging out since *Copious* sank?"

Logan smiles, "Pretty much, but we've been running around a lot, as you can imagine. You both must be hungry and exhausted. Follow me. I've got some food in the kitchen. We'll grab a snack, and then I've got to show you something downstairs."

Logan pours all three of them a drink. He pulls out a bottle of Max's favorite vodka, two chilled glasses, blue cheese olives, and their favorite deco martini shaker from their home in Beverly Hills. He smiles at Max as he begins to make their usual evening cocktail. But this time it seems even more special since their lives have been in turmoil the past two days.

Max is elated, "Oh, our favorite shaker! You've been to the house?"

Logan nods his head. "Yep, went there before our Chinese buddies had it ransacked, looking for you and me."

Max grins and shakes her head. "So, you have a quick trip to our house to get something special, and you grab this shaker? Did it occur to you to take anything a tad more valuable, like perhaps, my jewelry?"

"Oh, yes, of course, it certainly occurred to me."

"Wonderful, that's great, so you got everything in the safe?"

"Oh no, dear, nothing in the safe."

"What? What are you saying?"

"If I took anything obvious, they'd know I'd been there. Or you. It would ruin the whole disappearance scheme. If the sinking of *Copious* was an unexpected accident, how would it look if we just happened to take all our valuables before the sinking? Or after? It would certainly raise suspicions."

Max is so disappointed. "So, you didn't take anything? Just the shaker?"

"Well, let's just say a few other things we can talk about later, but nothing that the police or the FBI wouldn't expect to find in the safe when the police open it up. When they get a warrant.

After we're gone. That's why I left all your jewelry, and mine, in our bedroom. You saw it, no doubt."

Max nods. "I think I really need that drink now." She smiles and gives Logan a peck on the cheek, and they toast with their martini glasses.

"Seth, my dear boy, I haven't forgotten you. I have your favorite margarita mix in the fridge, all set to go, and we just need to add the tequila, your favorite Patron Silver, and voila! Here you go!"

Seth grins, takes a huge gulp, and then hoists his glass. His smile quickly turns to a frown. "I'm not exactly sure what we're celebrating. I have a feeling this isn't going to be a happy evening."

Logan tells them to fill their plates with the sliced steak, sushi, salmon, and salad and to then follow him downstairs. Tommy puts their drinks on a tray and takes them down the stairs to the theater.

Max smiles, as she strides down the marble stairs with the lighted side panels. When she sees the lobby of the theater with the lighted bar, she lets out a small laugh. "Oh, that little shit. He always does the same thing. I call it 'recycled decorating.' He charges exorbitant prices and just repeats the same theme and materials from job to job." She shakes her head as she surveys the room. "In the theater, oh, let me guess, there's deep-blue carpet, white kid-leather recliners that rock, teak tables, and glass wall sconces made in the shape of folded hands holding a golden orb? Please, tell me I'm wrong?"

Seth laughs. "Aubrey Worthington, the third! You're so right! How *does* he get away with it?"

Max nods. "I thought of him the moment I saw the living room furniture."

Seth agrees. "Me, too!"

Logan interrupts, "Okay, I realize the two of you would love to take a tour of the house so you can tear poor Aubrey to shreds, but may we save that for later? We have a movie to see."

Max grins. "A movie? How long are we going to be here?"

Logan waves his hand to show them into the theater. "Let's call it a short 'teaser.'"

As they are seated, Logan waves for Tommy to start the projector. He doesn't say anything. The photos are like what he showed Ethan and Jaclyn. "Before" and "after" pictures of each of them. Max catches on right away. She's even guessing if she knows the doctor who will perform the surgery. Logan smiles but says nothing.

Seth is quiet, almost somber. He isn't crying, but his eyes are tearing. Max notices first, and she reaches over to him.

"Don't like your new look, sweetie? I'm sure it can be changed."

He purses his lips and tries to smile. Max wipes his left eye with a napkin as a tear rolls down his cheek. She turns to Logan and shakes her head, no, subtly.

Logan whispers to her, "I agree. He should stay if he's okay with it."

After a few more shots on the screen of all three of them, Logan waves his hand to turn off the projector and turn up the lights. He leans forward to look at Seth and Max, sitting in chairs beside him. "Seth, I love you as my son. Max and I would love to have you with us the rest of our lives. But I must tell you that I think the best thing for you is to stay. Stay here in LA as Seth Boncola. You take over Max's design business. Make it your own. You're young. You have your whole life ahead of you. You're talented as a designer and as your alter ego, Lydia LaFon. That's a big part of who you are. You won't have that life where we're going. You'll feel you gave up everything. I'll let Max weigh in, of course, but I have a very nice package for you to stay and have a wonderful life here in LA, or wherever you choose for Seth Boncola to make his life."

By this point, Seth is crying. He puts his drink down and wipes his eyes with the napkin from his drink.

Max holds him. "You okay, sweetie?"

"You two are all I have. I don't have my real family. *You* are my real family. And now you're leaving."

Max is also starting to cry, as is Logan. Seth is looking down at the floor. Max gently takes his chin and holds his head up, so she can look into his eyes. "We will *always* be your family. You know that. I can't say I know all of Logan's plan, but I've got to believe that as time passes, this will all blow over and somehow, we can reemerge in your life." She turns to Logan. "Please tell me I'm right, Logan."

Logan nods his head, "In time, yes, maybe sooner than I think. Once we know we're safely hidden and the firm is disbanded and everything is settled, I think it would be safe for us to rendezvous, perhaps on a regular basis, in Europe or elsewhere. I just can't guarantee it."

Seth wipes his face and smiles broadly while looking at Logan. Still weeping, yet smiling, he speaks softly. "You are such a God-damn optimist, Logan. You are. You could always talk me into anything. You are the poster child for finding a pony buried under a pile of shit."

They all three laugh and wipe their tears.

Seth goes silent, obviously running through the scenarios in his mind. "My whole world is changing, no matter what, isn't it?"

Logan takes a deep breath. "Yes, and I'm sorry. The moment dear Laurent told me what the truth was with Viktor's client, I knew my life and Max's were changed forever. It's a breathtaking moment when you're confronted with that. Most often, you're confronted with that realization when your spouse or partner dies. Or you lose a parent or, God forbid, a child. That's a change initiated by grief, and you then come to terms with it. This is much the same thing. Something has died in our life, and we can't change it, no matter how much we want to. So, we grieve and then we must move on. I'm just sorry you got caught up in this, Seth. I truly am."

Seth shakes his head, gets up from his chair, and goes over to hug Logan. "I'd rather be with you and Max. Truly, I would. But I know the two of you so well. If I were with you, you'd be consumed about my happiness. What to do with your little designer and part-time drag queen, living in some small town in Europe or wherever. You two need to be happy, especially since you've lost your firm, your house, your life here. You don't need to be burdened with me."

Max starts to speak up, but Seth cut her off. "And you'll need someone here. Someone who loves you and waits for your return. Keeping the firm going won't be easy without you, Max, but it will let me go on living with a part of you. I'll feel the connection to you each and every day, and I'll work my butt off to show you I can carry on. Logan's already lost his business legacy, the firm. I don't want Max to lose hers too."

Logan and Max hug Seth, and they cry for a few minutes. Seth then pulls back, wipes his face, and holds up his margarita. "Well, I'm in because I'm out. I'm in your heart forever, and you in mine, but I'm out of this segment of your life. Only temporarily, I hope."

39

Not Suffering, Redemption

Logan asks Seth to go upstairs, while he and Max remain in the theater. Logan turns to Max, "You can likely imagine who I'm bringing in here next. To discuss our final plan."

Max nods. "You can't leave a soul behind, can you?"

"Would you want me to?"

Max is silent for a moment and then puts her arms around Logan's waist. "You did it for Jackie, didn't you?"

Logan slowly nods his head and then, after a loose smile, kisses Max. "You can always read my mind."

Logan motions to Jared, who is standing at the door by the side of the theater. As the door opens, Max sees Jackie first and then Ethan following behind her. Jackie is overcome with emotion and runs to Max, crying. They embrace, and Jackie tells Max she is so relieved that she's okay and how thrilled she was to see Logan earlier.

Ethan walks over slowly; his face is somber. He's embarrassed in front of Max that Logan rescued him for yet a second time. *Ethan screws up again; that's likely what Max is thinking now that she knows everything.*

Max turns to Ethan and puts both her arms out. Ethan falls into them, and before sobbing, he says, "I'm so sorry, Max. I just don't know what to say."

Before the situation gets too weepy, Logan tells them that time is short, and they need to listen carefully. Max, Jackie, and

Ethan sit down, while Logan leans against the back of the chairs in front of them. "We leave in about an hour, sooner if possible. I have just a few items I need to wrap up with Tommy and Jared, since we won't see them after they take us to the airport."

Ethan leans forward. "I know I dare not even ask, but is there anything I can do to help? You said you wanted me to apologize to Rebecca?"

"Thank you for reminding me. Ethan, you get off easy. Rebecca has decided to stay at the firm. She's going back to the firm tomorrow morning. She called the SEC and told them she had a panic attack this morning and had to compose herself. She's ready to work with the SEC and FBI to help them see what happened, what I did with the A Fund and why."

"Won't she give your scheme away?"

"She never saw me. Or Max. I asked Jared to contact her. He lured her downstairs at the office this morning, knowing Ethan would take a lot of this out on her. Jared called her at her desk after she was excused from the meeting by Ethan. He told her he's a friend of mine and that I had always spoken highly of her. He said he could help her financially, especially if she wanted to get away. As my friend, he was going to do it for me, since I was dead, all very confidentially. She said some very nice things, one of which was she wanted to help clear my name. If I was dead, she didn't want my legacy to end with an illegal fund redemption. I think she's sincere. She decided to stay and declined the offer to get away."

Ethan asks, "Does she know all the details about the B Fund?"

Logan responds, "Not that I know of. I think it's just Maria, at this point, but it will all come out."

"Maria, oh my God, Maria. I forgot about her. May I call her to say good-bye?"

"Ethan, you're dead. Dead men don't make phone calls. She's likely cursing both of us by now. Poor dedicated Maria. She's dumped with everything. At some point, even if it's years from now, we must make it up to her."

Ethan sits silently.

"Here's how our new lives begin. Thanks to the government of the Cayman Islands, we'll be transported to Grand Cayman early tomorrow morning on a private Gulfstream jet. We leave from the Burbank airport at three tomorrow morning. We'll be escorted by a Cayman government official, as the flight will be classified as 'diplomatic' in nature. We will each receive a Cayman Islands passport, identity cards, and entry documents, and will be staying under our new names in a rented house, for a month. Our surgeries begin the day after tomorrow. Here's the background on our plastic surgeon. He's from Miami, but he performs most of his surgeries in the Caymans. We're at a private hospital, with private nurses afterward for recovery at our rented house. I'm told we'll be fit for travel in thirty days, maximum. During that time, we'll receive Italian passports for me and Max and Swiss passports for you two. Here's the home that has been purchased for you in Switzerland. Berne, Switzerland, to be exact. You'll get more details, including your local bank and your sponsor once we're recovering in the Caymans."

Ethan and Jackie are stunned. Now that they've seen more details, it's apparent to them that their life is completely changing. Jackie, becoming tearful, asks, "Why Berne?"

Logan smiles. "Why not? It's a beautiful place."

Max is taken aback. "Can't you tell Jackie more than that?"

"Because it's Switzerland, and they're pros at doing this. I had to use an international relocation broker, and that's where it was easiest to establish your new identity. If you don't like it there in a few years, I'm told you can move about. Anywhere but the US or China. And you'll be safer sticking to Europe. They have stricter privacy laws than we do here in the US, and you'll be less subject to discovery if you be careful where you use your new passport. More on that later."

Jackie brightens up a bit. "So, what about you and Max? Where will you be, and how will we contact you?"

"Italy. Same situation for us. I'll tell you more later, but that's enough for tonight. Let's freshen up and be ready to leave for Burbank by 1:00 a.m. Ethan, you and Jackie can use the guesthouse to get ready. Everything you need is in there. There's fresh clothes and toiletries. If anything's missing, just let Jared know. Otherwise, meet in the living room by 1:00 a.m."

Ethan puts his hand out to Logan. "Thank you. Thank you. I don't know what to say."

Logan waves his hand and says, "No worries."

"But how are you paying for all of this? Where is all this money coming from? For our new lives?"

"Good question, Ethan. As a money man, I'd be disappointed if you hadn't asked that. The Caymans are our starting-off point, of course. Those expenses are significant, but fortunately the Royal Britannia Resort Hotel really paid off for us."

Ethan frowns. "How so?"

"I'm surprised you can't put that one together in your head. Think about it for just a moment."

Ethan puts his hand on his chin and frowns. "Beautiful property. I love it there. It's one of the star holdings in the B Fund."

"Yes, yes, and quite valuable!"

Ethan thinks for a few moments. "Well, the Chinese connection is obvious. They built it. The Chinese construction company even flew in their own labor. We financed it, or I should say, the fund financed it, and owns it. We pay those five-star hotel robbers to operate it, but even with that, we've made a great return."

"You're absolutely right, Ethan. And the new Cayman owners are just thrilled to have it. A real trophy property, now back in their hands and no longer Chinese owned. What a great business deal."

Ethan is lost in the conversation. He doesn't say anything, at first.

Logan says, with much excitement, "One of your best business decisions, ever!"

Ethan is shocked. "Oh shit, Logan, did you sell that property?"

"Of course not! Ethan, I'm not half the business investment wizard *you* are. I could never dream of such a profitable and well-timed transaction."

Max and Jackie can feel the tension mounting between Logan and Ethan. Logan had pulled something off, and Ethan is unaware. Perhaps he was even set up.

"A Cayman business consortium paid us, the fund, $360 million for the property."

Ethan perks up. "That's great! Didn't we only have about $200 million of the client's money invested in it?"

"Bang on, Ethan. Bang on."

"Okay, but I still don't get it. What does that have to do with us and how you're paying for all this."

"Oh, no, it's not me, Ethan. It's you! You're such a smart guy, that you sold the property, took the proceeds, and used 100 percent of the $360 million to buy Puerto Rican bonds, at such a discount, the return was 18 percent. What a genius. Just a shame that the Diego cartel went bust and the B fund lost everything. Oh, there was that brokerage fee to the broker who arranged the deal in the Caymans—oh, what's his name? Closely tied to the government. Seems his fee was about $50 million, so what a deal for everyone. Oh, and quite a bit of spare cash that found its way to Switzerland by courier."

"You bastard. Was this in my name?"

"Of course. You deserve all the credit for such a shrewd transaction. And of course, the other two, equally brilliant transactions."

"Shit. So, you raided some assets in the B fund, sold them, pocketed some of the money here and there, brokers, referral fees, all that. You gave great deals to the buyers, kept a bunch for you, for us, and that's how we finance our new lives? And the client, the secretary, gets screwed. You saddled the B Fund with the loss?"

"And we have you to thank for it."

"My name's all over these transactions?"

"The credit you amply deserve."

Max jumps up and goes to Ethan. "Logan, please, stop. *We* get it. *He* gets it. You began to sell things in the B Fund, under Ethan's name and instructions, to get money for us and to, well, stiff the client? The general secretary? You've been raiding the fund?"

"Just a bit. There's still plenty there. Well, plenty of shit. I sold off some of the good stuff to finance our new lives; pay off the Cayman, Swiss, and Italian governments we needed to; and to send a message to the secretary, even if he's in jail, that he didn't have the last word and a subtle message to the new general secretary of the Chinese Communist Party that the funds he thought he would now share with his family and cohorts have suffered a little 'haircut.'"

Jackie takes a deep breath. "Wow, the Logan I knew would never have done that."

Logan turns to Jackie, takes her hands, and says softly, "The Logan you knew died when he found out his business was a sham."

They all four stand there in silence for a moment. Logan says nothing but downs what's left of his martini.

Ethan walks over to Logan. "One question. I'm sure I know the answer, my friend, but did *you* blow up *Copious*, or was that an accident?"

"No accident. I'm sure you figured that out."

Ethan shakes his head and looks down at the floor.

Logan grabs Ethan's arm. "I know you loved that boat. It was your symbol of ultimate success. But it was over, whether *Copious* blew up Saturday night or not. The secretary wanted his dirty money back, we couldn't deliver, and even if we docked back in Dana Point Sunday night, everything was over at the firm. You know that. Either our biggest client would have killed you this week, or you'd have been arrested by the FBI by now. Your former life is over. At least I'm giving you a chance at a new life, Ethan."

"Do I deserve yet another chance?"

"Jackie does. That's what matters. Our wives shouldn't suffer from our bad judgment. And having your name on the final transactions is a bit of insurance you won't look back. Or come back."

Ethan nods and begins to walk out to the guesthouse. When he gets to the door, Jackie is standing there waiting for him. He turns to Logan and yells out, "Was it one bomb or two?"

"Two."

"Thought so. Did Clint know anything about it?"

Logan shakes his head. "No one knew about the explosives except me and Jared."

Ethan nods and puts his arm around Jackie's shoulders, and they walk out the door.

After Jackie and Ethan leave and close the door, Max turns to Logan. She looks at him intently. "Maybe he'd have been better off going down with *Copious.*"

Logan hesitates for a moment. "How so?"

"Nice of you to save him, from himself really, but are you going to keep rubbing it in? Hasn't he suffered enough? Losing the firm and everything?"

"It's not about suffering."

"Then what *is* it about?"

"Redemption."

40

One Less Frenchman

Brigitte sits alone at Viktor's favorite table in the Polo Lounge. She stares across at an empty seat, wondering why Viktor hasn't shown for their 11:00 p.m. dinner. Detective Carter sits at the bar, where he can clearly see Brigitte. He contacted her earlier when Viktor failed to show for their 6:00 p.m. appointment at the firm earlier that evening. She told Carter to come to the Polo Lounge at 11:00 p.m., as she was having dinner with Viktor, and he could speak with him there.

Outside the Polo Lounge, where the patio overlooks the pathways to the bungalows, there is much commotion. Police and paramedics are running along the path and about a dozen Beverly Hills police officers run from the lobby down to the bungalows in the opposite direction. Detective Carter walks over to Brigitte, who is by now, teary-eyed about being stood up by Viktor. "You stay here. Have another cocktail, and I'll go to his bungalow to see what's up. The phone line to his bungalow isn't working."

Brigitte nods her head.

Detective Carter walks out of the Polo Lounge to see a crowd of law enforcement and paramedics in the lobby. Most of them are congregating around the doors leading to the bungalows. He observes some plainclothes officers escorting three men in handcuffs out through the lobby. All three are Chinese, and two are badly bruised. A fourth man is wheeled out on a stretcher. He also appears to be Chinese. *What is going on?*

Carter first tries calling Viktor again on the house phone. The line still isn't working, so he makes his way through the crowd, hoping to get to the back door leading to the bungalows. As Carter tries to leave through the back door, a police officer stops him. "No admittance, sir, sorry."

Carter flashes his badge. "Orange County Sheriff. Detective Carter. I need access to the bungalow of a Mr. Viktor Lucienne."

The policeman at the door stands on his toes and scans the crowd. "There, that man over there in the gray suit. He's with the FBI. Go see him. He's calling the shots here tonight."

Carter shoves his way through the crowd and across the hallway to the gentleman in the gray suit. "Excuse me, sir, I'm Detective Carter with the Orange County Sheriff's Office. I have business with Mr. Viktor Lucienne. He was to meet for dinner at 11:00 p.m. I'd like access to his bungalow."

"I'm Winters. Special Agent Hank Winters. FBI. Winters flashes his badge. "What's your business with Lucienne?"

"Not the Feds' type of business, I can assure you."

Winters is not amused. "That's not what I asked you. And I don't need assurance from you. Why do you want to see Lucienne?"

"Murder, if you must know. Suspicion of murder, or at least a person of interest."

Winters's phone rings, and he puts his hand up to Carter, indicating for him to hold on for a moment. "Got it, yep." He hangs up and looks at Carter. "Murder, eh? Well, hate to disappoint you, but Mr. Lucienne won't be of much help to you tonight. Well, not at all. He's dead."

"What? How? His assistant is in the Polo Lounge, expecting him for dinner."

"Well, unless she's expecting a soggy corpse, I'd suggest she find another dinner companion. *You* look hungry!"

Carter is upset at the flippant remarks made by Special Agent Winters. "That the way the FBI speaks to everyone? Even fellow law enforcement? Oh, excuse me for using that word *fellow*. We aren't quite good enough for you, are we?"

Winters takes a breath, wipes his chin, and says, "Sorry. My apologies. This has been a fucked-up day. Kidnappings, murders, stolen money, all under our nose. Look, I'm sorry. If you want to see Lucienne, they're bringing him out here shortly. He took a swim earlier tonight with a kettlebell tied to his feet."

Carter, not the type to go to a gym, says, "Excuse me? What type of ball?"

"Not a ball. *B-E-L-L*. Kettlebell. Like you use at a gym. It's a thirty-pound weight. He tied it to his feet and took a swim in the pool. Left a suicide note. I had an appointment with him too. Tomorrow morning. So, we both get stood up. By a soggy corpse."

Carter is silent for a moment. "Suicide?"

Winters shakes his head. "That's what I'm told. Paramedics thought they saved him. Got a pulse after they fished him out of the pool. Didn't last long. Brain dead, so guess that was it. Up to the coroner to determine cause of death, but Mr. Lucienne won't be keeping any appointments, that's for certain."

"May I ask you why you were wanting to speak with him?"

"He was an investor in a Beverly Hills hedge fund that went tits up this morning. My staff is investigating, and he just happened to be in the office when we raided it, so naturally we're curious why he was there."

"Global Protocol Strategies? Logan Aronheart and Ethan Chandler? *That* fund?"

"Hmmm, yep. How'd you know?"

"We should talk tomorrow. I need to go back in there, to the Polo Lounge, and tell his associate that her boss is dead."

Winters points to an attractive Latino lady across the lobby. "You know that lady over there? Her boss is missing, too. Same firm." Winters is pointing to Maria, who is standing against the wall, watching all the commotion. Winters was interviewing Maria at the fund offices when the call came in from one of his FBI associates about the arrest of the Chinese men and the Lucienne drowning. Winters brought her down to the hotel. Maria is, by now, practically despondent.

Carter walks over to where she's standing. "Maria? I'm Detective Carter, of the Orange County Sheriff's Office."

Maria is startled.

"Don't worry. All I am here to tell you is that in there"—he points to the Polo Lounge— "is Ms. Brigitte Langevelle. She was expecting Mr. Lucienne for dinner. I need to tell her what's happened. Would you like to join me? I'll buy you a drink."

"Thank you for your kindness, but that might be awkward."

"Awkward, why?"

"Because her boss ... well, let's just say that I'm not sorry he's dead."

Carter is taken aback and says nothing.

"I just wouldn't be the right person to console Brigitte in her grief. If you know what I mean."

Carter nods. "I'll leave you be, ma'am."

Maria smiles and then looks away.

Across the lobby, Alton and Oksana are watching the mayhem from the concierge desk. Alton thanked the concierge with his usual generous gratuity and told him he'd be in touch in the morning to settle the final charges for the bungalow. The concierge is relieved Alton is leaving, given all the commotion that has unfolded this night.

Alton takes Oksana by the arm. "Shall we depart this sinking ship?"

"Of course! My feet are already getting vet, bubee! I'm starved."

"Me too. Where would you like to dine?"

Oksana thinks for a moment. "How about something ... *French*?"

"French? That doesn't sound like you."

"For tonight, French sound good. One less Frenchman on earth tonight so we celebrate, no?"

Alton smiles. They go to the motor court where Jimmy is waiting, with a string of apologies for losing Max. Alton doesn't care. He lets Jimmy rattle on, apology over apology. When they arrive at Taix, one of the oldest French restaurants in Los Angeles, Jimmy gets the biggest tip of his career and a huge thank-you from Alton. Alton is both celebrating and mourning. He's celebrating yet another successful end to an assignment but mourning the loss of three people he cares so deeply about.

As they enter Taix, Alton is ushered to his favorite table, as the bar patrons stare at Oksana when they walk by. *Big gal. Is she really a woman? What's that good looking guy doing with her?*

As he is just getting seated, Alton's phone rings, so he excuses himself from the table. It's the last call he will ever get from Logan Aronheart. He asks Alton to look after Seth because he's chosen to stay behind. *Alton, please care for him as I would. You'll be looking after my son.*

When Alton comes back to the table after taking the call, Oksana says, "Vhy you smile like dat? You get lucky in the men's room?"

Alton smiles, "No. Not quite. But I did just get a brand-new assignment. The best assignment of my life!

41

Finis, Dieu Merci!
(The End, Thank God!)

After Ethan and Jackie go to the guesthouse to get ready for their journey to the Cayman Islands, Max and Logan go upstairs to get Seth. They had him wait there so he wouldn't see Ethan or Jackie. Seth is sitting on the bed when Logan and Max arrive.

Seth looks up at both of them, rather somber. "Your secret guests are gone?"

Max smiles lightly. "Well, not gone, but out of sight."

"So, is this good-bye?"

Logan shakes his head. "Not good-bye, just *ciao*. We *will* be together before too long."

Max puts her arm around Seth and kisses him on the cheek. "And we'll be in touch, Seth. Maybe not in an obvious way but stay aware and watch for signs from us. When it's safe, we'll see each other again."

Logan comes over, and they all three hug and cry a bit more. Logan takes a deep breath, wipes his eyes, and takes Seth by the hand. "I'd like you to spend just a few days with Alton. Before you can object, please just listen. I want Alton to be sure your apartment is safe before you move back in. I just spoke with him, and he feels quite confident that the secretary's goons will be sent back to China by the State Department. In return, the State Department will cast the events of the past few days as just an angry client who got caught up in a web of fraud and deceit by their American asset managers, and—"

Seth cuts Logan off before he can finish. "But that's a lie. Why would you let them do that?"

Logan grins. "Well, it's not the way I would frame it, but hear me out. Alton is sure you'll be safe once it's apparent that Max and I are gone, and Ethan and Jackie are believed to be dead or in the custody of the secretary's goons. Plus, the SEC will have to wind down the fund, and once they discover the complex holdings of the B fund, they'll have to arrange liquidation with the State Department and FBI looking over their shoulder. Alton's FBI contact says he's quite certain the Chinese will turn this over to their securities regulator, and they'll work quietly to retrieve their funds. What's left of them. You'll be out of the picture. Nonetheless, we'd all feel better if you just stay close to Alton for a few days. I've also given Alton quite a bit of money to deposit in an account for you. And Jared has a wad of cash for you to keep in a safe place, like Alton's safe. If we replenish the business account for the design business now, it will look suspicious. So, Alton, or his associates, will feed it to the business, slowly, from a new design job he'll arrange. A very lucrative job. So, you'll have plenty of money to get on your feet and get the projects going again."

"It won't be the same without Max. It'll be so lonely."

Max smiles and holds Seth's face between her hands. "Not for long. You hire an assistant. Someone fun to keep you company and someone very talented. You can raid Aubrey's firm. There's a couple of talented people there. They must get tired of recycling the same design projects over and over. You have a lot to offer."

Seth purses his lips and nods. "Right, you have a good point. There're two guys that work with Aubrey who come to my show often. One is quite talented. Aubrey pays him well, though."

Max shrugs her shoulders. "Then make him an offer he can't refuse!"

Jared knocks on the bedroom door and opens it slowly. "Car's here, sir."

Logan nods to him. "Thanks. Tell them their passenger will be right down."

Jared smiles. "Yes, sir."

"That's your car, son."

"Where are they taking me?"

"Just to Alton's house tonight. It's late, and he'd rather check out your place tomorrow, and be sure it's safe to go back. He wants to swing by the office with you, to check that out, too."

"Crap, I'm back to Alton keeping an eye on me?"

Max and Logan both shake their heads. Logan pipes up. "He's just getting you settled; that's it. He'll always be there for you, but he'll leave you alone. I promise."

Max agrees, "Plus, you'll love seeing his home in Trousdale Estates. It's small, but quite something."

"You design it?"

"Well, of course! What do you think? Tell Alton it needs refreshing, and he'll be the first job you do completely on your own! He's got a lot of money to spend!"

Logan and Max escort Seth downstairs and stop at the front door. Logan doesn't want the driver to see him or Max, just in case. Logan asks Jared to escort Seth to the car. After a long and tearful hug between the three of them, Seth blows a kiss to them both and walks out the door to the waiting car. Max turns to Logan, embraces him, and begins to cry.

It is nearly 1:00 a.m., and Tommy goes to retrieve Ethan and Jackie from the guesthouse. Jared pulls into the driveway with a new Cadillac Escalade. He picked up the new SUV just in case the secretary has other people who know the license number of the Suburban, which is now safely tucked away in the garage.

"All set, sir?" Jared looks to Logan for approval, and Logan nods. He hands Jared and Tommy each a package, which are very thick.

"Thank you both so much for all you have done. When we get to the airport, you two stay in the car. I'm sure everything is okay, but no need for our Cayman friends to see you if they don't have to."

Jared speaks, "But, sir, we'd feel better if we know you got safely on the plane, and we see it take off."

"You each have your device, right?"

They both nod.

"Okay, then, I'll text A-OK when we're taxiing down the runway."

Tommy picks up the small travel bags Logan prepared for himself, Max, Ethan, and Jackie. Jared waits a moment for Tommy to go out the front door. "Sir, I don't quite know how to say this, but I'm really going to miss you. Please, will you contact me when you can. I need to know that."

"Of course, Jared. We discussed that. Be patient. Take your long vacation and watch for the signs I give you once you're back. I'm sure you're both safe but should anything go wrong before I give you a sign, go to Alton. Immediately."

Jared wipes one of his eyes and shakes his head.

"All set. Everything loaded up." Tommy waves his hand to show the four of them to the Escalade.

As they're driving down Laurel Canyon Drive toward the valley and the Burbank airport, Logan turns to the other three. "The gentleman who will be our escort tonight is with the government of the Cayman Islands. These are your passports. We'll be driving directly to the executive terminal and boarding the plane. There's no one who approves our departure. Once we land in the Caymans, our host has arranged for us to be taken directly to the residences I told you about."

Ethan, thumbing through his information in the passport, askes, "So we won't need these tonight?"

Logan says, "Likely won't need them at all, but just in case. You'll get Swiss passports before we leave Grand Cayman next month."

The Escalade pulls up in front of the executive terminal, and a young man in a tuxedo greets them by their new names. "Good morning. I'm Edward, and I'll be taking care of your luggage and escorting you to the aircraft." He looks at Logan and Max, who exit first. "Mr. and Mrs. Damiani?"

Logan nods his head. "Yes, this is my wife, Genevieve, and I'm Stefano."

"I'm very pleased to meet you." He glances in the back seat, "Then this must be Mr. and Mrs. Ramseyer?"

Ethan nods. "Please call me Luca, and this is my wife, Allegra."

Edward points to the lobby of the executive terminal. "Please make yourself comfortable in the waiting area. There's food and refreshments. We'll be leaving very shortly. I'll come and retrieve you after your luggage is loaded. Mr. Bancross has just arrived, and he'll meet you in the waiting area momentarily."

The four of them walk into the plushly appointed waiting room. Small sandwiches, fruit, wine, and an array of liquor and mixers are arranged on a table. In the lounge area, a sofa and chairs face a wall filled with art and a large-screen TV. The early morning edition of CNN is playing. There is no sound, but the closed caption feature is on. Logan, now Stefano, motions to the other three, asking if he can fix them a drink.

Ethan nods. "The usual."

Logan smiles. "The new usual, or the old usual?"

Ethan grins. "Well, I hope that not *everything* will change!"

Max and Jackie are sitting on the sofa when suddenly Max turns around to get Logan's attention. "Sweetheart, Stefano!"

Logan looks up, only to see Max pointing to the television.

It is a picture of the former secretary general of the Chinese Communist Party. The caption reads, "Former secretary arrested yesterday, whisked away to what will be a secret trial for treason, corruption, and improper execution of duties."

There's a picture of the new secretary general, and the caption discusses his efforts to uncover corruption in the former regime.

Then, there is a quick picture of the building where Ethan and Logan have the offices of the fund, Global Protocol, in Beverly Hills. The caption says, "In a related development, the Chinese government has accused a Beverly Hills hedge fund of fraud and improper management of business assets for a number of Chinese immigrants and businesspeople." It doesn't name

Ethan or Logan or the name of their firm. The caption ends by saying more details on this developing story will be on CNN Business later that morning.

All four of them are speechless, not sure if it's all right to publicly discuss what they have just seen or if it's best to ignore it.

A moment later, a tall older gentleman with thick, wavy gray hair enters the waiting area. Dressed in a dark-blue suit and red tie, he's grinning widely. He extends his hand to Logan. "Good morning, Mr. Damiani. I'm George, George Bancross."

Mr. Damiani smiles, clasps the hand of Mr. Bancross, and introduces him to his wife, Genevieve, and his two associates, Luca, and Allegra.

"Please, join me on the aircraft. We're ready for our journey. Edward has prepared a light snack for us. You may then sleep for a while, and breakfast will be served before we arrive in Grand Cayman. Our flight time is about five hours."

Mr. Damiani says, "Thank you." He waves for Allegra and Genevieve to accompany Mr. Bancross, who stands between the two ladies and puts out both arms to escort them to the plane.

As Stefano begins to follow them out, Luca grabs him by the arm and turns Stefano to look at the television, which by then is on to a different story.

"How can that not tear your heart out?"

Stefano nods. "Of course, it does. But it's not the last word."

"What do you mean? Ethan and Logan are gone. They're not here to tell the truth. They're muzzled forever."

"No, that's not true, Mr. Ramseyer."

Mr. Ramseyer looks very confused. "Then who will tell the story? How will the truth come out?"

Stefano takes Mr. Ramseyer by the arm and escorts him out the door. The others are already ascending the stairs to the plane.

Mr. Ramseyer goes on, "You didn't answer my question. How will the truth come out?"

"A book. It will be told in a book, by a writer who knows the truth."

"Who? Who would that writer be, Mr. Damiani?"

"Someone you don't know."

Mr. Ramseyer and Mr. Damiani smile at each other. Then they turn and follow their wives and their escort up the stairs to the plane.

Not, of course …

The End

Learn More About the Author

https://gregoryseller.com/
https://www.linkedin.com/in/gregoryseller
https://www.facebook.com/gregorysellerbooks
https://www.goodreads.com/book/
show/36821375-vanquish-of-the-dragon-shroud

Gregg is at work on his third novel, to be published soon. Please find more information on the author, his current and upcoming books at https://www.gregoryseller.com

Milton Keynes UK
Ingram Content Group UK Ltd.
UKHW012349150324
439374UK00014B/700

9 781737 168225